TWINS FOR THE TEXAN

BY
CHARLENE SANDS

MILLS & BOON

First Published in Great Britain 2016
By Mills & Boon, an imprint of HarperCollins*Publishers*
1 London Bridge Street, London, SE1 9GF

© 2016 Charlene Swink

ISBN: 978-0-263-91859-5

51-0516

Printed and bound in Spain
by CPI, F

Charlene Sands is a *USA TODAY* bestselling author of more than forty romance novels, writing sensual contemporary romances and stories of the Old West. When not writing, Charlene enjoys sunny Pacific beaches, great coffee, reading books from her favourite authors and spending time with her family. You can find her on Facebook and Twitter, write to her at PO Box 4883, West Hills, CA 91308, USA or sign up for her newsletter for fun blogs and ongoing contests at www.charlenesands.com.

To my sweet mother-in-law, Nancy, with love.
Thanks for having twins, inspiring
this story and giving me a great husband!

One

Brooke McKay had no clue where this deserted Texas road was taking her. Gazing past a dozen squished bugs on the rental car's windshield, she saw flatland stretching before her for miles and miles. After living in California near mountains and beaches, this kind of vast flatness was foreign to her.

Red warning lights blinked from the car's dashboard. She looked down at the indicator. Her gas tank was nearing empty. "Don't do it, don't do it."

Decked out in her best black lace dress with all the necessary trimmings and red heels so high they'd put the balls of her feet to the test in the walking-to-the-next-gas-station department, Brooke pushed the car to its limit.

She spotted something lying in the middle of the road. "Oh!"

Roadkill.

Apparently someone had driven on this road recently. It was good news for her, but not for the poor possum.

As she drove on, she removed her sunglasses and squinted into the afternoon sun searching for a miracle. A gas station would be nice, with an attendant who knew where in heck she was.

The car sputtered, the engine wringing out its last breaths.

She sucked in oxygen, praying that her worst nightmare wasn't coming to life.

And then the car crawled to a stop.

She pumped the gas pedal, but there was no more wringing to be had.

Oh, boy. Not only wouldn't she make it to Heather's wedding on time, she might have to camp out here in the wilderness for heaven knew how long.

She stared at her cell phone lying beside her on the seat. She already knew *that* miracle wasn't happening. She had no cell service. She hadn't for the last ten miles. She knocked her head against the leather steering wheel a few times and decided it made a good pillow, a place to rest her head and close her eyes while she thought of a way out of this predicament. She didn't have many choices. She'd have to get out and start walking.

"Excuse me, miss," came a deep voice from out of nowhere. "Are you okay?"

Her head popped up, and she looked into the bone-melting blue eyes of the man standing beside her driver-side door. Her heartbeat immediately picked up speed. There in the flesh was a dauntingly handsome, iron-jawed cowboy.

Her miracle.

"I, uh, I didn't hear anyone drive up." She glanced in her rearview mirror and sure enough, a shiny black Cadillac SUV was parked behind her car. "Yes, yes. I'm okay."

She took a closer look at him. Goodness, they grew them tall in Texas. Her miracle wore a black Western suit, a sterling silver belt buckle and one of those sexy string ties. "I th-think I took a wrong turn somewhere. Now I'm out of gas."

He nodded and scrubbed at the dark blond facial hair on his jaw. "Not a good thing to do on this road. There isn't a gas station for at least ten miles or so. I'm Wyatt Brandt, by the way." He stuck out his hand and she took it. It was a little awkward shaking hands through the car window, but his firm grip, beautiful eyes and rich Texas drawl put her at ease.

He could be a serial killer.

That thought flittered through her mind, but she dismissed it. The butterflies winging around in her stomach as he enveloped her hand, ever so briefly, told a different story. "I'm Brooke. I was heading to a friend's wedding, and now I'm afraid I'll never make it."

"Nice meeting you, Brooke," he said. "You wouldn't by any chance be heading to Blake and Heather's shindig, would you?"

Her eyebrows drew up. How did he know? *Serial killer* flashed in her mind again. Had he been stalking her? Her brother Dylan had almost lost his life to a stalker out to get revenge. Luckily, he'd survived the murder attempts and decided to get his wife away from the Hollywood scene for a while. Emma, Dylan and Brooke were all in Texas now, while Dylan was shooting a movie. She still had stalker on the brain but immediately dismissed the notion where Wyatt was concerned. How many stalkers drove Cadillacs and dressed like *GQ* models? No, Wyatt Brandt either was psychic or had been invited to the wedding, too. "Yes, that's the one. The GPS told me to take this road. I was running late, and this is supposed to be a shortcut to their wedding venue. Do you know them?"

"Sure do. I'm on my way to the nuptials, too. Blake's a friend of mine."

She smiled. This miracle was getting better and better.

"Heather and I went to college on the West Coast together. I've never met Blake."

"He's a great guy. Just so you know I'm not anyone you have to worry over. I own the Blue Horizon Ranch, about fifteen miles back that way." He pointed behind them. "And yes, this is a shortcut, if you know the roads. I'd be happy to give you a lift. I was running a bit late, too, and if we hurry, we'll make it before the ceremony begins."

"Gosh, that sounds great."

He opened the door for her and she got out. Their size difference was immediately evident. Even wearing three-inch heels, the top of her head reached his chin. His very rugged, strong chin.

"What about your car?" he asked.

"It's a rental." He closed the car door for her and she went on to explain, "I've been a little distracted lately, and forgot to fill the tank when I took off earlier. I'll lock it up and leave it here for now. I don't have much choice if I want to make the wedding."

He nodded. "Sounds good."

"Just let me get my bag." She clicked a button and the trunk popped open. He followed behind and before she could reach for her bag, he stretched a long arm around her, grazing her waist, and grabbed her suitcase. Warm shivers cascaded down her body from the contact. It was ridiculous how instantly attracted she was to him. She knew nothing about him other than his left hand was bare of a wedding ring and he had incredible eyes and pretty great manners.

"Anything else?" Her pink Gucci bag looked tiny in his grasp.

She'd heard about Southern charm, but experiencing it firsthand was refreshing. The men in other parts of the country could take a lesson from Wyatt Brandt. "No, that's it. Thank you."

"So you're staying overnight?" he asked as he guided her to his SUV.

"Yes. I figured the reception might go late, and I didn't think I'd be any good driving these roads at night. I'm not too great on them during the day either, apparently."

Rich laughter rose from his chest. "Probably a smart move." He opened the passenger-side door and she climbed into the seat.

Once she had settled in, she caught him gazing at her legs. A wave of heat passed through her as his eyes lingered just long enough not to be creepy.

After he put her suitcase in the back end, he took his seat behind the steering wheel and gave her a smile. "Do you have a last name?" he asked matter-of-factly as he started the engine. "Or are you just Brooke?"

Goodness, she didn't want to be Brooke McKay, not today, not with Wyatt. As soon as a guy got wind of who she really was, the sister of ultra-famous movie star Dylan McKay, he began treating her differently. She loved Dylan to pieces, but she'd had enough of that role, and it had caused her too much heartache with men who'd played her fast and loose just to get close to her famous brother.

Maybe it would be different in Texas than it had been in Los Angeles, where everyone it seemed, was trying to break into the movie business. But Brooke was too scarred now to test out that theory. "I'm Brooke *Johnson*."

The fib fell easily from her lips. For just one day. Was that asking too much?

"Okay, Brooke Johnson. Are you ready?"

"I think I was born ready," she said.

He laughed and they took off, leaving her little white Ford Escort in the dust.

Wyatt hadn't had a one-on-one conversation with a woman since his wife, Madelyn, had died some nine months ago. He wasn't including Henrietta in that, since his housekeeper was nearing retirement age, and besides, he was never really alone with her. Either Brett or Brianna or both of his eighteen-month-old twins were usually with them when they spoke, or rather when they tried to have a conversation. Raising twins was chaos in motion most of the time.

Yet Wyatt wasn't one for parties anymore. He preferred staying on the ranch, working long hours while trying to be a good father. But even he recognized his grief needed a swift kick in the ass, and his best friend Johnny Wilde had been the one to deliver it. "Go to that weddin', man. What you need is to get out and start livin' again."

Now he was wearing a monkey suit and heading for Blake's wedding, making conversation with a dark-haired woman with a sultry voice, great legs, and dark chocolate eyes with lids heavily shadowed and rims outlined in black.

"You're not from Texas, are you?" he asked.

"What was your first clue?"

He'd gotten a load of clues: the raven hair curling wildly down her back, the red painted lips, the dark made-up eyes and the manner of her dress. Sexy as it was, no woman in Texas would wear a skintight black lace dress to a wedding. At least none of the weddings he'd ever attended. "Oh, I don't know. Just a hunch."

"I'm from Los Angeles."

Her lips puckered as if she expected him to make some comment about her appearance. He wouldn't disrespect her that way. She was different from Madelyn, who'd been the epitome of Texas style and grace with sweet features, rosy cheeks and soft blond hair. Brooke certainly had her own style, but he wouldn't say she was unattractive. Quite the opposite, and he wished to hell he wasn't constantly noticing.

"So, you've come all this way for the wedding?" he asked.

"Yes, and for a little vacation. It just sort of worked out that I'd be able to attend Heather's wedding. I haven't seen her in years, but we've kept in touch. I'll be here for the rest of the summer."

"Where are you staying?"

"With a friend just outside of Beckon."

He nodded. "Nice."

"Yeah, it would be, but I co-own a business and I've put it in the hands of a new manager while I'm gone. It's a little nerve-racking."

"What kind of business?"

"It's called Parties-to-Go. We do all sorts of party and event planning. My partner is pregnant and well, it's a little complicated, but we both decided we needed a break. So we're here, enjoying the muggy end of the summer."

And he was enjoying her.

"What do you do, Wyatt? If you don't mind me asking? You said you owned Blue Horizon Ranch? Does that mean cattle?"

"Sure does. I've been raising cattle nearly all of my life. When my granddaddy started the ranch back in the forties, it was a small operation. My daddy built it up some, and then I took over when my folks moved to the East Coast. Blue Horizon's success had always been a dream of mine."

That and living to a ripe old age with his high school sweetheart, Madelyn.

"And now you're seeing it through."

"I am. The ranch does well, but I tinker in other things, too."

"Ah, you're an entrepreneur?"

"I suppose some might call me that."

He took pride in the investments he'd made in other companies that had paid off well. He'd made his first million before his twenty-seventh birthday, and he'd worked hard ever since to ensure a comfortable future for his family. Now he had all the money he'd ever need. Without Madelyn to share in his success, all of his hard work would've seemed pointless, but for his twins.

That was what getting off the ranch this weekend was about, him trying to move on with his life.

Start livin' again.

He glanced at Brooke, her red-lipped mouth in a pout as she tried to catch some cell service by waving her phone up in the air, putting it out the window for a few seconds. He couldn't seem to keep his eyes off her. She was a breath of fresh air and that alone stirred his juices. She was different and, he supposed, a lot of fun if he'd ever let himself find out.

"Nothing?" he asked once she gave up with her phone.

"Nope, not a blasted thing."

"We'll be at the hotel soon," he said.

The Inn at Sweetwater was known for lush gardens and scenic bridges along a natural lake. It was the destination spot for lovers and known as the ultimate venue for a romantic wedding. It was like the cherry topping on a hot fudge sundae for a bride and groom to speak their vows there. And it was why he'd resisted coming to this wedding.

Not on this day, of all days. It was Madelyn's birthday.

Hell, it was the exact reason Johnny insisted on his getting off the ranch. Wyatt needed the distraction, the time away. Wyatt had been restless and pensive and even Henrietta, bless her soul, had insisted he needed time to clear his head and gain some perspective. He'd be leaving his kids in her care overnight. Something he'd never done before, so with Johnny on his back and Henrietta pushing him, he'd accepted the invitation.

"What's wrong?" Brooke asked.

He turned to look into her pretty brown eyes. "Why do you think something's wrong?"

"Because I know you so well," she replied, grinning.

He laughed. "Sorry, just deep in thought."

"No apologies necessary. Aha! Finally, I'm getting bars on my cell. We must be nearing civilization. Excuse me while I call a tow service for my car."

"No problem." Wyatt listened to the deep, sensual lilt of her voice and tried to keep his eyes focused on the highway—not on Brooke Johnson, the engaging woman he'd picked up along the road.

As they drove through the intricate wrought iron gates of the venue, they entered a vibrant world of golf-course-green grass and tall swaying willows shading the lane leading up to the hotel. The Inn at Sweetwater was a plantation-style structure with palatial columns and snow-white shutters on every window. The gardens were ablaze with purple azaleas, pink peonies and stargazer lilies, and bluebonnets were interwoven among the stepping-stones. The paths all led to picturesque bridges arching over placid ponds. Off to the right fifty yards away, Sweetwater Lake sparkled in the late-afternoon sun.

"It looks like something out of a painting," Brooke said, hearing awe in her voice. She had an eye for creativity, and whoever landscaped these grounds knew how to set the mood. "Have you ever been here before?"

"No," Wyatt said. "But I've heard about it enough. It's my mother's favorite place. She'd have luncheons here with her friends."

"I can see why she'd like coming here."

Close to the lake's bank, there was a flowered canopy with descending wisteria vines waiting for the bride and groom. Hundreds of chairs tied with delicate satin bows were lined up in rows. Most of the guests were already seated.

Wyatt pulled the car up to a valet. And once they climbed out, he asked, "Want to make a run for it?"

"I think we have to. The wedding is supposed to start any minute."

"Okay, after you," he said, gesturing for her to take the lead.

She trotted along on her high heels, not an easy task even though the lush grass was as thick as a carpet. But after a few strides her heel dug into the rich earth and got stuck. Her leg twisted and she tipped sideways, stumbling. "Oh!"

Wyatt reached out and snagged her waist, catching her fall just in time.

"I've got you," he said, confidently. "You okay?"

They were locked together now, and her sensitive skin prickled under his touch. She liked being in his arms, and he seemed reluctant to let her go. A few seconds ticked by before he did.

"How many times are you going to save me today?" she asked breathlessly.

"As many as it takes," he offered, his blue eyes sparkling. She didn't know what to make of her miracle cowboy who'd caused her body to heat up with just one playful look. Was he teasing or flirting?

"I've got a solution to this problem," she said, snapping out of her insanity.

She slipped a finger into her shoes to pull at the straps and then wiggled out of them. Straightening, she came up holding her scarlet-red sandals between her fingers and nodded. "Okay, now I'm ready."

He blinked, grinned at her bare feet and then offered her his hand. They took off at a very brisk walk, making it to the last row of seats just seconds before the brides-maids began their trek down the aisle.

Brooke sighed in relief and sat back. A few minutes later, everyone in attendance rose to their feet as Heather glided down the aisle in an ivory satin wedding gown, her father walking beside her wearing a proud tearful smile. She held a gorgeous bouquet of new roses and fresh natural greenery that looked as though it had been handpicked just moments ago.

She met her handsome groom under the canopy, love shining in her eyes. Brooke looked on, happy for her friend who'd found love here in Texas. She'd probably start a family soon. Brooke's future wasn't quite so rosy. She didn't begrudge her friends, who'd already found happiness, but she'd always wondered what it was about her that seemed to repel any form of long-lasting relationship with a man. Being Dylan McKay's younger sister was like a noose around her neck. *Just hang me now,* she'd say to herself, whenever a man she'd dated starting hinting at meeting her celebrity brother. Of course, then came the teeny favors they'd ask of her.

Would your brother mind reading my script? I know it's gonna be a blockbuster.

I'm writing an autobiography and your brother would be perfect to star in the movie.

I'm starting a new business venture. I'm sure Dylan would love to get in on the ground floor once you tell him about it.

Riiiight.

Brooke was fed up with men who used her for their own personal gain. Leaving LA when she did had been a necessity. After the debacle with Royce Brisbane, who'd kept his cards close to the vest, and only showed his hand once she'd fallen in love with him, she'd written off relationships for the extended future. She'd been convinced her Wall Street–type boyfriend didn't give a lick about Dylan, until he handed her three scripts for her to show him. *Three*, for heaven's sake!

No man would ever use her that way again.

And then there was Wyatt Brandt, the polite, mannerly cowboy whose presence beside her made her heart pound in her chest. She didn't want to be Brooke McKay today, not while Wyatt Brandt was stealing glances at her when he didn't think she was looking. But she'd noticed, and it boosted her deflated ego to have a gorgeous hunk of a man checking her out without an ulterior motive. And if the tingles she was experiencing now weren't one-sided, this wedding could prove intriguing.

The *I do*'s were said with a flourish, and Brooke teared up as she witnessed these two people in love speak vows of undying commitment to each other. She felt Wyatt's eyes on her as a sole tear dripped down her cheek. Did he think her foolish for crying at a wedding? How cliché. Brooke wasn't a traditional kind of girl, yet weddings always seemed to get to her.

Wyatt gently placed a handkerchief in her hand. As she dabbed at her eyes, she sent him a silent nod of thanks. He gave her a brief smile.

After the vows were spoken, the loving couple garnered a round of applause as they marched down the aisle hand in hand, newly married. Row upon row of guests made their way from their seats to head toward the tented area where the cocktail hour was about to begin.

Brooke and Wyatt, seated in the back row, stood up and waited patiently for their turn. "It was a beautiful ceremony," she said, handing him his handkerchief.

"It was. But it made you cry."

She shrugged and slight embarrassment heated her skin. "I'm silly that way. Most people don't think of me as the sentimental type, but I guess I am when it comes to weddings."

"Maybe that's why you enjoy your business so much. You like seeing other people happy."

She stared into his eyes. Was he for real? How did he know that about her, after only meeting her two hours ago? Was he psychic after all? "You amaze me," she blurted.

"I do?" He rubbed at the scruffy dark blond hairs on his chin. "Well, now, it's been a while since I've amazed a woman."

"Don't stop on my account. It's been *too* long since I've been amazed by a man."

The look in his eyes suddenly grew dark and intense. "You flirting with me, Brooke Johnson?"

Yes. It was hard not to.

She glanced away for a second, making note of the two-hundred-plus guests milling about the large white wedding tent, and suddenly all she wanted was to be alone with Wyatt Brandt again.

"Just stating a fact, Wyatt."

"C'mon," he said, tamping down a smile and taking her arm gently. "Let's see if Blake and Heather had the good sense to seat us together."

She liked the sound of that.

A lot.

Two

Brooke wasn't seated with Wyatt. She sat between two of Heather's female cousins she'd met once or twice back in college. Two other male cousins and their wives rounded out the table. Everyone was pleasant. The ladies, dressed in florals and pastels appropriate for a late-afternoon wedding, were doing their best to make small talk. Brooke engaged in conversation with them and sipped white wine while giving the entire lakeside reception a cursory scan, keeping her eyes peeled for signs of Wyatt.

During the cocktail hour, she'd spent time with him, munching on appetizers and enjoying Sweetwater Lake until dinner had been called and they'd had to go their separate ways. She sensed that Wyatt had been just as disappointed as she was to discover that not only weren't they seated together, but their tables were separated by twenty others.

She spotted Wyatt standing just outside the perimeter of the decorated tent, sipping whiskey from a tumbler as he spoke to the groom. The sight of Wyatt shouldn't have made her heart race, and yet it was sprinting as if in an Olympic event. The two men shook hands and then Blake took off, most likely in search of his bride. Two women took Blake's place, sidling up next to Wyatt with giddy smiles on their faces.

She felt something possessive deep in her belly. He wasn't her date, but he seemed to want to spend more time with her, and now it didn't look as if that was going to happen.

Brooke's attention snapped back to her table when Connie, the younger of Heather's cousins, asked her a question. "Yes, I'm enjoying my stay in Texas so far," Brooke replied. "And I'm happy I was able to attend Heather's wedding. It was a beautiful ceremony."

"Heather's very happy with Blake. He's one of the good guys."

"There are so few of those," Brooke said, recognizing her tone was too cynical for a wedding.

Luckily, Connie chuckled. "I know what you mean. My mama says if you find a good one, land him and never let him go."

"She's a smart woman."

"She should know, she's been married three times. She kicked two losers to the curb before marrying my daddy. They've been married twenty-eight years now."

"I like your mother more and more."

"What about your folks?" Connie asked.

"Oh, my biological parents have issues. I don't see them much, but I was raised by foster parents and they were awesome. Without them, my life wouldn't be what it is today."

"So there's hope out there. I shouldn't be so skeptical— especially at my cousin's wedding—but my boyfriend and I have just broken up and it still stings."

She caught sight of Wyatt finally taking his seat for dinner. "I get the stinging part, Connie. I've been there." More than once. "It gets better, believe me. Just concentrate on what you enjoy doing most. That's what I do."

"Heather said you could've put this wedding together without blinking an eye."

"Heather is too kind, but if I lived here, yes, I would've loved to work on this event. There's so much natural beauty that only the fine points need accenting, and the event planner did a terrific job of not going overboard. I would've done the same."

"I guess that's the reason the inn is perfect for a wedding. It doesn't need too many added frills."

Dinner was served, toasts were given and the reception continued on smoothly. Brooke dug into her meal, enjoying the perfectly seasoned and cooked salmon, quinoa salad and freshly grilled veggies. The meal was light and tasty, and after she was finished and her plate was being cleared, a band began to make noises as they set up on a platform stage.

"Excuse me," she said to the guests at the table. She rose and walked over to the sweetheart table. This was the first chance she'd gotten to congratulate Heather and her new groom. After the ceremony, they'd been inundated by a swarm of well-meaning guests and Brooke hadn't entered the fray, deciding to bide her time until she could have a quiet conversation with the newlyweds.

"Heather, congratulations!" Brooke's friend rose and they immediately embraced.

"Brooke, my goodness, I'm so glad you were able to make it to our wedding. Blake," she said, turning to him, "I'd like you to meet my friend from Los Angeles. We went to UCLA together, back in the day."

Blake stood up and took her hand. "Nice meeting you, Brooke, and thanks for being here."

"It's a special day and I'm glad I could make it. Heather has been trying to get me to make a trip to Texas for years."

"Oh, yeah? I hope you're getting a big Texas welcome."

"I am. Everyone's been gracious and nice. I'm on vacation, staying with friends in Beckon, so I'll be here for several more weeks."

"That's wonderful," Heather said. "Maybe we can get together when Blake and I get back from our honeymoon."

"I'm taking her on a cruise of the Mediterranean. We'll be gone ten days."

"Sounds perfect. And I'd love to see you when you return. Heather, you look stunning and it's not just the gown...you're glowing. Blake must be doing something right," Brooke said, giving him a wink.

"You know it." Blake took Heather's hand. "I like your friend already."

"I told you you would," Heather said.

The master of ceremonies called for the newlyweds' first dance. "Well, I guess you're on, you two. Congratulations again. I'll speak to you later."

A crowd formed around the parquet dance floor set up under the glorious white tent. Brooke took a position in the outer circle as the two lovebirds danced to a George Strait ballad. The lights were dimmed, and a sole spotlight shone on them like a halo. Heather really was glowing now.

Once the dance was over, there was a round of applause, and the bandleader urged the guests to join the bride and groom on the dance floor. Brooke headed to her table. Before she reached her seat, a man approached. He was in his midforties, she guessed, his tie crooked, his entire body seemingly angled to the left, as if he'd fall over any second. "W-would...you like to d-dance?"

His breath reeked of alcohol. "Uh, no thank you."

"Just one dance, missy, is all I'm asking."

"No, thank you," Brooke said as politely as she could

manage. She turned away from him and started for her table again. But he snagged her arm from behind, thick fingers digging deep into her skin. She whirled on him and yanked her arm free. "What part of no don't you get?" she said quietly. The last thing she wanted was to make a scene at Heather's wedding.

"You're a f-feisty little th-thing." He reached for her again and it was easy to step out of his grasp.

"And you've obviously had too much to drink."

"Is there a problem here?" Wyatt got between her and the pesky man, towering a good six inches above the guy. Wyatt's glare made it clear he wasn't one to mess with.

The man leaned way over, nearly toppling, and Wyatt quickly caught him.

"No p-problem. Nope. N-not a one," he said, chuckling.

"I think you need some air." Wyatt held the man upright and turned to Brooke, his mouth twisting in a smirk. He winked at her. "I'll be back as soon as I can."

He escorted—or rather supported—the guy out of the tent and Brooke returned to her seat. The man was probably harmless, but Brooke didn't like being manhandled that way. She'd been ready to raise her voice and call security, which would've dampened the festive mood. Once again, Wyatt was there, stepping in to save the day.

A quiet hum strummed through her body and she smiled.

"That's weird Uncle Hal," Connie said into her ear as Brooke lowered down into the chair beside her. "I caught some of what happened out there and my whole family apologizes to you." Connie made a face. "Hal likes to drink…when the liquor is free. Heather almost didn't invite him to the wedding. She was afraid he'd cause a scene. But he seems to have been neutralized."

"Neutralized?"

"Yeah, once he's been set straight, he doesn't cause any more trouble. He'll probably come over to say he's sorry."

"I hope not." Brooke shivered.

"Who was that hunk who took him outside?"

"Oh, um, he's a friend of the groom's. I met him earlier today."

"Does he have a younger brother, if you know what I mean?"

Brooke sighed. "Yeah, I do know what you mean. And honestly, I don't know."

"You're three for three, Wyatt," Brooke said.

Wyatt held her at arm's length as they danced to a light and breezy love song. His touch, though highly appropriate, thrilled her from head to toe. There was something steady and sturdy about him. He made her feel female, which seemed silly, but those deep blue eyes studied her with keen intent, as if she were a secret art treasure or a delicious hot fudge sundae. Either way, she was happy to be the object of his attention.

"How's that?" he asked.

"You saved me thrice, my lord," she said with a mock curtsy. "The last time with big Uncle Hal."

He laughed. "You were handling the situation just fine."

"You think so?"

"I do. But I also saw the indecision on your face. Where I come from, a man doesn't lay a hand on a woman 'less he's invited. When he didn't back down I figured you didn't want to make a scene."

"You're right about that. I don't like to draw attention to myself."

He drew her closer and spoke into her ear softly, "Then you shouldn't have worn that dress."

His gaze dipped past the lace on her scooped neckline

and touched upon her breasts. From under the material, her nipples tightened. Wyatt could do that to her with one look.

"You don't like it?" she asked, a little uncertain. "Or was that a compliment?"

Emma, her bestie, business partner and sister-in-law, was always telling her to put some color in her wardrobe, but black was her thing. She wasn't a floral kind of girl.

"Every guy in this place has his sights set on you. And I'm the one dancing with you." Appreciation shone in his eyes and she almost forgot all about Royce what's-his-name. "I like it, all right."

"Thank you."

"Welcome." His hands snaked around her waist, and the space between them lessened to inches. Brooke wasn't complaining. He smelled like whiskey and something woodsy and natural. She took deep breaths of him, drinking in his scent and enjoying the way his dark blond hair curled at his collar.

"I have a confession," he said in a quiet rasp. "I'm glad your car ran out of gas today."

Something broke apart inside her then, and her cynicism crumbled away. At least for the present, she wasn't going to question her actions. Or his. This perfect guy seemed to come straight out of her dreams, and she wasn't going to play it safe tonight. Not with Wyatt. She brought her fingers to the curls at the back of his neck and smiled, titling her chin up. Her eyes had to be gleaming now. "I'm glad, too," she said.

Wyatt's gaze heated. Thrills ran up and down her spine as she waited for him to do something bold, something daring.

He brought his head closer, never losing eye contact with her. "Are you inviting me?" he said, but he didn't wait for her answer. The connection they had was real and happening fast. He had to feel it, too.

His lips brushed hers softly, once, twice. Shock waves traveled the length of her body. She hadn't realized how much she'd needed this, how much she'd missed the simple reality of connecting with a man on an elemental level. The pure masculine taste of him washed completely through her, and a soft purr escaped her lips. She kissed him back and things got hot and heavy really fast. He cupped the back of her head, weaving fingers through her long, wild hair. "Oh, man," he murmured, pressing his lips more forcefully to hers, making exquisite demands on her. Demands she was eager to answer.

Was it lust? She'd been attracted to Wyatt from the second she'd laid her eyes on him. And now he was kissing her as if he'd been starving, and let's face it, she hadn't even nibbled in a very long time. Now she was ravenous.

Wyatt broke off the kiss before things got completely out of control on the dance floor and sighed loud enough for her to hear his frustration. Her ego was lifted to new heights as he tugged her tightly into his embrace, pressing their bodies closer. The slow ballad continued, but she barely heard the music. All she knew, all she felt, was her connection to Wyatt. They were so close, so incredibly in tune with each other.

Tension sizzled between them in a crazy way that upset her newly regained balance. She wasn't ready for this, for him. But when the dance ended and he stared into her eyes, she was lost.

"Let's get some air, darlin'."

She gave him a tiny nod, and he grabbed her hand and tugged her toward the edge of the draped tent that led to the lake.

Soft blades of grass tickled her ankles as Wyatt wove a path to the bank of Sweetwater Lake. Moonlight reflected off the rippling waters now, the sun having long ago bid farewell to the day. The air was still damp with humidity, but since sunset the temperature had cooled considerably. They stood facing the lake.

"Better," he said, taking gulps of air into his lungs. "It got a little heavy in there."

He dropped her hand, seeming to compose himself.

"It did."

"You surprised me, is all," he said, looking away from the lake to connect with her again. "I mean, I didn't expect…"

"I know. I'm different." He didn't have to say it. He didn't expect to be attracted to her. "I'm no Texas girl. I dress weird most of the time. Believe it or not, I toned it down for the wedding." No leather wrist bracelets, giant hoop earrings or multiple long chains around her neck for this shindig. As a matter of fact, she'd left most of that stuff back home in LA. Maybe she was entering a new phase in her life.

"I like your style, Brooke. There's nothing weird about you."

"Thanks for that."

"I mean it. When I saw you with Uncle Hal on the dance floor, I had an irrational urge to knock his block off."

"Is that equivalent to punching his lights out?"

"It is," he stated plainly.

"Why, Wyatt, that's the nicest thing anyone's ever said to me." She stood toe-to-toe with him, grinning. It felt good to break the tension and get back to easy conversation with him.

He laughed loud and deep and she joined in, too.

"I like you, Brooke," he said easily.

"Feeling's mutual," Brooke said. "Isn't that how they say it out here?"

"Stop poking fun at Texans." Wyatt's eyes twinkled. "We're a proud lot."

"I've heard as much."

A wicked Texas breeze blew strands of hair into her face.

With his finger, Wyatt innocently pushed a barrel curl resting on her cheek behind her ear. From the second his finger glided across her skin, the ridiculous yearning reared up again, putting a halt to their pleasant banter. Her laughter died in her throat, and as she focused on the man touching her tenderly, his smile changed into something less animated and playful. He gazed at her with dire want, his eyes dipping down to her pursed and needy mouth.

"Brooke," he rasped. There was a distinct hitch in his voice.

"It's okay, Wyatt," she said. Whatever he wanted, she was ready for.

A groan rose from his throat and he began shaking his head as if he couldn't believe what was happening. Brooke was in the same boat. They were sailing along at break-neck speed. She wasn't about to throw down the anchor; she wanted the wind at her back taking her wherever this was leading.

Wyatt wrapped one of his hands firmly around her waist, his fingers inching her closer, while he lifted her chin to meet his beautiful giving mouth with the other. The kiss was sweeter, more leisurely than before. She instantly felt safe with Wyatt; it wasn't about his saving her from empty gas tanks or pesky older men. It was something more, something she'd never experienced before. Utter trust.

The little voice in her head said, *It's because he doesn't know who you really are.*

But that wasn't it. A Texas rancher couldn't care less about her being a celebrity's sister. Wyatt had no agenda in that regard, and this uncanny faith she had in him came from a deeper, more soulful place within her.

Only seconds later, Wyatt whispered a curse over her lips and deepened the kiss, making it hard for Brooke to think straight. Helpless to curtail the sizzling connection between them, she flung her arms around his neck and his kisses immediately became inferno hot. Her lips were on fire, set ablaze by this amazingly strong, gorgeous man. He walked her backward until she met with the solid breadth of a cottonwood tree. She leaned against it, out of view of the wedding tent and the two hundred other guests.

He urged her mouth open and their tongues tangled. Explosive sensations rocked her back and a potent stream of desire coursed through her body, making her feel more alive than she'd felt in a long, long time. Wyatt had her trapped, his arms on either side of the thick tree. There wasn't any place else she'd rather be.

He brought his arms down to cup her face and tilted her head at an angle that was to his liking. His kiss was more deliberate this time, packed with intensity and precision. Oh, he was a yummy kisser.

He began an exploration of her body with both hands grazing her shoulders and traveling down her sides, along the inward curve of her torso and caressing the slight flare of her hips. She could tell he wanted to touch her in more intimate places but his keen sense of propriety wouldn't allow it. She wanted more, but couldn't deny how incredibly sweet and sensitive he was to her.

They came up for air a minute later, both shaking, both completely turned on. The music inside the tent stopped and the bandleader's gleeful voice carried over the microphone, announcing it was time for the bride and groom to cut the cake.

"Brooke." He whispered her name on a sigh and touched his forehead to hers, his warm breath caressing her cheek. "We should really go back inside."

"Mmm." He was right, of course, but how on earth would she stop her legs from trembling, her body from quivering? "I think so, too."

"You go first," he said, encouraging her with a nod. "I'll need a minute. Oh, and be sure to save the last dance for me."

She straightened her disheveled dress, took a swallow, steadied her out-of-whack nerves and then headed up the embankment toward the tent. Halfway there, she swiveled her head around to find Wyatt's discerning eyes still on her.

She turned to continue her trek, purring with quiet delight like a kitten lapping up a bowl of rich cream.

"Here you go," Wyatt said so quietly she barely heard him. He set her luggage down outside her hotel room door as she slid the key card into the lock.

"Thank you," she said, turning to him. "I, um, had a great time tonight. The wedding was pretty cool."

"I had a good time, too. Thanks to you."

She stared at him, quaking inside. She didn't want to make another mistake. But looking into Wyatt's eyes, she didn't believe him to be one. "You give me too much credit."

"I don't think so. I was dreading coming here today. And then I met you."

She blinked. He had a way of saying the right things. He wasn't a clever charmer, but he was charming. And he was a gentleman, in every way that counted. "Why were you dreading it?"

Pain entered his eyes. "Let's just say I'm new to bachelorhood and leave it at that."

"Oh." She got that. She didn't want to rehash her past relationships, either. One of the best parts of meeting Wyatt tonight was not having to think about the Royce Brisbanes of the world. She was fine with forgetting all about her own lousy relationships. "Okay."

Wyatt tilted his head. "You're not like most women."

"That doesn't sound like a compliment, Wyatt."

"Believe me, it is. Most women want to nose around and fix what's broken, but I'm not into that right now."

He was broken? Now that was a revelation, because from where she stood all of his parts seemed to be in excellent working order. "Wyatt," she said softly. She didn't want him to leave. Gosh, how she didn't want to say goodnight to him.

"I'd better get to my room."

She didn't miss the reluctance in his voice. "Okay. Thanks for being my miracle cowboy today."

He blinked, seemingly surprised at her comment.

She smiled and lifted up on tiptoes to brush a soft kiss to his cheek.

He kissed her back, a gentle peck on the mouth. "Welcome."

She loved the taste of him, the way he smelled, the sturdy breadth of him.

He gazed at her mouth, his eyes holding a lingering dark gleam as if he wanted more. As if he wanted to devour her. The bone-melting effect reached all the way down to the tips of her toes. If he touched her again, she would be lost.

And then he did just that. He splayed his hands on her waist and drew her closer. "I need one more kiss, Brooke."

His rich baritone voice did crazy things to her, especially when he was asking to kiss her again. *Oh, man.* "Anything you need." Her voice was a breathless whisper.

And then their mouths came together in an amazing onslaught of potency and possession. Heat immediately rose up and flared like a lit match. It was as if everything fell into place again. His hands wound tighter around her waist. Her arms wrapped around his neck. Their lips smacked, and moans and sweet sighs of pleasure surrounded them.

"Take it inside, you two," a passerby said, chuckling as

he headed down the hallway, obviously having had one too many.

"Good idea," Wyatt stated softly over her lips.

"Yes, Wyatt. Yes."

With one hand, he pushed the heavy door open and then lifted her luggage and plunked it down just inside the room. Then the door closed behind him and they were alone in the dark hotel room.

"Just tell me you want this," he said, bracing her against the wall.

"I want this."

"God, Brooke. You're the one who's the miracle."

It was the sweetest, most beautiful thing anyone had ever said to her. She squeezed her eyes closed briefly and drank it all in. She drank *him* all in, too. His kisses set her body on fire, and now that they were out of the public eye, they were free to unleash their passion full force.

"I need to touch you," he whispered.

"Touch me."

His palms traveled over the slopes and curves of her body. His hands were large and rough, but he was gentle in his approach, making her want him all the more. He lifted her leg up under the knee, and she gasped as he slid his hand under the tight confines of her dress, stroking her thigh back and forth, over and over. "You're soft," he murmured between kisses. His body pressed to hers was a wall of granite, so big and hard, and she was overwhelmed with sensation after sensation. Between her thighs, pulsing heat gathered and her breaths came in short, rapid bursts.

He lowered her leg to the floor and flipped her around to face the wall, her back to his front. He probed her backside, skimming his hands over black lace. Through the material of her dress, the heat of his palms scorched her skin and she sighed, surrendering her body to him.

Finally, he inched the zipper of her dress down. She felt

the cooling fresh air on her skin as he pushed her dress away. Planting kisses on her shoulders, he undid her bra and then reached around to cup her breasts. He filled his hands, massaging and caressing her until she could barely stand the pleasure, tiny moans escaping her lips.

He skimmed his hands down her torso and back up again, navigating her body as if he were exploring points on a map. "You're soft everywhere."

She loved the quiet words he spoke over her shoulder and the way he held her so preciously. She breathed in the aroused scent of him as he reclaimed her aching breasts, his body pressed to hers, fully aroused, his scent intoxicating.

"We need to move this onto the bed," he said. "Unless you like—"

"No, the bed is fine," she managed.

He helped her remove the remainder of her clothes and then lifted her into his strong arms. He carried her to the turned-down bed and laid her there carefully.

Without saying a word, he kicked off his shoes and undressed for her, undoing his string tie, removing his jacket, shirt, belt and pants.

From what she could see from the sliver of moonlight streaming into the window, Wyatt met and exceeded her expectations. God, he was glorious above the waist, with brick shoulders and hard abs. And below, well, she took a huge gulp. He was definitely all man.

"Don't ask me why," he said, quite earnestly, "but I have protection."

"That's a relief," she said softly. "I don't."

She hadn't exactly planned on hitting the jackpot tonight, but she thought it odd that he would be apologizing for carrying protection. He'd said he was new to bachelorhood. She assumed he was divorced, yet she needed to ask. "Wyatt, just tell me one thing. You're not married, are you?"

He stared into her eyes for a beat of a second and then shook his head. "No, I can promise you that."

Relief took on a new meaning with that promise. "Then, as much as I like looking at you, I'd like to touch, too."

He sighed, perhaps equally relieved. "Absolutely, dar-lin'."

The first time Wyatt made love to her, it was an exploration of newness. They were careful with each other as she learned what he liked, while he provided what she wanted. There was heat and pleasure and a development of trust. She did trust Wyatt. She knew he wouldn't abuse her in any way; he was far too much of a gentleman for that. But now, after a short respite, Wyatt was pulling her atop him, kissing her senseless again, and this time both of their guards were down.

"I want you again." The urgent plea tore from his throat.

"I'm here," she whispered, climbing up his body and giving him access to her breasts.

"I'm glad you are," he said, tickling her nipple with the tip of his tongue. Both peaks pebbled up immediately, and wild stirrings began at the apex of her thighs.

Wyatt was the best lover she'd ever had. He could take her from zero to ninety with just a heated look or a bold caress. And he was doing just that with exquisite strokes of his tongue on her breast, the full circle of his mouth drawing her out, making every nerve ending ping and jump.

When he was through making her squirm in delight, he moved down her body, his hand gliding past her waist and his fingers tucking into her sensitive folds. He knew exactly how to caress her. He knew where she needed to be stroked and oh, he was merciless. She cried out, the pleasure so exquisite it was almost painful. Electric sensations rocked her back and forth until she could barely take it another second.

"Kiss me," he ordered, and she obeyed.

And just as their tongues met, her body splintered apart, the amazing orgasm rocketing through her body with enough force to jerk her off the bed. She came down panting, the effects of her release almost mystifying her until she opened her eyes and saw Wyatt staring at her, his darkened gaze hot as fired metal.

He rolled her over onto her back and lifted her hips, positioning her. And then he was inside her again, this time without hesitation. He began thrusting, his erection hard and thick, pulsing with new life. He moved deeper and harder and brought her to the brink of insanity once more. "Come with me this time," he rasped, his throat thick.

And they moved together, arching, aching, a beautiful joining of bodies in complete sync with each other. And when she was primed and eager and staring into his eyes, he tipped his head in acknowledgment. He knew she was ready. Then they rose up and bucked and cried out, her sighs meeting his groans. Her body shattered, just as his came apart.

It was glorious.

She was in heaven.

And she stayed up there awhile before slowly easing down.

Her limbs were weightless now. She felt like a sated rag doll, too limp to move. Wyatt scooped her up in his strong arms and surrounded her with his hot, perfect body. He kissed her cheeks, wove his fingers through her hair.

"Brooke," he whispered over her lips.

"Mmm." She'd never been happier. Or more tired.

"Sleep, darlin'."

"Sorry, can't help it."

"It's okay," he said.

Wrapped up in his arms, she closed her eyes.

Wyatt opened his eyes to a dawn that had long ago broken through the shuttered windows of Brooke's hotel room, streaming bright light inside. The digital clock read eight o'clock and he cursed silently as he untangled himself carefully from Brooke. His heart thumped in his chest as he glanced down at her, looking so peaceful, her eyes closed, that mane of raven hair falling down her back. His body strummed to life again, but he had no time to indulge or to say goodbye to Brooke. No time to look into those pretty brown eyes or hear the sultry tone of her voice.

He should've been on the road an hour ago. He was late, and he'd made Henrietta a promise. He couldn't take advantage of her good nature. Weekends were precious to her.

"Dammit," he muttered as he scrambled to step into his clothes. He hated leaving this way. There was a reason widowers shouldn't have one-night stands. He was out of his element here. He had seconds to make a decision and God only knew if it was the right one, but time was wasting. He scribbled a note to Brooke and left it on the nightstand.

He had nothing to offer Brooke. He was still in love with Madelyn and he had no room for another woman in his life. Not that Brooke seemed to want anything but this one night together. She hadn't asked him a bunch of questions the way women tended to do, and she hadn't hinted at anything more. She was vacationing in Texas and had a life and a business on the West Coast.

The thoughts crowded his mind as he gave her one last glance.

He'd be forever grateful to her for this night. Brooke

had helped him get through a tough day and they'd had a good time.

Actually, they'd had *multiple* good times during the evening.

End of story.

He walked to the door, not surprised by the regret burning a hole in his stomach. He didn't usually walk out on women. But he couldn't stay, either. It was better this way. For her. For both of them.

He turned the doorknob and strode out of the room, leaving Brooke and the Inn at Sweetwater behind.

More than an hour later he'd reached the gates of Blue Horizon Ranch. He was home, back where he belonged. But he'd thought about Brooke most of the way and he'd cursed his best friend, Johnny Wilde, for practically daring him to go to the wedding. Now he had guilt. And memories he couldn't wash from his mind.

Was he a fool to think he was betraying his late wife by enjoying himself with another woman? Johnny would certainly think so. But then, what did he know? He'd been with too many women to count and he'd never found the right one, while Wyatt had met the love of his life and had married her. For that short time—only five years—they'd had together, he'd been happier than he thought possible.

And now he had his precious twins to think about.

He parked the car in front of the house and gave it a quick glance, just as a wave of pain jabbed his gut. He'd never quite gotten over the fact that Madelyn wouldn't be here, greeting him after a trip. That her birthday had come and gone yesterday and there would be no more sweet kisses between them, no emerald sparks of joy in her eyes when he surprised her with a gift. "Sorry, Maddy."

That day nine months ago had ripped his gut in two. Seeing the sheriff at his front door, hat in hand, his face solemn. *Madelyn's had an accident. I'm sorry, Mr. Brandt.*

Wyatt shook off the memory. He had to get his ass inside the house. Henrietta's youngest niece was coming to help him with the twins, so Henrietta could spend the weekend camping in their fifth wheel camper up at the river. Ralph, her husband, wasn't a patient man. He'd been pressing her to retire, and she'd promised him she would as soon as Wyatt found a suitable nanny for the twins. Henrietta was as loyal as they came, and she was good with his kids, but she was exhausted lately. He'd catch her rubbing at her back and taking short naps in those rare times when the twins were both asleep. She'd been here since his folks lived at the ranch, and she was more like family than the help. Clearly, she didn't want to leave Wyatt in the lurch without someone he trusted to care for his children, but the search wasn't going well.

He entered his house and stood in the foyer, listening for baby sounds. "I'm home," he said quietly, just in case Brett and Brianna were napping. And then he heard their voices coming from the great room, which substituted now as a giant playroom, and strode in that direction. His heart warmed immediately when he spotted his kids. The twins were toddling around on the floor, paying Carly no mind as she read them their favorite book, *Goodnight Moon*.

"Hi, Carly," he said to the teenager.

"Oh, hi," she said, glancing at him through her black-rimmed glasses.

At the sound of his voice, Brett, who was scooting a Lego truck along the hardwood floor, and Brianna, who was clutching her doll, abandoned their toys, flapped their arms excitedly and toddled over to him, their smiles lighting him up inside. He scooped both twins up in his arms. "Hello, my babies."

He gave each a kiss on the cheek.

Brianna was more vocal than little Brett. "Daddy! Home. Daddy kisses."

Brett stared at his sister first and then hugged Wyatt around the neck. Nothing was sweeter. Nothing helped his healing more than their unconditional love. He was constantly enveloped in sadness thinking that Madelyn would never know her children. And that his twins had been cheated out of a wonderful mother.

Henrietta walked into the room. Her sturdy build and cinnamon red hair piled in a tight bun atop her head gave her the appearance of a stern woman, but nothing was further from the truth. She was an old softy at heart. "Sorry I'm late," he said, feeling like a heel.

"Not a problem, Wyatt. I hope you had a nice time at the wedding."

An image of Brooke Johnson, naked and asleep in the bed he'd just left, popped into his head. "I did. It was good to see Blake again."

"That's nice. My Ralph is on his way. Carly's been here, playing with the kids. She'll help with feeding them later, and getting them down for their naps. I've got the weekend's meals ready for you in the fridge."

"Thanks, Etta."

Carly stood, picking up a few toys from the floor as she rose. "I can stay overnight if you need me to, Mr. Brandt."

"Thanks, Carly. Let's see how the day goes. I might just need you to come back tomorrow, if you can."

"I can do that, too," she said.

"Okay, great." Wyatt set the kids down and squatted onto the floor next to them. It was a tough balancing act, being in charge of a huge ranch corporation and being Daddy to his children. But he couldn't let them down. They needed the stability of having him here most of the time, knowing that they came first, no matter what.

After Madelyn's death, he'd relied heavily on Henrietta

for support with the kids. But if he didn't find a suitable nanny soon, old Ralph would march in here one day and threaten to knock his block off…with a shotgun.

He had three interviews with potential nannies later this week.

He could only hope.

Three

Brooke
You'll never know how much last night meant to me.
If you ever need me for anything, you can find me at
the Blue Horizon Ranch. Thank you.
Wyatt

Brooke sat on her bed in the guest room of Zane Williams's brand-new gorgeous ranch estate and reread the note for the tenth time this month. She hadn't been able to toss it away. The paper was crumpled and creased, but the words rang out loud and clear. Wyatt had blown her off.

The morning after the wedding, when she'd woken up alone at the inn, she'd read his words and been baffled. She'd been certain Wyatt wasn't the love-'em-and-leave-'em type. She'd been certain they'd wake up together and exchange phone numbers, at the very least. Maybe have breakfast together. Their connection had been powerful, so strong, in fact, it sort of scared her. She'd been sure it wasn't one-sided. Had her BS meter gone on the fritz?

After what Royce Brisbane did to her, she'd turned on her protective radar with all shields up. She'd come to Texas partly to forget about men and romance. And then Wyatt appeared, seemingly out of the blue, and gave her one miraculous day…and night.

Maybe that's all there'd ever be for her, snippets of passion, spread out here and there, but nothing real, nothing permanent. Oddly enough, it was the "thank you" at the end of the note that pissed her off more than anything. As if she'd done him a service.

If you ever need me for anything, you can find me at the Blue Horizon Ranch.

Hell, yeah, she needed him. But right now, her pride interfered with good judgment. Tears entered her eyes. Tears she didn't want. Tears that embarrassed her. She wasn't a teary-eyed romantic fool, but her hormones were out of whack and had been pretty much since she'd missed her last period.

She knew what it meant. She'd taken the test yesterday. She was going to have Wyatt's baby—a result of too much passion and not enough good sense.

She'd slept on the news last night, hoping when she woke up today it would've all gone away, like a bad dream you eventually forget. She hadn't told a soul, but Emma was raising her eyebrows at her lately, asking her why she was tired and looking pale. She blamed it on the Texas heat and humidity. She wasn't used to the sweltering temperatures, but Emma was five months pregnant and having just gone through these early months, she knew the signs all too well.

Dylan popped his head into her room. "Are you gonna come out to the set today, sis?"

"Oh, I don't think so. But thanks."

"What are you gonna do? Stay alone here all day?"

Zane and his new wife, Jessica, had graciously offered for the three of them to stay as his houseguests in the glorious new home Adam Chase had designed as a wedding present, while Dylan shot a Western movie here. Zane had been a neighbor for a time back in Moonlight Beach, California, and Dylan, Zane and Adam were all good friends now. But newlyweds Zane and Jessica were inseparable, and a few days back, they'd left on Zane's spectacular tour bus, heading toward New Orleans to do a round of country music concerts.

Now Dylan, Emma and Brooke had the house all to themselves for the next few weeks.

Emma barged into the room, her growing belly covered by a breezy floral handkerchief dress. "No, she's not spending the day alone. She's going to help me pick out baby girl clothes!"

Brooke forgot about her own problems and jumped up. "You're having a girl?"

Emma nodded, her laughter infectious. She lifted the pointed hem of her dress with both hands, and danced around the room singing, "Yes, yes, we're having a baby girl."

Brooke caught her midstride and hugged her tight. "Oh, this is wonderful. Boy or girl, it doesn't matter, but now we know!"

She peered over Emma's shoulder at her brother. His eyes were gleaming with love for his wife and new child. One would never know the child Emma carried wasn't his. But he loved both mother and child with all of his heart. And that's all that mattered.

Brooke stepped away from Emma and with arms reaching up, walked over to Dylan to give him a giant warm hug. Her big brother was happier than she'd ever seen him. "Congratulations."

Dylan kissed her forehead. "Thanks. We're excited."

"You're going to be outnumbered, you know, with all these women around."

"He's used to it," Emma said, her eyes sparkling with mischief.

"That's right, the big mega movie star has women falling at his feet," Brooke said.

"Not anymore. They know I'm taken." Dylan went to Emma and took her hand. She smiled and then both of them looked Brooke's way. "So, you'll drop by the set with Emma later?" he asked.

"Sure, we'll come by and see you."

She couldn't burst his bubble. She'd been a downer lately, and hadn't been able to concentrate on having a good time. They sensed something was up with her, but hadn't pried. Not yet, anyway. She didn't want to raise any more suspicion. She was having enough trouble accepting the fact that Emma wouldn't be the only new mother around here. And she had no clue of how or when to tell Wyatt Brandt he was going to be a father.

Wyatt sat upon a black gelding with white socks named Oreo and faced the rushing waters of the Willow Springs River. Twenty miles north of Beckon and even farther from his ranch, he was doing Johnny a favor today by coming here. Aside from Johnny Wilde, no one else in the area had as much commonsense knowledge about horseflesh and cattle as Wyatt did. Not that he'd wanted this job. Hell, he was no consultant, but his friend had called him in a panic. Johnny had come down with the flu, hopefully just the twenty-four-hour kind, and he'd needed a replacement, pronto. "You're the only one I trust to do the job," he'd said.

It wasn't the plea, but the weakness in Johnny's voice that had Wyatt agreeing to haul his butt away from Blue Horizon Ranch and his kids today.

He glanced at the men milling around, decked out in fringed leather chaps, Stetsons and snakeskin boots. Actors.

Dressing room trailers—honey wagons, Johnny had called them—were set up in the outlying area and a crew of about fifty were pulling wires, setting up cameras and shouting orders. He'd already spoken with the director today about the scene they were to shoot along the river's edge. The horses and cattle would be crossing in shallow waters, but it was a key concern that no animals or actors be hurt in the highly technical shot.

From a distance, he spotted the star of the movie, Dylan McKay, stepping out of his trailer decked out in a chambray shirt, jeans and a red paisley kerchief around his neck. And then Wyatt froze. He blinked and refocused.

Yep, he wasn't imagining it. Dylan was with a woman. It was *her*.

Brooke Johnson.

What was she doing here? She looked awfully chummy with Dylan, laughing at something he'd said and walking along with him as though she was accustomed to being close to the mega superstar.

Seeing her again sent blazing fireworks off in Wyatt's head. "Uh, Tony?" He took his eyes off Brooke for a second to get the assistant wrangler's attention. "Do you know who that woman is walking with Dylan McKay?" He pointed. "Is her name Brooke Johnson?"

The wrangler scrubbed his jaw, his eyes narrowing a bit to gain a good look. "It's Brooke all right. All the single guys on the crew have been eyeing her. But her name's not Johnson. That's Mr. McKay's sister, Brooke McKay."

"She's Dylan McKay's sister?"

"Yep, that's what they tell me. She's a looker, but she's not the friendly type, if you know what I mean."

No, he didn't know what Tony meant. A knot formed

in the pit of his stomach. The woman he'd met on the road had been friendly and fun and sassy. He'd never describe Brooke as unfriendly. But then, he hadn't known the real Brooke, had he? She'd given him a fake name. Now that wasn't cool.

And just like that, Brooke turned her head and met his gaze. She halted abruptly, her face going as white as newly plowed snow. Dylan kept walking, but Brooke stood there, some twenty feet away, staring at him as if she couldn't believe it. As if she wanted to hide under a rock.

God, when had his effect on women taken a turn for the worse?

She said something to her brother, and then did a one-eighty and hightailed it back to the trailer. Before stepping inside she glanced in Wyatt's direction. To see if he was watching? Their eyes met again and for all he was worth, he couldn't, wouldn't stop looking at her. Then she was gone, the trailer door slamming shut behind her.

"Crap," he muttered, climbing down from his horse. He planted his feet on solid ground and held the reins in his hand, trying to decide what to do. He'd worked hard to put Brooke out of his mind, and now here she was infiltrating, invading and trying her best to take up space again.

He was so busy being in his own head, he didn't notice Dylan McKay until he was standing right in front of him. "Hello, I'm Dylan. I understand you're taking over for Johnny Wilde today?"

"Yes," Wyatt said, distracted. He got it together enough to refocus and pay the star some attention. "Wyatt Brandt."

Dylan put out his hand. "Nice meeting you."

"Same here."

They shook hands. "I understand you think the river's too fast to do the crossing scene today?"

"That's right. I told the director we should wait. I know the area, and that current is only going to get stronger as the day progresses. It's not safe for the animals. Clouds are starting to gather and those breezes are gonna turn ugly in a few hours. The winds will only complicate things. Sorry, I know it's not the news you hoped to hear."

"No need to apologize. We can shoot around it. Keeping the animals and crew safe is a priority. I just wanted to hear it from you."

"Sure thing."

"So, you're from around here?"

"I've lived in Texas all my life. I own Blue Horizon Ranch some twenty-five miles from here."

"Horses?"

"Cattle, but we have a string of Arabians and cutting horses on the ranch, too."

They spoke about horses and Texas for a while, and Wyatt came away thinking that Dylan McKay wasn't a stereotypical prima donna celebrity. It was on the tip of his tongue during the conversation to ask him about Brooke. But that didn't happen. Dylan had been called away. Just as well. Wyatt had come to the conclusion that he needed to speak to Brooke himself.

Sure, she'd lied to him about who she was.

But he'd left her alone in a hotel room after a wild night of sex, without much of an explanation.

He marched over to the honey wagon with a clear vision of what needed saying, but as he came close to knocking on the trailer door, his mind began to blur. Visions of Brooke slapping his face a good one flashed in his head. She might call security to toss him off the property.

He'd like to see them try.

But his hand clenched into a fist and he rapped on the door regardless. Things needed saying. It was as simple as that.

The door opened, and he was shell-shocked when a

pretty, pregnant redhead stood facing him. "Hi, can I help you?"

"Uh, sure. I wanted to speak with Brooke. I'm Wyatt Brandt."

"Okay, Wyatt. Let me see if Brooke is available. What can I tell her this is about?"

Hell, the wagon wasn't that big. Brooke was probably hearing this whole conversation. "Just mention my name. Tell her I hope she'll see me."

"I'll see him, Emma." Brooke said, her voice stony. And then she appeared in the doorway. She wasn't happy about seeing him, yet her beautiful brown eyes widened a bit when she looked at him, turning his brain to mush. The words he wanted to say fled him faster than a jackrabbit running from a hound.

"Hello, Brooke."

"Wyatt."

Emma gave them both a curious glance. "You know, I just remembered I have an errand to run."

Out here? There wasn't a town for miles.

"You don't have to leave, Emma. This won't take long," Brooke told her.

"No, no. I've really got to, to, uh…talk to Dylan. He's waiting on me to meet him down by the river."

Emma ducked her head and scooted down the steps quickly, giving them privacy.

Brooke's curvy body blocked the doorway. "I'm not inviting you in."

"There's no need for that. I just wanted to say…" Brooke's arms were folded and any minute now, she'd be tapping her foot, schoolteacher style. "Listen, I have some explaining to do. But so do you. You lied to me."

"About what?"

"About your name. You faked your identity."

"I have my reasons for that. But you skipped out...and oh, never mind."

"Can we talk?"

"I thought that's what we're doing."

"No, I mean really talk. I feel badly about how I had to leave you that morning. I do, and I want to make it up to you."

If body language had anything to do with it, she'd surely refuse him, but something stopped her. Instead, she seemed to be considering it. "What did you have in mind?"

"Come out to the ranch and have dinner with me. We can talk there, uninterrupted." Well, that depended on two little rascals and their sleep schedule, but he couldn't offer her anything more right now. His sense of honor was at stake. He didn't usually treat women the way he'd treated Brooke, and he wanted to make amends. "I can pick you up later and take you to the ranch."

"No. I don't think so," she said, and he felt the disappointment all the way to his toes. "I'll drive out. Just give me directions...*easy directions*, or I may not find it," she said.

She was agreeing? Why was he so damn happy about that?

"Great. It's about half an hour's drive from here and it's practically a straight run. I'll write down the directions. But I'd be happy to pick you up."

"No, I'll drive to you," she said, in a tone that meant business.

He got it. She wanted to be able to leave at a moment's notice. He didn't care. At least the nagging thoughts plaguing his mind would be put to rest after he explained the whole one-night-stand business.

The trick was trying to sort it all out in his own head first.

With her windows rolled down and a light drizzle dotting her windshield, Brooke was actually enjoying the ride.

The muggy Texas day had given way to an evening of fresh scents and cooler temperatures. Her windshield wipers clicked on and off and her driving arm was hit with an occasional raindrop as she steered over remote terrain toward Wyatt Brandt's ranch.

If it weren't for the baby she was carrying, she wouldn't be making this drive, but the opportunity to tell Wyatt the truth presented itself today when he shown up on the set of *The Price of Glory*. Seeing pigs fly would've shocked her less than having Wyatt Brandt appear at the river.

But as luck or bad karma would have it—she wasn't sure which—Wyatt had come out of nowhere again, her not-so-miraculous cowboy. Talking to him had become inevitable. She certainly couldn't speak with him on Dylan's set; there were too many opportunities to trigger gossip and speculation. And at Zane's home, there'd be too many eyes and ears around to have a private conversation, namely her brother's and Emma's.

Country music filled the silence of the road. Brooke sang along with Reba to keep her mind off what she was about to do. The words of "Cowgirls Don't Cry" poured out of her as she traveled over a lovely wooden bridge, the creek below surging with water. Alongside the water's edge, a carpet of healthy bluebonnets stretched out as far as the eye could see.

The picturesque image stayed with her and gave her a sense of peace. Soon white fences lined with Mexican oaks standing tall and probably designed for privacy came into view. Long branches with leathery leaves waved at her as she drove by. Within a minute, she came upon brick columns and iron gates and a pretty metal sign embossed with the sun rising over the land, welcoming her to Blue Horizon Ranch.

She sighed. Grateful to have made it without getting lost or running out of gas, she now had to contend with the fact that she was *here*. And one way or another, her life was going to change forever when she revealed her pregnancy to Wyatt Brandt.

As she drove through the open gates, the sudden strong scent of cattle filled her nostrils. Texans told her she'd get used to the smells around these parts, but it wasn't exactly vanilla sugar she was breathing in and she sincerely doubted that smell would be a treat to her nose anytime soon.

But oh man, the ranch was beautiful. The branches of whispering oaks formed a canopy over the road leading to a beautiful slate-gray stone ranch house. Wide windows gave the place an open feel. Across the way, the barns and outer buildings were faced with white wood and gray-toned shutters. It was homey and contemporary at the same time. Brooke immediately loved Wyatt's home. From the outside.

What lay in store for her on the inside was another matter.

She drove the circular drive and parked the car. She was on time for a change.

She'd dressed for dinner in old Brooke style, wearing basic black hip-hugging slacks, a silver-and-black shimmery top, and a wide belt. Her shoes were skyscrapers in red suede. She wasn't entirely sure she'd dressed this way out of defiance or as a shield of armor. She knew one thing: she felt comfortable in her own skin, and right now she needed that burst of confidence to confront Wyatt and tell him the truth.

She knocked at the door, and when nothing happened, she hit the doorbell. Inside, she heard the chimes ring out. A moment later, the door opened and she stood face-to-face with Wyatt.

Holding a squirming baby boy dressed in tiny denim overalls.

It was the last thing she expected. The child's melt-your-heart blue eyes were a perfect match to Wyatt's. The baby took one look at her and turned his head into Wyatt's shoulder and clung on for dear life.

"Wyatt?" She was rendered speechless after that, staring at the man who'd made her insides quiver just one month ago. Now he looked the picture of domesticity, his pale blue shirtsleeves rolled up, a stain that looked like sweet potato on his collar, his short blond hair disheveled.

"Come in, Brooke. I'm glad you made it okay."

She stared at him, still not believing what she was seeing. He'd never mentioned having a child. Although there'd seemed to be a silent agreement between them not to delve too deeply into their private lives. But being a father? Having a child was news he should've shared with her.

When she stood rooted to the spot, Wyatt moved aside and nodded, encouraging her to enter the house.

She stepped inside, instantly aware of her surroundings: the planks of light gray flooring under her feet, the brightness of the rooms even as dusk was settling. But what struck her the most was seeing the parlor crowded with toys: a fire truck and princess car suitable for a toddler and musical instruments and blocks everywhere. Everything was tidy and yet, it was *there*.

Wyatt closed the door behind her. "This is Brett, my son. He was supposed to be sleeping by the time you arrived. Obviously that didn't happen. Babies tend to make liars of their parents."

"You never mentioned you had a child, Wyatt." She tried hard not to put accusation in her tone.

"Would that have made a difference?"

"I don't know." It was the truth. She'd been so incredibly drawn to Wyatt that if he'd been open with her and told her he was a father, would she have fallen so easily into bed with him? She wasn't sure.

The baby inclined his head toward her, his rosy face so sweet, so curious. "Hello, Brett."

Brett clung tighter to Wyatt's neck.

"He's not much of a talker yet."

"How old is he?"

"Going on nineteen months."

"He's beautiful, Wyatt."

"Thanks, he's the best part of me. Well, him and his twin sister, Brianna."

"There's two of them?" Her ears twitched at the sound of her own voice. Twins? Wyatt had two children. This was all a bit much for her to take in. Her crazy hormones brought the threat of tears. She forced them down and tried not to think about what his reaction would be when she told him her news.

"Yes, and they're a handful, believe me. Listen, I want to explain all this to you. Why don't you have a seat in the dining room?" He started walking and she followed. "There's wine and cheese and other snacks ready. My housekeeper, Henrietta, is gone for the day, but she put out a nice spread for us. It'll just take me a few minutes to put Brett down to sleep and change my clothes."

He gave her another cursory glance. "You look pretty, by the way," he said, his miracle cowboy charm taking hold again. He was such a freaking gentleman, she had trouble remembering how he'd dumped her after a spectacular night of sex.

A night that they'd conceived a child.

"Please," he was saying, "have a seat."

Robotically she obeyed. And once he excused himself, she sat there stunned and feeling foolish. Her perfect miracle cowboy had engaged in lies of omission. Was he at that wedding just to hook up with a woman? Was her man radar off that much that she couldn't recognize a player?

But deep inside, she kept telling herself it wasn't true.

She couldn't have been that much off the mark with Wyatt. He'd been wonderful that night, and today, he'd invited her to his ranch to explain. Yet it nagged at her that if they hadn't accidentally met today, it would've been solely up to her to seek him out. It put her in an awkward spot.

A waterfall of rain poured over the gutter above the dining room bay window, drawing her attention. Lit by surrounding lights, it was a pretty distraction even if the skies were dark and filled with dreary clouds. It sort of mirrored her mood right now. Her nerves were jumping, and she bounded up to walk around the room, stopping to look at the pretty things in the china hutch, expensive yet tasteful pieces of crystal, delicate dishes and gold-rimmed teacups.

"That teacup set dates back to post-Civil War," Wyatt said quietly.

She hadn't heard him enter the room, but he stood behind her now and when she turned around, he was a breath away, staring into her eyes. The faint hint of his cologne brought reminders of being naked with him, of his hands on her and…

"It was my grandmother's favorite…" His voice trailed off as his gaze dipped down to her mouth.

Brooke felt the jolt down to her toes and looked away, pretending interest in the rain.

She wasn't going there with him, not again. There was too much unsaid between them.

He sighed and stepped away, pulling out a chair for her. The table was set perfectly, with some of the same fine china from the cabinet. She sat back down. Before he took a seat, he offered her a glass of wine.

"No thanks," she said. No alcohol for her.

He nodded, probably thinking she was being careful because she'd have to drive home. Well, there was that, too.

"You haven't touched anything," he noted.

"I'm not hungry right now, Wyatt." She was queasy about being here and queasy in general due to being pregnant.

"Okay, we can wait on dinner."

He braced his elbows on the table, matched the fingers of both hands in a steeple under his chin and sighed. "Brooke, I'm very glad you're here. The way I left you that morning was…unforgivable. I was out of my element and unsure what to do."

"You didn't appear unsure of anything the night we were together."

"Maybe it was you…"

"Don't butter me up, Wyatt. I can't get past the fact that if we hadn't accidentally met today, I would've never heard from you."

"You gave me a fake name."

"And you ran out on me after we…" She shook off the thought. She'd been over this in her mind a hundred times.

"I guess we both have explaining to do."

"You go first," she said. "And then I'll let you know if I want to share my reasons with you."

He nodded. Of the two sins, his was by far the worst, and he seemed to know it by the miserable look on his face. "My explanation is simple, but hard to admit. I lost my wife about ten months ago. She got in the car one day to pick up diapers for the twins and she never returned. She was pushed off the road by a semitruck. Her car plummeted off the shoulder and crashed into a tree."

Brooke gasped quietly, surprised to learn of Wyatt's loss. It explained a lot about why he hadn't spoken much about his past. He was probably still in a great deal of pain. When she'd met him he'd told her he was newly single. She'd thought that meant he had broken up with a girlfriend, or he was divorced. It never occurred to her that he might be a widower.

"That's awful, Wyatt. I'm so incredibly sorry."

She couldn't imagine losing someone she loved that way. One minute they were alive and vital and then in the blink of an eye, they're gone. How terribly sad it was for the mother who would never know her children. And those poor little babies, too. It was tragic all the way around.

She'd never forget how she felt when Dylan's life was in danger. She'd been absolutely terrified for him and she couldn't imagine losing him. But Wyatt had had to face that reality. He'd become a widower at a very young age.

"Thanks. I've been wallowing in self-pity and grief and as you can see, I have my hands full with the twins. They're about all I can handle. Two is like having four. Henrietta keeps reminding me how hard it is on her. I'm trying my best to find a suitable nanny, but it isn't easy. The last two who worked for me were mediocre at best. The babies didn't seem to respond to them, and they flaked on us a few times. I can't have that. I need someone reliable. Henrietta is sticking with me for the short term. She's getting on in age and she just can't do both jobs. I offered to hire more help so she could take the kids on full-time, but her hubby is chomping at the bit for her to retire. I can't say as I blame him."

Wyatt's shoulders lifted in a shrug that spoke volumes about his frustration. "My friend Johnny Wilde pressed me to go to that wedding. He said I had to get out and start living my life again. So, between him and Henrietta urging me on, I decided to go. The wedding was a way to distract me from the real issue that day. It was Madelyn's birthday. She would've been thirty."

Brooke was beginning to get the picture. "Was *I* your distraction, Wyatt?"

He gazed into her eyes, and his head made a slight movement. Was that a yes or a no? She couldn't tell what he was thinking or what he was about to say by the solemn expression on his face. "You were…but in an unexpected way."

"What does that mean?" She found herself speaking quietly, and not because of the sleeping children. This was delicate subject matter and Wyatt was looking so miserable.

"I thought I'd attend the nuptials, wish Blake well and bide my time during the reception. There'd be some drowning of my sorrows in whiskey, too, and then I'd planned on turning in early. I didn't go there with anything else in mind. I couldn't stop thinking about Madelyn and how we would've spent the day celebrating her birthday together. But then I found you broken down on the road, and I couldn't drive on by. I stopped and well, that's the unexpected part. For the first time since Madelyn died, I started enjoying myself again. Just being in your company changed my outlook and made me glad I'd made the trip to the inn. You made me forget some pretty awful days and I…well damn, this isn't easy to admit."

He pushed his fingers through his hair and sighed from deep in his chest. "I was attracted to you, Brooke. Madelyn was my whole life and I can't even remember a time that I wasn't infatuated with her. But then I had this one day with you."

"So I was a hall pass from your grief and guilt?"

He nodded. "Sounds awful, but maybe that's exactly how it was."

"So you woke up the next day and ran…because the guilt came back? You couldn't face me? Why didn't you wake me or at least wait until we could say goodbye?"

Wyatt reached across the wide table and touched her fingers, as if he needed the connection with her. Sparks ran up her arm, but she wouldn't make anything out of it. Wyatt was clearly still in love with his wife.

"No, Brooke. It wasn't that. It was Henrietta. She'd

stayed overnight with the babies, and I'd promised her I'd be back early in the morning. She had a trip planned and I didn't want to ruin her day or abuse her good nature. I woke up later than expected that morning. Believe me, there was so much I wanted to say to you. But that note was all I had time for, and that's the honest truth. On my babies' lives, I swear to you."

Brooke was quiet for a time. He was giving her time to absorb it all. She took a swallow of her drink and began nodding her head. "Okay, I get that. But you know what part of the note insulted me more than anything? The thank-you at the end."

Wyatt stared at her and shook his head. "You're mad because I thanked you?"

"It was as if...as if I'd done a service for you or something. I can't explain it, but that's how I felt when I woke up alone and found your thank-you note."

"Oh, man." He rubbed his forehead and closed his eyes. "I had no idea it would come off that way. I wasn't proud of how I left that day. It's bothered me all this time. Believe me, Brooke, I never intended to hurt you."

Thunder boomed off in the distance and she jumped. Was it a heavenly omen, a sign to take Wyatt at his word?

"I'm out of practice with women, Brooke. And I never expected to have..."

"Sex?"

He nodded. It wasn't in his wheelhouse to be crude; she'd already figured that out about him. But she had no problem telling it like it is.

"It was an amazing night, Brooke. But I didn't think past that night or what the next day would bring."

"I didn't either, if I'm being honest."

"But you didn't expect me to run out on you."

She nodded. "It made what could've been a good memory for me feel cheap."

"No!" Wyatt scraped his chair back and stood. "No, Brooke. That night…it was real and honest. I needed to feel alive again…and it was you, and only you, who helped me with that. And if I'm not mistaken, you needed the same from me, too. Am I right?"

She opened her mouth, but her denial didn't come. Slowly, she closed her trap and nodded. She would give Wyatt that. She'd needed someone who'd cared—if only in the moment—for her. She was still healing from Royce's duplicity. She would've almost rather had her ex throw her over for another woman than to use her the way he had.

Wyatt was a different breed of man. That much she knew. "You didn't tell me you had children."

"I didn't. I just wanted to be me, not a father, not a widower, that night. My pain-in-the-ass pal Johnny is forever saying I need to find myself again. That's what I was trying to do."

She inhaled a sharp breath, everything becoming clear in her mind now. He was lost without his wife.

A flash of lightning lit up the night sky behind Wyatt and reflected off the window. The bright beam illuminated a backyard filled with patio tables and chairs, toys and a gated pool. This was a home for a family to live and love and thrive in, but sadly there was a missing piece now. The family wasn't whole anymore.

Her anger faded as fast as the lightning. Oddly, she understood how Wyatt wanted to be private about his past when they'd met, wanting one night to just be himself and not a responsible father, not a grieving widower. Wasn't that the same reason she hadn't been totally honest with him? She just wanted to be Brooke, not Dylan McKay's younger sister, not the girl who'd had men use her to get close to her famous brother.

If she were brave, she'd reveal her pregnancy to Wyatt and try to cope with the decisions they would make together. But her courage failed her. She couldn't lay this on Wyatt right now.

As she grappled with her decision to cut and run, a baby's wail broke into her thoughts, loud and panicky.

Wyatt's squeezed his eyes shut momentarily. "That's Brianna. Sorry. I think she's having a bad dream. I've got to check on her. "

"Of course. Go."

As soon as Wyatt took a step out of the dining room, another howl erupted, the second one huskier and deeper than the first. Both babies had woken up. And their cries blasted through the house without interval. Double trouble. Brooke rose and followed Wyatt up the stairs.

At least this was one crisis she could help manage.

Four

Brett and Brianna both howled, one in each crib, their little bodies facing up toward glow-in-the-dark neon stars illuminating the ceiling. Madelyn had chosen nursery decor that would bring a sense of peace and calm, but there were times that nothing much soothed cranky twins. Thunder boomed outside, rattling the windows, and their cries grew louder. Wyatt picked up Brett first, bouncing him in his arms, and then turned to Brianna. But Brooke was already picking up his little girl.

Brianna was groggy at best, her eyes half closed. But she looked so sweet, her blond curls falling onto her face as she clung to Brooke's neck. She had no clue she was in the arms of a stranger. Heaven help them all when she discovered that fact. Bri was his wild child. She didn't take to newcomers, which was something her previous nannies had learned the hard way.

Brooke bounced Brianna in her arms, taking her cue from him. Not that he knew exactly what he was doing.

His kids were a constant bafflement to him. One minute they were happy as clams, the next, they'd be wailing about something he couldn't begin to fathom.

Bouncing them was clearly not working. Tears continued to fall, and then Brooke began to sing as she rocked the baby in her arms. Not just *sing*: her lilting voice filled the room with sweetness, a serene siren's song that mesmerized with its beauty. And damn if Brianna didn't stop crying right then and there. Her big blue eyes opened wide and she sniffled a few times, stunned into silence by her own curiosity and…awe.

Brett followed suit, and Wyatt walked him closer to Brooke, so he, too, could be enchanted. Brooke clearly had a talent, which seemed to pour out of her effortlessly. Within minutes, his crab apple little ones were quieted. Brooke rocked Bri and he rocked Brett and once they'd fallen asleep in their arms, Wyatt nodded to Brooke. Carefully, she laid the baby down in her crib. Then Wyatt kissed Brett on the forehead and also set him in his crib.

Brooke tiptoed out of the room, allowing Wyatt a minute to simply stare at his babies. God, he loved them. They were all he had left of Madelyn, and they truly were the best part of him. He would do just about anything to ensure their happiness. But with one strike against them already—losing their beautiful mother—the weight of his responsibility sometimes scared the stuffing out of him.

He left the nursery door open and went in search of Brooke. He found her at the top of the stairs, waiting for him. "They're both sweet," she whispered. "You're very lucky."

"Thanks. You have a beautiful voice, Brooke. Hidden talent? Or did you lie to me about your profession?"

Her body went rigid. Fueled by anger, her brown eyes lit up. "I didn't lie to you about anything but my name."

"Yeah, and why was that? You feel like telling me

now?" he asked softly, trying to tread carefully. He'd pissed her off unintentionally, but he really wanted to know.

Her shoulders relaxed some, and she studied him a moment, then nodded. "All right. I'll explain."

"Great. Let's talk downstairs." He took her arm and led her to the parlor sofa. "Have a seat."

She sat on the couch and he took a seat on the opposite end.

"It's not a big deal," she began, "that I lied about my last name. My brother is famous and it gets old real fast, having people act nice to me only because of him."

"That's it? That's why you lied? You get tired of answering questions about him?"

"No, Wyatt. I get tired of men using me, getting my hopes up and pretending to care about me only to get close to *him*. I get tired of men giving me scripts or screenplays to show him or using me to ask him to invest in their pet projects."

Wyatt shook his head, finally getting the picture. It wasn't pretty. It would take a strong, secure woman not to be affected, but then, Brooke was all those things, which made the creeps using her horrible slugs. "You've been burned."

"To a crisp."

"Man, that's rough. I'm sorry. Was it someone in particular, someone special?"

"I thought he was special at the time. It was a man who worked in finance, a real pencil pusher, a numbers man, a guy I thought wouldn't care who my brother was. As it turned out Royce was a closet wannabe screenwriter. And when he lowered the boom I didn't see it coming. It floored me and hurt me, and coming to Texas was a way to mend and heal. And gain some perspective. So, what I did that day by lying to you wasn't too different than what you'd done. I just wanted a day without questions. One day to be me. Just plain Brooke."

"You could never be plain," he said, and realized how much he meant it. From the get-go, he'd found something unique in Brooke.

"Thanks." She shrugged and looked away as if she didn't believe him, as if what he was saying to her was merely a platitude to make her feel better. Yes, he wanted her to feel better, but he wasn't lying.

"It's the truth. And I do understand. I'm sorry you got hurt, Brooke. Honestly, it makes me feel awful about running out on you the way I did."

She snapped off a quick smile. "Story of my life."

"You're terrific, Brooke. I mean that. And any creep who would use you isn't fit to call himself a man."

"Present company excluded?"

"I didn't use you. Tell me you don't think that."

Her eyes squeezed closed and she shook her head. "No. I don't think that. Not anymore."

Which meant she'd gone the entire month thinking he had. Crap.

Wyatt closed the gap between them on the sofa. He had to get closer to her now, and make sure she was okay. Hell, she was more than okay. She was amazing. It wasn't easy being this close without touching her, holding her in his arms and making her feel better. But sanity prevailed just in time and took over his brain. Touching her again would be a colossal mistake. A change of subject was needed.

"You're very good with children. Do you have a big family?"

"Not really. I'm Dylan's foster sister—his folks are my folks. It was just me and him growing up. He's always been my rock, my best friend, and sometimes, my bitter enemy. You know, your usual brother/sister dynamic."

"Sounds like fun."

"Yeah, it was. Still is. I love him to death. What about you? Brothers or sisters?"

"Nope, just me and those two powerhouses you helped put to sleep. They're a handful and a half. I don't know how people with big families do it. One boy, one girl, and I'm done. Especially now."

"You mean because you're doing it without their mother?" Brooke's voice lowered and nearly cracked. She wouldn't look him in the face.

"Two's enough, when both parents are in the picture. But yeah, I suppose it's because I'm trying to move on and it's tough going sometimes. That's why when I met you…well, it was nice. *You* were nice, and I suppose I—"

"Don't, Wyatt. I get the picture."

She went rigid all over and lowered her lids to her red suede shoes. They looked great on her feet, but weren't exactly perfect footwear for a rainy night. "Maybe you don't."

"Oh, believe me, I do." Her voice was stronger now, but pained, as if he'd hurt her all over again.

Just then, lightning flashed, and a second later thunder cracked, the loud boom shaking the house. Wyatt bounded up quickly and moved to the window. Rain was coming down in buckets. This raging storm wasn't moving on anytime soon. "Dammit. I should've been paying closer attention."

"To what?" Brooke asked.

He turned to her while releasing a you're-a-fool sigh aimed at himself. "The rain. The storm. This isn't good, Brooke."

"Won't it pass?" She rose and marched over to the window.

"Not before doing a lot of damage. The bridge is washed out by now. Happens every time we have a major storm."

"What bridge? Not that pretty little bridge I drove over a couple of hours ago?"

"That's the one. It's the only way in and out of the ranch. Can't get to the highway without it. You're going to have to spend the night here."

Her face twisted up, and those chocolate eyes went dark as coal. "That's ridiculous, Wyatt. I. Am. Not. Spending the night here."

"Hey, I know you don't want to, but this storm is dangerous. And you won't get over that bridge. Trust me."

She shook her head. "I'm betting it's not too late. If I leave now, I'll make it. The rain only just started coming down hard."

"Nope, not happening. I can't let you do it."

"You can't order me to stay here." Her voice rose. "I'm going to try, Wyatt."

She found her purse, grabbed her car keys and made a dash for the front door.

He followed her. "Brooke, be reasonable." But the determined look on her face said reason wasn't a factor.

"Thanks for dinner."

"You didn't eat a thing."

"Thanks anyway. I'll…we'll talk. I have to go."

He blocked the door with his arm. "Don't. It's not safe."

It wasn't safe for her to stay overnight either, but he wasn't going there.

She gazed into his eyes. There was something more going on with her. Something that he didn't understand. Was she worried about a repeat of the night they'd shared? He'd hurt her, and she wasn't forgetting that anytime soon, but for some reason he didn't believe that was it. He thought they'd cleared the air. They'd talked openly and honestly, but something had jarred her and he wasn't sure what it was.

"You don't have to worry about, about…"

"Don't be an idiot, Wyatt. You think you're that irresistible?"

She blinked her eyes; her sarcasm was hiding something else. Something she wasn't saying. Having her spend the night here wouldn't be easy on him. He wasn't immune to her, the way she claimed to be to him. She was the only other woman beside Madelyn to touch something deep inside him and bring out his protective instincts. Was it a bad case of lust? He'd gone months without sex, and Brooke had been the perfect partner, guileless and beautiful and giving. Having her here would test his willpower, but the very thought of her going out in that storm gave him hives. She didn't know the roads like he did. She didn't know the treachery that lay in her path. She came from California, where a few sprinkles meant storm watch. But here in Texas, they had real storms, ones that could wipe out entire towns.

"Brooke, listen to me. You're being stubborn."

"And you're wasting my time. You can't keep me here against my will," she hissed out.

Holy hell, she was right. "I am trying to keep you safe."

"I don't need you to rescue me anymore. You're through being my miracle cowboy, Wyatt. Now, unblock the door."

Slowly and against his God-given good judgment, he stepped away from the door.

She exited quickly, and he watched her get into her car, start the engine and pull away.

The windshield wipers weren't doing a very good job. Or was it her tears causing her vision to blur? She slowed the car down to a snail's crawl and inched her way along the dark road leading her away from Wyatt, his kids, his grief and his declaration that he wanted no more children. Period. *Two's enough.* Two, as in his adorable twins who were motherless now, and being raised by a dad who was lost in his own way.

And where did that leave her?

More tears spilled onto her cheeks, mingling with the raindrops that had slashed across her face just minutes ago as she got into her car. Damn her hormones. She was usually stronger than this. But usually, she wasn't pregnant by a virtual stranger whose only sin, other than running out on her in the morning after a one-night stand, was that he had no clue how her heart had shattered and was still shattering when she realized that he wasn't going to jump for joy at having another child.

And dammit, her child deserved more than that. Her child didn't deserve being cast aside. She should know. The McKays had taken her in and loved her like their own. She was grateful every day of her life, but it still didn't heal her secret pain of knowing that she'd been unwanted. Unloved. It was classic foster-child syndrome. But now, her baby, the sweet life growing inside her, wouldn't have what Brooke had vowed any child she bore would have: two loving parents.

"Not fair," she mumbled while trying to slosh along the flooded, muddy road.

A flash of lightning lit up the skies and thunder followed, the loudest she'd ever heard. Her hands trembled on the steering wheel, and she sobered. Maybe Wyatt wasn't trying to be Prince Charming again. Maybe this storm was really as bad as he'd said.

An animal skittered across the road and she braked hard. "Oh!" She barely missed the critter, and the car skidded, careering to the right. She gripped the steering wheel tighter, her knuckles white, as the car spun out of control. The back end dipped into a muddy ditch and hit a brick fence post. The force pitched her forward and her thick skull slammed into the steering wheel.

The jolt startled her, and her forehead immediately throbbed. She sat there, dazed, as big drops of rain pelted the windshield. Her head pounded, her eyes burned and she felt as if she'd been hit by a giant dump truck rather than mixing it up with a fence post. She closed her eyes, a sense of déjà vu hitting her. She'd been in this car once before and laid her head on the steering wheel, clueless as to how to proceed. God, she was an idiot.

Tears sprang anew from her eyes, and she welcomed them this time. She needed a good cry. What secretly pregnant girl didn't?

She took a tissue out of her purse and blew her nose. That's when she realized it wasn't just tears streaking her face. Blood colored the white tissue. Not a lot, but enough for her to take another tissue out and adjust the mirror in the dark to catch a glimpse of the damage. She had a knot the size of a plum erupting and a scrape two inches long. No doubt tomorrow, it would turn from hot red to dark purple. Wonderful. Now she'd have to explain all this to Dylan and Emma and endure their worry and concern.

If she ever got home tonight.

A knock came on the driver's side window, startling her out of her self-pity. Oh, no. It couldn't be. The man wearing a rain slicker and big Western hat gestured for her to roll down her window.

She did. He shone a flashlight on her face and then quickly lowered it. But it must have been enough for him to see her stricken expression and bruised forehead. Curses spilled from his mouth. Really ugly words hissed out, not exactly the words of a knight in shining armor. Lucky for her, the pound of the rain washed away the worst of them from her delicate ears.

"Wyatt."

"Dammit, Brooke. You're bleeding."

"Not that much," she said numbly.

"Are you okay?"

"I… I think so."

He yanked the door open and reached for her.

"I can walk."

"Quiet, Brooke," he said through clenched teeth. There was fierceness in his voice she'd never heard before. So she clamped her trap shut as he lifted her out of the car and carried her to a big four-wheel-drive Jeep. He dumped her in the front seat, but not before her eyes drifted to the backseat. And her stomach plummeted. Two beautiful children, strapped into their car seats wearing pajamas and shivering, were rustling around back there, restless, cold and sleepy-eyed.

Brett rubbed his eyes and Brianna was barely holding back sleep-deprived tears.

Wyatt had risked going out in the storm with his babies to save her sorry butt.

He slammed the door shut behind him and didn't look at her. "I'm…sorry about this, Wyatt."

Nothing.

She bit her lip. His seething anger was almost tangible, and she felt the slap of his silence as he pulled out onto the road and slowly navigated his way through the storm. The rain didn't let up, and the windshield wipers fought a crazy swish and slosh of water. But she felt safe again and knew he would steer them cautiously home. Lights from the ranch house appeared out of the darkness like a beacon of all things good, and Wyatt drove into the attached garage and killed the engine. He would've probably liked to kill her, too, at the moment. Brett had started crying halfway through the drive home and Brianna had joined in shortly after. The cacophony of their cries only added weight to her blunder.

She was a heel.

A thoughtless fool.

She hadn't once thought of the risk to her own baby in all this.

And Wyatt's innocent kids had been dragged through the storm in the dead of night.

Of course, she'd thought of none of this beforehand. She'd only wanted to make a clean getaway. She didn't think she could bear staying the night under Wyatt's roof, and guess what? *Hello.* Now she had no choice in the matter. And instead of Wyatt being a gracious host, she'd be privy to his wrath.

Which she deserved.

Wyatt gave her a cursory look, only to gauge her injuries. "Stay put in the Jeep. I'll be back for you," he ordered.

"You don't need to do that," she said, opening the door and practically falling out. It was a long way down, and she'd been in a hurry. "I'm helping with the kids. You take Brett, I'll get Brianna."

"Brooke," he said, his sigh weary and frustrated, but he didn't argue the point. It was too loud in the garage to hear much beyond the babies' cries.

"Let me help, Wyatt," she said softly. "It's the least I can do."

"You're not dizzy?"

She was dizzy in the brain lately, but that wasn't what Wyatt meant. "No. I'm not. It's just a little bump."

He grunted and she took that as a yes to helping with the kids.

She opened the back door of the Jeep, ignoring the throbbing pain in her head, and concentrated on unfastening Brianna from the car seat. The baby was pushing the heels of her hands into her tired eyes, whimpering. "Come with me, Bri baby. We'll get you warm and back to sleep."

Apparently at some point, Wyatt had tossed two blankets over them, but now they lay on the Jeep's floor. She grabbed one and wrapped it around the baby, while Wyatt was doing his best with Brett. Once they had their two unruly packages all bundled up, they entered the house. Immediate warmth settled around them as they made their way up the stairs.

The nursery was illuminated by a night-light. Brooke and Wyatt stood quietly in the center of the room rocking the babies. Their cries simmered some, but they were still restless.

"Wyatt?" she whispered.

"Hmm?"

"Do you have your cell phone handy?"

"Yeah, why?" he whispered, still swaying little Brett in his arms.

"I need it for a minute."

He gave her a look, but then handed it to her.

"Thanks."

She set Brianna down in her crib and covered her with a blanket. Brooke then fidgeted with the phone until she found what she was looking for. "Okay," she said, "put Brett in his crib."

Wyatt gave her a dubious look, but set the baby down and covered him.

Then she turned up the volume on the phone and the gentle humming of a box fan filled the room.

"They should be asleep in minutes," she whispered to Wyatt.

"What in hell is that?" he asked, staring at her as if she'd grown horns.

"White noise."

She tiptoed out of the room. Wyatt glanced at his quieted babies, not quite asleep yet, but soothed and calmer now, before following behind her.

In the hallway, he grabbed her hand. "Come with me."

His grip was tight, but not in a loving way. She felt a lecture coming on. But to her surprise, he led her into his master bedroom. It was a beautiful room filled with white oak furniture in tasteful shades of cream and lilac. Madelyn's touch was all around, from the top-notch drapes and bed linens to the delicate crystal perfume bottles on the dresser to the impressionist pastel artworks on the wall. It was hardly a manly rancher's room, and Brooke had trouble picturing Wyatt in here. Yet it was a testament to his love for his wife. He'd let her decorate, allowing her to do whatever made her happy.

"Wyatt, what are you doing?"

They bypassed the bed and entered a foyer that led to a massive master bathroom. She was sure she could put her whole apartment in this room. There were two of everything, which was the way Wyatt seemed to roll, having twins and all: two long granite counters with dual sinks, two toilets and two walk-in closets. Just one tub though, sunken and luxurious, surely big enough for two consenting adults to share. The thought made her hot all over.

He picked her up and set her on the countertop. "Gosh, you've got to stop doing that," she blurted.

"Doing what?" he asked, distracted. He was busy gathering supplies, peroxide, washcloths and a first aid kit.

"Carrying me places."

"You don't seem to have sense enough to keep yourself out of harm's way."

"I keep out of harm's way."

He snorted.

"I said I was sorry. I never meant to endanger your children. I wasn't…thinking."

"There's a lot of that going around."

Did he mean the night they'd slept together? Was he regretting it? Of course he was. She'd been nothing but trouble from the moment they'd met.

He placed a warm washcloth on her forehead, and she flinched.

"Sorry, Brooke. I've got to clean this wound."

"It's nothing."

"Nothing?" He placed his hands on her shoulders and swiveled her partway around. She got a good look at her wound in the light.

"Oh!" It was three times the size she'd seen in the car's mirror. Blood had caked on her forehead. It looked like a red rose atop a lumpy cupcake. Only this was not sweet. "I didn't realize."

"You could've been seriously hurt," he said through tight lips. He dabbed at the blood some more.

"But I wasn't. I never expected you to drag your babies out into the storm to rescue me."

"You left me no choice. What else was I supposed to do? Let you crash your car and get hurt or…or—"

"You put your children in danger for me."

"I could let you believe that. It would serve you right. But the truth is, I know the land and the four-wheel-drive Jeep has weathered lots of storms. I wouldn't deliberately put my kids in danger."

"But still, you dragged them out of bed to come get me."

"I won't be disagreeing with you."

"I'm so sorry, Wyatt. I promise you won't know I'm here and in the morning I'll—"

"You're not going anywhere in the morning, Brooke. This storm is pounding the land, and the weather reports aren't good. Looks like we're in for a few more days of it. There's another storm right behind this one."

"There is?" She took a swallow.

"I'm afraid so."

He finished washing her wound and dried her forehead, then took a pad of gauze and soaked it with peroxide. "This is gonna sting a bit," he said.

"You're going to love every second of it."

He leaned back to look into her eyes. His were still cold, hard and so amazingly blue, she wanted to cry. But she'd already done enough crying. She'd take her medicine like a big girl and pay the price for her stupidity.

"You should've listened to me. Then none of this would've happened. You put your life in danger, Brooke."

And then she got it. She knew why he'd come after her. She'd put him in a terrible position. Shoot. She wished she was wrong on this, but her heart told her the truth. He couldn't let her go it alone to possibly crash her car or worse. His wife had died in a car crash. Those memories must have tortured him tonight. Wyatt couldn't stand by and let another woman die on his watch. He had to come after her; his conscience wouldn't allow anything else. And whatever he'd said to the contrary, he *had* risked his kids and his own safety to rescue her.

"Ouch!"

The hardness in his eyes evaporated some. "I told you it would sting."

She almost choked on the pungent smell of peroxide. When he finished ministering to her gash, he capped the bottle and put it away. She jumped down from the counter before he picked her up again.

"It only lasts a minute or two," he said.

She nodded. "I'm really sorry I behaved so selfishly. Really, Wyatt. I wish there was a way for me to make it up to you."

His dark blond brows rose and the intense glint in his eyes put wicked thoughts in her head. Was he thinking about their night together? When they had labored long and hard to satisfy each other's hunger? When they'd spoken of nothing consequential and yet said so many things in the heat of passion?

Wyatt's landline phone rang in the master bedroom, breaking up the moment.

He walked over to it and glanced at the number, then

winced, his frown even deeper than the one he had for Brooke.

"I'll leave you so you can answer that."

"No, it's not necessary. I'll return that call in the morning. Right now, you're going to eat something."

"I'm not—" She was about to say she wasn't hungry, but then she remembered the life inside her needed nourishing. She'd been selfish enough tonight. She needed to eat, if only to maintain her strength for the baby. "Okay, yes. It's a shame to let the dinner go to waste."

"Fine," he said. "And you should put some ice on that bump."

"Right. Ice. Just what I need. Gotcha."

He turned around at her sarcasm, and that brow rose again. Did he have to be so darn appealing, even when he was scowling at her?

She made the gesture of zipping her lip with her fingers. Wyatt's eyes gleamed and a smile threatened to emerge on his face, before he turned around and kept going.

She followed behind without another word.

Dinner was a quiet affair of stilted conversation and reheated food. Nevertheless, she downed her meal with gusto. It was either a result of Henrietta's expert cooking or the fact that Brooke was eating for two now. She filled her tummy with chicken piccata, scalloped potatoes, yeast rolls and salad until she thought she would explode. "My compliments to the cook," she said once she was all through.

"I'll tell Henrietta. It'll earn me brownie points, relaying the compliment," Wyatt said, sipping coffee. He hadn't looked at her during the dinner. The vibe she got was that she'd pissed him off and now he was stuck with her. What was his demeanor saying? Don't mess with Texas? Or Texans, for that matter.

She kept her lips buttoned and spoke only when spoken to.

"How do you know about white noise?" he asked finally, pushing away his empty coffee cup.

She shrugged. "Years of babysitting, I guess. You pick up hints and tricks along the way. And I've been doing some reading. My, uh, sister-in-law Emma is pregnant."

And so am I. If only she had the courage to make that announcement.

"I'd never heard of it," he said, staring at her mystified. "There's so much…"

"You learn as you go, Wyatt."

"I suppose. But sometimes I feel behind the eight ball on all this."

"You're a businessman with a company to run. You can't possibly keep up on the latest baby trends. And the old ways of doing things aren't so bad."

He pushed his hands through his hair. "You mean like rocking a baby to sleep instead of brainwashing them with digital noise?"

She laughed. "Yes. Both ways work."

He chuckled, too, and his whole demeanor changed. It was nice to see his smile again, if only for a few seconds. She could faint dead away from how his eyes touched upon hers. They lingered for a while, sparkling brilliant blue like the sea on a sunny day. It was killer to see him unguarded and free of any pain or anger.

"So are you hating me right now, or have I moved up the scale to mild dislike?" she finally asked.

A deep sigh broke from his throat. "Brooke."

"I'm sorry. But we are going to be stuck here together for a few days."

He shook his head at her comment. "I don't hate anyone. Dislike is reserved for my enemies."

"You have enemies?" Now that was a surprise.

"A few. You can't get to this level in business without ruffling feathers and pissing people off. I've done my share of negotiating but I've always done it fairly. Some of my competitors haven't been so scrupulous. I don't abide ruthlessness in business or anywhere else."

"So, you dislike your competitors. That's probably the case for a lot of business owners. What did they do, undermine your good name?"

"I can fend for myself. And my name is just fine. But they hit me the hardest when Madelyn died. I was struggling with her loss and my babies being motherless, and my rivals swooped in during a vulnerable time in my life to steal contracts away. At the time, I was too grief-stricken to take much notice or to care."

"That sucks, Wyatt. That's a really rotten thing to do. Okay, so I'm not in that category. Thank God."

"Brooke, there's no need to put a name on any of this. I sure as hell don't know what to call…us." He gestured with his hands to both of them.

Us? As in, the two of them? Brooke wouldn't get her hopes up that he meant anything serious by using the term. There was just no other way to describe the two of them. Still, while they were on the subject of babies and white noise and all, why couldn't she bring herself to tell him she was carrying his child?

And the devil's voice in her head was only too glad to explain, *Because you couldn't bear for your baby to be unwanted, the way you were.* And that was the crux of the matter. She was just coming to terms with being pregnant herself, and having Wyatt rebuff and reject the baby would be a knife to her heart.

Outside, the storm didn't let up. Windows rattled and winds howled with frenetic energy. It was the gloomiest of gloomy and yet there they were having a cozy meal together in the warmth of the house with two sweet babies asleep in their cribs upstairs.

"Do you have to check on the animals or anything?"

Wyatt ground his teeth and nodded as if she'd hit upon the very thing he'd been thinking. "I probably should, but I…"

But he didn't want to leave the babies alone with a stranger. She would remedy that right now. If there was one thing she could do for him, it was that. "I'll watch the twins, Wyatt. I'll sit in their room if you'd like. And I promise no more stunts. I'll be right there if they need something. Although I wasn't hinting for you to go out in this god-awful weather."

"The weather doesn't bother me, but I should check on the horses in the barn at the very least. I've gotta make sure they have feed and water. And it's not necessary for you to sit with the babies. I'll look in on them before I go out. They should sleep the rest of the night. Why don't you get ready for bed? You must be tired. You can listen for them in the guest bedroom."

She was exhausted. And the idea of cuddling up with a pillow and a warm blanket over her suddenly became appealing. Usually a night owl, her energy cells shut down after nine o'clock these days.

"Sounds good. But first, let me help put some of these things away," she said.

Wyatt didn't stop her from picking up plates and taking them to the kitchen. They worked silently, moving about the room tidying up and making very sure they didn't accidentally bump into each other. She couldn't have him touching her tonight, not while the storm raged outside and her innermost feelings were so close to the surface. She liked Wyatt a whole lot, and the iron barriers she usually put up with men seemed to falter when he was near. And that was a bad, bad thing.

"Follow me. I'll get you something to wear for the night."

He was halfway up the stairs before she started the climb, trying to keep her eyes down and not on the precise cut of his jeans and the rear end that was pretty near perfection. It was darn hard not to notice as his boots clicked and clacked upon the shiny wood steps, accentuating what was going on with every long-legged stride he took. Then she caught a glimpse of his shoulders in the tight cotton shirt. He was one of those cowboys whose muscles bunched under the shirtsleeves.

It wasn't as if she hadn't seen him naked. But somehow this was more intimate: being alone with him in his home with his children sleeping just steps away from her room.

"Here we are," he said, once he reached the room that was two doors down from the nursery and on the opposite side of the hallway from his master bedroom. "You can bed down in here. There's new toothbrushes and towels and everything you might need. If you don't find something, just let me know."

"I'm sure it's fine. Thanks."

"Oh," he said, remembering something. "Just a sec."

He walked away and then came back holding a red plaid flannel shirt. "This is the best I can do right now. It's clean."

She'd wondered if he would give her one of his wife's garments to wear, or if he still had any of her clothes around. Wearing something that was Madelyn's would be too darn weird, so the flannel shirt was a good choice.

He handed it to her and she hugged it to her chest. "Thanks."

Maybe hugging his shirt wasn't the brightest idea. His gaze dipped down to her chest and his eyes flickered like a newly lit flame.

She took a big breath.

He did the same. "Well," he said, lifting his eyes to meet hers.

"Well," she said, captivated.

He made a face, then pushed his hand through his hair. "I'd best go see to the animals."

"And the twins?"

"Are sleeping tight. But you can check on them if you'd like while I'm gone. I hope to be only ten minutes or so."

"Fine, I'll be listening for them."

"Appreciate that."

Five

It was a mother of a storm. Wyatt wasn't a small man, and yet as he exited the warmth of his home, he was thrashed about quite handily by sweeping thirty-mile-an-hour gusts that nearly stole his hat from his head. He pushed it down with the flat of his hand and trudged toward the barns. He had a string of Arabians that wouldn't take kindly to Mother Nature's outburst. A few years back, he'd installed floor heating in the barn, but those animals were feisty and high-strung and they sure as hell didn't like the boom of thunder and the sound of rain pelting the rooftops overhead. It was not quite hurricane weather, and he was grateful he had the means and the cash to provide the best structures for the animals. If the cattle had any sense, they'd take shelter in the overhangs on the property he'd set up every forty acres or so to provide a source of cover for his crew.

He reached the barn and made quick work of checking on the horses, pitchforking a layer of extra straw in their stalls, and making sure they had enough alfalfa and oats to fill their bellies. It would be at least two days before his crew would return. His weekend crew couldn't get onto the ranch anyway, and he'd texted them all earlier, telling them not to try. It was too dangerous.

With his work done, he latched the barn doors. He fought his way back, putting his head down and trudging through winds that could likely lift him off the ground and carry him to parts unknown. But he made it to the house just fine.

He stood in the foyer, shedding his cold, rain-soaked coat and gloves. The warmth inside the house seeped into his bones. It would take a hot shower to completely thaw him out.

He climbed the stairs two at a time, ready for this night to be over, and checked on the babies. But he damn well wasn't prepared for the sight before his eyes. He halted and swallowed hard.

Brooke.

She was leaning over Brianna's crib, her mile-long tanned legs giving him quite a show. As she bent further, he caught a powerful glimpse of the slip of white cotton panties she wore and the plump, perfect cheeks peeking out.

He blew breath out of his lungs and admired the view, his groin tightening up, his heart racing. What he wouldn't give to have her here under different circumstances. To have the freedom to take her to his bed and make wild love to her again and again.

He groaned, the sound penetrating the room, to his chagrin.

Brooke startled and turned around, catching him in the act of lusting after her. She gasped, a beautiful breathy sound that stirred his senses even more as they met eye to eye across the darkened room.

Brianna quieted back to sleep, thanks to Brooke, and then Wyatt remembered his place, the fact that Brooke wasn't here by choice and that he wasn't available to her. Not in the way he craved. But judging by the spark of heat in Brooke's eyes she tried to conceal, she might be craving him, too.

She tiptoed out of the room, edging her way past him in the doorway, her breasts teasing his chest as she passed by. That wisp of a touch nearly undid him.

"Brooke."

She whirled around, her eyes knowing and hungry. "She was fussing. I calmed her back to sleep."

"Thanks."

"You're cold and wet," she said. He liked having her eyes on him.

"I'm getting ready for a warm shower."

She nibbled on her very plump bottom lip and drew his attention there. "Good idea."

Crap. Did she have to have such a kissable mouth? Now all he could think about was kissing her senseless, stripping her of his shirt and having her join him in the shower.

"I'll be off to bed now," she said, without making a move.

"I, uh…okay."

The staring match continued. Wyatt could look into her pretty coffee-brown eyes all night. Her hair was falling off one shoulder, all those lush rich raven strands close enough to reach out and touch.

"Brooke," he said again, giving his head a regretful shake.

"I know, Wyatt. It's okay… Good night."

He sucked in air. She felt it, too, and there wasn't a damn thing either of them could do about it. "Night."

Finally, she turned and headed down the hallway to

her own room. Before closing the door, she wiggled her fingers at him.

Once she was out of sight, Wyatt breathed a sigh of relief. Two more days of this could mean trouble. What a freaking mess he was. Hungering for another woman in the very home he'd once shared with Madelyn.

It wasn't going to happen.

But oh, it wasn't going to be easy, either.

When morning dawned, the sky was just as dreary as the night before. There was no sign of sunshine, just gray threatening clouds. A steady light cascade thudded against the roof, but without the theatrics of thunder and lightning. Today's storm was the second-class citizen to yesterday's deluge.

Wyatt pulled himself out of bed, splashed water on his face and shoulders, toweled off, threw on a pair of jeans and a shirt, and padded barefoot to the nursery. Would Brooke be in there again wearing his shirt and nothing else? A small tortured part of him sorta hoped so, crazy glutton for punishment that he was. But as he stepped into the room, he saw that only his precious two were in there, still sleeping. Brianna was on her back, looking so much like her mother it pained him. Her hair was the same honey blond with slight curls and her eyes were shaped like almonds, wide across her little face. She had the same fair complexion and sweet smile as her mother, and it melted his heart every time he looked at her. Brett was blond, too, but his hair was a darker shade that might just change to light brown when he got older. He was a good mix of both Wyatt and Madelyn, although people who didn't know Madelyn thought his son looked exactly like him, which made him puff up with pride.

He smiled and exited the room. Any minute now, they'd wake and all hell would break loose. It was always the same, the welcome quiet before the toddler storm. And he'd learned to take advantage of these quiet times. Having a cup of coffee in peace was a luxury. He descended the staircase, smacking his lips over the prospect of a simple bowl of cereal and a steamy brew. As he neared the kitchen, the scent of coffee filled his nostrils.

Before he could gather his thoughts, a sassy female voice greeted him. "Morning, sleepyhead."

He entered the kitchen, smiling. But his fantasies were extinguished quickly. Brooke was wearing the same clothes she'd been in last night, only this time, her silvery silk blouse wasn't tucked in. "Sleepyhead? It's six in the morning."

"I thought cowboys rose at the crack of dawn."

He glanced out the window. "Today, who could tell?"

She chuckled. "You got me there. It's nasty out there. Want some coffee? Oh, I hope you don't mind, but I sort of helped myself to your kitchen. I've got bacon under the broiler and I was going to crack some eggs. Are you in?"

"I don't mind at all. I figured cereal would be my breakfast and lunch of choice without Henrietta. Hell yeah to coffee, and I'm *all* in. How's the head?"

"Surprisingly, not bad. I thought I'd wake up to a huge headache. I guess I got lucky."

"You got damn lucky." Her hair covered her bruise. He imagined it had turned fifty shades of purple by now.

"How long do you suppose we have?" she asked.

Wyatt knew exactly what she meant. "Maybe fifteen minutes, maybe half an hour. The kids usually wake up around six thirty."

"Do they eat anything special?" she asked, pouring the coffee into the one mug she'd laid out on the counter.

"Well, they've been eating just about everything these days. So eggs and a bit of bacon is fine. I think Henrietta used to make them baby oatmeal or something. "

"Okay, we'll figure it out."

He liked the way Brooke took over his kitchen. She wasn't a wilting flower who needed to have everything handed to her. She'd stepped in and helped out and didn't seem uncomfortable in her surroundings.

"How did you sleep?" he asked, being a good host, though his mind automatically flashed back to an image of her lying next to him in that hotel bed. Things were different now and he knew it for fact, but his groin was having issues that didn't surprise him. He switched gears, thinking about his children sleeping innocently in their nursery right now. They were his splash of ice-cold water. They were the buffer he needed.

"Like a baby," she said. "The bed is comfy and the sound of the rain sorta lulled me to sleep. How about you?"

"Good. I slept good."

He removed the bacon from the broiler while she cooked the eggs. He made toast, too, and within a few minutes, they were sitting in the kitchen eating breakfast. "You're not having coffee?"

She shook her head, her gaze dipping to his chest. He hadn't buttoned up, and now he caught her stealing a glimpse. When his lips curved up in a smile, she pulled her gaze off him immediately and made a production of buttering her toast. "No, I, uh… I'm not one for coffee. I'm fine with orange juice. Want some?"

Her dark hair was in wild disarray, looking natural and untamed and gorgeous falling past her shoulders. He hadn't thought to give her a hairbrush last night. He had other things on his mind, such as how in hell he was going to steer clear of her this weekend.

"No thanks. I'm good." He sipped his coffee and they both concentrated on the meal, keeping the conversation to a minimum.

Cries erupted upstairs ten minutes later. "Peace as you

know it has just ended." He rose from his seat. "I'll go get them."

"I'll go with you."

Wyatt wasn't going to argue. When it came to his kids, without Henrietta here to guide him, he was on a bucking wild horse without a saddle.

Brooke scooped Brett up just before he slung his taxi-cab-yellow dump truck at Brianna's head. She took the truck out of his hands and twirled him around and around. "Here we go," she said, giving Brett an airplane ride. "Zoom, zoom." Brett's legs shot out and his giggles made Brianna stop attacking the seventy-inch flat screen's remote controller with a spoon to look up at her brother in envy.

"Your turn next," Brooke said, almost out of breath. The little ones weighed a good twenty-five pounds if they weighed one pound. Brooke figured this was the best workout she'd get while she was here. Wyatt had offered her his private gym in the basement of the house, and maybe when the twins napped, she'd head down there to check it out, but until she got the okay from a doctor to do some mild exercise, all she would be doing was looking.

Brianna raced around the great room, which seemed to have inadvertently become the twins' playroom. As a matter of fact, every room downstairs had signs of toddler-dom. There were dolls and trucks, cars and dress-up clothes everywhere, though neatly arranged, thanks to Henrietta, Brooke presumed. Yet the entire stunning ranch home, with all the latest perks and privileges and modern digital conveniences, showed signs of children.

Not a bad thing at all. Maybe that's why Brooke felt comfortable instead of out of place here. The house was grand not but austere. So what if she didn't want to be here. She was stuck and she might as well make the best of it.

Brianna came running into her arms and she lifted her up and flew her across the room. "Zoom, zoom, zoom. You're flying, Bri." Sweet laughter poured from the child's tiny mouth and her joyous smile put a sparkle in her bluebonnet eyes.

"Daddy, lookee me."

"I see, Bri. You're flying," Wyatt said. His eyes were filled with so much love, Brooke's heart lurched. This family was missing one vital part and she saw the hint of that sadness, even as Wyatt smiled at his daughter and held his son.

"I flied too," Brett said.

"Yes, you did," Brooke said, setting Brianna down and drawing deep breaths into her lungs.

Wyatt made note of her labored breathing and announced, "Okay, flying school is closed for today."

The children protested with whines and whimpers.

"But maybe if Daddy says it's okay, we can have ice cream?" She gave Wyatt a sheepish smile. "Is that okay?

"Yay, Daddy, pleeeeze," from Brianna.

"Pleeeeze, pleeeeze," Brett parroted.

"Oh, um…" He glanced at his watch. The children had eaten a good breakfast and lunch, and it was now approaching dinnertime. "Sure, why not?"

The twins squealed with joy. Wyatt lifted Brett in one arm, and picked up Brianna in the other, giving Brooke a break as they headed for the kitchen.

Twenty minutes later, the ceiling had nearly caved in from Brianna's screams and Brett was covered from head to toe in fudgy ice cream. There wasn't a clean spot on his shirt, despite the bib. Apparently bibs weren't foolproof, not with little hands pulling and tugging at them constantly.

"Okay, well, maybe ice cream wasn't such a bright idea," Brooke said.

"You think?" Wyatt frowned at the mess that was his kitchen, splattered walls and all.

"I'll take care of it. You mentioned you have work to do?"

"I can't leave you with this…them." He spread his arms out wide. Which only made her want to jump into them. Getting away from him today would be imperative for her peace of mind. They'd been together all day, dealing with the children, and she'd been all too aware of him. His presence beside her. His heart-stealing blue eyes. The intoxicating scent of his cologne. When he was close she felt safe, and that scared her most of all. She couldn't give up her heart again. She was scarred by Royce's deception and didn't trust herself to make the right decisions when it came to men. Especially since she had no idea what Wyatt would say about the baby she carried. And she was too chicken to find out.

At times, she'd catch him ogling her with an intense look that even she, a novice when it came to knowing a man's mind, understood as hunger and desire. And her ego would rocket like a shooting star.

Wyatt looked ready to escape the chaos. He was struggling to balance his fatherly duties with tending to business.

"Wyatt, I can manage just fine. Piece of cake."

"Oh, yeah? What's your plan?"

"My plan? Well, a bubble bath works wonders."

His brows arched and he gave her a sardonic smile. "Sounds perfect."

"For them, Wyatt."

"Oh, right." At least he could tease about the tension that sizzled between them, despite the double kid duty. "I knew that."

Her ego soared again.

"I don't know." He scrubbed his face, pulling at the

golden stubble on his jaw. "It's a lot to ask of you. They're a handful and a half."

"Hey, it's not as if you're far away. Your office is down here, isn't it?" she asked over Brianna's meltdown.

"Yep, but it's in another wing of the house."

"You have an intercom system, right? I'll use it if I need to. And that's a promise. Now go, and let me put these little ones out of their misery."

And you out of yours.

He finally agreed. After he helped get the twins upstairs, she took over, giving them both a bath full of light airy bubbles. The kids immediately simmered down, their sugar high from the ice cream leveling off. Brooke splashed them silly, until the room filled with their giggles, until their little fingers and toes shriveled to wrinkled raisins. When the bath was over, Brooke wrapped each one in a My Little Pony towel and snuggled them to her chest, drying them off. She dressed them in their jammies and then all three squatted on the floor to play. The twins had so many toys, and they played with each and every one before they got bored of the games. Then Brooke laid them down on a pastel-colored quilt and sang them silly songs. When she couldn't remember the lyrics, she made up the words, and every song brought big grins to their faces.

"Piece of cake?"

She swiveled her head to find Wyatt blocking the doorway, his arms folded across his chest, blue eyes filled with admiration.

"Putty in my hands," she said.

"I know the feeling," he said under his breath.

Oh, God.

"Actually, I know the *secret*," she said.

"And what's that?"

He came to sit beside her and ruffled both of the children's hair. Again, those blue eyes were alight with love for his kids.

"Play with them 24/7. Entertain and delight them, give them what they want."

"And exhaust yourself…"

"Do I look exhausted?" She turned her face to him. When their eyes met, his nearness suddenly made it very hot in the room. It was a mistake to ask him that leading question, because his expression went dewy soft and he reached out to touch a strand of her hair. Focusing on the dark lock, he shook his head. "No," he rasped. "You look beautiful."

He touched her then, with his smile.

She gave him an uncertain smile back. "Thank you."

He backed off, noting her hesitation. "You've been up here two hours."

"Really? I lost track of time. Probably should think about dinner."

He nodded and cleared his throat before standing up. He reached for her hand and helped her rise. Pretending nonchalance, she pulled her hand away and made a fuss about cleaning up the room when all she wanted was for him to touch her and keep on touching her.

Dangerous thoughts.

"Come on, you two. Let's race and see who can put the toys away the fastest." She dumped the first one into the toy box and the twins followed suit, grabbing toys two at a time, competing in another fun game.

Forty-five minutes later, Brooke and Wyatt were eating spaghetti in the kitchen with the twins. "Good move, not giving them sauce," Wyatt said.

"Butter and cheese keep the bath monster away."

He chuckled. "Yeah, you sure are an arsenal of helpful hints."

"Maybe when dealing with children." The same couldn't

be said in her dealings with men. In that regard, she was clueless.

Wyatt tipped his head to stare at her, a question in his eyes.

"That didn't come out right," she said, easing diced pasta into Brett's mouth as Wyatt fed Bri. It was a subject that needed changing quickly. "Hey, looks like these guys are ready to conk out. I bet they go to sleep right after dinner. Then you can finish up your work."

"I'm finished for the day," he said.

Oh, great. It was coming up on eight o'clock. Too early to turn in. Of course, Brooke could claim fatigue and watch television in her room or read a book.

"I thought I'd get a fire going, relax some and have hot chocolate," he said, giving her a glance.

"With marshmallows? Gosh, that sounds like heaven," she cooed, thinking out loud. Peace and quiet by a crackling fire, sipping hot chocolate, and relaxing with Wyatt after a long, tiresome day would be pretty amazing. Hot chocolate was something she *could* drink and not endanger her baby. But uh-oh, she'd just stepped in it. Now there was no legitimate way out without sounding lame.

"With marshmallows," he said on a nod. "Then you'll join me?"

When would she ever learn to button her lips?

"Uh, yeah. For a little while. Unless you'd rather be alone, with your, uh, thoughts?"

He grinned. "Men never want to be alone with their thoughts."

"Okay, then."

As expected, the twins had fallen asleep right after dinner without much coaxing. Now the big ranch house was quiet. She padded on bare feet down the stairs, wearing Wyatt's ginormous flannel plaid robe, which tied around her waist twice. The robe hugged her like a big teddy bear, a teddy bear that sported Wyatt's appealing scent. She'd been wearing the same outfit for two days straight and had asked Wyatt for something to throw on over his shirt while she laundered her clothes. The rain hadn't let up; just as the weatherman had predicted, a new storm had piggybacked on this one.

She entered the living room, where a floor-to-ceiling bedrock fireplace blazed. "It's beautiful in here," she said, hugging herself around the middle. The entire room was softly lit by the glow of the fire. Wyatt looked up from his place on the floor and gave her a heart-melting smile. Two mugs of steamy hot chocolate sat on the hearth, a bag of marshmallows beside them. "Have a seat," he said, and arched a brow when she sat down on the floor, leaning her body against the part of the sofa farthest away from him. He couldn't think she'd sit directly next to him, could he? Not in this lifetime. It was hard enough seeing him all day, as he interacted with his children and sauntered about in those perfect-fitting jeans, with that sexy pirate beard going on. A girl could only take so much.

"At least move closer to the fire," he said, a knowing tone in his voice. "It'll warm you."

"I'm warm enough, thank you very much."

"Suit yourself."

He sprinkled mini marshmallows into both mugs and handed her one. Then he leaned back against the sofa and stretched out his long legs. Sipping the cocoa, he quietly watched the fire for a while. "Don't get much peace around here. This is nice."

"It is."

"You're good with the little ones," he said.

"They're precious, Wyatt."

"They're all I have left..."

She let that comment go, but she knew he was thinking of their mother, Madelyn. Oh, to be loved like that, so strongly that even in death the bond couldn't be broken.

He put his head down. "Sorry."

"No need to be, Wyatt. You went through a trauma. All of you did, and I get it."

"It's just that… I'm feeling all this guilt now." His eyes lost their gleam, and he looked absolutely miserable.

"Guilt? About what happened between us?" Her stomach clenched. At times, she forgot she was carrying his child, but the baby made his presence known. Her breasts were becoming increasingly tender. She got tired more easily now, and she often bordered on nausea, especially in the morning. As far as symptoms went, hers were mild, but they were there reminding her daily that she couldn't just pretend all was right with the world. Not until she shed her secret. She wanted to tell him to forget about what had happened between them, to put it in the past and save himself from his torment, but she couldn't. She couldn't say those words when she had more profound words to say.

"About what I'm feeling now. About how much I want you, Brooke."

Her hand shook and the mug nearly tipped on its way to her mouth. Goodness, he'd just come right out and spoken his mind. She wished it would be that easy for her. She set her mug down and stared at the marshmallow circles melting as fast as her heart. "What if I said…the feeling is mutual, but we both know better?"

"Do we?" he asked, his voice registering doubt. She glanced at him again, and his dubious expression caught her off guard. Firelight reflected in his eyes and she noted the torment in them. His expression gave her pause.

"What do I say to that, Wyatt?"

"I don't know. Maybe one of us needs to be reckless," he added.

"I thought both of us were, at the wedding."

His Adam's apple bobbed up and down as he swallowed. "Meeting you that night was the best thing that happened to me in nine months. You helped me through a rough time, and I'll be forever grateful."

She didn't want his gratitude. What exactly did she want from Wyatt? She knew the score. He was emotionally unavailable and she'd be fooling herself to think anything else. She was pregnant and a little bit frightened about telling him, because then they'd have to face reality and make appropriate arrangements for custody and all the ugly painstaking plans that went along with a child being born out of wedlock. Gosh, it was so much easier to put her head in the sand and not deal with any of this. Pretty soon, her body would betray her with a belly bump that would expand, and then she'd have no choice but to reveal her pregnancy. But tonight she wanted to sip hot chocolate with Wyatt and just *be*.

She heard one of the babies' cries from upstairs and just *being* was immediately eighty-sixed. "Is that Brianna crying?" she asked softly, her ears perking up.

"I think it's Brett," Wyatt said, putting his mug down and listening. "Yep, that's him. Bri will be right behind him. She doesn't sleep when he's in a state. Stay here by the fire. I'll see to them." Wyatt popped up.

"I'll help." She rose and nodded. "It's okay. I want to."

"Appreciate that. Double rocking them doesn't always work."

"I can't see how it ever works, Wyatt. What do you do, hold one in each arm?"

"I try." He sighed. "Usually Henrietta is here to help out."

He really did need a nanny. Or two. How could one aging housekeeper keep pace with twins? Brooke was younger by thirty years, and even she was exhausted after watching them most of the day.

As she followed him up the staircase, Brianna started wailing. Now both babies were rocking the nursery walls. Wyatt and Brooke entered the room and she took one quick, assessing look at Brett. "He's soaked through his jammies."

"Ah," Wyatt said. "That explains it."

"I'll change him and get him back to sleep," she said. "Why don't you rock Brianna?"

"Sounds good. If you're sure…"

"I'm sure."

And then on an afterthought, a storm of indecision crossed his face. "Their mother didn't want the babies separated. In a house this size, they could each have their own room, but Madelyn thought this way was best."

"There's time for them to have their own rooms later in life. I think it's a good plan for now, Wyatt. Twins have a special bond, I think."

He let out a relieved sigh. "Okay."

The poor guy. He was second-guessing his decisions regarding his kids and trying like mad to honor his late wife's wishes.

"You take the rocker, Brooke. I'll walk Brianna in my arms. She likes that."

Twenty minutes later, Brett was dressed in clean pajamas and sleeping soundly. Wyatt wasn't far behind putting his daughter back into her crib and covering her. He kissed her forehead so lightly, it might have been an air kiss, and then did the same to Brett.

With a hand to Brooke's back, he guided her out of the room and down the hall. "Thanks," he said. She found herself wrapped in his cushy robe, standing just outside her bedroom door. "You've been pretty darn great. I'd kiss you good-night, but we both know where that would lead."

Her lips formed into a pout. She couldn't hide her disappointment. She felt closer to Wyatt tonight. Maybe it was the intimacy of putting his little ones to sleep and working as a team, sharing meals and personal thoughts. Maybe it was the strong pull of his deep gaze that told her beyond words how much he wished things were different.

Maybe it was his body language and the way his eyes were on her mouth now, looking as if he'd devour her if given the chance.

"What if *I* kissed *you*, Wyatt?" She rose up on tiptoes, absorbing the heat of his skin as she laid her palm on his jaw. Not giving him a chance to answer, she brushed her lips over his.

"Good night," she whispered, and as she backed away, Wyatt's lids lowered, his breath rushed out in a groan, and before she knew what was happening, he reached out and pulled her into his arms. As he crushed her against his chest, his mouth came down on hers and his kiss stole her very breath. It wasn't hard to melt into him, to give up her denials and simply feel. And oh, how good it was.

"God, Brooke," he rasped over her lips, and then drove into her mouth in a fiery surge that she met with equal eagerness and enthusiasm.

"Wyatt," she murmured, raking her fingers through the short tufts of his hair.

The connection between them might only be physical but it was strong, real and overpowering, judging by how fast her heart was racing, how every nerve in her body was standing on end.

He cupped her face with both hands and positioned her head to give him more access.

His kisses went deep, and raw, elemental lust rose up. Suddenly, she wanted his hands all over her again; she wanted to feel his flesh against hers and have him inside her making her splinter apart.

He gripped the tie of her robe to pull her closer. "I've been wondering all night what you have on under here."

"Not too much," she offered softly, the need in her voice ringing in her ears.

A painful groan emerged from his throat. "That's what I thought."

He kissed her again, his mouth ravaging and greedy. She didn't mind being the recipient of his hot, passionate hunger. She wasn't going to stop him. She wasn't going to let any rational thoughts enter her head. Not tonight.

"I don't think I can walk away from you tonight, Brooke."

Her chin up, she captured his gaze. "I don't think I'd let you."

She turned the knob on her bedroom door and entered backward, keeping his face in her line of vision the entire time. He followed her, and the door flew shut with a kick of his foot.

He came toward her, stalking her like a wild animal, limber in his approach. His blue gaze was as dark as midnight. He tugged her forward by the sash on her robe. It opened and hung from her shoulders, the cool evening air replacing the warm furnace of material and leaving her naked but for the panties she wore.

Wyatt sucked in a breath and gave her a glowing look of admiration. Then he sifted through the material of the robe and laid his hand on her breast. She closed her eyes from the pleasure of his touch. And when he began a slow, deliberate massage with the flat of his palm, squeezing the skin together and flicking her nipple, everything below her waist began to throb. Like crazy. Sweat broke out on her forehead.

"Are you sure about this?" he asked.

Totally not fair of him to ask. "Yes. Oh, yes."

Six

Wyatt's hands roamed her body as his kisses drove her to the brink. It wasn't any different, any less urgent, than the night they'd shared at the inn. In the guest room of his beautiful ranch home, amid horses and cattle and yes, children sleeping a few rooms away, she gave in to the storm of desire enveloping her with a force that she could no longer fight. If she was being stupid and foolish, then so be it. She'd pay the price later, but for now, in this moment, she wanted Wyatt. No, she *needed* Wyatt.

A shudder passed through her entire body. Wanting was one thing, but needing him? Fear slammed into her heart and brought her up short momentarily. The blood froze in her veins.

Wyatt immediately stopped midkiss. He sensed something was up, and didn't that tell her all she needed to know about him? He was sensitive enough to know she'd balked. "What's wrong, darlin'?"

The corners of her mouth lifted as she touched his

cheek, her palm grazing the rough stubble of his beard. His eyes bore down on her, waiting. "Nothing."

He pulled her palm to his mouth and kissed the inside of her hand. "You sure?"

She nodded, plastering on a smile. "Positive."

Other than she was falling hard for the Texan, the father of twins and her unborn baby, and there was nothing she could do to stop it.

He gave her a soft, loving kiss and murmured. "Climb into bed, sweetheart. Stay warm. I'll be right back."

She was pretty sure he was going to his room to get protection. Oh, man.

After he left, she gazed out the window at threatening stark gray clouds and the pouring rain that was keeping her trapped here. Now, that was a notion: being shut in with a gorgeous guy who you're pretty sure is the best man you'd ever met in your life. Only he was still hung up on his late wife. And he'd made it clear in no uncertain terms, quite a few times, that having two children was quite enough for him.

The debate in her head raged like the storm outside. She pulled the material of her robe together tightly, and crossed her arms over her chest, ready to tell Wyatt everything and pay the consequences.

And then, there he was standing in the doorway, shirtless, bootless, in jeans riding low on his waist, holding a batch of purple-hued flowers in his hand. His hair was damp and there were raindrops sprinkled on his bare shoulders.

"These are for you, Brooke," he said. His eyes blazed bright blue as he sauntered over to her and set the flowers in her hand.

"They're beautiful," she said. "Where did you get them?"

"Out back. There's a garden, and these are pretty hardy

this time of year. Asters and violets. This one here is a tiger lily."

She stared at the flowers as he pointed them out.

"I figured you might like them."

She pressed them to her chest and felt tears coming on. "I love them, Wyatt. You went out in the rain for these?"

"You deserve them," he said. "I, uh, wanted you to know, I'm not the jerk who ran out on you at the inn."

"I think I know that now."

As her arms slid down her sides, the robe opened again. Now both of them were standing in the middle of the room, nearly naked. He began rubbing her arms up and down briskly, getting her circulation going and heating her up inside. "I thought you'd be in bed. Aren't you freezing?"

"I, uh, no. You're pretty good at keeping me warm."

"Ah, Brooke," he said, circling his arms around her entire body, warming her with his own heat. "I like the sound of that."

And then his kisses rained down on her and for all those beautiful minutes, she kissed him back, loving the taste of him, loving the poignant sound of his passion-filled groans, loving the way he held her as though she was precious and sacred.

They moved to the bed together, locked in each other's arms. Wyatt gently removed the robe from her shoulders and lowered her down until the mattress met with her bare back and the pillow cradled her head. He loomed above her, all those straining muscles holding him back from crushing her with his body, and brought his mouth down to hers. He smelled of fresh rain and outdoors, and she roped her arms around his neck and played with the dark blond strands of his hair.

He began to lightly massage her shoulders. His fingertips dug in to release tension there before he moved lower still to caress her tender breasts. Smoothing them over with gentle hands brought relief, and then he molded them with a propping motion making ready to take her into his mouth. She held her breath, waiting. And then he dipped his head and sucked on her, his tongue circling the round orb and lashing her with moisture. An almost painful pleasure coursed down to her belly, and a tiny moan escaped her lips.

Down below, his erection strained against his jeans and ground into her body, pulsing and ready. She thrashed her head against the pillow, biting her lip as electric currents outraced her heartbeats. "Wyatt," she breathed.

He tore his mouth away from her now-aching breast and slid down her body, pulling her free of her panties. Lifting her legs up, he positioned himself, and the hot, wet slide of his tongue teased her core. She stilled, absorbing the sensations washing through her like waves on the ocean, one right after another, his stroking creating tingles and light shocks.

"Oh," she whimpered, biting her lip.

Everything inside her tightened up and as his relentless tongue bathed her, her body absorbed the pleasure until it was too, too much. The pulses grew heavier, tighter, and then, then a spasm burst inside her and claimed her breath.

She hurtled back down to earth, sated, her body limp and her endorphins causing the highest high.

Wyatt released her then, his eyes glazed and hungry.

"So good," she said, instead of admitting it was the best.

He brought himself up, kissed her soundly on the lips and then rolled away to unzip his jeans. "I'm glad. It was for me, too."

He moved his pants down his legs and a sigh escaped her throat as she caught a glimpse of him in all his glory.

She rolled on her side and took him in her hand. "Thank you for the flowers," she whispered, and began long, slow, deliberate strokes. He was hot silk in her hands, so smooth, so inspiring. Scooting closer, she pressed her mouth to his and began kissing him. "Lie back and enjoy."

And if the grunts and noisy sounds he made were any indication, she was giving Wyatt just as much pleasure as he'd given her tonight.

"I'll never make it," he rasped, "if you go on doing what you're doing."

He gave her no time to respond. He flipped her over onto her back then, and she was captured by the inferno in Wyatt's eyes. With his knee, he parted her legs and rose over her. A heady rush of adrenaline pulsed through her veins. She remembered the last time they were joined; this was going to be equally good, if not better. She saw the promise in Wyatt's eyes and believed it.

He touched the tip of his manhood to her. "Oh, man, Brooke," he murmured so quietly, it was more of a sigh. Her breath caught in her throat. She couldn't manage a reply; she couldn't utter a word. Sensations rippled through her as he pushed deeper, giving her time to adjust, time to accept him.

She pulled him down to her mouth and kissed him. It was beautiful and crazy good and from then on, Wyatt locked in on her body and she was done for. Completely and utterly in his zone. She gave everything she had to him and then some.

The furious passion in his eyes, his hands exploring every part of her and his magnificent erection kept her body on the brink. She was close to combusting in the very best way. He pumped and she bucked, he grated and she rubbed, he climbed and she followed.

A vivid curse pushed from his lips and the word vibrated in her ears. Everything below her waist tightened.

Talk dirty to me, Wyatt. I can take it.

The fact that he'd lost a bit of control pushed her over

the edge. There was nothing higher, or better, than being at this same place with him. Going the distance together.

He lifted her hips from the bed, squeezing her cheeks tight with his powerful hands as he thrust deeper still.

"Oh…oh, Wyatt."

"We're here, Brooke."

Her spasms of release joined his, a continuing series of shudders and moans that filled her ears. They were in their own place now, a few moments of exquisite flurry shared equally. Her heart was racing like mad, her body tight.

Wyatt kissed her gently, his hands softly tangling in her hair as he whispered sweet words in her ear. When he lifted up and moved beside her on the bed, his heat evaporated and cool air touched her skin. But it didn't matter; she was flushed and hot enough to warm up Wyatt's entire ranch house.

Wyatt brushed hair from her cheeks. "You're beautiful, Brooke."

If he kept saying it, she might just believe it.

"And this was…"

He didn't finish. Brooke understood his dilemma, how he must be feeling. What happened between them was better than good, better than great. It was freaking amazing. But Wyatt's admitting that would be disrespectful to Madelyn in his eyes. That had to be it.

Right now, as she came down from the most satisfying blissful sex of her life, she didn't want to think too much. She hugged a pillow to her chest and faced him. "Wyatt, you don't have to say anything. I think we both know."

He stared up at the ceiling and when she thought he'd checked out, he slipped his hand over hers and held on until her eyes closed and she drifted off.

Wyatt was sex-starved and Brooke's appearance in his life was a scratch to his itch. Or so he thought. But as he lay beside her on the bed they'd shared last night, watching her chest rise and fall in deep slumber, the rosy hue he'd put on her face making her appear even more beautiful, he realized he was full of crap.

He wasn't going to get her out of his system anytime soon.

He wanted her here. But as Sunday morning dawned, the worst of the storm was gone, leaving only a light drizzle in its place that would slow to a stop sometime this afternoon. Texas sunshine would dry the land, and the bridge would be repaired and drivable again. By tomorrow, Brooke would be heading away from Blue Horizon Ranch and he would have to let her go.

As she rolled over, the sheet covering her fell away and her breasts teased his chest. The gentle scraping of her nipples stirred everything male inside him. *Shoot.* He was hard again and ready to take her once more.

Lazy eyes opened to him and she smiled. It was a sweet, aftermath-of-good-loving smile that tugged at his heart. She blew her messy brown locks out of her eyes on a soft puff of breath.

"Mornin'," he croaked.

She chuckled, stretching her arms over her head. "Yes, it is," she said on a long, sexy sigh. "You look good enough to eat, Wyatt."

His lips curved up in a smile. Brooke always surprised him. "I was thinking the same about you."

She rose on her elbows, and his gaze drifted to her small, round, perfect breasts. "Have you checked on the babies?" she asked.

"I have. Ten minutes ago. They're asleep."

"Is it still raining?" she asked, taking a peek out the window.

"Yep, drizzling."

"Guess you're stuck with me another day."

"Guess so." He leaned in, inches from her mouth, and whispered, "It's a hardship."

She tried to swat at him, but he was too fast and caught her wrist midmotion. "Now that I've snagged you, what will I do with you?"

"Whatever you want," she said coyly.

He snapped his eyes to her. "God, Brooke. You're killing me."

"Am I?" she asked, her smile gone, her dark brown eyes soft and steady on him.

"Yeah."

She looked under the sheet draped at his waist. "You seem very much alive from where I'm sitting."

"I am alive, when I'm with you." Rising over her, her pinned her arms above her head and held her there. Her lips parted slightly, and the intake of her breath told him she wanted him again. There would be no protest, and he wasn't gonna leave this bed without making love to her again.

One minute later, his cell phone buzzed. He had a mind to ignore it. But he gazed over at the lit-up screen on the nightstand and bit back a curse. It was his mother again. Man, she had bad timing. He'd dodged her call the other night and managed to leave her a voice mail afterward telling her everything was all right.

But Mom was nothing but persistent.

Brooke looked at the phone. "It's your mother. You should answer it, Wyatt. She's probably worried about the kids and the storm."

He backed away from Brooke and sat up on the bed, gritting his teeth. "Yeah, you're right. I'm sorry I have to get this."

"It's okay," Brooke assured him.

"Don't move a muscle. Not an inch. Okay?" he asked.

Her arms were above her head, her breasts exposed and gorgeous. "I promise."

Releasing a low guttural groan from his throat, he picked up the phone, walked out of the room and ducked into another bedroom.

"Yeah, hi, Mom."

"Wyatt. I've been trying to reach you. Is everything all right? The storm is all over the news here in New York. Lord, I remember those hurricanes. I know how dangerous they can be. How are my grandbabies?"

"The babies are fine. We're staying in and the storm's ready to pass. Did you get my message?"

"Yes, but, honey, I needed to speak with you in person. You have to understand how I worry. I haven't seen Brett and Brianna in months. You know that I was planning on coming to Texas for the cancer foundation's big fund-raiser in Dallas, right?"

"Yes, I know, Mom."

"And I was going to come to the ranch for a visit after that?"

"Uh-huh." He began to feel an ache in the pit of his stomach. Something was up with her, and he wasn't going to like it.

"Well, my plans have changed. I'll be coming to Blue Horizon before the fund-raiser, rather than after. I should arrive day after tomorrow. I'll stay about a week."

His heart stopped. He'd thought he had at least a month before she arrived. "What?"

"Sorry for the short notice, but it's just worked out better this way."

"For who?" he asked.

"Now, Wyatt, you know I have a busy schedule. You're all alone there, except for my Henrietta, and well, I miss the babies so. Have you managed to find a nanny yet?"

"It's in the works, Mom. I'm getting close." It was a

lie. He had some interviews scheduled, but nothing was concrete yet.

"That's what you said the last time we spoke. And poor Henrietta is being run into the ground trying to keep pace with my precious grandkids. Honey, I know you don't think I'd do a good job, but my offer still stands. I'll come back to Texas to live. I'm willing to help out. There's nothing I'm doing here that can't be postponed or canceled if you really need me."

Wyatt always thought her offer was an idle threat, but lately, she'd been speaking more and more about moving back to Texas and leaving high society behind to care for her grandchildren. It was an offer that he'd patiently and tactfully refused on several occasions.

She'd hate it here. Genevieve Brandt wasn't meant for country living, and when Wyatt was growing up, she'd reminded him and his father daily of the sacrifice she'd made for love. She was a city girl, through and through. As soon as his father retired from Blue Horizon, she'd dragged him off the ranch and moved him to her home-town and the faster-paced city life of New York. George Taylor Brandt passed on three years ago, and Wyatt was convinced that if he'd stayed on the ranch he loved after his retirement, he would still be alive today.

"Mom, we're managing just fine." It was a blatant lie.

"We'll see, honey," she said, a dubious tone in her voice. "I can't wait to see you and the babies."

"Uh, same here, Mom."

After the call ended, Wyatt stared at the phone as dozens of thoughts filled his head. He had to do right by his kids. But having his mother move in with him wasn't the answer. Oh, yeah, he loved her. She'd been a good mother, and she did adore his children, but she was also high-main-tenance and somewhat self-centered. And she would drive him absolutely nuts.

He shook his head and remembered Brooke, the stunner he had waiting for him in bed just steps away. She, too, drove him nuts, in another way entirely.

He left all that behind and returned to the bedroom.

"What's wrong?" Brooke asked the second he walked in. She read his expression and must've seen his concern.

He sat down on the bed and ran a hand through his hair, staring at the opposite wall. "You don't want to hear it."

"Sure I do." She covered up and took a place next to him on the bed.

"My mother is coming for a visit."

"That's a good thing, isn't it?"

"It is if it was only that. But I get the feeling she's coming to check up on me and the kids. And if she doesn't like what she sees, she might just stay on *to help out*."

He shuddered and Brooke bit back a laugh.

"It's not funny," he said, focusing on the Dalí print on the wall.

"I know." He appreciated that she managed not to chuckle again, though he must've looked pretty comical, sitting almost buck naked on the bed, twitching because his mother was coming for a visit.

"I've been trying to find just the right nanny to relieve Henrietta of her duties. A new housekeeper I can always find, but a nanny, someone to watch my kids all day, that person has to be special. And I haven't had any luck finding anyone that meets my requirements."

Someone who could stand in for Madelyn.

"Sorry, Wyatt. Those children are treasures and they do deserve someone special." Brooke laid her hand on his shoulder, and her warmth and comfort seeped into his skin. Her touch, or maybe just having her understand his situation, helped a great deal. With Brooke beside him, he didn't feel quite so alone and devastated.

He covered her hand and turned to give her a smile.

When she returned the smile, his body stirred and his mouth sought hers again. Kissing her helped untangle his mind, and he indulged over and over again. It seemed that he needed lots of untangling. And when kissing wasn't enough, he pushed her down onto the bed, pulled off the sheets and fell headlong into Brooke's willing arms.

Making love to Brooke McKay was the best medicine for what ailed him.

"I'll do it," Brooke announced, coming to stand over Wyatt on the bed. He looked edible, lying with his arms over his head, his eyes still dusted with sleep and his luscious muscled chest calling for her touch. Dawn was long since gone. She'd just finished checking on the twins. They rustled about and made sweet noises, on the verge of waking. Any second now, they'd be up and ready to start the day, and she and Wyatt wouldn't have a moment to gather their thoughts. That's when the idea came to her. She wasn't ready to leave Blue Horizon yet. She needed more time with Wyatt. "I'll stay on during your mother's visit and pretend to be the twins' nanny."

"What are you talking about, darlin'?"

"You need a nanny, Wyatt. I'm here. I've got nothing on my agenda until Dylan's movie wraps, and I owe you."

Wyatt sat up, hung his legs over the side of the bed and planted his hands on the edge of the mattress. "After last night, and this morning, I'm thinking I'm the one owing you."

He was teasing. They'd satisfied each other and there was no measure to that, no payment for deeds. "That was mutual and equal. Wasn't it?"

He gave her an earnest look. "Yeah. So what do think you owe me?"

"You came after me in the storm with your kids in the

car. I'll never forget that. You risked them to save me. It's the least I can do. I want to help."

He heaved a big sigh and ran his hands through his hair, tousling it even more. Bed head looked incredibly sexy on him. "How can I ask you to do that for me?"

"You're not asking. I'm offering."

He thought about it awhile as she stood there, her heart in her throat. God, he had to say yes. Once the offer was out there, she realized how very much she wanted him to agree. She wasn't ready to leave him. She wasn't ready to reveal her secret and part company, all businesslike. She was falling in love with him. More time would confirm her feelings, and she could test out her new and wishful theory that Wyatt was getting over his late wife's death. Silly her. At the very least, she could bide her time and try to find the exact right moment to tell him she was carrying his child.

He lifted his eyes to her. "My mother isn't easy."

"I can handle her."

"She's got a mouth on her."

"So do I."

His gaze dipped to her lips. "Lord, I know."

She smiled.

"She's impetuous, rude sometimes, and likes to get her way."

"Sounds like my kind of girl."

"She'll drive you crazy."

"I won't hold it against you."

"You're determined then? You want to do this?"

Brooke nodded.

"I mean, hell... I'd be lying if I said I didn't want you here longer."

That was encouraging. "Ah, but if I stay, Wyatt, we can't..."

"Yeah, yeah, I get it. I agree. It won't be easy."

No, it wouldn't be easy going to bed at night, knowing that forbidden pleasure and the satisfaction of being in Wyatt's arms were just down the hallway.

Wyatt rose from the bed, shedding the sheet, and stood before her, fully aroused. "You think we can pull this off?"

Her bones melted. She wanted him so badly. She gulped air and nodded. "Yeah, I think we can. It's only for a week, right?"

"Yeah, a week should convince her." He sighed. "Now I'd best get me a cold shower. Seems I'm gonna be taking a lot of those from now on."

Seven

The stage was set. The sun had come out. The land was dry. The roads were clear. All was back to normal.

Well, sort of.

To Genevieve Brandt, Brooke would be Brooke Johnson, the newly hired nanny. The very best Wyatt had ever found. The twins loved her. She had all the right credentials. Wyatt made her a promise to take care of any probing questions his mother might ask when she arrived.

Brooke wasn't a liar by choice. In fact, she hated people who bent the truth to suit their needs. And wasn't she sliding right into that persona now, pretending to be someone she wasn't? In essence, she was also fibbing by omission to Wyatt, too.

By the end of the week, she promised herself, one way or another, Wyatt would know the truth about her pregnancy and all would be settled. A shiver ran through her. She was in deep now and she would have to wade through the days hoping to convince Genevieve that the babies were in good hands. Hoping that Wyatt would...what? Beg her to stay?

Her cell rang and she muttered a choice word as she glanced at the screen. Putting pep in her voice, she answered the call. "Hi, Dylan. How's it going?"

"How's it going? I'm sitting here in my trailer, trying to read lines, wondering why the hell my sister is spending the week with a total stranger. A man with two kids, no less."

"Oh, I explained it all to Emma when I picked up some of my clothes yesterday. He's a good guy really. You know him. He's the consultant to the film. Wyatt Brandt. The storm struck while we were having dinner and I sorta got stuck here."

"It's not raining anymore. Aren't you coming back to Zane's place?"

"Well, as I told Emma, I'm staying here helping him with his twins this week. It's a long story, but trust me, I'm fine."

"Is this a paying job?" Dylan knew damn well it wasn't.

"Hey, I'm a big girl, Dylan. I can take care of myself."

"It's not a job. Oh, right, because you have a job waiting for you back home in California. Are you forgetting that we're leaving for home in less than two weeks? So what's really going on, Brooke?"

"Nothing. God, Dylan. Please, back off. I...kn-know what I'm doing. I'm helping someone out."

Her brother's overprotective groan traveled through the receiver. "All right, I'll back off. I'm only looking out for you, you know."

She sank into the bed Henrietta had made sometime while Brooke was feeding Brianna and Brett their lunch. "I know. I'm... I'm going to be fine." Even to her ears, she sounded uncertain.

"I'm trusting that you are. But I want to hear from you every day, Brooke."

"I'll call. I promise to check in with you and Emma."

Dylan grunted his farewell, and after she hung up, she was torn between loving Dylan to death and wishing he wouldn't treat her like a child. She was twenty-six years old, for heaven's sake. And yes, granted, she'd had a tough year and he didn't want to see her hurt again, but that might happen anyway. Regardless.

The sound of tires crunching gravel on the road put her on alert. She rose and walked to the window. Outside, Wyatt was opening the Jeep door for Genevieve. At first glance, Brooke's eyes widened. Wyatt's mother was beautiful, with sterling platinum hair and a tan complexion complemented by just the right amount of makeup. Wearing a blue silk blouse, a flowing crepe scarf, cream slacks and ankle boots, Genevieve looked every bit the part of New York high society.

Bolstering herself with a pep talk, Brooke headed toward the nursery. Brett and Brianna fidgeted in their cribs, waking from their naps. Just in time.

Brooke made fast work of cuddling them with hugs and kisses, then diapering and changing them into clean clothes. Brianna wore a pink dress with ruffles at the skirt, and Brett wore a new pair of blue jeans, à la Wyatt Brandt, and a little man shirt in red. She was just putting a bow in Brianna's hair when she heard footsteps on the polished wood floors.

"My babies." Genevieve rushed into the room—her pleasant floral scent following her—and picked up Brett immediately. She smothered the boy with kisses, and Brett, love his soul, watched her carefully, as if trying to piece together who this woman was exactly. Genevieve turned to Brooke, looking her up and down. Had she passed the test? "And how's my little Breezy Peezy doing?"

"She's on the verge of being a crank pot. I think she woke up too soon from her nap." Brooke held a fussing Brianna to her chest. "Hello, I'm Brooke," she said to Genevieve.

Genevieve's chin rose. "Wyatt tells me you're good with the children."

From behind his mother, Wyatt shook his head, his lips twitching. Brooke wasn't fazed. She'd dealt with tough cookies from her Parties-to-Go business. "We think alike."

Genevieve laughed. "Do you, now?" She ruffled Brianna's light blond locks and bent to kiss her cheek. Anyone with that much love shining in her eyes couldn't be that bad. "I'm Genevieve. Their grammy."

"Nice to meet you, Grammy Genevieve."

"You can call me Mrs. Brandt."

On the other hand…

"Mom." Wyatt pushed into the room. "Brooke doesn't have to—"

"No, it's okay, Mr. Brandt," Brooke said, giving him a big smile. His eyes bugged out and she almost laughed. They hadn't spoken about what she should call him, but now, it was clear in her mind, she needed to distance herself from him while Grammy was here. "I most certainly will call you Mrs. Brandt. It's not a problem. I was guessing it might be confusing for Brett and Brianna. There's so many names being jostled about, but I'm sure the twins know exactly who you are."

"Of course they do," Genevieve said, just as Brett kicked away from her, reaching for his daddy's arms.

Wyatt grabbed his son and Brett immediately turned his head into his daddy's chest. Genevieve's confident expression slipped a little. "Well, they may need a little reminder," she said. "It's been too long. I miss them."

"I'm sure they miss you, too," Brooke said, swaying her

hips and rocking Brianna side to side. "Bri, would you like your grandmother to hold you now?"

Brianna didn't make up her mind right away, and Mrs. Brandt began smiling and encouraging her. "Come on, Bri Bri. Grammy will rock you."

Genevieve clapped her hands, wiggled her fingers and twirled around in a circle. "And I don't mean on my hip. Wanna dance, Breezy Peezy?"

Brianna giggled, the sweet sound penetrating the tension radiating off Wyatt's body. He needed to lighten up. His mother wasn't all that bad. A bit huffy and pretentious maybe, but she did love her grandchildren.

"Maybe we can all dance," Brooke said, handing Brianna over to her grandmother and giving Wyatt a big nod as she began singing a Taylor Swift song about shaking it off. Wyatt grinned for half a second and began to move. He wasn't light on his feet—that was for sure—but he did have good moves elsewhere. And she loved that he didn't balk at the idea of acting silly with his kids.

The children cackled as they moved throughout the room.

Just then her stomach notched up, a weird kind of hollow, dull ache pulling her out of the dance mentally. Was this what morning sickness was like?

And wasn't that supposed to happen in the morning?

Then she remembered Emma telling her it can hit at any time, day or night. Something would set it off, the smell of food or too much activity or nothing at all. It would just sweep in and make you feel like you could empty your lunch at any second.

Lucky for her, Genevieve put a halt to the fun, claiming fatigue, and Wyatt showed her to her room. It was the second master suite down the hall. Henrietta had told her that after the Brandts retired to the East Coast, Wyatt had a contractor tear down walls in two rooms and construct his very own master suite. The house was certainly large enough for two master bedrooms, and Wyatt had wanted to keep his mother's room intact. Or as Brooke imagined, Genevieve wouldn't have it any other way.

Henrietta walked into the nursery carrying folded baby laundry. Brooke's savior. "Oh, um, Henrietta, can you watch the babies for a few minutes?"

"Of course." Henrietta had gentle eyes and a kind heart. Brooke had only met her yesterday, but she could tell the woman was a nurturer. And loyal to the Brandt household. She didn't know the truth—the less deceit the better—yet she had to be suspicious of how Wyatt had pulled a new nanny out of his cowboy hat over the weekend. But she hadn't said a word about it. Instead she'd readily accepted Brooke, probably greatly relieved to have additional help.

The children were playing with giant interlocking blocks on the floor. Well, munching on them was more like it, giving them a good toothy chew. Henrietta set the laundry aside and squatted on the floor. "Oof."

If Brooke didn't get out of this room immediately, the three of them would witness her double over. "I promise I'll only be a minute," she called, racing out of the room. She sprinted to her bathroom, leaned up against the wall, her hand on her tummy, and took deep solid breaths, praying she could hold it together.

Minutes later and lucky for her, the need to empty her stomach had passed. Only slight tremors rocked her belly now. She splashed water on her face, took a comb to her hair, pulling it back into a ponytail. She felt much better now. She opened her bedroom door.

To Wyatt. He blocked the doorway, his hand fisted, ready to knock. Her jaw dropped and he seemed quite pleased that he'd startled her.

"Wyatt, I'm sorry, I can't talk to you right now. I've got to get back to—"

He shoved at her chest and followed her as she stumbled into her room. He gave the door a quick kick and it quietly clicked behind him. The next thing she knew, she was pinned to the back of the door, Wyatt's hands on her wrists, his beautiful face inches from hers, wearing a wry smile. "I'll show you *Mr. Brandt*," he whispered. And then his mouth was on hers, hungry, possessive and wild.

God, payback was a bitch. She should've known he wouldn't let that go. Her bones liquefied instantly and she kissed him back with a fire that started from deep inside her belly. She was helpless to push him away. "We can't," she pleaded blandly, between kisses. "Your mother—"

"Is locked far away in her room, probably already napping."

Was the locked part wishful thinking? "But the children?"

"Henrietta is doing fine with them."

"But we agreed..."

He nibbled on her throat and then ran his tongue down to her collarbone, taking bites there, too. The secrecy of meeting him like this was a turn-on, but then so was *he*—anywhere, anytime. Just one touch from him turned her brain to jelly. "I'm breaking the agreement. Just for now."

"Wyatt," she sighed, giving in to sensations driving her crazy. They groped at each other like teenagers hiding out behind the stairwell.

If only her teen years had been this exciting.

Finally she put a stop to it. Wyatt, breathing heavy, clunked his forehead to hers. "I don't want my mother bullying you."

"Is that why you came in here?"

"Yes. No."

Something about his confusion tugged at her heart. He wanted her, and that gave her all kinds of happy butterflies, but he wasn't ready and he was clearly battling with his emotions. "I've got your mom pegged already, Wyatt. She's not all that. I can handle her. Now, I've got to get back to the twins."

She made a move, but his hands were still splayed around her waist, and he didn't let go. He gave a yank and their bodies met, thigh to thigh, hip to hip, pulse to pulse. He kissed her once more, a killer kiss that left her trembling. His gaze sharpened on her, a hot blaze of blue lashing her as he opened the bedroom door. "*Mr. Brandt* is leaving now."

Then he walked out of the room.

The land was dry enough to take the children outside. Lord knew, they all had cabin fever. Getting out of the house for some fresh air seemed like a great idea. Until Mrs. Brandt got wind of it and decided to come along.

"Too bad my son couldn't join us today," she said, pushing the double stroller toward the stables. "We could've spent some time together, just the four of us."

Brooke let the comment pass. In Genevieve's eyes, she was just the nanny and didn't rate in a family outing. Wyatt had a meeting this morning and he wouldn't be back from Beckon until later this afternoon.

It was silly how much she missed him. They'd spent the entire weekend together and it had been like a dream. But reality was staring her in the face now. "I'm sure you'll be able to have more time together before you leave. I think Mr. Brandt would like that. I used to love family outings with my folks."

"You're from Ohio, right?"

"Yes, born and raised there."

"Do you have any siblings?"

"Just one brother. Well, technically, we're not related, but we're as close as any brother and sister could be. I was in the foster care system and then was adopted by the…

the Johnson family." Eek. She didn't want to expand on the lies. "But my family is solid and tight. It was my lucky day when Mom and Dad took me in and then adopted me."

"I did some charity work for the foster care program. It appears the system worked for you."

"I was one of the lucky ones. My good friend was in the system and wasn't as lucky as I was, but she's doing well now. She married my brother and life is good."

"Is that why you became a nanny?"

"Oh… I guess. And because I adore children. I babysat my way through high school."

"Madelyn was the same way. She adored children. It breaks my heart that the twins will never know their mother. Wyatt was crushed when she died."

"It had to be rough."

"She was a sweet girl, the perfect match for my son." Sadness seemed to steal Genevieve's breath. "I still can't believe she's gone. A horrible tragedy. Wyatt wouldn't have made it through if it wasn't for his children. Madelyn was the love of his life. He had no choice but to go on."

Such strong words. Oh, to love someone so much that you didn't want to live without them. Yeah, Wyatt would feel that way about Madelyn. Brooke had no delusions about what she was up against. She couldn't fault Wyatt's mother. But she had no idea how hurtful it was hearing her go on about Madelyn. Genevieve couldn't possibly know what Wyatt meant to her.

They walked in silence the rest of the way, the thick-wheeled stroller bumping over rougher terrain, keeping the twins quiet until they reached the stables and a white-fenced corral. Playful horses nudged each other, then raced around the perimeter in an equine game of tag.

"Horsey," Brett called out the second he spotted them.

Brianna followed the direction of his pointed finger and bounced in the seat of the stroller. "Horsey," she squealed, too.

Brooke laughed at how animated they'd become. They lived on a ranch and probably saw the horses every day, but that didn't seem to diminish their enthusiasm.

"Mrs. Brandt, if you'll get Brianna out, I'll get Brett. Henrietta packed carrots. We can show the kidlets how to feed the horses."

Mrs. Brandt chuckled. "The kidlets?"

Brooke shrugged. "I nickname everyone."

"Heavens, don't tell me what name you've picked out for me."

"I promise I won't."

Mrs. Brandt gave her a sideways glance, and then chewed on her lip to keep from smiling. "You have one for me already?"

She was rescued from answering when a tall man in jeans approached. "Is that you, Genevieve?"

Wyatt's mother whipped around and appeared startled. "Oh, uh, hello, James."

James was about the same age as Genevieve, and the hair under his black hat was almost the same silvery-pearl tone. A goatee shaped his chin and jaw and looked marvelous on him. He stared at Wyatt's mother for almost five full seconds, his green eyes sparkling. "Hello."

Brooke made herself busy taking Brett out of the stroller.

"And who is this young lady?" he asked.

"Hi, I'm Brooke. I'm the twins' nanny." With Brett on her hip, she walked over to shake his hand.

He took her in from top to bottom and nodded. "James. I'm the foreman here on Blue Horizon."

"Nice meeting you."

"'Bout time Wyatt saw fit to hire himself a decent nanny."

"Th-thanks. We were just letting the children get some fresh air and hoped they could feed the horses."

"Sure thing," he said, his gaze going back to Genevieve. She did her best to ignore him.

Brianna made noises, stretching her arms up, and James bypassed Genevieve to lift Brianna out of her confinement. "There, there, now, Brianna. Uncle James has you now." He bounced the toddler in his arms and Brianna reached up to pull at the hairs of his goatee, as if she'd done it a dozen times.

Rich, deep baritone laughter poured out of him, the sound amazingly sensual, and Wyatt's mother began fidgeting with the collar of her blouse.

"Don't you have work to do?" she asked, her tone ice-cold.

"Well, now, I've done all that needs doing so far." His chest expanded and he dug his heels in where he stood. "Like always." He bounced Brianna again and she cackled.

Oh, wow. He wasn't a man to be put down by the likes of a strong-willed woman. Watching James with her granddaughter, Genevieve looked lost for a moment, her light aqua eyes filled with something…longing or regret? It was sad in a way, but it wasn't any of Brooke's business.

"Here, let me have her," Genevieve said to James, putting her arms out.

"Grammy needs a hug," he whispered to Bri and when he made the transfer, his arm brushed Genevieve's—maybe deliberately, Brooke couldn't be sure. Wyatt's mother sucked in a breath and stiffened her body.

"I get plenty of hugs," she barked at him, cradling the baby to her chest.

"Not enough, I'd bet." He stared into Genevieve's eyes and for a moment, Brooke felt as if she needed to give the two of them some privacy so they could hash out whatever they really needed to say to each other.

"Brooke, you said there were some carrots?" Genevieve

needed an escape from James's intense gaze, and the excuse of feeding the horses came to the rescue.

"Oh, yeah. Let me get them." Brooke reached for the bag under the stroller and by the time she had the carrots sorted out and ready, James had said a quick goodbye. She caught Genevieve watching his retreat, her gaze on his backside as he sauntered into the stable.

Wyatt's mother turned around, her face flushed. It was hard not to notice…or comment.

"I'm a good listener, if you want to talk about it," she said quietly.

"There's nothing to talk about." Genevieve's eyes flashed in cold defiance, a reminder for Brooke to mind her own business. There *was* something to talk about, but just not with the family nanny.

Brooke recovered quickly and handed Genevieve a few carrots, then grabbed a few for herself. "Shall we?" They walked over to the corral fence. The horses had a sixth sense when it came to treats, and they'd wandered over, nudging each other to get to the carrots.

"Here you go, Brett. Hold it out," Brooke said.

Genevieve followed suit, giving little Brianna instructions.

"You know your way around a ranch." Brooke was impressed at Genevieve's ease with the animals.

"I know horses," Genevieve said. "And cattle for that matter. My husband saw to it that I knew everything there was to know about his business. God, I loved him, but ranching wasn't in my blood the way it was with him."

It was obvious Genevieve's tastes were far more refined. She wasn't one for living out on a remote ranch, gorgeous as it was, without people, nightlife and high fashion.

"But I miss these babies. And my son." She stroked the bay's mane gently. "Though I think he'd rather not have me here."

It was a confession that surprised Brooke. "I don't think that's true."

Genevieve shook her head and chewed her lip, most likely regretting letting that nugget of information slip. Maybe Wyatt didn't want his mother here right now, but James sure had his eye on her. From all indications, he'd probably like her to stay on at the ranch indefinitely.

Genevieve reached into her pocket and unfolded a hand filled with sugar cubes. "Watch this, Brett and Bri." She put out her hand and moved from one horse to another feeding them the sugar. Afterward, she graced each horse with a loving pat on the head. "Sugar cubes are like cupcakes to horses," she said. "Who here likes cupcakes?"

Brett and Brianna grinned and shouted, "Me! Me!"

"Well, maybe tonight, Grammy will give you some, if you eat a good dinner."

Brooke smiled at the joy on their faces.

So far, so good.

The twins' accidental nanny hadn't blown her cover.

Brooke's tummy heaved and bile rose in her throat. Henrietta had insisted on cooking liver and onions for dinner, and the steamy aroma filled the entire room. Apparently, it was a Brandt family favorite. Lucky for Brooke, the housekeeper also fried up a plate of chicken fingers for the twins. Okay, so she wouldn't starve; she'd eat with the children. But the pungent smell and onion was doing a number on her. Blood drained from her face, and she imagined she'd turned a pale shade of avocado right then.

She wanted so badly to put her hand on her stomach, to somehow make it feel better. But standing near Henrietta and Genevieve, two women who'd carried a child, she feared that gesture would be like drawing a bull's-eye on her belly.

Instead she rubbed at her forehead.

"Something wrong?" Wyatt asked, coming up from behind. She hadn't seen him enter the kitchen.

She gave him a half smile. "Just a little headache."

Struck by the concern in his eyes, she put her head down. "I'll be all right in a minute."

"Why don't you go lie down?" he said.

"Yes, dear," Henrietta said. "I think between the three of us, we can manage the twins. Dinner will keep."

Darn right it would. If she ate a bite right now, she wouldn't be able to hold it down.

"Are you hungry?" Wyatt asked.

"Not really."

"Then go lie down. There's headache medicine in your bathroom."

He glanced at Henrietta and she nodded.

Wyatt, Henrietta and even Genevieve had sympathetic expressions on their faces.

"Okay, but just for a little while. I'll get the twins their baths and put them to sleep later."

"Take the night off. I can do all that." Genevieve seemed eager to spend precious time with the children.

"Thank you, Mrs. Brandt."

Wyatt's lips went tight. He wasn't a fan of his mother's insistence on formality.

"I'll walk you up," Wyatt said.

"No, no. That's not necessary." She gave Wyatt a solid, don't-argue look, and he relented. "Thank you," she said to everyone.

She made her way up the staircase and entered her room none too soon, flopping on the bed facedown, and closed her eyes. Getting away from the ungodly smell of liver and onions was half the battle. She immediately felt less nauseous and was grateful she hadn't made a spectacle of herself in the kitchen. She gave herself up to rest.

A gnawing ache in her stomach woke her and she

snapped her eyes open to darkness. She waited a second for her eyes to adjust to the barest glimmer of moonlight streaming into her bedroom. Slowly, she sat up in the bed and got her bearings. The bedside clock read midnight, and another grumble of her stomach reminded her she'd gone to bed without dinner.

Now she was famished.

She rose and walked into the bathroom. Under dim light she washed her face and changed out of her wrinkled blouse. She ran a brush through her unruly hair, then wove the strands into one long braid, letting it fall down the middle of her back.

Barefoot, she ambled down the hallway and peeked in on the twins. She smiled at their peaceful sweetness and air-kissed both of them. The rest of the house was equally quiet. Carefully, she tiptoed down the stairs and into the kitchen, bracing herself for the awful scent of liver. Thanking all things holy, she was happy to find that the horrid scent was gone. Instead the kitchen smelled sweet, and she remembered Genevieve had promised to bake cupcakes for the twins. The aroma of chocolate was a much better scent, but she wouldn't dare. She opted for a piece of French bread, no butter.

She sat at the kitchen table with the bread and a glass of milk.

"Want some chicken to go along with that?"

She jumped in her seat, startled by Wyatt's voice. "My God, you scared me half to death."

He grinned. "Sorry."

"Why don't you look sorry?"

"Because I heard a noise and was hoping it was you."

"You mean, you'd rather face me than a burglar?"

"I'd rather face you, period."

Oh, wow.

He grabbed a chair, turned it backward and straddled it.

His feet were bare, his jeans riding low. A T-shirt stretched tight over his arms and chest, exposing his solid strength. He didn't look like a filthy rich billionaire, but a father of twins with a bad case of drop-dead gorgeousness.

"Sorry about the meal tonight. Liver's a staple around here. I'll make sure Henrietta doesn't cook it again while you're here."

"Thank you."

"How's your head?"

"My head?"

"You had a headache."

"Oh, I slept it off and then woke up hungry."

"Well, eat up."

She nodded and chewed for a few seconds, aware of Wyatt's gaze resting on her.

"How was your day with my mother?"

"It went well."

"Really?"

"Really." She wouldn't tell him that Genevieve had been curt at times and seemed out of sorts when James showed up. "We took the babies for a walk and I met some of the crew and your foreman, James." She searched Wyatt's face hoping for a clue about his relationship with Genevieve. "He seems comfortable around the babies. Brianna adores him."

"He's a good man, likes kids. He's been with us for twenty years."

"Hmm." She took a swig of milk.

"I bet my mother wasn't thrilled to see him."

She snorted and milk spewed from her nose and mouth.

He chuckled. "That bad?"

She nodded her head and grabbed the napkin Wyatt offered. Dabbing at her mouth, she kept her thoughts to herself.

"Ah, that's what I was afraid of. It's no secret James is

smitten with my mom. They dated once, last year when she was here for a visit. James was over-the-moon happy and then Mom called it off. She didn't want to have anything to do with him after that."

"Do you know what happened between them?" She was dying to know. It was a great diversion from her own problems. And maybe she could help.

"I have my suspicions. Mom likes James, a whole lot. And that's the problem. He's a threat to her life in New York. If she got seriously involved with him, it would mean moving back to Texas."

Brooke mulled it over for a few moments. From what she gathered about Genevieve, it made perfect sense. "Maybe that's exactly what she needs, Wyatt. She misses the babies very much, and being near you."

"Ah, but she made her choice when she pulled Dad away from the ranch as soon as he retired. I think she believes it would be a step backward if she gave in to her feelings now."

"So James, I take it, isn't a pushover. He gave her grief over it, right?"

"That would be my guess."

She nodded. Now she understood Genevieve's reaction to James today.

Wyatt took hold of her hand, lacing their fingers together. It was clear the conversation about Wyatt's mom was over. Tingles ran up her arm, and her mind got a little fuzzy.

"Come into my study with me, Brooke," he whispered, leaning close. She suppressed the urge to run her hands through his thick hair. "I want...us."

God. She squeezed her eyes shut. She wanted "us," too. It was wrong. They'd made an agreement. While she was here as his nanny, they had to keep their distance. And yet, as she glanced at their entwined hands, the power of his simple suggestion was a pull she couldn't resist. She wanted to be with him. He excited her and made her long for more. They shared a child, and whether he knew it or not, the bond was there, nestling inside her.

She nodded.

A gleam sparked in his eyes and he smiled, pushing all her female buttons. He stood to pull the chair out for her. Then he grabbed her hand and gave a squeeze as they ambled down the long hallway that led to his study.

With a *click*, they were locked in.

"The babies?" she whispered.

"We'll hear them if they cry out."

And then his mouth was on hers and his kisses washed away all her worries and doubts. Within minutes, they were naked on a wide comfy leather sofa. Atop her, his body was steel to her softness, his chest rock solid as it grazed her tender nipples, his hands threading through the braid that had come loose. In haste and urgency, they explored and pleasured each other in the near-darkness. Wyatt spoke sweet words, loving her body, offering her anything she wanted. He wanted to please her, to make it good for her. The gesture made her fall deeper under his spell.

She loved him.

It was not a big surprise. She'd been falling steadily. He was the kind of man a woman didn't forget. Wyatt made her see and feel the difference between the superficial kind of love she felt for Royce and the love she had for him. He was a real man. A good, kind, solid man, and she had fallen head over heels in love with him.

She rode the wave of his passion, giving him all she had to give, making it good for him, too. When they were joined, his flesh deep inside her, she felt safe. Protected. The connection was real, and not just physically. They shared something wonderful, a compatibility and understanding that carried over to their day-to-day living. She'd never felt more encouraged than now. The urge to speak the truth and get it all out in the open was never stronger. Tonight was the night she would tell him about the baby she carried. His baby.

The joy in her heart led to a wild, furious release. Wyatt joined her, and they shared the amazing climb together, the grind and arch of their bodies in complete sync with each other. "Let go, sweetheart," he rasped, his voice tight and tense.

"Wyatt," she moaned, and the pressure rose to an extreme high.

Both shuddered. Both cried out. Both were bathed in sweat and heat. And then they both came down, Wyatt cupping her head and bestowing kisses on her face.

She'd never been happier.

And afterward, when they were poking around in the dark, retrieving their clothes and attempting to dress, she whispered, "I can't find my panties."

Wyatt chuckled. "It's all part of my plan."

"Wyatt!"

"Hold on a sec," he said, and scrambled for the light switch. Soon the dark study was awash in dim light. And oh, if only her panties weren't missing. If only she could've walked out of that room blindly and gone on with her plan.

But clarity was a bitch. Clarity brought pain. Clarity made her see what she didn't want to admit. Wyatt's study, his most private place and the room where he relaxed and retreated to whenever he needed an escape, painted a very telling picture. There on all four walls, the fireplace mantel, the massive desk and bookcase, were dozens upon dozens of framed photos. Madelyn smiling into the camera. Madelyn riding a horse. Madelyn pregnant with the twins. Madelyn in her bridal gown. The two of them, the four of them, the entire Brandt family. Everywhere.

Yes, she'd seen photos of Madelyn in some rooms in

the house. Henrietta said Wyatt wanted to make sure the babies never forgot their mother. Brooke got that. It was understandable. She'd worry if there were no pictures around of his wife and the mother of his children.

But *this*? The room Wyatt considered his sanctuary wasn't merely a study, but a cluttered cathedral meant for worshipping at the altar of Madelyn. *This* was a wall-to-wall depiction of their life together. Every photo, every scene, every unabashed smile told the story of their love.

His love. For his late wife.

Brooke's mouth gaped open and every good thing inside her fizzled like the bubbles of stale champagne. Her shoulders slumped in defeat.

"Brooke." Wyatt reached for her.

She jerked away. "Don't, Wyatt," she breathed in a hush. "I've been a fool."

"No," he said. "You're not a fool."

She found her panties and finished dressing. "Oh, yes, I am. I get the picture now. Literally. How could I not? I can't do this anymore." She lifted her chin to Wyatt's baffled expression. What did he think? That she'd be overjoyed seeing his devotion to his dead wife? Did he think she wouldn't be affected by his homage to Madelyn Brandt, the true love of his life? "We need to stick to the original plan. While I'm here acting as nanny, we need to keep our distance. And this time, I mean it. Don't come looking for me, Wyatt. Got that?"

He stood facing her, his hands on his hips and his mouth pulled tight, refusing her an answer.

"Do you understand?" she asked.

"Let me explain."

"This," she said, gesturing around the room, "is all the explanation I need."

She spun on her heels and exited the study.

Nausea kicked in big-time. Her stomach gurgled and ached and there was no holding back.

Once she got to her bathroom, she was going to throw up.

Eight

Two days later, the babies sat in their high chairs, making a game of tossing toys off their trays. "Now, now," Genevieve said. "Patience, little ones, we're going as fast as we can fixing your breakfast."

Brooke stirred the oatmeal to cool it down, tossing in some fresh cut-up strawberries.

"There once was a pair of silly twins," Genevieve began in a singsong voice, a deliberate diversion from the great twin toy drop. And sure enough, the children's heads popped up, smiles emerging. "Who liked to *drop, drop, drop* their toys onto the floor." Her voice was lovely, sweet, engaging.

"With a *mop, mop, mop* of curly blond strands," Brooke chimed in singing. "On the *top, top, top,* of their heads."

Genevieve chuckled. Brooke danced the bowls of oatmeal over to the table and took her seat in front of Brett while Genevieve sat down beside Brianna.

"The food goes *plop, plop, plop* into their mouths," Genevieve harmonized.

Brooke giggled and aimed the spoon into Brett's mouth. "And they couldn't *stop, stop, stop* filling their tummies."

Genevieve speared a spoonful into Bri's waiting mouth.

The babies giggled at the rhyming verses, enjoying the silly song and their meal. Once the bowls were emptied and the twins were sipping milk from their sippy cups, Genevieve looked over to Brooke. "You're not half bad, Brooke."

A compliment? "You're pretty good yourself, Mrs. Brandt."

Genevieve chewed on her lower lip, giving Brooke a thoughtful stare. "You know, I think you were right. We don't want to confuse the babies. Call me Genevieve or Grammy."

"You mean in front of the twins?"

"I mean, always." When she smiled, her eyes lit up. In the last few days, Brooke must have passed some sort of test with her.

"Okay, I will. Thanks."

Genevieve seemed pleased with herself. "Good. Now what are we going to do with these two today?"

The morning sun was at Brooke's back, streaming warmth into the kitchen. "I think it's going to be a beautiful day."

"Fall has arrived. It's a shame to let it go to waste. There's a nice playground in Cahill. And if I'm not mistaken, the diner there is pretty good. We can let the babies play at the park and then God willing, they'll nap while we have a peaceful lunch."

"Sounds wonderful to me." It meant spending the day away from the ranch and away from Wyatt. That was a good thing, because she was hurting. Seeing him day in and day out was difficult. Her heart hadn't stopped aching. She was doing everything in her power to keep her distance. He wasn't making it easy, though. He was always around. He loved his twins and wanted to be Daddy to them at every turn. There were times when she wanted to run into his arms and other times when she wanted to run far and fast in the opposite direction.

His eyes always found hers during meals, and although she kept out of his path she couldn't help seeing him when he popped in to play with the twins, or feed them or help put them to sleep at night. Thankfully, Genevieve unknowingly made a nice buffer. Brooke and Wyatt were rarely alone.

Which was a good thing.

But it also broke her heart.

"Will you tell Wyatt our plans, Brooke? I have some phone calls to make before we leave later this morning. Give me a couple of hours."

"Uh, okay. I'll make sure he knows where we're going today."

Genevieve gave the children each a kiss on the cheek. "I'll see you later, my babies."

Once she exited the room, Brooke rose to help Henrietta with the dishes while the twins were still in a happy mood. The great toy drop began anew, but it kept them occupied in their high chairs while Brooke was busy. At least one good thing had come from Brooke being here: Henrietta wasn't exhausted anymore. The older lady actually had pep in her step.

"Did I miss breakfast?" Wyatt walked in, looking sharp in a blue plaid shirt and faded denim jeans. That particular cobalt color brought out the deep hue in his eyes and Brooke had to force herself to keep from staring. Her heart beat hard in her chest.

"I've got eggs and bacon cooking for you, Wyatt," Henrietta said.

"Thanks, Etta." He approached his babies, giving them

a pat on the head and kissing their cheeks. "Morning, my darlins'. Brooke." He turned to her, his gaze unreadable.

"Good morning, Mr. Brandt."

He winced. He hated the formality but she'd kept it up for appearances. And now she was grateful she had that crutch to fall back on. It was just one more way to keep her distance. Often, over the past few days, she'd wanted to simply tell Wyatt the truth and be done with it. The duplicity was killing her, but she'd made him a promise she would stay until Genevieve was satisfied and left the ranch. She wouldn't go back on her word. Besides, they'd have a lot to work out once he learned about the child she carried, and having his mother here would only hamper the process.

In a very real way, Brooke was trapped here by her lies.

Her stomach grumbled. She hadn't eaten yet, either. But bacon and eggs would only make her sick. Morning smells did a number on her very sensitive tummy lately. Luckily, her stomach wasn't on the fritz all day long. If she made it past breakfast eating bland foods, then she was usually good to go the rest of the day.

"Have you eaten?" he asked.

"I, um, no. Not yet. The babies woke early and seemed hungry. No big deal, I'll have some oatmeal later."

"Have it now. I don't like eating alone."

Henrietta glanced at him. Her brows gathered at his less-than-friendly tone. Wyatt was clearly out of sorts.

"Fine." She gave him a fake smile and Henrietta handed her a bowl of oatmeal, then dished up the bacon and eggs for him. She placed biscuits on the table, too. How did any Texas woman retain her figure with biscuits, breads or muffins being served at every meal? Brooke was tempted to grab a biscuit and slather it with butter, but thought better of it. Her tummy could only hold so much food, and oatmeal was the far better choice.

"Would you like cinnamon or sugar with it?" Henrietta asked.

"I'm good with this. Thanks."

After she served them, Henrietta exited the kitchen mumbling something about getting down the fall decorations.

Great, now they were alone. Well, except for the babies. Brooke put her head down, concentrating on eating her oatmeal.

"When I said I didn't like to eat alone, I didn't mean this."

"What?"

"You're giving me the silent treatment."

"It's for the best," she whispered.

"Depends on who you ask."

"Wyatt, don't."

"I'm sorry, okay. It was really a dumb move on my part bringing you into that room."

She bit her lip and looked away. Taking her in there in the heat of passion was one thing, but that his shrine to Madelyn even *existed* was the heartbreaker. Seeing his private sanctuary put everything into perspective. He had every right to hold on to his love for his late wife. But why did he have to make love to Brooke as if it meant something to him? Maybe he shouldn't have made love to her at all. "I don't want to talk about it. Okay?"

He sucked in a breath and then sighed. "Okay. Listen, I want to spend some time with the twins this morning. I'd like to take them for a ride."

"A ride? Where?"

"On the grounds."

"In your car? That seems silly."

A smile emerged, transforming his sulky face. "Not in the car. On horseback."

"You've got to be kidding."

He glanced at his children, who were beginning to wiggle and squirm in their high chairs. "Nope. I rode my first horse when I was one year old. Got the pictures to prove it. If you ask me, they're overdue."

"Okay, suit yourself."

"I'll need help."

"James or your mother could probably help."

"I need your help. Mom's not much for riding and James is too busy today."

"Wyatt, I can't ride a horse."

"You've never ridden before?"

"I have. That's not what I meant. I'm not exactly an expert." She was pregnant. She shouldn't get atop a horse, should she?

"You don't have to be. Do you think I'd risk my kids' safety? I have all the rigging to keep them and you from any danger."

"Well, we can't do it today. Your mom and I are taking the twins into Cahill."

"When?"

"In a couple of hours."

"That gives us more than enough time."

Holding Brett in his arms, Wyatt motioned for Brooke to climb atop the horse. She came forward tentatively, the hat on her head shading her troubled eyes from morning sunshine. He wasn't being fair to her. As sure as the sun rose in the east every day, he knew it. But once a notion took root inside his brain, he had trouble removing it. He'd dug his heels in insisting on Brooke's being a part of the twins' first ride. Now he couldn't imagine doing it without her.

Since their argument, she was on his mind constantly. She'd sidestepped him every moment of every day since, whenever she possibly could. He'd hurt her without intending to, and if he had a lick of sense, he'd let these next few days pass without interjecting himself more into her life. But he couldn't do it. He had a powerful need to spend as much time with her as possible.

It wasn't a conscious move on his part to include her on the ride this morning. Hell no. But after hearing her singing that silly ditty to his toddlers, something snapped inside him. He'd practically ordered her to share the morning meal with him, and then insisted she ride with him and his babies. When she left the ranch for good, he'd miss her like crazy.

If only he had something to offer her. But he wasn't over Madelyn and he couldn't bear hurting Brooke again.

"Step on up to the mounting block," he said to her, holding the reins. "These two mares are the gentlest in the string."

"I know how to mount a horse, Wyatt."

He ignored her and helped her up into the saddle, his hand on her rear end giving a little push. Brooke lanced him with a look that could cut ice.

He bit back a laugh. "This is Maple. She's five years old and sweet as her name."

"Good to know."

Brooke placed her boots into the stirrups and adjusted her position. "I'll hand Brett up to you. And then I'll put the rigging around both of you. You'll be snug and locked in. Just keep one hand on him at all times."

"Okay, got it."

He handed the baby up and immediately, Brett started kicking up a happy fuss. His smile was worth a zillion bucks. "There you go, boy. You like that, don't you?" Once they were secure, he gave Brett a pat on the head. His kids liked the ranch animals. They had no fear, and Wyatt's chest puffed out seeing Brett take to being in the saddle.

"Horsey, go!"

Brooke cracked a smile. If anyone could get that sour

look off her puss, it was Brett. "Not yet, little guy. We'll go as soon as Daddy says so."

Wyatt lifted Brianna out of the stroller and then holding her tight, mounted his mare with ease. He wrapped the protective rigging around both their bodies and clicked his heels, guiding the horse over to Brooke. "Can you tighten this strap?" he asked her.

Brooke leaned way over, took the strap he offered and gave a tug. "That's perfect," he said. "All set?"

She nodded. "Bri's all smiles, too."

"You both look cute in those hats."

Brooke rolled her eyes. Wyatt was too damn happy to take offense. "I'll lead. Try not to fall too far behind."

"We'll keep up, don't you worry."

"Okay," he said. And off they went.

They left the stables and got as far as the house when Genevieve came running out. "Wyatt! Stop! You can't take the twins without documenting this." She had her cell phone in her hands. "It's their first ride."

God, he hadn't thought of that. "Thanks, Mom. You're right. I wasn't thinking."

"Yeah, that happens a lot with you," he heard Brooke mumble.

He gave her a sideways glance. "Maybe because you make me forgot my own name."

Brooke had no response to that, but he liked the way her face flushed pink.

"Maybe you'd like to take my place, Grammy G?" Brooke called out. "You should be in the pictures, not me."

Grammy G? When had Brooke started calling his mother that? When his mom didn't react to the nickname, he was totally baffled.

"No, no, Brooke. I'm a better photographer than I am a rider. You two go on. I'll get some video of this, too. Bri and Brett, look over here at Grammy."

The children were in awe, being atop their favorite animals. There wasn't a peep out of them as they rode by the stables and corrals. Wyatt's ranch hands stopped what they were doing to wave. The twins giggled and gave a wave back. James had a big smile on his face, too, until he noticed Wyatt's mother standing in front of the house with camera in hand. All joy was wiped clean from James's face and just like that, he marched over to the house.

Whatever was going on between James and his mother, Wyatt was keeping his nose out of it.

"Uh-oh, looks like trouble is brewing," Brooke said.

At least she was talking to him. Lately Brooke had barely given him the time of day, except when it came to something regarding the children. How did he turn out to be the bad guy, while his mother and Brooke were such good buddies now? "Mom can be a lot to handle. James has his work cut out for him."

"I think James is just what Genevieve needs. She just doesn't know it yet. Women need lots of encouragement, especially when their mind is set on the wrong thing."

"Do they now?" Wyatt gave her an intense stare.

"Yeah, uh, never mind. I'm the last one to give advice." She looked straight ahead. "How far are we going?"

He let her comments drop, but logged them into his memory. Brooke was good at giving him a female perspective. "Oh, don't know exactly. The kids are enjoying it. I guess we'll head back when they start to fuss."

They ambled down a path heading away from the grazing cattle toward one of Wyatt's favorite spots on his property. The meadow was a mix of bluebonnets and tall grass. It was pretty scenery. "Here's where my granddaddy came up with the name of the ranch. Sitting on the ground looking out, he said the bluebonnets appeared to meet the sky like a blue horizon."

"Wow, I can picture that. It's lovely here."

"Yep. There's a pond up ahead. We can water the horses."

The twins were amazingly quiet, satisfied and thrilled to be riding. One day, they'd own their own horses, learn how to care for and groom their animals. Learn how to respect them. They had time for that, though. He wouldn't rush them. Hell, he still needed a nanny for them. He had two preliminary interviews scheduled on the day his mother was due to leave the ranch. He didn't hold out much hope; replacing Brooke in any capacity would be hard. She was great with his kids and, well, great overall.

And in two days, his mother and Brooke would be long gone.

He wasn't ready to say goodbye to Brooke, but he couldn't ask her to stay. He didn't want to hurt her any more than he already had. The dilemma plagued his mind, but he had to think of the twins. They needed someone steady and constant in their lives. Someone they could rely on. Henrietta and Brooke weren't an option anymore.

"Lookee, Daddy. Duckies," Brianna said, pointing toward the pond.

Brett got wind of it, too. "Duckies! Duckies!"

Brooke laughed. The joy on her face and the way she squeezed little Brett tight, as if she loved the little guy, tugged at Wyatt's heart.

"I see them. They're swimming and taking a bath."

"They look like the duckies in the book I read to you," Brooke said. "*One, Two, Three Ducks*. You remember, right?"

The twins nodded without taking their eyes off the birds, their smiles brighter than sunshine.

Wyatt hadn't known this much joy since before Madelyn's accident. It was as if they were a family, similar to the ducks swimming in his pond, sticking together, having a fun time. A knot twisted in his gut. He knew better. He wouldn't dwell on what couldn't be. But still…

Fifteen minutes later, they were back at the stables and off the saddles. The twins were pooped and ready for a morning nap.

He carried the heftier Brett over his shoulders, while Brooke carried Bri as they headed for the house. Dust kicked up, stopping them midway on the driveway as a slick midnight blue sports car came to a halt right in front of them.

And Johnny Wilde stepped out of his convertible.

Nine

"So that's Brooke?" Johnny said to Wyatt after they'd put the twins down to nap. Brooke was upstairs getting ready for her outing with his mother and the children. "You finally found someone suitable as a nanny, then?"

Wyatt gave Johnny a thoughtful look here in the privacy of his study. He'd learned his lesson the hard way and removed the shrine of photos he'd had of Madelyn in the room. Now only a few of his favorites graced the wall. "Not exactly."

Johnny was his best friend, someone he trusted, a rancher and part owner of the Dallas-based Wilde Corporation he ran with his brothers. They'd grown up together and once upon a time, Johnny had even had an eye for Madelyn. But Wyatt had won her over.

"What does that mean?" With the twist of his wrist, ice shuffled around in the glass of lemonade Johnny held.

"It means, and I know I can trust you…" He eyed him carefully and Johnny nodded. "Brooke is a woman I picked up on the road. We were both going to the same wedding and her car had broken down and…well, it's a long story."

Johnny leaned forward in his chair. "You got my attention at *Brooke is a woman I picked up on the road*. Trust me, Wyatt, for this, I have the time."

Wyatt took a swig of his drink. "I know, it doesn't sound like me, does it?"

Wyatt spent the next ten minutes explaining the situation to his best friend. Johnny listened, keeping his thoughts to himself and nodding.

"So that's it. Brooke is leaving in two days, right after Mom leaves."

"Weird coincidence that she's Dylan McKay's sister."

"Tell me about it. Are you still working on the set?"

"Yeah, part-time. The show wraps in less than a week."

"That means Brooke will be going back to California."

Johnny's dark brows rose and white lines appeared in his otherwise tan forehead. "And you're letting her go?"

Wyatt nodded. "I have to."

"Why?"

"Because I've already hurt her. And I can't… I can't." He began shaking his head. "Listen, you know how hard I took Madelyn's death. I'm still grieving. There's a hole in my heart that will never fill up again. If I got involved with Brooke and it didn't work out, I… I'm just not ready for that."

"Too bad, pal. If it were me, I'd ask her to stay. You said she's great with the kids, and well, if she's that hot in the sack…"

"Watch it," Wyatt warned, his blood ready to boil over. He'd told Johnny that he and Brooke had a good time together. He hadn't elaborated, but it was true, Brooke was hot in bed. Yet hearing it come out of Johnny's mouth rankled him no end. "Don't make me sorry I confided in you."

"Okay, okay. Mellow out, Brandt."

"It's just that, Brooke is…"

"Special? Amazing? Beautiful? Oh, yeah, I noticed."

"You only spoke with her for two minutes."

"Two of the best minutes of my life."

Wyatt gave a half groan, half laugh. "Johnny, you're hopeless."

"I'm just trying to help. If you've got feelings for her, Wyatt, don't run from them. You may never come across another woman you like as much."

"That's just it, I'm not looking for another woman. I need a nanny for my kids. Preferably someone with warts and knobby knees. Someone who doesn't distract me every second of the day."

Johnny laughed. "Man, you are tortured."

"Tell me about it. Come on," Wyatt said. "Mom's probably downstairs by now. She'll want to see you."

"She's the main reason I came by. I couldn't let your mama leave for home without saying hello."

An hour later, Wyatt and Johnny were in the garage helping Brooke load the kids into their car seats. Johnny gave Brett and Brianna high fives and then kissed them on their cheeks. "I'll see you next time I come by, kids. Love you both," Johnny said. "Brooke, it was very nice meeting you."

"Same here, Johnny."

"What do you mean, *next time*? You're staying for dinner tonight," Genevieve said. "I haven't seen enough of you today and the twins would love to see more of their Uncle Johnny. Wyatt, didn't you invite Johnny for dinner?"

"Yeah, Wyatt," Johnny egged him on. "I didn't hear anything about dinner."

"You're welcome to stay for dinner," Wyatt droned.

Johnny glanced at Brooke and gave her a big smile. "I'd like that very much."

Brooke smiled back, and Wyatt's jealousy radar went crazy.

"There, it's settled." The queen of England herself would stand up and take notice at his mother's tone. "We'll see you later tonight."

"Sounds good. And hey, will James be sitting down with us? I promised him a visit, too."

"No, James doesn't usually dine with us," Genevieve was quick to point out.

"But I'll ask him to join us," Wyatt said. He wasn't about to throw James under the bus because of his mother. James deserved better treatment. He'd been loyal to the ranch for decades.

"Well, that's just great." Johnny glanced at Brooke, then Genevieve. "You two ladies have a fun outing. I'll see you all later."

Deliberately, Wyatt didn't look at his mother. If she was pissed, she'd aim her wrath at him, and he had enough to worry about lately.

Dinner at the Brandt house tonight wasn't going to be dull.

That was for darn sure.

"Genevieve, your mouth is going to stay that way if you don't untwist it. At least that's what I was always told," Brooke said.

As Wyatt's mother slumped on the wrought iron and wood park bench, her face wrinkled even more. The usually strong woman appeared diminutive sitting next to Brooke. "Sorry, I'm lousy company today."

The children were playing in the park, shoveling sand into a variety of sifters, pails and animal molds. They were getting filthy and having the best day ever. Horsey rides, ducks at the pond and now the sandbox. Brooke loved seeing the joy in their eyes. They were the sweetest kids.

"Why?"

"It's complicated."

"Life usually is." And wasn't that the truth. She was keeping secrets from Genevieve and Wyatt. And one of those truths was beginning to show in the form of a tiny baby bump.

Genevieve nodded. "I like my life. It's full and rich and when I'm helping others, I feel better about myself. I work for charities and foundations and pour my heart and soul into the work. It's what I love. I've made friends. I have a beautiful home in New York."

"Why do I feel a *but* coming here?"

"It's just one big fat *but*. James."

Brooke laughed.

Then Genevieve laughed, too. "I didn't mean it that way. James is…"

"Nice? Handsome? Persistent?"

"Yes, all of it. He and I, well, we began seeing each other and it was marvelous. I mean, we really had a good, good time. But he wanted more."

"And you're afraid to give it?"

"He used to work for my husband. He works for Wyatt now. I mean…what would people say? How would it look?"

"Like maybe two lonely, intelligent people found each other?"

Genevieve smiled sadly. "I don't think so."

"Why do you care what anyone says?"

She shrugged and tears entered her eyes. "I don't. Not really. But it's taken me all this time to get what I really wanted in life—to live on the East Coast, to be part of society rather than being tucked away on a remote ranch. To have friends, go to the theater and enjoy all the city has to offer."

"There are pros and cons to every issue, Genevieve. What if you gave James a chance and found that you were happier than you could ever imagine? You'd be close to your grandchildren and your son. And I'm sure James could be persuaded to do some of those things you enjoy so much with you."

Genevieve's gaze rested on the children playing so heartily in the sand. Little Bri was standing, wearing an accomplished expression and ready to dump the contents of her tiny bucket into a pile. Brett was busy playing with another child's red toy truck. Behind them, a group of older kids were tossing a football back and forth, their laughter and country music filling the park. "I know. I know. All that might be true," Wyatt's mother said. "Lord knows, I'll never have any more grandchildren. Wyatt is through having babies, and I'm missing out on the ones I do have. I'm just…so afraid."

The comment about having babies stuck like a knife in Brooke's heart. Genevieve had just reaffirmed the reason Brooke was being so cowardly. Wyatt wouldn't want their child, and it crushed her to face that fact. How could she tell him? How could she possibly confess her pregnancy knowing how he felt about having more children? "Fear is something I understand. It can stifle you and cause you to make bad choices and wrong decisions."

But Genevieve's reply was interrupted when a football sailed over her head. Brooke saw the wild pass heading straight for Brianna and leaped into the sand, tackling her to the ground and then *thump*! The football smacked the side of her head. Hard. Pain slashed through her temple and her eyes crossed. She closed them until Brianna's cries reminded her that she had the little one tucked safely beneath her body.

"Brooke! Are you okay?" Genevieve came rushing over and Brooke slowly gave her a nod.

"I think so. I'm a little dazed."

"Goodness, Brooke. You saved Brianna. That ball would've really hurt her. Can you sit up?"

"Yes, I probably can." Although everything seemed to be going in slow motion at the moment, with Genevieve's help, she sat up.

Brianna was dazed, too. Then startled by Brooke's quick reaction, she started wailing. "It's okay, Bri. I'm sorry if I scared you."

Brett had gone pale. Any minute now, he'd start sobbing, too. Genevieve cradled both children, hugging them to her chest.

"Gosh, lady. I'm sorry." It was one of the football players. "Are you okay?"

"No, she's not okay." Genevieve's voice carried across the playground. "She was hit by your football. But it would've been worse if my granddaughter took that hit. Why are you playing so close to the playground? You boys should know better."

"Yes, ma'am. Sorry again."

The boy, joined by his friends, grabbed up his football and slumped away.

"My goodness, Brooke. You dived in to save Brianna. I, uh…" Genevieve choked up, shaking her head. "Thank you," she managed in a whisper.

"I just reacted," she said. "I couldn't let anything happen to Brianna."

Genevieve gave her an intense stare. "Are you sure you're okay? Maybe I should take you to see a doctor."

"No. I'll be fine." She touched the sore spot on her skull. Luckily, her arm had come up to partially divert the knock she took to the head. "I'm a little shaken up. You'll probably have to drive us home though."

"Not a problem. Let me get the kids into the car and we'll get you some ice."

One of the mothers from the playground came running

over. "Gosh, I saw what happened. I have an ice pack. Here you go." She handed it to Genevieve. "That was really brave of you," she said softly to Brooke. "Nice tackle. The momma bear in you came out, didn't it?"

She was about to correct the woman. Brianna wasn't her child, but Genevieve didn't give her the chance. "It sure did. I'm impressed."

"Me, too," the woman said. "Well, I hope you'll be all right."

"Thank you."

The woman gave her a sympathetic smile and walked off.

Brooke figured she must be dizzy in the head, because her first thought after that was that she'd managed to impress Wyatt's mother. What would he say to that?

"How about joining me in a glass of wine, Brooke?" Johnny Wilde offered after he'd poured his own glass on the side bar of the dining room. "It'll help heal that injury you took in the line of duty." He gave her a smooth smile, the wine bottle tipped and ready to pour. Thanks to Genevieve, everyone around the table had heard about the incident at the park.

"No thanks, Johnny. I'd better not."

Standing beside him, Wyatt held a shot glass to his mouth and downed the liquor in one swallow.

Brooke looked away. The babies were down for the night and without them as a shield, she had to deal with Wyatt on her own. They'd had a wonderful morning together, taking that ride with the twins. Now he studied her face and head, looking for signs of her injury, no doubt. There was a perpetual frown on his face aimed at her. It was a bit intimidating.

"You sure?" Johnny asked, ready to put the bottle down. "Being the hero of the day has its perks."

"I'm sure. My head is clear and I'd like to keep it that way. Thanks anyway."

When they returned home this afternoon, Genevieve had insisted that Brooke take a nap, while she took over tending to the children. The rest had done wonders. Her head no longer ached. And the bump on her head was teeny tiny, hardly noticeable. Still she felt uncomfortable with everyone staring at her as if she'd rushed into a burning building or something. Her save hadn't been that dramatic, but Brianna would surely have been hurt if that football had knocked her down.

Genevieve was already sipping wine at the far end of the dining room and speaking with James. It appeared to be a civil conversation from the smile on James's face. If a man could beam, he was surely doing it, and Genevieve's occasional quiet laughter was sweet to the ears.

Wow.

During the first course of dinner, glazed walnut and pear salad, Johnny entertained them with stories of growing up with Wyatt as his best friend. They'd gone to high school together and were teammates in baseball and football.

"*Rivals* is a better word," Wyatt was saying. "You were always trying to best me."

"Trying? I always did," Johnny added.

"In whose world?"

"In my world, Wyatt. Don't you remember who ran for more touchdowns? Who had more home runs?"

"I do recall. That would be me. The numbers don't lie. Maybe your recollections need a little tune-up. Check out the stats."

"I bet you still have them."

"They're here somewhere. Madelyn saved them for me." Wyatt's voice quieted.

Johnny's smirk didn't falter. He loved the banter, and the

mention of Madelyn didn't stop him from teasing Wyatt. "If you'd told that girl the moon was made of blue cheese, she would've believed you."

Wyatt didn't smile. Instead he glanced at Brooke, his soft gaze penetrating her defenses. That's all it took: one apologetic look from Wyatt to crumble the walls she'd tried so hard to maintain. He cared about her, she understood that, but it wasn't enough. Not nearly enough.

Genevieve and James rose from their seats to help Henrietta serve the entrée. When Brooke stood to lend a hand, both Wyatt and Genevieve stopped her immediately. "Don't you dare," Genevieve said.

Wyatt's stony stare said the same.

"I'm fine," Brooke said to everyone, but she lowered down in her seat.

"That's the way we want to keep it, right, Wyatt?" Genevieve gave Wyatt a glance and he nodded.

"I'll help, too."

"No need. Your mom and I have this," James said.

Genevieve gave James a smile and off the two of them went.

"Well, would you look at that," Johnny said. "And here I thought Genevieve had no use for good ole James."

Good ole James was a silver-haired, intelligent man of the earth. He was no country bumpkin, and maybe Genevieve was finally seeing his merits. If something good had come from this little deception she and Wyatt were engaging in, maybe it would be that those two were finding common ground.

"Did you have anything to do with my mother's change of heart?" Wyatt asked.

"Me?" She thought to refute it, but that wouldn't be totally true. And she needed to tell as much truth as she could to atone for all the lies. "Maybe. We had a nice talk today. She's a little confused about some things."

"Mom? Confused? She seems to know exactly what she wants."

Brooke shrugged. "I noticed a change in her after what almost happened to Brianna. She's got some thinking to do."

Wyatt blinked at the suggestion that he didn't know all there was about his mother after all. "I suppose. Maybe you saved more than one person today, Brooke."

"Deserving of a Purple Heart," Johnny said, giving her a winning smile. "Or at the very least a pat on the back and a kiss on the cheek."

Johnny leaned over, put his hand on her shoulder and then brushed a kiss to her cheek. It was short and quick, a chaste kiss, yet he'd stunned her. Heat climbed up her neck and one glance at Wyatt's murderous stare at Johnny had a bubble of laughter erupting from her lips. Only Johnny Wilde could get away with something like that.

"What the hell?" Wyatt rasped.

"What?" Johnny feigned innocence and chuckled.

Brooke couldn't contain her laughter, either. But Wyatt was not amused.

The conversation halted when James walked into the room with a sizzling platter of Blue Horizon prime rib roast. "Here we go," he said, setting the platter down carefully in the center of the table. "Wyatt, I'll do the slicing, if you don't mind. And Gen can serve the roast up. Is that okay with you, Gen?"

Genevieve gave him a smile and nodded. "I'd love to."

It was almost comical watching Wyatt struggle to keep his mouth from dropping open. Admittedly, from what Brooke gathered, James and Genevieve hadn't been this civil with each other in quite a while.

Henrietta walked in with a side dish casserole and then retrieved a basket of home-baked buttermilk biscuits. The room immediately filled with mouthwatering aromas.

It was time to concentrate on the scrumptious meal that looked and smelled delish.

With her stomach on the fritz and her head a little sore, Brooke only hoped she could hold it down.

The knock on her bedroom door came at precisely nine thirty. From her bed, Brooke stared at the door, fearing who was on the other side. She didn't want to speak to Wyatt tonight. She had two more days here, and she was trying to make the best of them. Wyatt seemed to have other plans.

"It's me, Genevieve. Are you awake?"

Surprised, she set her novel down and tossed off her blanket. "Just a sec, Genevieve. I'm coming."

She slid her arms into her robe and tied it before opening the door. "Hello."

Genevieve had a helpless look on her face. "I'm sorry to bother you. Do you have a minute?"

"Of course I do. Come in."

Genevieve entered her room and Brooke led her to the pair of wing chairs that looked out onto Blue Horizon property. The night was dark but for a sliver of moonlight. "Have a seat."

"Thanks." She sat.

So did Brooke. "What's on your mind?"

Genevieve tilted her head to one side. "James. We took a walk after dinner."

"Yes, I saw the two of you leave after dessert. So how was it?"

Genevieve inhaled a deep breath. "Wonderful. So sickeningly wonderful, I can't describe it. I, uh, well, I hope you don't mind me confiding in you. I can't imagine talking about this with Wyatt. But James kissed me goodnight and it was beyond amazing. It was bells and whistles going off."

"That's wonderful, isn't it?"

"I hope so. We talked at length and decided to take it slow. But I am going to continue seeing him. Do you think that's the right move?"

"I do, Genevieve. I think taking it slow is a good thing. You can spend more time here in Texas, and maybe he'll come to visit you in New York."

"That's what we're going to try to do. Maybe split our time and see how it goes. It'll give me more time with the twins, too." She nibbled on her lip. "Brooke, is it crazy to do this at my age?"

Brooke smiled. "Not at all. My goodness, Genevieve, if you see what I see when James looks at you, I'd say it'd be crazy not to. If you have feelings for each other, why not explore them?"

Wyatt's mother began nodding, taking in her suggestion. "I don't think I would've come to this conclusion without you."

"Me?"

"You're easy to talk to. I know I can be bitchy at times, but I respected how you managed me."

"You're not bitchy, exactly. And I wasn't managing you."

"Saying how calling me Mrs. Brandt might confuse my grandchildren? That was just the right comeback for me. And well, after your quick reaction with Brianna today, it was like a boulder being dropped on my head."

Brooke rubbed her sore skull. "Make that a football and I'd understand."

"Oh, dear, and I haven't even asked you about your head."

"It's fine. I'm fine. Go on," she said.

"Okay, I won't keep you much longer, I promise. But I wanted to thank you for listening and for your advice today. I have been sort of lost, coming here and seeing James again."

"Well, if I helped you in any way, I'm glad."

"You did. I realized today how badly I want more time with my grandchildren. It all seems to fit now. James and me, more visits to the ranch, less city, more country. I think I can do it."

"I'm happy for you, Genevieve."

"I'm sad I have to leave day after tomorrow. I haven't spent any time getting to know you. It's all been about me. Next time I come out I plan to spend time getting better acquainted with you."

"Uh, well, that would be nice." She felt like a heel, letting Genevieve Brandt believe she'd be here when she returned. Not only wasn't she really the twins' nanny, she was carrying Wyatt's baby and couldn't confide in Genevieve. The woman would probably end up hating her once she found out about all the lies Brooke had told.

What a deep hole she'd dug for herself.

Another soft knock came at her door and she froze. Her heart beat like crazy in her chest. Before her new visitor—more than likely Wyatt—could say something, Brooke called out. "Just a minute!"

Genevieve appeared genuinely surprised. "Who could that be?"

"Probably your son. I promised to give Mr. Brandt my… my schedule for next week. I have to take a few days off and he'd wanted to check with Henrietta to make sure she could cover."

"Goodness, I wish I could help out. I'd love to, but I've had this commitment in Dallas on the books for months."

Brooke swept over to the door. "It's going to work out, don't worry," she said, opening the door to Wyatt's somber face. "*Mr. Brandt*, I'm sorry I forgot to give you my schedule."

Wyatt stared at her as if she'd grown bull horns, and then noticed his mother walking toward him. He scratched his chin, buying time, and finally catching on. "No problem, I just wanted to remind you. And see how you're feeling. Hello, Mom."

"Wyatt. It's late for Brooke. Don't keep her up too long. Gosh, you are so much like your dad. He couldn't go to bed until he dotted his *i*'s and crossed his *t*'s."

"Yeah, the hazards of being a Brandt, I guess."

"Good night Brooke, get some rest." Genevieve patted her shoulder gently and then eyed her son for a moment. "Remember, you can discuss business in the morning."

Wyatt nodded and waited until his mother walked down the hallway and closed the door to her room. Then he sighed. "What was that all about?"

"Mostly about James, but I can't discuss it."

Wyatt didn't press the point. "May I come in?"

"If you have to."

He frowned and stepped inside her room.

Ten

Brooke tightened the ties on her robe and hugged herself around the middle. Wyatt was giving her his signature devilish blue-eyed look that threatened to devour her in one huge gulp. She didn't need any more private time with him. She'd told him to stay away, but he didn't listen very well. "Why are you here?" she asked on a sigh.

He frowned at her bluntness. "I'd like to see your bruise, Brooke."

"Why? The last time I checked, you didn't have 'MD' behind your name."

"Are you saying you need a doctor?"

"No, it's just a bump. It hurt like hell before, but the pain's gone now."

"Well, then. Show me. I couldn't see a damn thing at dinner."

"What's the point of having long hair if I can't cover up my wounds?" She was being deliberately obtuse with him tonight. Because…because, darn him, he was standing in her bedroom like her miracle cowboy again, with doggone sympathy and admiration in his eyes. The two didn't at all mesh, but on him, it looked appealing.

He stood with feet planted wide, hands on his hips, his jaw made of granite. "How bad is it?"

"Oh, for heaven's sake, Wyatt." She stepped closer to him and under a halo of lamplight angled her head slightly, pushing her hair to the side. "See, it's not that bad."

He winced and his breath rushed out. "There's definitely a bump there. Dammit. I wish to God you hadn't gotten hurt."

She believed him, because Wyatt was a decent man. That was the good news and the bad news.

"I told you at dinner, I'm fine now."

"What you did for Brianna…" He shook his head as if he couldn't find the words.

"I'm happy she wasn't hurt," Brooke said softly. "There's no need for you to be here worrying about this."

"Thank you for protecting her."

"You're welcome."

"You're making it impossibly hard for me to find a real nanny, you know."

"You're just saying that because your mother likes me." *I even impressed her today.*

"You're likeable, but Mom never takes a shine to people this quickly."

"She's not that bad, Wyatt. I feel terrible lying to her about all this."

"Just for another full day. Then she'll be on her way."

Brooke backed up a step and stared into his eyes. "And so will I."

Wyatt cleared his throat and nodded. "I know. Brooke, listen," he said, his voice deep and raspy. He came toward her, all iron-jawed handsome, and she closed her eyes.

"Don't, Wyatt."

"There are things I need to say to you. Things that need explaining."

"Look, you're off the hook, okay?" She smiled, softening her words. "I don't need to hear all about your heartache and your undying love for your wife. I don't need you to say nice things to me. I'll be leaving soon and…and…"

I'm having your baby.

God, it was on the tip of her tongue. But she held back. In less than forty-eight hours, she'd be gone from Blue Horizon. She needed more time before she told him. She needed to gain some perspective. She needed to discuss her situation with Emma and Dylan. Why hadn't she done that yet? Why had she jumped in with both feet without seeing how deep the bottom was? Without knowing how far she would fall?

Her decision made, she walked to the door and opened it. "Wyatt, I'm tired. I really should get to sleep."

"All right," he said, striding to the door. "Good night, Brooke," he said quietly, and then landed the softest kiss on her cheek. "Sleep well."

She gazed into his eyes. "You, too."

He shot her a dubious look, as if the last thing he would do was get a good night's sleep. He left her at the door and sauntered away. She fixed her focus on his retreating form, all cowboyed up, tight-jeaned and hunky.

Then she closed the door and put her hand to her tummy as tears spilled down her cheeks.

Brooke sat cross-legged in the great room among wooden alphabet blocks, dolls and two little people cars, playing with Brianna and Brett. The twins were a lot of work, but they were also adorable and sweet and Brooke's heart broke thinking she'd be leaving them tomorrow. Not only had she fallen for Wyatt, but she'd fallen for his kids, too.

"Here you go, Breezy Peezy." She handed Brianna a red block.

Brianna flung it across the room.

"No, we don't do that."

Brett giggled and it only egged Brianna on. She picked up another block and tossed it as hard as she could. It nearly hit Wyatt's gazillion-inch flat-screen TV. "Bri. No!"

She grabbed Brianna's hand and the little girl's face turned cherry red and she broke down in sobs. "Oh, it's okay, Bri. It's okay. Come here." Brooke cradled her in her arms, absorbing her genuine, honest-to-goodness tears. They soaked her blouse.

She'd been having so much fun playing with them, she didn't realize their nap time had come and gone, and the twins were both on the verge of hysteria.

Wyatt walked into the room, took one look at Brooke with Brianna and then scooped up Brett. "Nap time."

"Yeah, it's overdue. My fault."

His eyes warmed on his daughter and he ruffled her hair. "They're just having too much fun with you. It's hard not to." He kissed the top of Bri's head and she immediately stopped crying. "You're gonna be okay, sweetie." Then he planted a kiss on Brett's head. "Up we go."

They climbed the stairs and entered their nursery, his compliment humming through Brooke's system. "My mom thinks it's time for the babies to have their own rooms."

Brianna had nearly conked out in her arms during the climb up the stairs. Brooke lowered her down gently and the little one curled her body up, nestled down and fell fast asleep. "Well, I've told you before, I don't think there's any rush. You can do it in a year or so when they develop different tastes."

"You mean like blue for boys and pink for girls?"

She chuckled quietly. "Only if it's their choice. Boys

do tend to prefer trucks and tractors over princesses and castles. At least that's how it worked in my family."

He nodded. "So you think I've got some time? They've had so many changes in their young lives, I don't want to make things harder on them."

"Yes, I think there's time."

"Book?" Brett's tiny voice rang in her ears.

"I'm here," she whispered. It was so cute how the babies called to her.

He put out his chubby arms and Wyatt made the transfer. Brett liked the way she rocked him to sleep. She bounced him up and down, to and fro, and slowly his inquisitive blue eyes closed. She laid him down.

"You're good for my kids," Wyatt said, almost as if he was thinking aloud.

Brooke bit down on her lip to keep from crying herself. She'd been weepy lately, and only part of it was due to her pregnancy. She left the nursery and Wyatt followed her into the hall.

"I'm taking Mom out for dinner on her last night here. James is going and I'd love for you to join us," he said.

"Oh, Wyatt…no, I don't think so. I'll stay home and watch the twins so you can have a peaceful meal."

"The babies are coming. It's nothing fancy, but it was my mom and dad's favorite barbecue place."

"Suddenly, I have a craving for barbecue again," Genevieve said, walking up to them. "And I insist you join us, Brooke. It'll be fun."

"Oh, uh?" What could she say; it was two against one. "Okay, sure."

"I'll drive with James and you and Wyatt can bring the twins."

Three hours later, the four of them were seated in a booth at the Brickhouse, James sitting next to Genevieve and Wyatt next to Brooke. She was as close to him as she wanted to get tonight, breathing in his incredibly rich scent of musk and lime. At times, they brushed shoulders. At times, they brushed thighs. It was hard not to react. Hard to pretend there wasn't more between them. Being here with his family, it dawned on her she really didn't fit in. She wasn't part of the love they shared. Even James belonged here more than she did. He'd known the Brandt family for decades.

A pitcher of beer sat on the table, and all three of them had offered at one time or another to pour her a glass. She shook off their attempts, claiming to prefer lemonade to quench her thirst.

But when the ribs were served, with coleslaw, mashed potatoes and corn soufflé, oddly, her stomach didn't rebel. She dug in as heartily as the others. "Mmm, this is good."

"I knew you'd like it," Genevieve said.

"How long have you been coming here?" Brooke asked.

"Since the place opened," Genevieve said.

"I think it's going on forty years, right, Mom?"

Genevieve smiled. "I worked here as a hostess."

"You did?" James seemed to eat up anything he learned about Genevieve. "I didn't know that."

"It was only for a few months. But I got to eat all the free food I wanted. It was my first job."

They shared a sweet glance.

"My first job was mowing lawns in Ohio. Hostessing sounds like more fun," Brooke said.

The babies were indulging in mashed potatoes and cut-up chicken tenders.

Everyone seemed content.

Until Brooke looked across the restaurant and nearly spit out her lemonade. There, seated in a booth in the far corner of the place, sat Dylan and his very pregnant wife, Emma. Dylan's disguise, a cowboy hat and thick glasses, might fool some, but Brooke would know her brother anywhere. She froze in her seat. She couldn't panic. Thinking fast, she glanced at Wyatt. "Uh, would you excuse me for a second? I need to use the restroom." She shrugged. "Too much lemonade, I'm afraid." TMI, too, but it couldn't be helped.

"Sure thing." Wyatt scooted out of the booth and she slid out after him.

"Thanks."

She strolled down the aisle and hoped like hell no one at the Brandt table was watching her. Luckily, she heard the twins begin to whine and grumble, which usually drew all attention their way.

Thankful the restaurant was crowded, with not a single table empty, she made a quick turn to the left, passed two booths and then scooted in next to her brother. He jumped, his eyes going wide seeing her suddenly sitting beside him. "Brooke? What are you doing here?"

"Same thing as you. Having dinner and hoping not to be recognized." She slid a quick glance at her bestie. "Hi, Emma. How're you feeling?"

"Hungry. Seems I'm always feeling that way lately. It's good to see you, Brooke. We miss you."

"Miss you, too."

"What's all the mystery?" Dylan asked, noting how strange she was acting.

"Shh," she said to both, slinking down in the seat. "Please don't ask why right now, but I don't want the people I'm with to know I'm your sister. But it's not what you think. Just trust me, okay? I promise I will explain everything tomorrow when I come back to Zane's place."

"You sure you're okay?" Dylan asked, giving her a good once-over with his eyes.

"Yes, I swear everything's fine."

"And I would know that, if you called me every day like you promised."

Emma came to her defense. "Dylan, she's called me several times since she's been gone. We know she's doing well. You have to trust her."

Dylan shot his wife a baffled look and then sighed. "Fine, then. I'll see you tomorrow."

"Thanks. Oh, and nice disguise, Dylan."

She slid out of the booth quickly, before he had time for a snarky comeback, and leisurely strolled back to the table.

Disaster averted.

As she sat in the kitchen enjoying the morning sunshine, Wyatt came in, surprising Brooke and disturbing her peace. He sauntered inside with that lazy *I'm Texan* way he had of getting her attention. Wyatt's presence always seemed to surround her, even when he was ten feet away. "Mornin'," he drawled.

"Good morning."

He homed in on her sipping hot cocoa and nibbling on a slice of toast. She'd hoped to have a few moments of solitude before the household woke, but instead she found herself gazing into the clearest blue eyes she'd ever seen. So blue it hurt her heart.

"I'm gonna be driving my mother into Dallas today."

"I know." She'd dreaded this conversation.

He slid into the seat facing her and leaned in real close. "I don't know how to thank you for all you've done." He reached across the table and took her hand.

"There's no need." She glanced at the door. Genevieve or Henrietta could walk in any minute.

"There is a need. You've been amazing in so many ways, Brooke. And you've meant something to me."

Would he care to name that something? No, she didn't think so. It wouldn't be what she wanted to hear anyway. She reached for a napkin with the hand he'd held and dabbed at her mouth. It was a way to break the connection without being totally obvious.

"We're all going to miss you."

"I'll… I feel the same," she said, setting both of her hands in her lap. No sense tempting fate. She couldn't bear to have him take her hand again. It was hard enough gazing into his eyes and knowing things would never be the same between them. "I feel bad leaving the twins with Henrietta. She does so much already."

"It won't be for long. I've got two interviews today that look promising. Whoever I hire could never replace you, but we'll make it work."

"I'm glad, Wyatt. Really. And you know, if your mother moved back to Texas, it wouldn't be the worst thing in the world," she said quietly.

"Yeah, I know. That's a long way off still, but I'm going to build her a cottage on the property. It's something she and Dad had always talked about. They drew up the plans and everything. So, if she wants to come back, she'll…" He cleared his throat. "She'll have some privacy."

Brooke smiled. "That could be the best of both worlds."

"If only everything was that easy." He kept staring at her, his voice husky. She would embed that voice in her memory bank.

She didn't feel much like finishing her toast. And this conversation was just about over. They'd said all there was to say to each other. "Well, I've got some packing to do myself," she said, standing. Wyatt immediately stood, too. "I'll say goodbye now. I'll be gone before you get back."

He stood silently and studied her. There was no *stay and give us more time together* or *I don't want you to leave.*

No, Wyatt only sighed, nodded his head and stared at her lips so long she thought they'd catch on fire. And then he leaned in and kissed her. As far as kisses went, this one was subpar. It was a cautious, someone-might-burst-into-the-room kind of kiss that spoke to Wyatt's unending sense of propriety and decency. It was one of the traits she loved most about him. He always did the right thing, no matter what.

Her eyes stung. Tears threatened. She had to make a clean break and get out of here before she confessed all of her sins and told him she loved him. "Goodbye, Wyatt."

And then she marched out of the room, her head held high, her face perfectly masked in a performance worthy of an Academy Award.

Later that afternoon, with a hole in her heart and missing the twins and their father like crazy, Brooke entered Zane's magnificent custom-built home with two pink bakery boxes in hand. She had a lot of explaining to do, and sugar always seemed to help.

"Hello? Anyone home?" she called out. She might as well get this over with, but on the drive from the bakery in Beckon, she suddenly felt lighter, the weight lifted, knowing she was about to unburden herself of the truth.

"We're out here," Dylan called from the backyard.

She found Dylan and Emma stretched out comfortably on chaise longues on Zane's veranda overlooking the countryside. They sipped from tall glasses of iced tea. "Hello, my family," she said.

"Ah, the prodigal sister has returned bearing gifts, I see," Dylan said.

Emma rolled her eyes. "Hi, Brooke. What did you bring us?"

"A peace offering," she squeaked.

"And why do you need a peace offering?" Dylan asked as he sat up on his chair, all jest aside.

"Because I have a confession to make and it's a big one."

Dylan and Emma exchanged glances.

"I've got red velvet cupcakes for you, Em, your favorite. And for Dylan, I brought an assortment of bakery cookies."

It was a throwback to when they were kids. Dylan had an eye for only the best, even then. He longed for the better decorated, fancier cookies he'd see displayed at the local bakery on his way to school every morning. But Mom couldn't afford the luxury, so she brought home the grocery store brand every week. When Dylan finally made it big, he began sending home fresh-baked cookies on a regular basis to their folks.

"Raspberry shortbread?" he asked.

"And chocolate-dipped macaroons. Take a peek," she said, holding open the box.

Not only did he peek, he grabbed two and gave one to Emma. "These are the best," he told her.

Emma chuckled. "You're like a little boy getting his favorite cookie."

"You're my favorite cookie," he said to her with a wink. "Brooke, take a seat, have a cookie and tell us your big confession."

She lifted a shortbread cookie out of the box and sat down. "Hmm. I've been *craving* these." She bit down and the soft cookie crumbled in her mouth.

"Craving?" Emma asked, scooting up in her lounge chair. "As in the way I have cravings?"

There was another exchange of looks between her and Dylan.

Brooke nodded. "Let me start from the beginning. You see, I met my miracle cowboy on the road to Heather's wedding…"

When Brooke was through telling her story, shedding her guilt about hiding the truth from them and begging for their understanding about the baby, Emma wrapped her up in her outstretched arms. Brooke snuggled into her embrace and breathed a sigh of relief. "Brooke, of course we understand. And to think, our babies will be very close in age. They'll be cousins."

The acceptance in Emma's voice did wonders. "Yeah, that part is exciting."

But Dylan sat pensive, staring at her, absorbing all the facts. "This guy's got to be told he's the father of your child, honey. If he's as decent as you say, he'd want to know."

"You're right, Dylan, he should know, but I'm… I'm in love with him. And he's still grieving over his late wife. The love of his life," she said quietly. "I've heard him say half a dozen times his two children were quite enough. He doesn't want any more. I don't think I could take seeing disappointment or fear enter his eyes when he learns the truth. I wanted to tell him the entire time I was staying there, but…it just wasn't the right time."

"You were too busy playing nanny to his kids and deceiving his mother," Dylan replied.

"Dylan, please." Emma rose to her defense. "We both know some things are out of our control. Brooke did what she thought was right at the time."

Her brother ran a hand down his face. "God, I'm sorry, sis. I just wish you would've come to us first."

"You're right. I should have confided in you guys. I know I've handled this whole situation all wrong. I was hoping…"

"Hoping what?" Dylan asked.

"That Wyatt would fall in love with her," Emma answered.

Brooke gave her friend a nod. No more needed to be said. Heartsick, she choked up. Wyatt had said goodbye to her. He hadn't stopped her from leaving. He didn't love her.

Her bestie had her all figured out. It was most likely because a similar thing had happened between her and Dylan. For a time, Dylan thought the baby Emma carried was his, and when he found out the truth he'd been taken by surprise and deeply hurt. But he came to love both Emma and the baby with all his heart. They were one tidy little family unit now and happy as clams.

Dylan came over and pulled Brooke into his arms. She rested her head on his broad shoulder and felt his love surround her. He really was the best brother ever. "We'll work it out, hon. Don't worry." He stroked her hair and kissed her forehead.

"Thanks. I feel better now that you know the truth. But I'm unsure what to do next."

"Give yourself a day or two," Emma said. "You need to be away from the situation for a while. I'm sure you'll figure out what to do."

"I'm gonna tell him, Em. Maybe just not to his face."

"Just don't text him," Dylan said, trying for levity.

"Maybe I'll send him an email."

Dylan tugged on her hair. "You're a goof sometimes. You know that?"

"Yeah, I know that."

Emma took her hand, and Dylan held her around the waist. The three of them were solid. "We're here for you, Brooke," Emma said.

"If you need something, just let us know," Dylan added. "You're feeling well?"

"Yes, just a bit of morning sickness, but it's not terrible."

"Good," Emma said. "It should pass soon."

"My shoot's almost over. Just a few pickup scenes and we're done and headed home. Don't rush into anything," her brother said. "Take Em's advice and think things through."

"I will. I promise. I already feel ten times better now that you guys know. Thanks. Your support means so much to me. Now I think I need a nap. Confessing is exhausting."

"Have at it, sis. We'll be here when you wake up."

"I think I'll take a nap, too," Emma said. "Our baby might grow up to be a soccer player with all the kicking he was doing last night. I didn't get much sleep."

"It's dangerous, you know," Brooke said, starting to feel her old snarky self again.

"What is?" Emma asked.

"Leaving Dylan alone with that entire box of bakery cookies. He might get pudgy around the middle and then the ladies won't buy tickets to see his movies."

"Funny," he said, reaching for the box, but Brooke was too quick for him. She snatched it up, tossed him a sole macaroon and then strolled away with the box under her arm as she headed for her bedroom.

"You're the one who'll be getting pudgy around the middle," Dylan called to her.

She grinned and thanked heaven for normalcy again.

Well, as normal as her life could possibly be from now on.

Without seeing her miracle cowboy every single day.

Wyatt sat atop Josey Wales, his favorite gelding in the string as the sun descended on the horizon. Riding had always been his balm, a way to cool off from a bad day, a way to let off steam. He'd pushed his horse hard this evening, racing against the sunset, going farther and farther out on Brandt land. Now that they'd turned around, Josey was taking his sweet time heading back to the house.

It was a lonely time of night. The babies were already asleep, thanks to the new nanny he'd hired just today, Loretta Martinez. She didn't have warts or knobby knees. Her résumé had been the best of the women he'd interviewed. Loretta was in her midforties, divorced, a little chubby, and her own children were all grown up. At first, the twins called out for "Book" each time Loretta went to pick them up. It broke his heart all over again that Brett and Bri would have to make another adjustment in their lives. They missed Brooke.

So did he.

He pushed his Stetson back from his forehead and sighed. The ride, the night air and cooler temperatures weren't working. He felt lonesome and isolated, cut off from the world. Abandoned by Brooke McKay. Though that made no sense, since the deal he'd made with Brooke was that she'd stay the week until his mother left for Dallas. She'd honored her part of the deal. He was the one having trouble with all of it.

You big dummy, you didn't ask Brooke to stay. Of course you feel abandoned. It's your own damn fault.

By the time he reached Blue Horizon stables, misery had set in. He dismounted and led the horse inside for grooming. When his cell phone rang, he had a mind not to answer, especially when he saw the caller's name pop up. But it could be important. His mother didn't usually call at night, preferring to FaceTime with the twins while they were awake.

"Hi, Mom," he said.

"Wyatt, what's wrong? I can hear it in your voice. Are the babies okay? Bri didn't catch cold. She was sneezing quite a bit when I left the ranch last week."

"Everyone is fine. I'm just in from a ride and the babies and I are all healthy."

"Okay, good. That's a relief. Actually, I'm looking for Brooke. She isn't answering her cell. Is she there by any chance?"

"Uh, no. She's not. Why do you ask?"

"She promised to give me her recipe for almond crusted halibut. She said it was foolproof and you know how appealing that sounds to me. My cooking skills are lacking lately. I'd like to perfect the recipe for the next time I come out. I'll make it for everyone."

"You mean, you'll make it for James, don't you?"

"Well, if he likes fish, he's welcome to come."

Wyatt chuckled. His mom was so transparent. "Maybe you can email her, Mom."

"Oh, right. I guess I could do that. Speaking of Brooke, I've been thinking about her, honey. Does she have someone?"

Wyatt cleared his throat. He hadn't broken the news that Brooke had been replaced yet. "Someone?"

"A boyfriend or anything? She never talked about her private life."

"Maybe because she wants to keep it private."

"She's great with the twins, Wyatt. But I couldn't help noticing for such a thin girl, she had a bump in her belly and well, she never touched a drop of alcohol even when she was off the clock. One morning I saw her take a look at the ham and eggs cooking on the griddle and turn pea green. I thought she was going to lose her lunch, right then and there."

"What exactly are you getting at, Mom?"

"Nothing. I'm being silly."

"Mom," he said more firmly.

"She's the best you're going to find as a nanny, Wyatt. I don't want you to lose her because she's pregnant."

"You think Brooke's pregnant?"

"I, um, it's just a hunch, son."

Wyatt ran a hand down his face. His whole body shook at the possibilities. He'd noticed a little thickening of Brooke's stomach lately, but hadn't thought anything of it. To him, she had the perfect body. But if he recalled correctly, Brooke didn't have any trouble drinking alcohol at Blake and Heather's wedding. Yet a month later, while she was there, she'd never accepted a drink from him. Little things were beginning to add up in his head now. All those little remarks he'd made about the twins being enough for him and Brooke giving him strange, almost pained looks after his comments. "Mom, I've got to go. I'll talk to you soon."

He ended the call quickly and slumped against the stable wall. Could it be true? Was Brooke carrying his child? Suddenly, and out of the blue, he came to the conclusion that he didn't need to know. It wouldn't matter anyway.

He pushed Johnny's speed-dial number. His friend answered on the first ring. "Johnny? Tell me what's going on with the production. Are they through filming yet?"

"Hello to you, too, pal."

"Listen, this is serious. I need to know if Brooke is still in Texas."

"Wow. You are serious. Yeah, she should be. As a matter of fact, I'm getting ready to go to the wrap party tonight. The whole cast is supposed to be there. I'm assuming she'll be there, too."

"Where is it?"

"They've rented out the Applewood. Are you crashing it?"

"Damn right I am."

"This I gotta see. Listen, I'll swing by and pick you up in half an hour. Deal?"

"Deal."

Wyatt showered and dressed fast, then began pacing the floor and glancing at his watch every fifteen seconds. When he heard the roar of an engine in front of his house, he was out the door instantly. "Hey, thanks for this," he said to Johnny. "But is it okay if we take my car?"

"Sure, why?" Then his friend caught a glimpse of what was happening over Wyatt's shoulder. "You're bringing the artillery?"

"Have to. I need all the help I can get."

Johnny smiled. "When you say it's serious, you mean it."

* * *

Wyatt walked into the Applewood Bar and Grill, an iconic honky-tonk that rivaled the famous Gilley's. The place was swarming with the cast and crew of Dylan McKay's Western movie. Wyatt spotted a few people he'd worked with on the day he'd filled in for Johnny.

Country music blared, a classic Zane Williams hit about loves lost and found. Wyatt moved through clusters of people chatting, scanned over the bar area and peeked into a small stadium arena where wannabe cowboys pressed their luck on a mechanical bull. There was no sign of Brooke.

He turned around and collided smack into someone's chest. The guy was built like granite and didn't offer an apology for blocking his way. When his gaze drifted to the man's face, he understood the reason. "McKay."

"What are you doing here, Brandt?"

They were nose to nose. "I didn't come for the food or the company. I'm looking for Brooke."

Dylan's chest puffed up with brotherly concern. "You weren't invited."

They could butt heads all day, but Wyatt was beyond that. If he had to make nice to Brooke's brother, he'd swallow his pride. "I know. I apologize. But this is important. I've got to speak with Brooke. Is she here?"

Dylan looked him up and down, his expression grim. "You plan on hurting her?"

"God no. I'm here to…"

"What?"

"To make things right."

"That means different things to different people," McKay said, still eyeballing him.

"You have my word, I'm not going to hurt her. That's all I can say for now."

They stared at each other for beats of a minute and then Dylan nodded. "Okay. I dragged her here, but she wasn't in the party mood. She's in one of the private offices. Follow me."

"No, it's okay. Just point me in her direction. I'll find her."

Dylan moved through the crowd and down a hallway. Wyatt followed quietly behind. When Dylan stopped and gestured to a room with a paneled door at the far end of the hallway, Wyatt made a move to pass him. And Dylan got in Wyatt's face again. "Remember what I said."

He tipped his hat. "Got it."

As soon as Dylan walked away, Wyatt whipped out his cell phone and called Johnny. Then he strode over to the door and knocked, his heart beating in his chest like crazy.

Brooke's eyes were just closing when a knock on the door broke her peace. She jumped and the phone on her lap fell to the floor. So much for the novel she was reading. Another knock boomed and this time, Brooke shook out the cobwebs in her head. "Hang on a second," she called.

Music filtered in, the lyrics muffled through the closed door, yet the sweet melody of the ballad came through softly. The din of conversation told her the party was in full swing. Too bad. She'd been ready to leave hours ago, which was weird, since parties were her business. Literally. Maybe Dylan and Emma had had enough country twang and porterhouse steaks for one night.

She rose and went to the door. "Ready to leave yet?" she asked just as she turned the knob and opened the door.

"Now that depends on you."

Her breath whooshed out as she took in the length and breadth of the man she loved. "Wyatt, w-what are you doing here?"

"Funny, your brother asked me the same thing. I guess I'm crashing the party."

She blinked. She couldn't believe Wyatt was standing on the threshold, one hip braced against the doorjamb.

He took his Stetson off, held it to his chest in true cowboy form and gave her a killer smile. "May I come in?"

"Oh, uh…yes. I guess so."

He walked in and turned to her, his smile wider and his face…well, how could a man get even more gorgeous in just a week's time? She was filling up on the sight of him, allowing her heartsick soul to take him all in.

"You look beautiful, Brooke."

"Thank you."

"Why don't we sit down?"

"Why?" She eyed him cautiously. Why was he here? Why were his sky blue eyes glowing like that? A girl could get her hopes up if she wasn't too bright.

"Because I've got things to say to you. And you're gonna listen. Now sit down."

She frowned.

"Please."

She sat on the cream sofa and he sat down next to her, as in, so close their thighs touched. She swallowed hard, planted her feet and waited.

Wyatt sighed as he set his hat on the sofa and then reached for her hand. It fit so nicely in his, and she trembled from his touch. "The truth is, when I married Madelyn, it was for life. I mean, I loved her so much, I could hardly breathe sometimes. She was everything to me. And we had this perfect little family. I was happier than I thought a man had a right to be. But you already know all that. What you don't know is that when you came into my life, I thought it was a brief interlude. I was instantly attracted to you and fooled myself into believing that it was lust. A simple case of lack of sex and female contact."

She gasped. "Are you insulting me, Wyatt?"

"Not at all, sweetheart. I'm trying to explain. And maybe I'm not doing the best job of it. You'll have to forgive me for that. But the honest truth is, I wasn't afraid to be myself around you, because I never thought I could have feelings for another woman. I never thought I would ever find love again. Certainly not so soon after Madelyn's death. She's been gone less than a year and my mind-set was that I'd be alone for a long, long time. Deeply caring for anyone before that time wasn't an option. But then you became the twins' nanny. Granted, it wasn't real, but it was. Wasn't it? I mean, you care for my kids, don't you?"

"Now I'm the one not able to breathe, Wyatt. Yes, I love those kids. They're amazing and sweet and…"

"They've been asking for Book."

A tear slipped down her cheek. "Really?"

He nodded.

"Are you trying to win me back as your nanny, Wyatt?"

"No. Don't cry, sweetheart. I'm trying to tell you I love you. I mean it. I've fallen crazy in love with you. And it took you leaving and a phone call from my mother to make me realize it."

Her heart bubbled up. "You love me?"

"I love you."

She caught her next tear with her finger and wiped it away. "I love you, too."

He squeezed her hand and then leaned in to give her the best kiss in the entire world. A sweet, simple brush of the lips that sewed her heart up good and tight.

"I want you to marry me, Brooke. I want you to come live with me at Blue Horizon. I want you to be my wife and help me raise my twins. But before you answer me, I want you know that my mother thinks you're carrying a child. She may be all wrong but after hearing what she had to say, I realized that yes, I'd want a child I'd conceived with you, but I'd want you to marry me, regardless. I missed you so much, I could hardly stand it."

He got down on one knee. "So I'm going to ask you again. Whether you are or aren't carrying my child, will you marry me? Oh, and wait one darn second."

He pulled out his cell phone and texted someone.

Really? In the middle of his proposal?

Johnny Wilde entered the room, holding two sleepy-eyed babies in his arms. He set them down and once they spotted her, they waddled right into her arms. "Book, Book."

"Oh!" The babies were here! Her eyes watered again. She scooped them up and kissed each one on the cheek. "I've missed you two."

"Mission accomplished," Johnny said, giving a salute and backing out of the room.

Brooke chuckled between her tears.

"They want you for their mommy, Brooke," Wyatt said. "And I just plain want you."

Brooke couldn't believe her ears. She was hopelessly and fully in love with Wyatt Brandt. And yes, she'd have to make some changes in her life, give up her business or run it long distance, but right now, all that mattered, all she wanted, was Wyatt Brandt and his two adorable children.

"You can answer me anytime now," Wyatt said, still on bended knee.

"Yes, I'll marry you," she said, snuggling the twins. "And yes, I'm carrying your child. I was going to tell you before I left Texas. I truly was. I just didn't know how to tell you to your face. I was afraid you wouldn't want me or the baby."

"It's okay, Brooke. I get it. I didn't make things easy on you. I was stuck in my grief and almost lost you because of it."

"I was wrong not to tell you sooner. I'm sorry, Wyatt. I just couldn't find a way."

"You would've told me, Brooke. I have faith in that. I only wish you would've trusted me more. But I get it. We were both raw and cautious from past hurts."

He took her hand and kissed her fingertips. "You have to know, I'm glad about the baby. *Our* baby. It'll be a fresh start for both of us." Wyatt grinned wide, and Brooke's fears were put to rest with that one gesture, that one affirmation of his true love for her.

"I'm so happy."

"So am I." Then he turned to the twins. "Did you hear that, kids? You're going to have a brother or sister one day soon. There's gonna be more little Brandts running around the house."

"It's going to be a madhouse," Brooke said, grinning and picturing it in her mind.

"I can't wait," Wyatt said.

"Really?"

"Really. I'm good with all of it, sweetheart."

Of course he was.

He wouldn't be her miracle cowboy otherwise.

And Wyatt Brandt was that, and so very much more.

* * * * *

The only prayer Gage had of cracking that ice was to give her something sizzling hot to grab on to with both hands.

"Your point—if I recall—was that you'd use all the information at your disposal to seduce me," Cass murmured throatily. "I don't think you have a shot."

"Guess there's only one way to find out."

The irresistible draw between them sucked him in, and finally his arms closed around her, and her mouth sought his. A scorching kiss ignited the pent-up emotions and desire Gage had been fighting since he'd first laid eyes on Cass in the parking lot of her building.

Yes. Her tongue darted out in a quest for his and he lost himself in the sensation of her hot flesh. She tasted of wine and familiarity.

Memories zipped by, of Cass spread out under him, hips rolling toward his in a sensuous rhythm, hair spread out, her gaze hot and full of anticipation and pleasure as they came together again and again. Memories of her laughing with him, challenging him, filling him.

He wanted her. Just like that. Right now.

* * *

The CEO's Little Surprise
is part of the Love and Lipstick quartet:
for four female executives, mixing business
with pleasure leads to love!

THE CEO'S LITTLE SURPRISE

BY
KAT CANTRELL

MILLS & BOON

First Published in Great Britain 2016
By Mills & Boon, an imprint of HarperCollins*Publishers*
1 London Bridge Street, London, SE1 9GF

© 2016 Kat Cantrell

ISBN: 978-0-263-91859-5

51-0516

Our policy is to use papers that are natural, renewable and recyclable products and made from wood grown in sustainable forests. The logging and manufacturing processes conform to the legal environmental regulations of the country of origin.

Printed and bound in Spain
by CPI, Barcelona

Kat Cantrell read her first Mills & Boon novel in third grade and has been scribbling in notebooks since then. She writes smart, sexy books with a side of sass. She's a former Mills & Boon *So You Think You Can Write* winner and an RWA Golden Heart® Award finalist. Kat, her husband and their two boys live in north Texas.

One

By the time Gage Branson's tires hit the Dallas city limits, Arwen had started howling along with the radio. Not for the first time since leaving Austin, Gage questioned the wisdom of bringing his dog on a business trip.

Of course, it wasn't a normal business trip—unless showing up at your ex-girlfriend's office building unannounced and uninvited counted as customary. And Arwen wasn't a normal dog. She was his best buddy, and the one and only time he'd left her at one of those pet hotels, she'd refused to speak to him for a week.

Arwen shared Gage's love of the open road and honestly, he didn't mind the company as he drove to Dallas to collect a long overdue debt from the CEO of Fyra Cosmetics.

GB Skin for Men, the company he'd just pushed into the billion-dollar-a-year category, had enjoyed a good run as the top skin-care line of choice for the discerning guy who spends time in the elements: professional athletes, outdoorsmen, even the occasional lumberjack.

Gage had spent millions designing a new product to heal scars. The product's launch a month ago had outperformed his carefully executed publicity strategy. GB Skin instantly cornered the market. But now his former lover's company was poised to steal his success out from under him with a product of their own. That wasn't going to happen.

A Black Keys song blasted through the speakers and the howling grew unbearable.

"Arwen! Really. Shut up."

She cocked her ginger-colored head and eyed Gage.

"Yeah, never mind," Gage grumbled good-naturedly and flicked off the music.

The exit for Central Expressway loomed and Gage steered the Hummer north. He drove a few miles and before long, he rolled into the parking lot at the headquarters for Fyra Cosmetics.

Nice. Of course, he'd done an internet search for pictures before driving up from Austin. Just to check out the company Cassandra Claremont had built alongside her business partners–slash–friends after graduating from the University of Texas. But the internet hadn't done justice to the sharply modern, glass and steel, five-story building. Cass's multimillion-dollar cosmetics company lived and breathed inside these walls, and the deep purple Fyra logo dominated the landscape.

"Stay here and keep your paws off the gearshift," he muttered to Arwen and got the trademark vizsla smile for his trouble. It was a cool day, so he parked in the shade and left her in the car with the windows cracked.

Cass had done very well for herself thanks to him. Gage *had* been her mentor for eight months and turnabout was fair play. She owed him. And he'd help her see that by reminding her of how he'd guided her at a time when she had no idea how to navigate the shark-infested waters of the cosmetics industry.

With any luck, Cass would be curious enough to see him on short notice. Gage couldn't call ahead and lose the advantage of surprise. Not when he was here to get his hands on Cass's secret formula.

So secret, he shouldn't even know about it since it wasn't on the market yet. His sources had whispered in his ear about a miracle formula developed in Fyra's labs that worked with a body's natural healing properties to eliminate wrinkles and scars. His intel adamantly insisted it was better than his. And he wanted it.

You didn't spring that kind of request on anyone over the phone, not even a former girlfriend. They hadn't even spoken in eight or nine years. Nine. Maybe it was closer to ten.

"Gage Branson. To what do I owe the pleasure?"

The husky feminine voice raked over Gage from behind before he'd managed to get ten feet from the Hummer.

He spun to face the speaker and did a double take. "Cass?"

"Last time I checked." High-end sunglasses covered her eyes, but her tone conveyed a hint of cool amusement just fine. "Did I leave my face in my other purse again?"

"No, your face is right where I left it." Gorgeous and attached to a hell of a woman.

But *this* überchic version in five-inch heels and a sexy suit with cutaway panels at her hips did not resemble the Cassandra Claremont who lived in his memories. Her voice wasn't even the same. But something about the way she held herself was very familiar. Confidence and the ever-present "look but don't you dare touch" vibe had always been a huge part of her attractiveness.

Obviously *he* hadn't changed much since graduate school if she'd recognized him from behind.

"Moving into the dog transportation business, are you?" she asked blithely.

He glanced at the Hummer. "You mean Arwen? Nah. She's just company for the drive. I came up from Austin to see you, actually. Surprise."

"Do you have an appointment?"

The lack of question in that question said she already knew the answer. And wasn't planning to adjust her calendar one tiny bit, even for an old boyfriend. He'd change that soon enough.

"I was hoping you'd see me without one." He grinned, just to keep things friendly. "You know, for old times' sake."

His grin grew genuine as he recalled those old times. Lots of late-night discussions over coffee. Lots of inventive ploys to get Cass's clothes off. Lots of hot and truly spectacular sex when she finally gave in to the inevitable.

She pursed her lips. "What could we possibly have to say to each other?"

Plenty. And maybe a whole lot more than he'd originally come to say. Now that he was here and had an eyeful of the new, grown-up Cass, a late-night dinner and a few drinks with a former lover had suddenly appeared on his schedule for the evening.

Everyone here was an adult. No reason they couldn't separate business from pleasure.

"For one, I'd like to say congratulations. Long overdue, I realize," he threw in smoothly. "I've been following along from afar and what you've accomplished is remarkable."

Once her name had been dropped in his lap as a potential game changer, he'd searched the internet for details, first with an eye toward how well she was executing his advice and eventually because he couldn't stop. Strangely, he'd liked seeing her picture, liked remembering their relationship. She was one of a small handful of women from his past that he recalled fondly, and for a guy who held on to very little in his life, that was saying something.

"Thank you." She inclined her head graciously. "It was a group effort."

He waited for her to say she'd been following his entrepreneurial trajectory in kind. Maybe a congrats or two on the major retail distribution deals he'd scored in the past few years. An attaboy for Entrepreneurs of America naming him Entrepreneur of the Year. If nothing else, Fyra's CEO should be brushing up on her competition the way he had.

Nada. She hadn't been a *little* curious about what he'd been up to? Was their time together such a blip in her life that she'd truly not cared?

But then, their affair had been brief, by design. Once he'd escaped his restrictive childhood home and overprotective parents, he'd vowed to never again let his wings be clipped. He owed it to his brother, Nicolas, to live on the edge, no regrets. To experience all the things his brother never would thanks to a drunk driver. Sticking to one woman didn't go with that philosophy and Gage liked his freedom as much—or more—than he liked women, which meant he and Cass had parted ways sooner rather than later, no harm, no foul. He could hardly blame her for not looking back.

"Come on." He waved off her "group effort" comment. "You're the CEO. We both know that means you call the shots."

She crossed her arms over that sexy suit, drawing attention to her breasts. In spite of the cool breeze, the temperature inched up a few degrees.

"Yes. Because someone has to. But Trinity, Harper, Alex and I run this company together. We're all equal owners."

Yeah, he'd figured she'd say that. The four women had been inseparable in college and it wasn't hard to imagine they'd extended their tight circle into the company they'd created together. Fortunately, he'd always gotten along with the quartet of savvy females, but Cass was the one he had his sights set on. She'd make this deal happen.

"Can we take this inside?" Hoping she'd like the idea of getting behind closed doors as much as he did, he sidled closer. "I'd like to catch up."

"Gage."

Her husky voice wound through him as she moved closer in kind, tilting her head toward his in a way that shouldn't feel as intimate as it did. A hint of jasmine filtered through his senses and it was a powerful punch. "Yeah, Cass?"

"You can save the 'Kumbaya,'" she murmured. "You're here because you've heard about Fyra's breakthrough formula and you want it."

Back to business, then.

He grinned and reined in his thundering pulse. Going toe-to-toe with Cass was such a turn-on. Smart, sexy women who didn't take any crap had always floated his boat. "Am I that easy to read?"

Cass laughed in his ear, a throaty sound he instantly wanted to hear again. "I'm afraid so. Sorry you've wasted your time. The formula is not for sale."

All right, then. Cass needed persuasion to see how his

tutelage had launched her into the big leagues. He'd anticipated that.

"Of course it isn't. Not to the rest of the world. But I'm not one of the masses," he reminded her. "I'm not unreasonable. I'll pay fair market value."

He turned his head at just the right angle to almost bring their lips together. The pull between them was magnetic, and he nearly forgot for a second that he'd instigated this sensual tease to get him closer to his goal—the formula.

She didn't flinch, holding herself rock steady. "You think you have special rights because of our former relationship? Think again."

His element of surprise hadn't worked to catch her off guard and, for some reason, that made her twice as attractive. Or maybe the unexpected draw had come about because they were equals now. It was an interesting shift in their dynamic he hadn't expected, and it was throwing him off.

So he'd up his game. Gage had never met a woman he couldn't charm. When he wanted something, he got it. "That's no way to talk to an old friend."

If he moved an inch, they'd be touching. He almost did it, curious if she still felt the same—soft, exciting and warm. Except he had the distinct impression Cass was all business and little pleasure these days. And that she wasn't interested in mixing them up.

"Is that what we are?"

There came that sexy laugh again and it did a powerful number on his already-primed lower half. She really shouldn't be so intriguing, not with his agenda and the lost element of surprise. But all of that actually heightened his sense of awareness, and he had a sharp desire to get under her skin the same way she'd managed to get under his.

"Friends. Former lovers. At one time, mentor and student."

"Mmm. Yes." She cocked her head. "You've taught me a lot. So much that I'm running a successful company I need to get back to. You'll excuse my rudeness if I request you make an appointment. Like anyone else who wants to talk business."

All at once, her heat vanished as she pulled away and clacked toward the entrance to her building. Ouch. He'd been relegated to the ranks of "anyone else."

He let her go. For now.

There was no way a former pupil of his was going to take away even a single point of his market share, and he'd pay handsomely to ensure it. But one had to do these things with finesse.

Remind her of what you've done for her. Remind her how good it was.

The voice in his head was his own conscience. Probably. But sometimes he imagined it was Nicolas guiding him from beyond the veil. A big brother's advice in times of need, which usually led Gage down the path of living life to the fullest. Because Nicolas couldn't.

The philosophy had never steered Gage wrong before.

He wasn't about to stop listening to sound advice now, especially when it aligned with what he wanted. Cass clearly needed a good, solid reminder of how tight they'd been. So tight, he knew every inch of her body.

Your best strategy is to use pleasure to influence business.

Nicolas had spoken. And that pretty much solidified Gage's next steps because that genie wasn't going back in the bottle. He wanted her. And her formula. If he did it right, one would lead to the other.

He gave her a good five minutes and went after her.

Turnabout was fair play in love *and* cosmetics.

* * *

Hands shaking, Cass strode to her office and checked her strength before she slammed the door behind her. That would only invite questions and she had no answers for why her entire body still pumped with adrenaline and… other things she'd rather not examine.

Okay, that was a flat-out lie. Gage Branson was the answer, but why seeing him again so severely affected her after all of this time—*that* she couldn't explain.

God, that smile rocked her to the core, even all these years later. And his still-amazing body had been hidden underneath casual-Friday dress, when it should clearly be on display in a pinup calendar. He'd always had the messiest, most casually cut hair that somehow managed to look delicious on him. Still did. Oh, yes, he was just as sexy and charismatic as he'd always been and she hated that she noticed. Hated that he could still put a quiver in her abdomen. Especially after what he'd done.

Breathe. Gage was just a guy she used to know. Put that on repeat a thousand times and maybe she'd finally believe it. Except he wasn't just a guy from college; that was the problem.

Gage Branson had broken her.

Not just her heart, but *her*. Mind, body and soul. She'd fallen so hard for him that the splat hadn't even registered. Until he casually declared their relationship over, and did she want the clothes back that she'd left at his place?

Nine years later and she was still powerless to move on, unable to fall in love again, incapable of forgetting and far too scarred to forgive. And that's why her hands were still shaking. Pathetic.

The only positive was she felt certain Gage hadn't picked up on her consternation. God forbid *he* figure out how greatly he'd affected her. Emotions had no place here, not at work, not in her personal life. *No place.* That's the most important lesson she'd learned from her former mentor. Thankfully, he'd taken her advice to make an appointment without too much protest, giving her much-needed regroup time.

Her phone beeped, reminding her she had five minutes until the meeting she'd called would begin. Five minutes to put her thoughts together about how Fyra should handle the leak in the company. Someone reprehensible had publicized Harper's nanotechnology breakthrough before they'd even gotten FDA approval or a patent. Five minutes, when she should have had an hour, but didn't because of the car wreck on Central and the surprise appearance of the man who'd laced her nightmares for nearly a decade.

And maybe a few need-soaked dreams. But he didn't have to know about that.

Great. This was exactly what she needed, a come-to-Jesus meeting with Trinity, Harper and Alex so soon after locking horns with the offspring of Satan. Who was here strictly because of a leak that never should have happened.

Well, she'd have to get her wild swing of emotions under control. *Now.* It wasn't as though she didn't already know how she felt about the leak—sick, furious and determined to find the source. They'd not only lost a potential competitive advantage, until they figured out who had spilled, there was also no guarantee the same person wouldn't leak the secret formula—or steal it.

But five minutes was scarcely enough time to settle her racing heart before waltzing into a room with her best friends, who would see immediately that Something Had Happened. They'd probably also realize "Something" had a man's name all over it.

Working with people who'd held your hair when you drank too much and borrowed your clothes and sat with you in a tight huddle at your grandfather's funeral meant few secrets. Most of the time, Cass appreciated that. Maybe not so much today.

In the bathroom, she patted her face with a blotting cloth and fixed her makeup, which was equal parts wardrobe and armor.

No one saw through Cass when she had her face on—with the right makeup, no one had to know you were hurting. The philosophy born out of the brokenness Gage had left her with had grown into a multimillion-dollar company. Best Face Forward wasn't just the company tagline, it was Cass's personal motto.

No man would ever put a crack in her makeup again.

Fortified, Cass pasted on a cool smile and exited the bathroom. Only to run smack into Fyra's receptionist, Melinda. Her wide eyes spelled trouble as she blurted out, "There's an extremely persistent man at the front desk who seems to believe you have an appointment with him."

Gage. When she'd said make an appointment, she meant for later. Much later.

Her not-so-settled nerves began to hum. "I don't have an appointment with him. I have a meeting."

"I told him that. But he insisted that you'd scheduled time with him, and he drove all the way from Austin." Melinda lowered her voice. "He was very apologetic and sweet about it. Even asked if there was a possibility you accidentally double booked your appointments."

Did his audacity have no end?

The stars in Melinda's eyes were so bright, it was a wonder she could still see around Gage's charm. Well, Cass didn't suffer from the same affliction. "When have I ever done that?"

"Oh, I know. Never." Her shoulders ducked slightly.

"But I…well, he asked if I'd mind checking with you and he just seems so sincer—"

"Why is Gage Branson in our reception area?" Trinity Forrester, Fyra's chief marketing officer, snapped, her short, dark hair nearly bristling with outrage. Since Trinity possessed the main shoulder Cass had cried on back in college, the statement was laced with undercurrents of the "hold me back before I cut off his fingers with a dull blade" variety.

Cass stifled a sigh. Too late to have Melinda throw him out before anyone saw him. "He's here with a business proposition. I'll take care of it."

As the woman in charge, she should have taken care of it in the parking lot once she'd figured out he wanted her formula. But he'd been so… *Gage*, with his wicked smile. He fuzzled her mind and that was not okay.

This was strictly business and she would die before admitting she couldn't handle a competitor sniffing around her territory.

"That's right." Trinity crossed her arms with a smirk. "You take care of it. You toss him out on his well-toned butt. Shame such a prime specimen of a man is riddled with health problems."

Melinda's gaze bounced back and forth between her employers, clearly fascinated by the exchange. "Really? What's wrong with him?" she asked in a stage whisper.

"He's got terrible allergies to commitment and decency," Trinity explained. "And Cass is going to hand him his hat with class. Can I watch?"

Strangling over a groan, Cass shook her head. This was her battle, and there was no way she'd deal with Gage for a second time today in front of a bevy of onlookers. "It's better if I talk to him in my office. Trinity, can you tell Alex and Harper I'll be there in a few minutes?"

Trinity harrumphed but edged away as Cass stared her down. "Okay. But if you're robbing us of the show, you better come prepared to spill all the details."

With Melinda dogging her steps—because the receptionist likely didn't want to miss a thing at this point—Cass marched to the reception area.

Arms crossed and one hip leaning on the desk as if he owned it, Gage glanced toward her as she entered, his deep hazel eyes lighting up at the sight of her. His slow smile set off a tap dance in her abdomen. Which was not okay. It was even *less* okay than his ability to fuzzle her mind.

Steeling her spine against the onslaught of Gage's larger-than-life personality, she jerked her head toward the hallway. "Five minutes, Mr. Branson. I'm late for a board meeting."

"Mr. Branson. I like the sound of that," he mused, winking. "Respect where respect is due."

Flirting came so naturally to him, she wondered if he even realized when he was doing it. She rolled her eyes and turned her back on his smug face, taking off toward her office in hopes he'd get lost.

He drew abreast with little effort, glancing down at her because he still topped her by several inches no matter how high her heels were, dang it. His powerful masculinity dominated the small hallway that had always seemed quite large enough for every other person who'd accompanied her to her office.

"Trying to score the first one-minute mile? You can't outrun me barefoot, let alone while wearing icepick stilettos." He eyed them appreciatively, his too-long hair flopping over his forehead. "Which I like, by the way."

Her toes automatically curled inside her shoes as heat swept over her skin. "I didn't wear them for you."

Why had she thought taking care of this in her office

was a good idea? She should have gone to her board meeting and had Melinda tell Gage to take a hike.

But he would have just shown up over and over again until she agreed to an appointment.

So she'd get rid of him once and for all.

Two

When she halted by her open office door, Gage raised a brow as he read its deep purple placard. "Chief enhancement officer?"

His amused tone rankled but she just smiled and silently dared him to do his worst. "Branding. We put incredibly careful thought into every single aspect of this business. Seems like I had a mentor once who taught me a few things about that."

He grinned in return and didn't acknowledge her sarcasm. Nor did he say a word about her outstretched arm, choosing to humor her and enter first as she'd meant him to, but he didn't miss the opportunity to brush her, oh, so casually. She pretended the skin he'd just touched wasn't tingling.

"Yeah, we did have a few lively discussions about business strategies," he mused. "Branding is why I drive a green Hummer, by the way."

Cass had decorated her office with the same trademark Fyra deep purple hue, down to the glass-topped desk and expensive woven carpet under it. He took it all in with slightly widened eyes.

"Because you want everyone to see it and think GB Skin has zero environmental consciousness and its owner is obnoxious?" she asked sweetly before he could make a crack about her decor.

Sleek and modern, the offices had been decorated by an expensive, trendy uptown firm. It had cost a pretty penny, but the results had been worth it. This company was hers, from the baseboards to the ceiling and she loved it. They'd moved to this building three years ago, once Fyra posted its first annual revenue of fifty million dollars. That was when she knew they were going to make it.

She'd do whatever she needed to do in order to keep her company alive.

He laughed as he slid into a purple chair and then swept her with a pointed once-over. "You know the name of my company. I was starting to think you didn't care."

How did he manage to make understanding the competitive landscape sound so...*personal*? It was a skill he'd clearly bargained with the devil to obtain.

"I'm good at what I do. Of course I know the names of my competitors." Cass remained standing near the door. Which she pointedly left open. "You've got your appointment. And about three minutes to tell me why you didn't take the no I gave you earlier and run back to Austin."

Casually, he swiveled his chair to face her and waved a hand to the empty chair next to him. "Sit and let's talk."

She didn't move. There was no way she could be in close quarters with him, not on the heels of their earlier encounter when he'd barely breathed on her and still managed to get her hot and bothered. At least by the door, she had a shot at retaining the upper hand. "No, thanks. I'm okay."

"You can't keep standing. That tactic only works if you inflict it on someone other than the person who taught it to you," he said mildly.

The fact that he saw through her only made it worse.

"Really, Gage," she snapped. "Fyra's executives are waiting in a boardroom for the CEO to arrive. Cut the crap. Why are you here?"

His expression didn't change. "The rumors about your formula are true, right?"

She crossed her arms over the squiggle in her stomach. "Depends on what you've heard."

"*Revolutionary* is the word being thrown around," he said with a shrug. "I've heard the formula works with your natural stem cells to regenerate skin, thus healing scars and eliminating wrinkles. Nanotech at its finest."

She kept her expression schooled, but only just. "I can neither confirm nor deny that."

Her lungs hitched as she fought to draw a breath without alerting Gage to her distress. The leak was worse than they'd assumed. When Trinity had stormed into Cass's office yesterday to show Cass the offending blurb in an online trade magazine, she'd read the scant few lines mentioning Fyra's yet-to-be released product with horror. But it could have been so much worse, they'd assured each other. The trade magazine had few details, especially about the nanotechnology, and they'd hoped that had been the extent of the information that had traveled beyond their walls.

Apparently not.

It was a disaster. Full-blown, made even worse by Gage's arrival on the scene.

Gage watched her carefully, his sharp gaze missing

nothing. "But if my intel is correct, a formula like that might be worth about a hundred million or so. Which I'm prepared to pay."

Oh, no, he had *not* just dropped that sum on her. She shut her eyes for a blink. Money like that was serious business, and as the CEO, she had to take his offer to the others for due consideration.

But she knew her friends. They'd agree with her that the formula was priceless. "I told you, the formula isn't for sale."

He stood suddenly and advanced on her, clearly over the power play she'd instigated by standing by the door. The closer he got, the harder her pulse pounded, but she blinked coolly as if lethally sexy men faced her down on a daily basis.

"It's smart business to consider all opportunities," he said as he leaned against the doorjamb not two feet from her. "If you sell, you don't have to worry about little things like FDA approval and production costs and false-claim lawsuits. You just roll around in your millions and leave the hard work to someone else."

The scent of clean forest and man wafted in her direction.

"I'm not afraid of hard work," she stated firmly as she fought to keep from stepping back, out of the line of his masculine fire. It was a battle of wills, and if she fled, he'd figure out how much he truly affected her.

The man was a shaman, mystical and charismatic. One glance, and she'd follow him into his world of hedonistic pleasure. Or at least that had been true in college. She'd learned a few tricks of her own since then, along with developing a shield around her fragile interior.

His gaze held her captive as he reached out and tucked

a chunk of hair behind her ear, his fingers lingering far longer than they should have.

"What *are* you afraid of?" he asked softly, his expression morphing into something almost…warm.

You. She swallowed. Where had that come from? Gage didn't scare her. What scared her was how easily she forgot to control her emotions around him.

This cat-and-mouse game had veered into dangerous territory.

"Taxes," she muttered inanely and ignored the way her pulse raced.

When was the last time she'd been touched? Months and months. She'd developed a reputation among single men in Dallas as a man-eater and unfortunately, that just made her even more popular as men vied for her attention so they could claim victory. Mostly she just shut them down because the whole scene exhausted her.

And she couldn't lose sight of the fact that the reason she chewed up men and spit them out was staring her in the face. He was very dangerous indeed if she'd forgotten for a second the destruction he'd caused.

And that's when it hit her. She was handling Gage all wrong.

This wasn't college and Gage wasn't her mentor. They were equals. And he was on her turf. That meant she called the shots.

If he wanted to play, she'd play.

Once Gage had tucked the errant lock of hair behind her ear, he'd run out of legitimate excuses to have his hands on her. Which didn't keep him from silently running through a litany of illegitimate excuses.

"Gage," she murmured throatily and the base of his spine heated. "The formula's not for sale. I have a board meeting. Seems like we're done here…unless you've got a better offer?"

Her eyelids lowered to half-mast and she didn't move, but the sensual vibe emanating from her reached out and wrapped around him, drawing him in. Those cutaway panels at her waist would fit his palms perfectly and with any luck, the mesh inserts would allow him to feel her while fully clothed. The thought sent a rush of blood through his veins and the majority of it ended up in a good, solid erection that got very uncomfortable, very fast.

"I just might have something in mind," he said, his vocal chords scraping the low end of the register. God, she'd even affected his voice.

Down boy. Remind her why the formula is *for sale… but only to you.*

Yeah, he needed to get back on track, pronto, and stop letting her get into his head. He dropped his hand but leaned into her space to see about turning those tables on her. "You're doing amazing things here, Cass. I'm proud of what you've accomplished.'

Wariness sprang into her gaze as she processed his abrupt subject change. "Thank you. I'm proud of what the girls and I have built."

He crossed his arms before an errant finger could trail down the line of her throat. Because his lower half wasn't getting the message that the goal here was to get *her* hot and flustered. Not the other way around. "Remember that project I helped you with for Dr. Beck's class?"

That was before they'd started sleeping together. He didn't recall being so magnetically attracted to Cass back then. Sure he'd wanted to get her naked. But at twenty-four, he'd generally wanted women naked. These days, his taste was a bit more refined, but no woman he'd dated over the years had gotten him this hooked, this fast.

Of course, he never looked up his old girlfriends. Maybe any former lover would affect him the same. But he couldn't imagine that would be true.

Her eyes narrowed a touch. "The project where I created a new company on paper, complete with a marketing plan and logo and all of that?"

"That's the one," he said easily. "You got an A plus, if memory serves. Except you didn't do that alone. I was right there every step of the way. Guiding you. Teaching you. Infusing you with CEO superpowers."

In fact, he'd done such a good job, here he was smack in the middle of her corporation negotiating over a Fyra product that was better than his. He appreciated the irony.

An indulgent smile bloomed on her face and he didn't mistake it for a friendly one. "Nothing wrong with your memory. As much as I'm enjoying this trip down memory lane, if you have a point, now would be the time to make it."

"Your success here…" He waved a hand at her office without taking his eyes off her. "Is amazing. Your C-suite is unparalleled. But you didn't get here without me. I'm a big factor in your success."

"Yes, you are," she agreed readily. Too readily. "You taught me some of the most important lessons I've learned thus far in my life. Fyra's business philosophy grew 100 percent out of my experience with you."

She blinked and undercurrents flowed between them but hell if he could figure out what they were. Regardless, it was a great segue. Exactly what he'd hoped for.

"I'm glad you agree. That's why I'm here. To collect on that long-outstanding debt."

"Oh, really?" Her head tilted slightly as she contemplated him. "Do tell."

"You know what I'm talking about. Without me, Fyra

might never have existed. You might never have achieved your goals, particularly not to this degree. Don't you think turnabout is fair play?"

"Hmm." She touched a finger to her cheek. "Turnabout. Like I owe you for what you've done. That's an interesting concept. It's kind of like karma, in a way."

"Kind of."

But he didn't like the comparison, not the way she said it. Karma was rarely a word used in the context of reward. More like you were getting what you deserved.

"What I'm saying," he interjected smoothly before this conversation went in a direction he didn't like. "Is that I want to buy your formula. My role in your success should be a factor in your decision-making process. In all fairness, you do owe me. But I'm fair, too. I'm not asking you to *give* me the formula for old times' sake. One hundred million dollars is a lot of tit for tat."

He watched her as she filtered through his argument, but her expression remained maddeningly blank.

"Here's the thing, Gage." She leaned in, wafting a whole lot of woman in his direction. "You did teach me and I'm grateful. But you must have been sick the day they taught corporate structure, so I'll clue you in. Again. I'm a quarter owner in Fyra. We're missing three-quarters of the decision makers, none of whom *owe* you a thing. I'll take your offer for the formula to the board and we'll consider it. Period. That's how business works."

Her mouth was set so primly, he had the insane urge to kiss her. But they were just getting into the meat of this and he needed to hone his focus. Not lose it entirely.

So he grinned instead and waved off her protest. "Not in the real world, honey. You need to get out more if that's your best line of defense. Deals are done and undone across the globe based on exactly that. Companies don't make decisions. People do and rarely are they united."

"Fyra is," she insisted. "We're a team."

"I hope that's true," he said sincerely. "If so, then it's in your best interests to convince them to sell. How would they feel about their CEO not honoring this lingering debt?"

Her brows drew together but it was the only outward sign she gave that she'd heard the underlying message. This was business at its core and he was not leaving Dallas without that formula. It had become more than just about ensuring Fyra didn't take any of his market share. GB Skin was number one for a reason and he liked being the top dog. His products should be the best on the market and Fyra's formula would put him there—assuming it checked out like he thought it would.

Not to mention that Cass's stubbornness had piqued his.

"Threats, Gage?" Her laugh thrummed through him. "You gonna tattle to my partners about how naughty I am?"

He nearly groaned at her provocative tone.

"Nothing so pedestrian." He shifted a touch closer because he liked the scent of her, tightening the cross of his arms. Just to keep his hands where they belonged. "I wouldn't go behind your back to manipulate the other executives. This is your cross to bear, and I'm simply pointing out that you don't want this on your conscience. Do you?"

"My conscience is quite clear, thanks." Her gaze fastened firmly on his, she crossed her arms in a mirror of his pose, intentionally sliding her elbow across his. And then hung around, brushing arms deliberately. "I'll take your offer to the others. Shall I show you the way out or can you find it yourself?"

Heat flashed where they touched. "As you're late for a board meeting where I suspect one of the topics will be the offer in question, I'll see myself out."

She didn't move, still partially blocking the open doorway. On purpose. So he'd have to slide by her like he'd done when he entered the room, to show she had his number and that whatever he dished out, he should expect to have served right back. It almost pulled an appreciative chuckle out of him but he caught it at the last second. Cass had grown up in many intriguing ways and this battle was far from over.

No point in letting her believe she had a chance in hell of winning.

So close to her that he could easily see the lighter colored flecks of blue in her irises, he palmed those cutaway panels at her waist like he'd been itching to do for an eternity and drew her against him. Yes, she was still as warm as he remembered and he ached to pull the pins from her tight blond chignon to let it rain down around her shoulders.

He leaned in, nearly nuzzling her ear with his lips. Her quick intake of breath was almost as thrilling as the feel of her skin through the panels. Instead of pulling her toward him like he wanted to, he pivoted and hustled her back a step into her office.

"Tell the girls I said hi," he murmured and let her go. Though where he found the willpower, he had no idea.

She nodded, her expression blank. He was *so* going to enjoy putting a few more cracks in her newly found ice-goddess exterior when they next met.

Three

Cass blew out the breath she'd been holding. Which didn't help either her shakes or her thundering pulse.

That hadn't gone down quite like she would have hoped. She and Gage might be equals now but that hadn't afforded her any special magic to keep her insides under control.

But Gage had left and that seemed like a small win.

Except now she had to go into that board meeting, where Trinity had most definitely told the others who Cass was meeting with. So she would have to give them the whole story, including his ridiculous offer for the formula.

Of all the nerve. Telling her she owed him the formula because he'd given her a few pointers once upon a time. Oh, she owed him all right, but more like a fat lip. Fyra's success had nothing to do with Gage.

Well, the broken heart he'd left her with had driven her for a long time. But she'd succeeded by her own merit, not because he'd mentored her.

If anyone decided to sell the formula, it would be because it made sound business sense. Like she'd told him. She squared her shoulders and went to her meeting in the large, sunny room at the end of the hall.

The other three women in the C-suite ringed the conference table as the governing forces of the company they'd dubbed Fyra, from the Swedish word for four. Alex Meer ran the numbers as the chief financial officer, Dr. Harper Livingston cooked up formulas in her lab as the chief science officer, Trinity Forrester convinced consumers to buy as the chief marketing officer and Cass held the reins.

All three of her friends looked up as she entered, faces bright with expectation.

"He's gone. Let's get started." Cass set down her phone and tablet, then slid into her customary chair.

"Not so fast," Trinity said succinctly. "We've been sitting here patiently waiting for juicy details, remember?"

They'd all been friends a long time. Juicy details meant they wanted to know how she felt about seeing Gage again. Whether she wanted to punch him or just go in the corner and cry. What was he up to and had they talked about their personal lives?

She didn't have the luxury of burdening her friends with any of that because they were also her business partners. There was no room at this conference table for her emotional upheaval.

"He wants to buy Formula-47. Offered one hundred million," she said bluntly. Better to get it out on the table. "I told him it wasn't for sale. That's the extent of it."

Harper's grin slipped as she wound her strawberry blond ponytail around one finger, an absent gesture that meant her brilliant mind was blazing away. "That's hardly the extent. What's the damage? Did he hear about my formula from the trade article?"

"No." Cass hated to have to be the bearer of bad news, but they had to know. "His information was much more detailed. Which means the leak is worse than we thought."

Hearing her own words echo in her head was almost as bad as a physical blow.

"What's wrong?" Trinity asked immediately, her dark head bent at an angle as she evaluated Cass. "Did Gage get to you?"

Dang it. It had taken all of fourteen seconds for the woman who'd been Cass's best friend since eleventh grade to clue in on the undercurrents. That man had put a hitch in her stride and it was unforgivable.

"I'm concerned about the leak. That's it. Forget about Gage. I already have," she lied.

Trinity's eyes narrowed but she didn't push, thank God. Gage's timing was horrific. Why had he waltzed back into her life during such a huge professional catastrophe?

Alex, the consummate tomboy in a pair of jeans and a T-shirt, fiddled with her ever-present pen, tapping it against the legal pad on the conference table in front of her. "A hundred million is worth considering, don't you think?"

Instantly, Harper shook her head so hard, her ponytail flipped over her shoulder. Trinity and Cass scowled at Alex, who shrank under the heat of their gazes, but didn't recant her traitorous statement.

"Worth considering?" Cass's stomach contracted sharply as she took in the seriousness of Alex's expression. How could she be talking about selling so coolly? To Cass, it would be like selling her own child. "Are you out of your mind?"

"Shouldn't we consider a lucrative income stream when it's presented?" Alex argued. "We can't categorically dismiss that kind of paycheck."

They could when it was coming out of the bank account of the man who had destroyed Cass. Didn't that matter?

"Wait just a darn minute, Ms. Moneybags." Harper rounded on Alex, who shrank a bit under the redhead's scowl. "Formula-47 is my baby, not yours. I spent two years of my life perfecting it on the premise that we'd hinge our entire future strategy around the products we can create from the technology. If we sell it, we're giving up rights to it forever for a lump sum. That's not smart."

Alex tapped her pen faster against the legal pad. "Not if we retain rights and structure the deal—"

"No one is structuring deals," Cass broke in. "I only mentioned it because you needed to know. Gage's offer will vanish instantly if the leak shares the formula's recipe. And since we still don't know who it is, we have to focus on that first."

Alex firmed her mouth and nodded. "That's true."

"What did our lawyer say?" Trinity asked, raising her eyebrows as Cass blinked at her. "Didn't you just come back from Mike's office?"

"God, I'm sorry." Cass slid down in her chair an inch in mortification. Gage had wiped that entire meeting out of her head. "Mike doesn't think we can involve the police yet. The article didn't contain enough detail and wouldn't stand up in court as proprietary information. He advised us to file for FDA approval immediately, in hopes that will stem future information from being released prematurely. Until we find the leak, we can't be too careful."

She had to regain control *now*. Gage wasn't a factor. Period.

"I'm not ready." Harper shook her head mulishly. *Careful* and *thorough* might as well be tattooed on her forehead alongside her credentials, a valuable trait in a scientist who created the products with Fyra's label on them. "This is our first product that requires FDA approval. We can't rush it."

"So our lawyer gave us advice we don't plan to take." Pradas flat on the ground, Trinity leaned on the table. "What else do we have on the agenda that we need to get busy shooting down?"

"The leak is the only thing on the agenda," Cass said firmly.

Alex zeroed in on her. "What's your plan for fixing this problem, then?"

"I'm still working on it."

"You're working on it." Alex's sarcastic tone couldn't have conveyed her disbelief any more clearly. "You mean you don't have something laid out already?"

Cass froze her muscles, a trick she'd perfected over the years. She refused to let on that Alex's words had pierced her through the chest.

Alex's point wasn't lost on her. Cass should have a plan. But didn't, which was the last thing she'd admit to these women who were looking to her for leadership. "I've got some ideas. Things in the works."

"Things?" Trinity repeated incredulously.

Trinity and Alex glanced at each other and foreboding slid down Cass's spine. She was losing her edge. And everyone knew she didn't have a blessed clue how to handle this problem.

"I said I'll take care of it," Cass snapped and then immediately murmured an apology.

She couldn't believe how the meeting had deteriorated, how much it hurt to have Alex on the other side of these critical company issues. There were fractures in Fyra she hadn't known existed. Fractures in the relationships with her friends and business partners that scared her. Was

Alex disputing her ideas because she had lost confidence in Cass's ability to run Fyra?

And what was with that look Alex and Trinity had exchanged? Did they know Cass had lied about how much Gage had affected her? And Trinity hadn't defended Cass, not when Gage's offer had come up and not when Alex had attacked Cass for her lack of a plan.

It all rubbed at the raw place inside that Gage had opened up.

Cass cleared her throat and forced her CEO mask back into place. Emotions had no place in a boardroom, yet she'd been letting them run rampant thus far. It was much harder than she would have expected to shut it down given all the practice she had.

"I've got this," she said a little more calmly. "Trust me. Nothing is more important than finding this leak. Let me take care of it."

Trinity nodded. "Let's meet again on Friday. You can give us a progress report then."

Cass watched the other ladies stand and leave the conference room. No one said a word but the vote of no confidence rang out in the silence, nonetheless.

With the room empty, she let her forehead thunk the table but the wood didn't cool her raging thoughts.

She needed a plan.

But Gage had messed her up. Of course he was the reason she'd slipped up in the board meeting. Why had he picked today to dismantle her careful facade?

Her head snapped up. What if the timing wasn't coincidental? It had been bothering her how accurate his information was and how quickly on the heels of the trade article publication that he'd shown up. What if he'd planted someone in her company who was feeding him information and the mention of Fyra in the trade magazine had been designed to throw her off?

But why would he do that? He was already success- ful in his own right and he was willing to pay for the for- mula. It wasn't as if he'd put a mole in her company in hopes of stealing it.

Or was it?

She had to make sure. She'd never forgive herself if she left that stone unturned.

She also had to make progress on discovering who the culprit was and the faster the better. If the leak heard the formula was worth one hundred million dollars to GB Skin, it was as good as stolen. And Gage probably wasn't the only competitor willing to ante up.

Fyra needed Cass to step up, to lead this company. So she'd keep her friends close and her enemies closer, no matter what sort of distasteful cozying up to the CEO of GB Skin she'd have to do. After all, she *did* owe Gage Branson and it was time to pay him back.

He'd used her once upon a time. Turnabout was fair play in Gage's book, was it? It was time for Cass to whole- heartedly embrace that mantra.

Whatever Gage's game was, she'd uncover it. And maybe exact some revenge at the same time. Karma in- deed.

Whistling as he rounded the Hummer's bumper, Gage went over his pitch as he strolled toward the entrance to Fyra Cosmetics only one short day after running into Cass in the parking lot. After she'd kicked him out, he'd really expected to have to push her for another appoint- ment. When she'd called, it had been a pleasant surprise.

The 9:00 a.m. appointment had been another one. Nice to be Cass's first priority for the day. Apparently she'd thought about the logic of his offer overnight and was finally on board. Or the other executives had convinced her that selling him the formula did make for smart business, like he'd told Cass. Either way, the tide had turned.

Which was good because Arwen didn't like the hotel, and she'd let Gage know about it. Loudly. He'd have to take her on a weekend camping trip to the Hill Country to make up for all of this. Hopefully, he could melt a little of the ice in Cass's spine, close the deal and be back in Austin tomorrow.

Depending how things went with the ice melting, of course. If Cass was still as hot as he remembered under her new bulletproof CEO exterior, he might stick around for a couple of days. Arwen could rough it.

Cass didn't make him cool his heels like he'd thought she would. After yesterday, with all the power plays disguised as flirting and Cass not letting him run roughshod over her, he'd come prepared for battle. Hell, he'd kind of looked forward to another game of one-upmanship. It was rare that a woman could match him.

She appeared in the reception area looking gorgeous and untouchable in another sharp suit with a microskirt, this time in eye-popping candy pink, and she'd swept up her hair into another severe bun-like thing held by lacquered chopsticks that he immediately wanted to take apart. Why was that so hot?

He dredged up a memory of her old look from college, which had largely consisted of yoga pants and hoodies, and he'd liked that, too. But this was something else. Something elemental. He wanted to explore this new Cass in the worst way.

"Good morning, Mr. Branson," she said, though the frost in her tone told him she thought it was anything but. "This way."

The chilly greeting and use of his last name put a grin on his face. So she planned to cross swords after all. Excellent.

This time, he didn't even hesitate at the door of her office. No point in beating around the bush when the upper hand was still up for grabs. He waltzed into the middle of all that purple and plunked down into a chair. Happened to be the one behind the desk—Cass's chair—but he figured that would be enough to get her into the room.

It was. She followed him into the interior, and without batting an eye, she crossed to the desk and perched on it. Two feet from his chair. Gaze squarely on Gage, she crossed her stocking-clad legs with a slow and deliberate slide and let her stilettos dangle. The little skirt rode up her thighs almost to the point of indecency.

His tongue went numb as all the blood rushed from his head, pooling into a spectacular hard-on. One tiny push with his heel and Cass's chair would roll him into a proximity much better suited to enjoying the smorgasbord of delights inches away.

This was his punishment for stealing her chair? She clearly didn't get how corporate politics, particularly between competitors, worked.

"Thanks for coming on short notice," she purred and the subtle innuendo wasn't lost on him.

"Thanks for having me," he returned and cleared the rasp from his throat. Maybe she knew a little more about this game than he'd supposed. "You ready to talk details?"

"Sure, if you want to jump right into it." She cocked her head, watching him. "The others don't want to sell. But I'm willing to talk to them."

Instantly suspicious, he grinned and crossed his arms, leaning back in the chair so he could see all of her at once. She was something else. "Along with what strings?"

"Oh, nothing much." She waved a French-manicured hand airily and leaned forward, one palm on the desk. Her silky button-up shirt billowed a bit, just enough to draw his attention to her cleavage but not enough to actually show anything.

The anticipation of catching a glimpse of skin had his mouth watering.

"Name your price, Cass," he murmured and wondered what she'd do if he pulled her off that desk into his lap. "I'm assuming one hundred million wasn't enough?"

"Not quite. You also have to help me catch the leak first."

His gaze snapped back up to her beautiful face as her meaning registered. "Help you catch the leak? You mean you haven't already?"

Unacceptable. Hadn't she learned anything important from him? Yesterday he sure would have said so, but obviously she needed a few more pointers about how to run her business.

"I have a plan," she explained calmly. "And you're it. Until the leak is stopped, Fyra can't make a major decision like selling our formula. Surely you understand that."

He did. This was a wrinkle he hadn't anticipated. But what she was proposing—it meant he'd have to stay in Dallas longer than he'd anticipated. He ran a successful company, too, and it was suffering from his lack of attention. If he stayed, he'd have to ship Arwen home, which she'd never forgive him for.

"You should have already handled the leak," he groused.

"I know."

Her voice didn't change. Her expression didn't change. But something shifted as he realized how hard this conversation was for her. She hadn't wanted to admit that.

Disturbed at the sudden revelation, he stared at her and

his heart thumped strangely. He'd been so busy examining the angles, he'd failed to see this was actually just a baseline plea for help that she'd disguised well.

"Work with me, Gage. Together, like old times."

She wanted to pick up where they left off. Maybe in more ways than one. The simple phrases reached out and grabbed hold of his lungs. It echoed through his mind, his chest, and the thought pleased him. Enormously.

It was a redo of college, where he was her mentor and she soaked it all up like a sponge with a side of hero worship that made him feel invincible. That had been a heady arrangement for a twenty-four-year-old. But they weren't kids anymore.

And he didn't for a moment underestimate Cass. She'd suggested this for some reason he couldn't figure out yet. Which didn't keep him from contemplating that redo. Who was he kidding? He'd wanted her the moment he'd turned around in the parking lot yesterday and gotten an eyeful of grown-up Cass. If he hung around and helped her, it gave him an opportunity to get her naked again.

And he could ensure the problem with the leak was handled like it should have been from the get-go. Not to mention he could dig a bit to uncover her real motives here.

Her eyes huge and warm, she watched him and he was lost. Dang. She'd played this extremely well. There was absolutely no way he could say no. He didn't want to say no.

But a yes didn't mean he'd do it without adding a few strings of his own.

"I'll help you. Until Sunday. I have a meeting Monday that can't be rescheduled."

Her smile hit him crossways. And then it slipped from her face as he leaned forward oh-so-slowly. Mute, she stared at his hand as he braced it on the desk a millimeter from her thigh. He could slip a finger right under the hem of that tiny skirt. And his mind got busy on imagining where that would lead.

"But you have to do something for me," he murmured. He got as close to her as he dared, crowding her space where all the trappings of business melted away and they were simply man and woman.

She smelled classy and expensive, and instantly he wanted that scent on his own skin, transferred by her body heat as she writhed under him. He could lean her back against that desk and at this angle, the pleasure would be intense. The image made him a little lightheaded as his erection intensified.

"I already said I'd talk to the others about selling you the formula," she said a touch breathlessly, but to her credit, she didn't allow one single muscle twitch to give away whether she welcomed his nearness or preferred the distance. "*If* we catch the leak."

That ice-goddess routine needed to go, fast. That wasn't going to happen here. Not under these circumstances. If he wanted to take things to the next level, he had to go bold or go home.

"Yes, but you're doing that because deep down, you know you owe me. If I help you find the leak, you owe me again. Turnabout, sweetheart."

"What do you want?"

Oh, where should I start? "Nothing you can't handle."

The knowing glint in her gaze said she already had a pretty good idea what gauntlet he was about to throw down. They stared at each other for a long moment and her breathing hitched as he reached out and slid a thumb along her jawline.

"You have to take me to dinner."

Four

Cass's laughter bubbled to the surface in spite of it all. Gingerly she dabbed at her eyes without fear thanks to Harper's smudge-proof mascara. "That's what you want? Dinner?"

She'd been braced for...anything but that. Especially since she had the distinct impression he was working as many angles as she was.

His fingers dropped away, but her face was still warm where he'd stroked her. She missed his touch instantly.

Why had she thought sitting on the desk would give her an edge? Seemed so logical before she actually did it. Gage had taken her chair in deliberate provocation that she absolutely couldn't ignore. So she'd trapped him behind the desk and put all her good stuff at eye level. It should have been the perfect distraction. For *him*. The perfect way to spend the entire conversation looking down at him, imagining that he was suffering over her brilliant strategic move.

Karma, baby.

Instead, she'd spent half of the conversation acutely aware that all her good stuff was at eye level. He'd noticed, quite appreciatively, and it hit her in places she'd forgotten that felt so good when heated by a man's interest.

The other half of the conversation had been spent trying to stay one step ahead of Gage while feeding him the right combination of incentives to get him to agree to help. If he was up to no good, what better way to keep tabs on him than under the guise of working together to uncover the source of the leak? Besides, she hadn't done so hot at resolving the leak on her own. If they kept their activities on the down-low, no one had to know she'd outsourced the problem.

If they caught the leak—*and* Gage wasn't involved— she'd absolutely talk to the other girls about selling the formula. She hadn't specified what she'd say…but she'd talk to them all right. The conversation might be more along the lines of no way in hell she'd sell, but he didn't have to know that.

It was a win-win for everyone.

Crossing his heart with one lazy finger, he grinned. "Totally serious."

"Dinner?" She pretended to contemplate. "Like a date?"

"Not *like* a date. A date. And you're paying."

A God-honest date? The idea buzzed around inside, looking for a place to land, sounding almost…nice. She'd love to have dinner over a glass of wine with an interesting man who looked at her like Gage was looking at her right now.

She shook it off. She couldn't go on a real date with Gage Branson. It was ludicrous. The man was a heartbreaker of the highest order.

Instead, she should be thinking of how a date fell in

line with her strategy. A little after-hours party, just the two of them. Some drinks and a few seductive comments and, oh, look. Gage slips and says something incriminating, like the name of the person he'd planted at her company. The one who was feeding him information he could use to his advantage.

And she would pretend she wasn't sad it had to be this way.

Coy was the way to go here. But she had to tread very carefully with the devil incarnate. No point in raising his suspicions by agreeing to his deal right out of the gate. "What if I already have plans for dinner tonight?"

She *did* have plans. If working until everyone else left and then going home to her empty eight-thousand-square-foot house on White Rock Lake, where she'd open a bottle of wine and eat frozen pizza, counted as plans.

"Cancel them," he ordered. "You're too busy worrying about the leak to have fun, anyway. Have dinner with someone who gets that. Where you can unload and unwind without fear."

"What makes you think I need to unwind?" she purred to cover the sudden catch in her throat. Had she tipped him off somehow that she was tense and frantic 24/7?

His slow smile irritated her. How dare he get to her?

"Oh, I'm practicing my mindreading skills," he told her blithely. "I see that things are rough around here. You can't be happy that word got out about your unreleased formula. You're at a unique place in your career where you have millions of dollars and a large number of people's jobs at stake. You want to keep it all together and convince everyone that you have things under control. With me, you don't have to. I get it."

Something inside crumbled under his assessment.

Guess that shield she'd thought she'd developed wasn't so effective after all. How was he still so good at reading her?

Now would be a good time for that distance she should have put between them long ago. She unglued herself from the desk and rounded it, an ineffective barrier against the open wounds in her chest but better than nothing. Let him make what he chose out of her move.

"You can't come in here and throw around pop psychology," she told him, pleased how calmly she delivered it. "You don't know anything about me, Gage. Not anymore."

Arms crossed, he watched her from behind her own desk, still wearing a faint trace of that smile. "Yet you didn't say I was wrong."

She shut her eyes for a beat. Dinner was going to be far more difficult than she'd anticipated.

If Gage was involved in corporate espionage, catching him in the act was the only way to prove to the others she could lead Fyra through these difficult circumstances. Plus it got rid of him, once and for all. His hundred-million-dollar offer wouldn't be a factor and the leak would be stopped.

He'd get exactly what he deserved.

Then she could get started on getting over him—for real, this time. She could stop hating him. And stop being affected by him. And stop turning down every man who asked her out. The chaos inside with Gage's name written all over it had driven her for so long. Wasn't it time to move on? That was what *she* deserved.

"I'm not what you'd call a fun date," she said. "I have a very boring life outside of these walls. Dinner is a chance to discuss the leak. Strictly business."

A token protest. She knew good and well it was anything but.

"Is that really what you want, Cass?" he asked softly,

as if he already knew the answer. "Because it sounds to me as if you need a friend."

Of all the things she'd thought he come back with, that was not one of them. The laugh escaped her clamped lips before she could catch it. "What, like you're volunteering? I have lots of friends, thanks."

But did she really? This time last week, she would have said Trinity would take a bullet for her. They'd been friends for almost fifteen years. It still stung that no one had stood up for Cass in the board meeting, but Trinity's silence had hurt the worst.

Alex's defection was almost as bad.

Cass and Alex had met in a freshman-level algebra class. It had taken Cass four months to convince Alex she had what it took to be the CFO of a multimillion-dollar corporation and Cass had been right. Alex's lack of confidence and all the talk of selling hurt.

Cass was afraid the cracks in Fyra's foundation were really cracks in *her* foundation. The last person she could stomach finding out about the division in Fyra was Gage Branson, and it would be just like him to sniff out her weaknesses.

So she wouldn't show him any.

"There's always room for one more friend," Gage countered softly. "In fact, I changed my mind. Let *me* take *you* to dinner and you can relax for a while. Wear a dress and we'll leave our titles at the door."

There he went again, working his magic because that sounded like the exact date she'd envisioned. He was the last man on earth she should be envisioning it with, though. "How do you know that's what I need?"

"Cass. I know you. You can't have changed too much over the years. At least I hope you haven't."

Before she could figure out how to respond to that, he

rounded the desk and took her hand to hold it tight in his surprisingly smooth one. For a guy who'd always spent a lot of time outdoors, his skin should be rougher. It was a testament to GB Skin and the effectiveness of his products that it wasn't.

She stared at his chiseled jaw, gorgeous hazel eyes and beautiful face framed by the longish brown hair he'd always favored and something unhitched in her chest.

Gage had broken her so thoroughly because she'd once given this man her soul.

That hadn't been an accident. A mistake, surely, but not because she didn't realize what she was doing. She'd fallen in love with Gage willingly. He'd filled her, completely. Because he understood her, believed in her. Taught her, pushed her, stimulated her.

All of it rushed back and she went a little dizzy with the memories of what had been holy and magnificent about their relationship.

"Say yes," he prompted, squeezing her hand. "I promise not to mention how boring you are."

Despite everything, she laughed, oddly grateful that he had figured out how to get her to.

"Yes," she said. There'd really never been another choice. "But we split the check."

He couldn't be allowed to affect her. The good stuff about their relationship didn't matter because at the end of the day, Gage didn't do commitment and never would.

"That part's nonnegotiable," he said with a wicked smile. "I'm paying. After all, I bullied you into it."

Mission accomplished. He had no clue he'd spent this entire conversation persuading her into exactly what she wanted to do. For that alone, she returned the smile. "You haven't seen the price of the obscenely expensive wine I plan to order."

"I'll pick you up at eight," he said, clearly happy to have gotten what he wanted, though why he considered dinner such a coup was beyond her. He had an angle here that she hadn't yet discovered.

She watched him leave. That gave her nearly ten hours to figure out how to keep Gage at arm's length while co- zying up to him. Hours she'd use to figure out how to pump him for information while keeping him in the dark about her motives.

Ten hours to figure out how to seduce answers out of Gage Branson without falling for him all over again. All she had to do was focus on his sins and the rest would be a walk in the park.

Gage knocked on Cass's door at seven fifty-five.

Nice place. A bit too glass-and-steel for his tastes but Cass's house overlooked a big lake with a walking trail around it. His own house in Austin was near a lake. Funny how their tastes in views had aligned all these years later.

She swung open the door wearing a sheer lacy dress that hugged her body in all the right places. Cranberry- colored, which was somehow ten times racier than red would have been, it rendered him speechless. When he'd told her to wear a dress, he'd fully expected her to wear anything but.

His body sprang to full attention. He could not get a handle on her.

"You're early," she said with an amused brow lift. "I like an eager man."

The blood that should have been stimulating his brain into a snappy response seemed to have vacated for a warmer locale in the south.

Cass wasn't a college student any longer. Not that he was confused. But he was having a hard time reconciling how *much* she'd changed. Cassandra Claremont, CEO, might be the most intriguing woman on the planet. She was also far more of a challenge because she seemed to have developed Gage-proof armor.

Dinner was supposed to level the playing field. Warm up that ice so he could get her used to the idea of selling him the formula because she recognized what she owed him. She might be willing to talk to the other ladies about the formula, but he needed her to convince them, not talk about it. For that, she had to be totally in his corner. How was he supposed to get her there when he couldn't get his feet under himself long enough to figure out what game she was playing?

"Uh…" *Brain not engaging.* He shook off the Cass stupor. "It's only early if you're more than fifteen minutes ahead. Technically, I'm right on time."

"Where are you taking me for dinner, Mr. Right-on-Time?" She cocked her head, sending her dangly diamond earrings dancing.

His body was not interested in food. At all.

"I'll let you choose," he allowed magnanimously. "Since you cancelled your previous plans."

Not for the first time, he wondered what she'd told the poor schmuck she'd ditched, who'd likely spent all day anticipating his date with Cass. Had she admitted to her date that an old boyfriend had unexpectedly come to town? A business deal had suddenly fallen in her lap that she needed to attend to? She had to wash her hair?

It probably didn't matter. She'd be forgiven for breaking the date regardless. Cass was a gorgeous, sophisticated woman who ran a multimillion dollar company and she likely had her pick of companions. Suave execs, successful doctors, cut athletes with Pro-Bowl or all-star credentials. The dating circles were wide open and she was most definitely sleeping with *someone*. A woman like Cass wouldn't be alone except by choice.

That burn in your gut? Feels a lot like jealousy.

Ridiculous. So Nicolas didn't get it right *all* the time.

Gage and Cass hadn't been an item for nearly a decade. Sure, he'd thought about her and wondered what might have been if he wasn't so averse to being tied down, but he hadn't spent all his nights alone since then either. Though lately, a couple of hours at the dog park with Arwen was more fun than wading through the pool of women in his circle. That was the one downside to guarding your freedom so ferociously—you went through eligible women pretty quickly.

"That's so generous of you to let me pick after leaving me so few choices otherwise," she said, infusing it with enough sarcasm to clue him in that she still wasn't clear on what she owed him.

"You always have choices," he countered. "One just might lead to a different place than the other."

"Well said." With a cryptic nod, she brushed past him onto the front steps, engulfing him in a delicious haze of jasmine and other exotic spices. On Cass, the scent was half "come and get me" and half "I'm untouchable." A thoroughly arousing combination.

Somehow, he managed to drive to the restaurant without veering off into a ditch. Or a shadowy hiding place between two buildings where he could ravish the cool beauty in the next seat. If he wanted her willing, he had to get back on track. But the ice in her spine seemed extra hard and cold tonight.

The restaurant was as highbrow as they came, making him glad he'd tossed a suit in his overnight bag, just in case. The maître d' led them to a secluded table in the back, exactly as Gage had instructed, and left them bless-edly alone.

Except Gage still didn't know how to play this dinner. Seduction or strategy? Which would get him an invitation through the front door of Cass's house at the end of the night? Because seduction might be the only way to get what he wanted in the end. A sated Cass might make for a much more reasonable Cass. But they did need to work together on the leak or the formula would be worthless. He couldn't ignore the need to discuss strategy.

Fortunately, what he apparently lacked in ESP, he made up for in charm and ingenuity. So he'd wing it. Like always.

Gage barely glanced at the wine menu before handing it over to Cass. "Since you called dibs on ordering the wine, here you go."

She arched one of those cool brows and took the leather-bound wine listing. The movement drew attention to her cleavage, where scarcely-contained nipples threatened to burst free of their cranberry lace cage at a moment's no-tice. A bead of sweat slid between his shoulder blades as he tore his gaze from her breasts.

"I was expecting more of an argument," she com-mented as if the sexual undercurrents didn't exist. "You're not a fan of wine, if memory serves."

No, but the fact that she recalled his preference put a good deal more warmth down south. As if he'd had room for more.

"I'll make an exception for you."

The more she drank, the less she'd remember to act like the ice goddess, or at least that had been the plan once upon a time when his faculties were in order. Back in her office, she'd seemed...brittle. As if she'd needed someone to pay attention to her. Cass was in sore need of a glass of wine and an orgasm, and not necessarily in that order.

That made up his mind. He wanted to give her a chance to relax, as he'd entreated her to. One of them should be able to anyway. Seduction first. And then they could talk leak strategy later. Much later.

With their food, Cass ordered a four hundred dollar bottle of wine—exorbitant, as promised—and once the waiter left to retrieve it, she folded her hands, contemplating Gage as if she'd found an amusing little puppy she didn't know whether to pet or send outside for peeing on the floor.

"Tell me something," she began in her boardroom voice that he should not find so sexy.

"Sure. I'm an open book." He spread his hands wide, earning a small, less-than-amused smile. She needed to drink more. Maybe her Gage-proof armor would fall off along with her inhibitions.

Once, they'd talked about everything under the sun and he'd enjoyed hearing her thoughts and soothing her through her angst. Just like he'd enjoyed being her mentor, shaping her, guiding her.

Maybe you hope to fall into that role again, with the hero worship and Pygmalion overtones, hmm?

Yeah. He did. And she needed his help to find the leak. Needed *him*. So what? Seduction *and* strategy, then. All of that worked together to get him the formula. Where was the harm?

"Why the interest in my formula?" she asked point-blank. "Other than the song and dance about how I owe it to you. For real. Why? You've expanded your retail reach enormously over the past five years and you just landed that endorsement deal. Something must have prompted you to show up on my doorstep."

"That's a fair question," he acknowledged, impressed that she'd done her homework on his company. And that's why he chose to answer her honestly. "It's simple really. My target consumers are starting to pay close attention to things like bar-fight scars and wrinkles. So I launched my own product. I don't want any competition."

"Gage, there are a hundred wrinkle creams on the market. Your competition is legion."

"No." He caught her gaze and held it. "There's only one person who's my equal."

"So this is a pride thing." Looking away, she sipped the glass of wine the waiter had placed in front of her and murmured her appreciation for the red blend. "You can't stand it when a competitor is primed to beat you."

He might as well be made of glass when it came to Cass and that was sexy, too. Dang if he could figure out why he was so drawn to her when all he should care about was whatever got him that formula.

Ignoring his own vile glass of headache in a bottle, he grinned because it would be pointless to argue when she clearly saw the truth. But that didn't mean they had to dwell on it.

Gage slid a palm across the table and captured her hand before she could prevent it. "Don't think of me as your competition, not tonight."

She glanced down at their joined hands but didn't snatch hers away. He could tell she was contemplating it, though, hopefully because she also felt the electricity between them—and it was working to loosen her up.

"But you are. Always and forever. We sell similar products or you wouldn't be here. Nor would you have been my mentor. Competition is not something you can will away."

"Maybe not. I can, however, ban all business talk until later. Then we're just old friends reconnecting. Like I told you in your office."

He had the distinct impression she didn't loosen up easily these days. If there was any competition going on tonight, that was it. And he didn't intend to lose this particular contest.

"I'm curious," she said, her gaze back on him but not nearly warm enough for his taste. "I never see you at trade shows. My email address is easy to locate on Fyra's website. If you have such an interest in reconnecting, why haven't we done so before now?"

A hot prickle walked across the back of his neck as he instantly recognized a spring-loaded trap, ready to close around his leg if he moved the wrong way. An unsettled feeling bled through his chest.

And in the end, *he* was the one to pull his hand back from hers, suddenly uncomfortable with the contact.

"I hate trade shows. They're stifling. And they're always on weekends when I'm…busy."

That had sounded much dirtier than he'd intended, especially when lately, his weekends had consisted of giving Arwen a bath or taking her to the lake so she could have fun practicing her pointer skills.

Cass watched him without blinking, silently waiting on him to stop stalling and get to the meat of her question, which was basically designed to force him to admit he'd developed an interest in her in order to get his hands on her formula.

Maybe it had started out as a little of both—seducing her to ensure she remembered what she owed him. He wasn't a saint.

But at this moment, he really did want to be a friend. None of her other so-called friends seemed to realize how brittle she was under her super-CEO costume. Someone had to banish the shadows of fatigue and uncertainty in her gaze. Give her a safe place to let her hair down, which would preferably be in his bed, like she'd once done.

Yeah. He'd like to pull those pins from the tight blond twist at her crown, all right. His lower half went rock solid as he imagined that fall of hair raining down around her bare shoulders as he peeled that lacy, sexy cranberry-colored dress from her beautiful body. It was crazy to be so hot for her again after not seeing her for so long—or to her point, after not actively pursuing reacquaintance for all these years.

He should have looked her up. Why hadn't he?

He blew out a pent-up breath. "Truth? I didn't drive up from Austin to reconnect over a drink. I want your formula. But that's just business."

Tonight was very personal.

Nodding at the wine bottle, she drained her glass and held it out for Gage to pour her another. "I'm surprised you'd admit it."

"I told you, I'm an open book. I don't mind being cagey when the occasion calls for it, but I don't have deep dark secrets." Who had time for that noise? Life was too short to care about other people's opinions, and that's all secrets were—things you didn't want others to know because you feared their judgment.

Cass leaned forward and the new angle did fascinating things to the deep V over her breasts. Not that he was a lecher, but come on. A lady didn't wear a dress like that if she didn't want her date to notice her spectacular breasts. And a lady who didn't want a man to imagine tasting her breasts definitely didn't *lean*.

"Really. No secrets?"

"Really, really." His tongue was still a bit thick.

"Sounds like we need to play a game of truth or dare, then."

Five

Cass held her breath as Gage's gaze flew to hers. It had been lingering somewhere in the vicinity of her cleavage, and the heat from his appreciation had been warming her uncomfortably for the better part of ten minutes. But what had she expected with such a daring wardrobe choice?

Gage's eyes on her body were far more affecting than any other man's hands would be.

Question marks shooting from the top of his head, Gage lifted a brow. "Yeah, truth or dare. That's what I was thinking, too. How did you know?"

She bit back the laugh. Even when he was being sarcastic, he was still charming. She wasn't falling for it. "I'm serious. If you don't have any secrets, should be an easy game."

And she could pump him for information about his involvement in the leak without raising red flags. It was brilliant.

Lazily he traced the rim of his untouched wineglass, watching her with undisguised calculation. But what all those equations added up to, she had no idea. The clink of silverware against china filled the sudden silence, along with snatches of conversation from other diners.

"You know how that game works, right?" he finally asked.

She waved dismissively. "Of course, or I wouldn't have suggested it. I ask you a question and if you don't choose to answer it honestly, you have to do whatever I dare you to."

"And you have to do the same." The once-over he slid down her body unleashed a shiver.

She'd considered that. Not enough, apparently. "Yeah, so? I'm not worried."

The waiter brought their dinners but instead of picking up a fork, Gage folded his hands in front of his plate of salmon and asparagus. "You probably should be. But now I'm insanely curious what you want to know that you feel you have to bury inside a game. You could just ask."

Her pulse tripped as she scrambled for a response. She was slipping. How had he seen through that ploy so *easily*? "That's no fun."

His laugh curled up inside her thickly. "It *so* can be, but it's all in the asking. No matter. I'm in. Truth or dare away. Truth for my first round."

Forking a bite of salmon into his mouth, he watched her expectantly and it bobbled her pulse again. This was why she sold cosmetics for a living instead of becoming an investigator. There was a skill to it apparently, one that she lacked. Too late to back out now.

"Have you ever…" She cursed silently. Thinking on the fly was one of her strong suits but not with Gage's hazel laser beams boring into her. *Say something.* "Cheated on your taxes?"

"That's your question?" He shook his head with a laugh. "I'm almost afraid to ask what the dare would be. But it doesn't matter because I have nothing to hide. As much as I think the corporate tax structure needs to be reworked in favor of businesses, no, I've never cheated on my taxes."

Taxes. Could she be more boring? Despite having warned him that she was not a fun date, she had a goal here and she needed to get on it by steering the conversation toward his ethics. "But you cheat at cards. All the time."

His slow smile did something X-rated to her insides. "That's only when we're playing strip poker, darling. And believe me, it's worth it."

The memory of messing around in college, using things like card games as foreplay, spiked through her. They'd always ended up naked and breathless. The anticipation had been drawn out over the length of a game she could hardly pay attention to because Gage had been revealing himself oh-so-slowly while she sat there in a similar state of vulnerability.

Kind of like now.

And she couldn't unthink it. Back then, when they'd finally come together, she'd exploded under his careful and thorough lovemaking. Because he had always thoroughly engaged her—mind, body and soul.

And that hadn't changed. The moment she'd recognized Gage in the parking lot, it felt as though she'd woken up from a coma. She hadn't realized how much she'd missed being so comprehensively engaged. How much she missed a man paying attention to her.

No. Not any man. This one.

Their gazes met over the table, burning up the atmosphere. Obviously he was recalling their hot and heavy times, as well, and his expression unleashed a shiver she couldn't control. Something unknitted inside, falling apart as if all the glue holding her together melted at Gage-point-five degrees.

They'd once been so close because they had so much in common. They'd shared the same goals, and she'd always been able to count on him to have the answers she sought. She'd counted on him to encourage her, to push her. Because he understood her.

It was so much more powerful now that they were equals. Gage Branson, CEO, was so much more attractive than he'd been as her mentor.

Fork suspended in midair, he tilted his head. "Weren't we playing a game?"

Cass blinked. The game. The suspicions. Her precarious position within Fyra. She bit back an unladylike swear word and took a fortifying sip of wine.

How had she fallen into Gage so easily that she'd forgotten what this dinner was supposed to be about? He'd cursed her with his magic voice and wicked personality, lulling her into believing they were former lovers reconnecting over a drink.

He wasn't on her side, not like he used to be. Maybe he never had been. As he was making love to her, he'd probably already be plotting his escape. Just like he'd almost assuredly plotted to steal her formula.

Gage Branson, CEO, wasn't any more of a good bet with her heart than he had been as a graduate student.

She steeled her spine against the good memories and dredged up the bad ones. She'd spent years working sixteen-hour days so she could fall into bed exhausted and actually sleep. Otherwise, she lay there in misery, aching over having lost the love of her life.

And here he was again, ripe for a comeuppance and

deserving of whatever she threw at him. She narrowed her gaze and shoved back the past. "We got off track. Sorry. Next question. Have you ever stolen anything?"

"I'm supposed to say whether I want truth or dare first." Warily, he eyed her. "What's with all these moral questions anyway? Admittedly, it's been a long time since I played truth or dare, but I seem to recall we always asked things like who was your first crush or have you ever gone skinny-dipping?"

"Those are great questions for eleven-year-olds. This is the adult version," she informed him pertly and was instantly sorry as something wicked flashed through his expression.

"Why didn't you say so?" His slow smile had all sorts of danger signs attached to it. "I'd like to take the dare, then."

She cursed. *Should have anticipated that he'd take the dare, dummy.* "I dare you to answer the question."

"Oh, no, honey," he said with a laugh. "It doesn't work like that. You promised me the adult version and I'm fully prepared to pay up for not answering. Lay it on me."

Clearly he expected the dare to come packaged in a thinly veiled sexual wrapper. So she indulged him with a sensuous smile. "I dare you to take your shirt off."

"Here?" He glanced around the crowded, high-class restaurant with a dubious line between his brows. "It doesn't seem fair to show up all these other guys. Can't you think of something else?"

Typical male machismo. Of course if his body still looked like it used to—and chances were high that it did—his point was valid.

"Chicken?" she asked sweetly. "You wanted the dare."

"I'd be happy to take my shirt off," he growled. "In the car. In your living room. In your office. No card game required. Pick another locale, sweetheart, and dare me to get naked to your heart's content. Unfortunately, there are both a dress code and health regulations in a restaurant. Which means your dare is invalid."

First the insistence he always paid his fair share of taxes and then he'd refused her dare because of *health regulations*? She bit back the noise of disgust. Barely. "When did you become such a boy scout?"

"I've never willingly broken the law." He shrugged. "So there's your answer since I can't take the dare. My turn."

"Your turn for what?" she asked, temporarily distracted by his claim to be a law-abiding citizen.

Honesty? Just because truth was the name of the game didn't mean he wasn't lying. But in reality, he'd never been anything but forthright in their relationship. Sure, he'd dumped her and broken her heart. But he'd been honest about it.

"To ask you a question." He finished off his dinner and chewed thoughtfully. "What's the name of the last guy you were in love with?"

Love. The word echoed through her chest cavity, which was still empty thanks to the last guy she'd fallen in love with. Her stomach rolled and the wine soured in her mouth.

Stupid game. She could lie. But he'd see through that as though he was reading her mind. And she couldn't take the dare—she'd bet his hundred million it would be something impossible like sit in his lap for five minutes or put her underwear in his pocket with her toes.

Why had she started this game? To prove he'd become someone untrustworthy, when she had no evidence of his involvement in the leak? To prove she wasn't affected by him any longer, when she'd only managed to prove the exact opposite?

Or some deeper reason that she couldn't admit, even internally?

Trapped and furious with herself, she stared at him as her frustration grew. And then she pictured the shock on his face if she blurted out *Gage Branson* in response to his question. That was perhaps what stung the most—he didn't even realize he'd detonated a landmine in her heart.

The emotional agitation inside boiled over. And that was unacceptable.

"Excuse me." She threw her napkin into the middle of her plate of uneaten chicken marsala and fled to the bathroom before the sob beating in her throat escaped.

What in the... Gage watched Cass do the hundred-yard sprint through the obstacle course of tables and waiters, presumably headed for the restrooms at the rear of the building.

She'd started this silly game. Was she really that upset he hadn't taken her dare? Why—because she wanted him naked and was too afraid to come right out and say it?

He shook his head and thought seriously about draining his untouched glass of wine to see if Cass made any more sense when he had a buzz. The subsequent headache would at least be more easily explained than the one Cass was giving him.

She didn't return for a long while. A little concerned, Gage followed her, hoping to find a female employee to check on her if need be. Except she was sitting on the velvet bench at the end of the long hallway, her vibe so edgy, he could almost feel the tension.

"Hey," he said softly as he approached. "What's up? Trying to skip out on me? I said I'd pay."

The joke didn't get the smile he'd hoped for. In fact, her expression remained completely blank. "I'm fine."

"Yeah. I can see that." Taking a chance that she'd welcome the company, he sat on the bench next to her.

She didn't move. He'd noticed she did that a lot, holding herself frozen. But this time, he was close enough to see the muscle spasms in her thighs as if she was fighting her body's natural instincts to flee in some kind of mind-over-matter contest.

"I'm sorry I didn't play the game fairly," he said sincerely. And gingerly, in case that wasn't the reason she was upset. Women and emotions were not his forte and he wouldn't be surprised to learn this was one of those situations where if he didn't know why she was upset—she sure wasn't going to tell him.

"You did." She stared straight ahead. "I'm the one who was playing unfairly. You were right, the dare wasn't valid."

Somehow, her admission of guilt managed to sound as if she felt it was anything but her fault. Which was a rare talent.

"Okay. You ready to get out of here, then?" He nodded toward the end of the hallway. "Or do you want to finish dinner?"

"What would be the point of finishing dinner?" she asked in a monotone that pricked the hair on the back of his neck.

This strange mood went well beyond her normal reserve. When he'd labeled her demeanor as *brittle* earlier, he'd had no clue how much more so she could actually become, as if he had to watch how heavily he breathed for fear of shattering her into a million pieces.

"The point of dinner is so I can spend time with you," he said. And…some other agenda items that had somehow slipped his mind in favor of the woman herself.

That earned him a sidelong glance. "I told you I wasn't a fun date."

"I'm having fun," he told her automatically and then had to clarify. "Well, I *was*. And then you disappeared."

Physically and mentally.

"That was fun?" She tilted her head toward the dining room, her eyes incredulously wide. "I made you drink wine, which you hate, and then foisted a teenagers' sleepover game on you. Which part did you find the most entertaining?"

"All of it." He grinned in spite of her mood and accepted her scowl with a nod. "You heard me. I have legs and I know how to use them. Trust me, I've got no problem walking out of a restaurant in the middle of a date. I don't waste my time on things that aren't fun."

"Really?"

"Honesty. It isn't just for breakfast anymore."

And finally, he scored a small laugh. Why did that make his chest feel so tight and full?

"I guess I'm done with dinner." She sneaked another glance at him and he pretended not to notice.

"But not with spending time together?" He resisted the urge to reach out. He wanted to touch her but he couldn't gauge if her mood had shifted enough to welcome it.

"Well..." She crossed her arms, hiding her hands underneath, as if she'd sensed that he'd been contemplating taking one of them. "We were supposed to be talking about the leak. I think we have to do that together."

Which wasn't an answer at all. "You know dinner wasn't about the leak. Don't be dense."

"I was giving you the benefit of the doubt," she countered. "I'm well aware that you're playing all the angles."

And that was the opportunity he'd been waiting for. Since her hands were still locked behind the cross of her arms, he opted to slide one chunk of hair from her cheek and lingered at her neck. Touching that beautiful alabaster skin had suddenly grown more important than breathing. So he indulged himself, letting his fingers play with her neck. And then he tipped her head back so he could meet her gaze.

A shield snapped over her expression. That look he recognized. The ice goddess returneth. Excellent. Now he could get started melting her, like he'd planned. Though the reasons that had felt so necessary at the beginning of the night weren't the same as they were now. At all.

"No angles," he murmured and drew her face closer. Almost within kissing distance. But not quite. "I asked you to dinner because I wanted to. You...interest me. I want to find out how you've changed since college. Discover what's still the same."

Cass didn't look away, challenging him with merely the glint in her eye. "So you can use it to your advantage."

God, that was sexy. In-charge, take-no-prisoners Cass was something else. His motor started humming. "Absolutely. I fully intend to use every scrap of information I learn to seduce you."

Not even a blink to show she'd registered that he'd shifted away from business and zeroed in on pleasure. Which was where they'd keep it if he had his way. Oh, he'd eventually wind his way back to the formula. But for now, it was all about Cass.

"I think you've forgotten that I specified this dinner should be strictly business. I was about to thank you for sticking to it."

Ah-ha. Her voice had grown a little huskier and it skated through his blood, raising the heat a notch. She wasn't as unaffected as she wanted him to believe.

"Sorry," he apologized without a shred of regret. "I

never agreed to that. But we're smart people. We can keep business and pleasure separate. Like we did in college."

He watched her expression smooth out, becoming blank. Which meant he'd hit a nerve.

"I can," she said firmly. "I'm not so sure about you."

"I'm good for it." *Press your advantage. Now.* "If you are, too, prove it."

Her gaze dropped to his mouth. "How?"

Heat and awareness shot through the roof. God, that dress clung to her curves like a second skin. Would it be terrible if he hooked both sleeves with his thumbs and yanked it down so he could feast his eyes on her beautiful bare breasts?

Gage tipped her chin up with a crooked finger to bring her mouth in range. But he didn't take it with his. Not yet.

"So, let me see if I've got this straight," Cass murmured, her breath mingling with his. "By your logic, if I kiss you, that'll prove I can separate business from pleasure?"

"Who said anything about kissing?" he countered. "Is that what's on your mind, Cass? Because I'm game if you think kissing me will make your point."

It was a dare and a challenge—guaranteed to get an in-control, powerful woman like Cass hot—and she caught both full force. Her mouth curved upward as she contemplated him. "I think it'll make your point, not mine."

"Oh?" Barely six inches separated their lips and he ached to close that distance. "What point is that?"

She leaned in, almost there but not quite, lips feathering against his, and it was more evocative than if she'd gone for it. Her perfume engulfed him in a sensuous wave that heightened the sparking awareness. Her breasts brushed his chest aggressively and he nearly groaned with the effort it took to keep his fingers from her dress.

One little signal and he'd slide his arms around her, pulling her into the fiercest kiss. The only prayer he had of cracking that ice was to give her something sizzling hot to grab on to with both hands.

Public place, public place, public place, he reminded himself furiously.

"Your point—if I recall—was that you'd use all the information at your disposal to seduce me," she murmured throatily. "I don't think you have a shot."

"Guess there's only one way to find out."

The irresistible draw between them sucked him in, and finally his arms closed around her and her mouth sought his. A scorching kiss ignited the pent-up emotions and desire Gage had been fighting since he'd first laid eyes on Cass in the parking lot of her building.

They twined together, shifting closer. As close as they could on the bench without turning the kiss into something too indecent for public consumption.

Yes. Oh, God yes. Her tongue darted out in a quest for his and he lost himself in the sensation of her hot flesh. She tasted of wine and familiarity, throwing him back to a time when she'd been a major part of his first round of freedom.

Memories zipped by of Cass spread out under him, hips rolling toward his in a sensuous rhythm, hair spread out, her gaze hot and full of anticipation and pleasure as they came together again and again. Memories of her laughing with him, challenging him, filling him.

He wanted her. Just like that. Right now.

He forgot about the hard bench and pulled her closer, nearly into his lap as he let the lace of her dress pleasure his fingers.

She tilted her head, sucking him deeper, her hands sliding across his back, gripping his waist. Driving him wild with the need she'd enflamed with a simple touch. He wanted to feel her again, feel like the world was his for the taking, like life had endless possibilities. How had he not realized that Cass had been such a huge piece of that?

Masterfully, purposefully, she kissed him, breaking down everything he'd thought he was doing here. Everything went out the window: plans, strategy, formulas. Who cared? This was pleasure at its finest and he wanted more.

Then she pulled back, separating from him before he was ready, and his knees went weak. She smiled, her expression heavy with something he couldn't identify.

"Nice," she said conversationally. "And now it's time for the business talk we've been avoiding. Join me when you're done with the pleasure part of the evening."

She stood, swishing away from him on her dangerously sexy heels and sashaying out of the hall. The ice in her spine appeared firmly in place.

Blearily, he watched her go, too floored to call out. That had been hotter than he could have ever imagined. Hotter than it had ever been with Cass in the past. Hotter than he would have credited, given the ice-goddess routine she'd perfected.

He'd goaded her into kissing him in hopes of getting past all that icy reserve, past her CEO exterior, past all this business talk so he could seduce her into his bed. Instead of melting her, he'd learned he wasn't quite over Cassandra Claremont. And she hadn't been affected at all.

That turnabout was anything but fair.

Six

Gage paid the tab and followed Cass out of the restaurant.

Thank God he was behind her. That gave her a good three minutes to get her shakes under control.

It wasn't long enough. By the time they hit the sidewalk and Gage gave the valet his ticket, she'd almost managed to stop hyperventilating.

That kiss still singed her lips. His touch still burned her back. Worse? She'd touched him, too. Her own fingertips had reacquainted themselves with Gage's broad shoulders, thick hair, muscular torso. They'd explored him thoroughly and she ached to memorize him all over again.

She was supposed to be seducing him so she could get some answers about his involvement in her company's problems. Somehow that hadn't happened. She had to get the advantage back. Pronto.

As they waited in tense silence for his Hummer to appear at the curb, she prayed he wouldn't try to corner her again, maybe in one of the shadowy alcoves off to the right, where he could back her up against the brick away from prying eyes and kiss her like that again. Because she could almost feel the bite of that brick against her back. Could almost feel his hands on her. His mouth.

That would be...too much. And it was all she could think about.

"Hi, Cass. I thought that was you."

The enthusiastic female voice on her right snapped her out of the fantasy where Gage had hiked up her dress as he kissed her in that shadowy alcove and... *Get a grip, for crying out loud.*

Cass turned. And her heart tripped as she came face-to-face with Fyra's accounting manager. Who was eyeing Gage with undisguised interest as she gripped her own date's arm.

"Hi, Laurie," Cass croaked before clearing her Gage-riddled throat.

"Fancy seeing you here," Laurie commented and gestured to the man with her. "This is my husband, Mark. You may remember him from the Christmas party? But I haven't had the pleasure," she said to Gage, sticking out her hand in expectation.

Oh, no. This was not the time or place to be caught with a rival CEO. They needed to play it cool and extract themselves without—

"Gage Branson," he announced cheerily, completely ignoring the elbow Cass had just shoved in his ribs.

Too late. She stifled a groan as Laurie's expression lit up.

"Not *the* Gage Branson of GB Skin? I'm a huge fan of your body wash. I use it all the time, but don't tell my husband," she said with a laugh.

Cass glowered at her but Laurie just shrugged. "What?

Ours is too flowery. Men's scents are more outdoorsy. Lemon and sage and such."

Gage grinned. "That's what I like to hear."

The mutual admiration club gained another member when Laurie's husband jumped into the mix to announce his own GB Skin product preferences. This was beyond uncomfortable. Not simply because it grated to hear that Gage had one-upped her, but also because he'd just kissed her.

Could Laurie and Mark tell? Of course they could—she was probably mussed, and she hadn't had a chance to slick on more lipstick. It was a cardinal sin to stand here on the curb with missing makeup. They'd probably noticed her naked lips the moment she'd turned around.

Okay, yes. She'd been kissing the CEO of GB Skin. Cass had kissed Gage. Strictly in the name of finding out whether he'd been the mastermind behind the leak, which had somehow turned into something else.

Her guilty conscience was probably seeping from her pores. She had to get out of here.

Cass gritted her teeth and broke in at an opportune moment. "Laurie, you know we welcome suggestions from employees on Fyra's products. Just send me an email with your thoughts about how to improve the scents in our body wash, and I'll get it into the right hands."

"Oh, I know I shouldn't be gushing over a competitor's products in front of my boss's boss." Laurie's giggle was the opposite of contrite. "But I figured it was okay to admit it. After all, I'm just using the products, not dating the CEO."

"Oh, this isn't a date," Cass interjected swiftly. "Mr. Branson is...uh—"

"Providing consulting services to Ms. Claremont," Gage finished for her smoothly. "Cass and I went to college together and she contacted me to ask for strategic advice."

"That's a pretty fancy dress for a business meeting." Laurie sighed a little over it. "I would love to be able to wear something that sexy."

Her husband murmured something in her ear and she laughed as the valet rolled up in a Lexus. "That's our ride. Nice to meet you."

The couple disappeared into the interior of the car.

"A consultant, Gage? Really?" Cass muttered as the valet parked the Hummer behind the Lexus. A horn blared behind her but she didn't take her focus off the traitor at her shoulder.

"Yeah." He opened her door and helped her into the monstrously high seat without asking. Which she appreciated because she hated needing help.

As he handed her up, she pretended she didn't notice that his fingers brushed her thigh and hung around a little longer than was absolutely necessary. Just like she was pretending she wasn't remembering what had happened a few minutes ago. But noticing was a little hard to stop once she'd opened that Pandora's box.

When he slid into his own seat, he glanced at her. "Would you have rather I corrected you? I can run up to the window of Mark and Laurie's Lexus and let them know it really *is* a date. I'm sure the company grapevine would catch fire as quickly as that news would travel."

"I get the point."

"Thank you, Gage," he mimicked in a high voice. "You're the best, Gage. Your quick thinking saved me, Gage."

A spurt of laughter burst out through her clamped lips. How dare he make her have a good time? He was not allowed to be funny and charming. And sexy. Or such a good kisser. There should be a law.

How in the world did Gage get her to have fun on this date that wasn't a date?

She sobered and crossed her arms. "It wasn't a terrible cover. Now you can come by in the morning to continue digging into the leak. The other girls know you were my mentor and they'll believe me if I say I'm consulting with you."

He shot her an amused once-over, brows raised and she resisted sinking down in the seat.

"Thank you, Gage," she said in a high voice, imitating him mimicking her because she was not about to admit she should have already thanked him. "You're the best, Gage. And so on."

She didn't like how masterfully he'd handled her. It was supposed to be the other way around.

"That's more like it." Oblivious to her sarcasm, he grinned and nodded out the windshield. "Where to?"

Everything rolled off him like water off a duck's back. She wished she had that skill; she had to work at making it *appear* as if she did, when in truth, nothing rolled off. He'd missed teaching her that back in college—how to not care about anything and always squeeze the maximum amount of fun out of everything.

Perhaps she needed to practice. Retreating wouldn't get her what she needed—answers. She threw her shoulders back.

"Turn at the next light," she instructed impulsively. "There's a great little area that overlooks the lake."

As it wasn't too far from her house, she often used the trail for jogging, though she'd never been there at night. The spot had nighttime assignation written all over it.

"Are you asking me to *park*, Ms. Claremont?" The innuendo in his tone was half amused and half *hell, yeah*.

She forced a laugh as he followed her directions and
pulled into the parking lot. "I'm asking you to stroll. It's
a walking path."

They could walk along the secluded moonlit path and
she'd get him comfortable enough so she could ask a few
pointed questions. And then when he least expected it,
she'd move in for the kill.

It was no less than he deserved.

And she'd keep the reminder front and center, no matter how good it felt to be with him again. He'd kissed her.
She'd kissed him back. No big deal. She didn't have to
fall in love with every man she kissed. In fact, she'd never
fallen in love with any man she'd kissed. Except one.

The key here was to work with Gage to find his connection to the leak and go on. A kiss was just a kiss. Emotions didn't belong in the middle of this and she'd make
sure to keep it that way.

No problem.

She wished she didn't have to keep reminding herself
of that.

"There's a gate with a keypad," she called over her
shoulder as they slid from the car. "This part of the lake
is only for residents. Follow me."

The area was secluded, with one dim light that illuminated only a small circle of the concrete lot. Trees marched
away from the lot along the line of the path, sheltering it
from the outside world.

"Sure." Gage's voice had deepened in the dark, skit-
tering along her bare skin and burrowing underneath to
heat up her insides, as if he'd whispered erotic instructions instead of merely agreeing with her.

Lights would be good here. Gage and the dark mixed like oil and water.

Except she didn't have any lights to turn on. The dark blanketed them both as they walked to the gate, wrapping them in a secluded bubble that felt entirely too intimate.

As she punched in the key code, Gage's presence swept along her back, igniting her nerve endings with sensuous heat. He wasn't physically touching her, but she could feel him, hear his breath. Maybe even sense the beat of his heart.

The urge to move backward, flush against his body, almost overtook her and she bit her lip. He'd be warm, solid. Her core flooded with sharp desire and she covered her gasp with a cough.

The key panel flashed red. Wrong code. Dang it.

"Problem?" Gage murmured and leaned forward, decimating the space between their bodies.

Who was she kidding? Gage and darkness went together like chocolate and peanut butter. The dark was where he did his best work, wove his best spells. Wreaked the most destruction.

"I...fat fingered it," she muttered back. "Give me a sec."

She got it right the second time. How, she'd never know.

The gate swung open on well-oiled hinges and that's when the moon blessed her with an appearance, washing the path and the lake below with a silver sheen. Perfect timing. Her nerves couldn't take much more and the dark would only tempt the devil to perform his black magic.

"There's a gazebo a few hundred yards up the path," she murmured. "We can talk."

Yes, talking. She grasped on to the concept like a lifeline, hoping the short walk would allow her to get her brain in working order again. If everything went according to plan, she'd have the solid proof she needed to implicate Gage in the leak and then she could drop him like a hot potato.

Gage, to his credit, strolled to the moonlit gazebo as instructed. The heady scent of man and sage wound through the stillness, distracting her. She never would have identified the faint herbal notes of Gage's aftershave without Laurie's comments in front of the restaurant and now it was all she could do to keep from sticking her nose in the hollow of his shoulder bone.

"So," she said as she glided up the gazebo stairs and leaned on the railing to peer out over the silvery lake. "You must have some great ears to the ground to have such detailed information about my formula."

He leaned against a post, arms crossed, and watched her as if the gorgeous panorama beyond the gazebo didn't exist. "Pardon me if I have very little interest in that subject right this minute."

She glanced at him and he wasn't even bothering to conceal his thoughts. Which must be very naughty indeed judging by the lascivious once-over he gave her. Answering heat gathered in her core, totally against her will.

All at once, she wished for a bunch of clouds to cover the moon. At least in the dark, she could pretend she didn't notice how he had such a beautiful body and gorgeous face, both of which had become more interesting with age. She shuddered as she recalled the way he'd kissed her. More heat flashed across her skin.

Why did he do that to her?

"It's a great subject," she corrected, ignoring the corkscrewing pulls inside her abdomen. "Very important. I'm just curious where you heard about it. If we're going to stop the leak, it might help to work our way backward."

"You think?" he murmured as he unwound from his

casual pose against the post to advance on her. "What if I want to talk about something else?"

She held her ground as he drew up within a hairsbreadth of touching her. "Like what?"

Without hesitation, he grabbed her hand, pulling her flush against him. Her body fell into alignment with his, nestling into the grooves like a mascara wand meeting eyelashes. His arms settled around her and somehow her head tipped back, exposing her throat to his hot perusal.

"Like how it would feel to kiss you when there's no danger of anyone interrupting us."

"Gage," she said and cursed the breathless delivery. She might as well announce how her core had gone liquid the moment his hard muscles came in contact with her curves. "Let go."

"Are you sure that's wise?" he murmured, holding her closer, which she would have sworn was impossible. "You sound a little faint. I wouldn't want you to collapse."

God, he felt good.

She needed to go on a real date, obviously, with a nice man who would treat her well and drink the wine she'd ordered. They'd have a pleasant evening ending with a romantic nightcap at her place and then he'd gently and attentively make love to her.

Above all, when she told him what to do, he'd do it.

"I'm okay. Thanks," she threw in before he started mimicking her again.

"*I'm* not okay." He bent his head to murmur into her ear. "And I like you where you are."

His breath on her skin and his hard thigh between her legs—hell, his voice alone—ripped through her in a whitehot streak of lust.

Insanity. She needed that nice man, pronto, so she could slake this thirst. A couple of rounds with Mr. Gentle-and-

Attentive and she'd be good for another year or so. Gage Branson wouldn't cause so much as a blip on her sex radar.

"This is supposed to be business only," she reminded him, but her voice cracked in the middle of the sentence and she doubted he was listening anyway.

"Hold still."

Eyes on her hair, he reached up and plucked one chopstick from her chignon, tossed it to the wooden slats under their feet and went for the other one as she yelped.

"What are you doing?" she protested as her hair spilled down her back.

"I couldn't help it." His own voice broke as he threaded both hands through the strands, winding up the locks around his fingers, a groan rumbling in his chest that vibrated her rib cage. "Your hair. It's so beautiful. Why do you put it up?"

"It's professiona—"

His mouth hit hers and stole the rest of her words as he kissed her into stunned silence. Hot and wet, his tongue slid through her lips and pleasured her relentlessly.

Tugs at her hair tilted her head back, and he took her deeper into the sensuous haze. She lost all sense of up or down, all sense period because, *oh, yes*, Gage was kissing her again and she wanted it.

The emotional tangle? Not on the agenda. If she could separate business from pleasure, she could surely separate pleasure from love. No broken hearts this time. She'd take a lesson from the King of Fun and have some.

Without warning, he pushed her against the wooden post. It wasn't brick biting into her back. Close enough.

His mouth drifted to her throat as his hands untangled from her hair to cup the back of her head, drawing her against his magic lips. She arched into him, and a moan escaped her throat, echoing in the still night.

All at once, his hands seemed to be everywhere, racing down her sides, at her shoulders. Pushing down the neckline of her dress. Her breasts sprang free of the fabric and he cupped one, bending to draw her taut nipple into his mouth.

She gasped. Exquisite. The pulls of his mouth and tongue buckled her knees but he had her. Yes, he did. He held her firmly in place as he pleasured her with his talented mouth. Shutting her eyes, she let the pleasure fork through her, damp heat gathering at her center until she thought she would burst if he didn't...

He did. One hand snaked under her dress and found her folds beneath the scrap of underwear. The barrier didn't exist to him. Clever fingers danced over her burning flesh, inside. Out.

Anyone could walk by. It heightened the pleasure... somehow. She hissed and opened wider, encouraging him to go deeper. Faster. Her breath came quicker as he drove her relentlessly, sucking at her breast, touching her intimately.

And then one final stroke shattered her resistance. She rode wave after wave of release, crying out at the strength and intensity of the pleasure he'd given her. *Gage.* Smart, funny, tender, amazing Gage. She'd missed him.

That was...not good. Oh, it had been *good.* But somehow he'd gotten below the surface, past her emotional armor.

When she floated back down from the heavens, he was watching her. He leaned in to set her dress back to rights, hands lingering, touching, pleasuring, and he murmured, "Take me back to your place. I want to do that again properly."

Again? She shook off the miasma of Gage and stared up at him, stricken with guilt. That beautiful face stared back at her and she longed to fall into him again without reservation, without fear. Without complications. Without agendas.

What was she *doing*? This wasn't the time to be playing around with fire, not with her career at stake and her company on the brink of disaster. Not when she wasn't sure she could actually stay emotionally uninvolved. She couldn't be vulnerable to him again, couldn't fathom how she'd pick herself up if he flattened her. *Could. Not.*

"I…can't."

And then her throat closed, forcing her to swallow the rest.

His expression blanked and he stepped back, releasing her. "Okay."

His tone said it was anything but. He didn't press her, though, which she was pathetically grateful for. Because if he had, he'd probably have broken down her resistance in about four seconds.

Yeah, she was a whiz at separating business and pleasure. The moment his flesh touched hers, all thoughts of business went out the window and she'd forgotten about digging for his secrets entirely.

That wasn't going to work. She had to get back in the game.

Gage dropped Cass off at her house with a terse goodnight.

They hadn't spoken at all after she shut him down. Apparently, she could flip the ice-goddess switch at will, melting in his arms for a gorgeous orgasm that nearly finished him off, as well, and then hardening her spine right back into place.

He was slipping if that hadn't gotten him an invitation into her bed. Cass had matured in many intriguing ways, but she'd also grown...distant. He had to figure out how to get rid of that space between them or he'd lose his bid for the formula. This was one competition he could not afford to lose.

When he got back to his hotel, frustrated and alone, Arwen greeted him at the door, leash in her mouth. He groaned. Last thing he needed right now. "All right."

Happily, she sniffed her way in the dark to the small park across from his hotel, zigzagging between clumps of bushes as she always did. It got a small smile from him. He hadn't been able to send her home and midnight walks in the park were due penance.

Unfortunately, Arwen didn't talk so he was left with his thoughts for company and they were anything but restful.

This thing with Cass was a problem. She was making him lose his focus on the end game. He still didn't know why she'd asked him to help her or what that silly game at dinner had been about, but one thing was for sure—he'd fully intended to find out. That was before she'd put on that cranberry dress and driven him to thorough distraction.

Of course, his solution to eliminating the distraction had been—and would continue to be—burning off their mutual, insanely hot attraction with a night of uninhibited passion. Then, with that out of the way, they both could concentrate on the business at hand: the leak.

He hoped. He couldn't deny he wanted Cass more fiercely than he could ever recall wanting a woman. Maybe more. He still ached with unfulfilled release and it was an unpleasant reminder that somewhere in the middle of all of this, getting his hands on Cass had started to eclipse getting his hands on her formula. Somehow, his plan to remind her of what she owed him had vanished and become a plan to reacquaint himself with Cass as a lover.

That was an even bigger problem. He was not going home without that formula. So far, he wasn't balancing his two agendas very well.

That changed *la mañana*.

Seven

"Hi, Melinda," he said easily to Fyra's receptionist the next morning. "I have a nine o'clock with Ms. Claremont."

"Good morning, Mr. Branson," she chirped. "She's expecting you."

Looked as though Cass had already cleared the decks for their leak discussion, which was masquerading as a "consulting" gig. The cover story had been quick thinking on his part, if he did say so himself.

He knocked on her open door. Cass was waiting for him, leaning on the front of her desk, arms crossed over a sleek pantsuit. Chopsticks peeked over the edge of her crown and dang if his fingers didn't curl at the sight of them, itching to yank them out.

He tore his gaze away. *Focus.*

"Ready to get to work?" Cass asked coolly as if last night had never happened.

"Sure." He grinned to dispel the heavy vibe and slid

into one of the chairs on the visitor's side of the desk. No power plays today. None of them had worked anyway.

Well…they'd worked to a degree. After all, he'd had Cass in his arms twice last night. That was progress. Very hot, very spectacular progress. His body sprang fully alert.

Focus, he reminded himself.

"I have a couple of thoughts I wanted to run by you," she said.

She seemed agitated, though he couldn't put his finger on what had given him that impression when she closely resembled an ice sculpture. A subtlety in her tone, maybe.

"Do any of them start with *Gage* and end with the word *naked*?"

Cass's mouth tightened. So that hadn't been the best tactic, even though he'd been kidding in an attempt to lighten the mood. Mostly. He could no sooner forget his outrageous attraction to her than he could leave without the formula. The dual agendas were supposed to complement each other, not be at war. It was killing him.

"Not in the slightest." The frost in her voice needed to go. "I've already done a couple of hours' worth of research. Now that you're here, I want to go over my notes with you."

Would she balk if he yanked her into his lap and kissed that frown upside down? Since the door was open, he resisted. But only just. And only for now.

It was better to deal with business during daylight hours. Probably.

"All right. Lay it on me. I am a fount of advice."

Her brow raised as if she didn't quite believe him. "I haven't even told you what I've got yet. How do you know you'll have anything valuable to contribute?"

"I'm motivated. Plus, you of all people should be aware of my résumé when it comes to that."

"Well, then. I'm dying to hear it, O Sage One."

Maybe her mood wasn't as volatile as he'd assumed if she was making jokes.

Memories of her, hot and pliant in his arms, damp heat against his fingers, all that hair like silk in his fingers... yeah.

It was totally worth taking a shot.

"My first piece of advice is to relax," he said smoothly. Cass hadn't moved an iota from her no-nonsense pose against the desk. Gage couldn't work his charm with her so uptight. "Second, I advise you to have dinner with me again tonight. But let's actually eat this time."

Other than a slight eye roll, she held herself impressively frozen with not even a leg tremor to give away her thoughts. "I can't display that on a presentation at a board meeting. I need results and I need them today."

"Then sit down and let's hash it out," he suggested with a nod at the other chair. "I'm starting to feel as though I was called to the principal's office the way you're towering over me."

With a piercing side eye aimed pointedly in his direction, she perched on the other chair but he had the distinct impression she didn't like the idea. He held his hands up in silent promise to keep them to himself, which she acknowledged with a muttered, "Yeah, we'll see."

The truth was he had as much of an interest in finding the leak and plugging it as Cass did—if nothing else, he wasn't prepared to hand over one single dollar until it was handled, or his investment would be worthless.

Nor could he afford to let the leak take the formula public. Then someone else might get the upper hand. The issues inside Cass's company needed to be resolved.

"Talk to me about your notes." When she hesitated, he

stuck his palms under his butt, and widened his eyes in an exaggerated *okay*? "Come on."

It was so subtle, he almost missed it. But he was watching her closely enough to pinpoint the exact moment she relaxed. The victory shot through him with a sharp thrill.

"My theory is that the leak came from someone in the lab. Has to be. No one else outside of the four founders knows how the formula works."

He'd considered that, too, and it was probably true, but she couldn't make broad assumptions. "Anyone could have hacked into your database or paid off a janitor to steal Harper's notes."

"True. But I don't think that's how it happened. So I'm thinking about planting some false information and watermarking the files. If it gets leaked, I can trace it back."

"Digital forensics? Like what banks use when they're hacked? That's expensive."

"Formula-47 is worth millions of dollars. Maybe billions."

Yes, absolutely. But you had to spend money where it made sense. "Regardless, you'd have to wait until the leak found the information and hope he or she didn't realize that the transferred files could be traced, then you have to assume the leak will decide to spill it, wait for the news to hit the industry and then try to track down who accessed the file on your server. You don't have that long."

Her lips pursed but she didn't give away anything else of her thoughts. "That's exactly why I wanted to run this by you. I knew you'd find the holes if there were any."

That small compliment from a tough customer like Cass held more weight than he would have imagined. It spread through his chest warmly. He could get used to that. Get used to combining business and pleasure in exactly this way, with a woman who could match him mentally and physically.

That's a new experience you can get behind.

Except it wasn't exactly new. This was like old times, but better because they were equals.

"It's not rocket science. I've just been around a while. Failed a lot early on and learned a few things. No big deal," he said, and he ducked his head.

She swept him with a once-over laden with—dare he hope it—some heat?

"You'll forgive me if I disagree. It's is a big deal. You're the CEO of a billion-dollar company for a reason. And I'm not. Also for a reason." Her self-deprecating shrug spoke volumes.

"Hey. You're being too hard on yourself."

Her gaze flew to his and something raw flashed in the depths, a stricken sense of anxiety. The brief spurt of emotion in her eyes sucked him in instantly, spreading through him with equal parts warmth and a desire to fix it. He almost reached out then to comfort her.

Because she needed him that way, too. And he liked being needed by a strong, independent woman like Cass.

It had nothing to do with sex, nothing to do with business—or even fun—and everything to do with why he'd recalled their relationship so fondly. Why he'd wanted to revive that between them. He liked being her go-to guy, being there for her. How had he walked away from that so easily?

Better yet, how did he keep it going now?

"Am I? How many times has one of your employees spilled company secrets?" she asked, and he didn't like how matter-of-fact she was about it.

She'd accomplished something really fantastic here at

Fyra. Insisting that a blip like the leak overshadowed that riled him up but good.

"That's not a yardstick," he insisted right back. "If it was, then you could also compare yourself to the CEOs of companies that went bankrupt or employed executives that ended up in orange jumpsuits. You're a star in comparison."

Her amused smile heated his blood unnaturally fast.

And if he could get Cass on the same page, this conversation could very well explode into something that didn't need words.

Cass let her smile widen.

She had Gage exactly where she wanted him. It had taken her a bit to shift the mood and even longer to convince Gage his charm was working on her. At this point, he was so busy flirting and shooting her heated glances, he was scarcely paying attention to the matter at hand—the leak. Advantage Cassandra.

Keeping it was another story.

"You really think so?" She leaned into him, letting her arm casually brush Gage's. His gaze darkened. "That means a lot to me."

"This is not the conversation I thought we were going to have." He shifted closer, crowding into her space and she almost flinched as the contact sang through her but caught herself in time.

That episode last night, up against the gazebo post, had kept her tossing and turning all night long. She couldn't forget it. She might never be able to jog by that gazebo again without reliving the feel of Gage's mouth on her flesh and the intensity of his heated gaze on her bare breasts as he watched her climax under his talented fingers.

It was enough to make her want to corner him, strip

him naked and let the passion between them come to conclusion. Where she got to watch *him* fall apart at *her* hands.

Which she totally planned to do…while extracting the information she needed. She could not, under any circumstances, let him dissolve that goal like he'd done last night. No more would she let her emotions run away with her. It was all business, all the time, especially while she was seducing him.

This was her career at stake, and the careers of her friends, poised to vanish into thin air if she didn't produce the name of the person responsible for disclosing company secrets.

Fyra was her life and no man could replace it. Especially not this one.

"This conversation is better," she said with a tiny smile guaranteed to pique his interest. "For example, I was just about to take your advice and ask you to dinner tonight. At my place."

That got his attention. He sat up so fast, his back teeth clacked together. "Don't toy with me, woman."

Oh, but he was so fun to toy with, especially as she gave him a taste of his own medicine.

"Does that mean you don't want to come?" she purred. "Or do you want me to tack the dinner discussion to the end of today's agenda?"

"Now I'm dying to know what topics we have to get through to reach that particular item."

"Business," she said firmly. "Then pleasure."

His hazel eyes lit up and a wicked smile spread across his face. "Just so you know, the fact that you label dinner at your place as pleasure warms my heart tremendously."

She held off the shiver because he didn't need to know he'd affected her *that* way. He *shouldn't* be affecting her that way. Her armor—the shield she easily employed with other men—seemed to soften far too easily when he was around.

"Business," she repeated. "We have to make more progress on the leak. The news broke on Monday. It's Thursday morning. I'm no closer to plugging the blabbermouth than I was then."

She'd done a considerable amount of digging this morning on her own and had found a couple of promising leads. Right before Gage had arrived, she'd ordered the most high-level background check money could buy on every last employee in this company. But he didn't have to know that. In reality, she didn't want him anywhere near her files or embroiled in a real discussion about her strategy.

His job was to tell her what his connection was to the leak. What strings he was pulling. Which angles he was playing. She needed to uncover every last secret, especially when he looked at her like he was right now, like he wanted to finish what he'd started last night in the gazebo.

Because as soon as she handed him over to the authorities, then she could remind herself with cold hard facts that he was the spawn of Satan. Somehow she kept forgetting that.

"It's a problem," he agreed far too easily.

Suspicious of his capitulation, she nodded. "Right. We find the leak and then we can think about pursuing a... personal relationship."

She caressed the term with her voice as suggestively as she could. She had to regain the upper hand.

"Oh, no, sweetheart," he growled. "You have it all backward. That orgasm last night? Only the beginning of what's in store for you. For both of us. It's an absolute necessity that we start there and then worry about the leak."

His heavy, masculine vibe snaked through the room,

engulfing her. Tempting her down the wrong path, where she craved that pleasure, that connection more than anything else. "That makes no sense."

His intense gaze zeroed in on her and she felt it deep inside, where he'd thoroughly woken up her latent sex drive. He didn't move, didn't touch her, and somehow that was more powerful than if he had.

"It's the only thing that makes sense. We're not going to get anything accomplished until this fire between us is extinguished. Admit it. You know it's true."

She hated to say it…but he might have a point. Worse, she couldn't think of one solid argument against it, but she had to try as a matter of principle. "That's your logic? We're not disciplined enough to work together so we should just screw around instead?"

He didn't flinch. "If you want logic, then do it for the best reason of all. You want to. And I want you, Cassandra."

His deep voice caressed her name, unleashing another wave of desire that grew very hard to contain. This was a seduction, plain and simple, but she'd lost track of who was seducing whom. Besides, dragging it out wouldn't change things. It was just sex. She wasn't going to fall for him again. Why deny herself what she wanted?

Maybe she'd failed thus far to get him to admit anything incriminating because she really needed to get him naked first. Naked and sated.

"I dug up some paper archives from Harper's research over the past few years that have names of the employees attached to each stage of the development. Can we at least pretend to do some work tonight?" she asked as the compelling force of his smile nearly drew her into his space, magnetically, like she'd transformed into a pile of metal pins straining toward him.

"Sure. If that's what turns you on, I'm game."

"Be at my place at seven." Her turf, her rules. And there was no way she'd let him get to her like he'd done last night. Ruthless detachment was the only way. "I'll bring the files and you bring the drinks since you're such a big baby about wine. I have until tomorrow to report progress back to the other executives. So we definitely have to do *some* work."

Hopefully she'd discover she did her best work between the sheets.

He grinned and saluted. "Wear something sexy and I'll read every one of those files word for word."

She'd removed all the proprietary information from the files and her employee's names were posted on the company website, so she had no qualms about sharing that information with him. With enough incentive, he might slip up and clue her in that he recognized one of the names. "It's a deal."

She just had to be very careful to ensure the only slipping going on was on his side.

Eight

Later that night, Gage picked up a bottle of cachaça, some limes and a bag of brown sugar, just in case Cass didn't have any on hand. Caipirinhas were a far sight more tolerable than margaritas, and women usually loved the way he made them. Plus the drink was about 85 percent alcohol, which gave a nice buzz but, because cachaça was distilled from sugarcane, the next morning didn't come with a busting headache.

On his way to Cass's house, Gage dropped Arwen off at a doggie daycare. With that heartbreaking task out of the way, he drove to Cass's house. She was worth a furious vizsla and the probability of an additional fee upon pickup after Arwen drove everyone at the daycare to the brink of insanity.

Cass opened the door, barefoot and clad in shorts that showed a mile of leg, thank the good Lord, and a fitted T-shirt that most women couldn't have done justice. On

Cass, it was legendary. She'd twisted her hair up in a messy waterfall of a hairdo that was somehow more suggestive than the chopsticks.

His mouth went dry.

"Hey," she said, opening the door wider, which lifted the hem of her T-shirt just a flash, revealing a slice of bare stomach. "Hope casual is okay. I thought low-key might help us get some work accomplished tonight."

Yeah, no. She needed a better mirror if she thought that what she had on was supposed to provide some kind of Gage repellant. Her toes were hot pink, for crying out loud, which drew his attention to her bare feet again and again.

"Oh, good," he said when he could speak. "I was worried I wouldn't be able to keep my hands off you. *Whew.*"

He mimed wiping his brow in relief and she shot him a sunny smile that heightened the flame inside his gut.

She motioned him inside and called over her shoulder. "Should we start on the paperwork first, then? Maybe later we can have a drink and relax."

Seriously?

"That was sarcasm," he said bluntly as he blew over the threshold, shutting the door behind him with a loud bang.

She whirled, clearly startled by the sudden noise, and smacked into his chest. Right where he wanted her. He set down his bag of goodies—caipirinhas had totally lost his interest.

"If you wanted me to keep my hands off you," he growled, hauling her into his arms. "A better plan would have been to move to Timbuktu."

He hustled her backward, against the wall, and shoved a thigh between her legs. Hard and high. She gasped, a throaty sound that crawled inside him and lit the fuse of a row of fireworks residing in his groin, threatening to explode without notice.

"In case you're not clear on this," he continued, nipping at her ear as he leaned in. The full body contact sang through him. "I want you. *Now.* Not later."

Her nipples pebbled against his chest as he rolled his hips to fit more snuggly against hers. Those shorts were made of much thinner fabric than he'd guessed and her heat engulfed his steel-hard lower half. Lust licked through his blood like a wildfire.

He needed her hot and pliant immediately, before he lost it. There was no way she would get the opportunity to leave him hanging like she had last night. Oh, he'd enjoyed every second of making her come against that post, moonlight spilling over her gorgeous body, while they were both fully dressed. It had ranked as one of the hottest experiences of his life. But tonight he deserved a turn, too.

He ached to reacquaint himself with her body, the way she tasted, the way she would respond to his touch. That T-shirt, soft under his fingers, promised delights underneath it and he was game to discover them.

No one was around and they had all night. He planned to make the most of it.

They gazed at each other and the ocean of desire in her eyes twisted through him. She was inside him already and he welcomed her with a sense of awe. How had she made him feel this way before they'd scarcely gotten started?

"I want you," he repeated hoarsely, but the phrase scarcely encompassed the sheer need he was trying to describe, as if he depended on her for his next breath. "And not because you're wearing a sexy outfit. Because you have a brain. Because you challenge me. Because I like being around you. Because—"

"If you're going to kiss me, shut up and do it."

"That might be the sexiest thing you've ever said."

Because it suited him, he tilted her head back and took her mouth with his, open and wet, pleasing them both with the force of his tongue. She tasted of fire and woman and he wanted more. So he went deeper, coaxing her to meet him with increased passion. No holding back. No ice goddess, not tonight.

Apparently of the same mind, she moaned and shifted against his thigh, her fingers working at his waistband. She pulled his shirt free and spread her palms across his back. Oh, yeah. *Heaven.* He'd captured his very own angel. Her touch raced down his spine and dipped into his pants, resting on his butt. She shoved, grinding his erection against her.

Nothing angelic about that.

Sensation exploded. In his body. In his head. She was taking over, taking her own pleasure, and he was hard-pressed to find an argument against it. Bolder now, she rubbed against his shaft, nearly finishing him off. He clawed back the release through will alone.

With her barriers down, she was hotter than he'd imagined. Duly noted.

With a groan, he fumbled with the hem of her shirt and finally, his fingers closed around it. Gone. Next? Bra. Also gone.

Her gorgeous breasts fell into his palms, heavy and hot. She was made for him, filling his hands perfectly. Locking his lips onto one erect nipple, he swirled his tongue around it as he worked the rest of her clothes into a heap, desperate to have her flesh against his. His pulse beat in his throat as she stripped him in kind, then urged him on with her hands against his thighs.

"Wait, darling," he murmured, and in moments, he'd sheathed himself with a condom.

Boosting her up against the wall, he slid into her heat and pinned her in place, reveling in the perfection of her tightness. *Yes.* Exactly where he belonged. Inside her.

She wrapped her legs around him and thrust her hips, drawing him deeper. And deeper still. She gasped out tiny moans of pleasure that drove him wild.

He needed to touch her…but he couldn't let go or she'd fall. From this angle, the sensation was unbelievable. Then she widened her hips, changing the pressure and his moans mingled with hers.

This wasn't the Cass he recalled. This woman was on fire, taking what she wanted, giving unconditionally. Finding his pleasure center easily and drawing him higher and higher, against his will. He'd planned to savor. To reclaim.

But this Cass, who was every inch his equal, was claiming him, wholly.

He couldn't hold back one second longer, but somehow managed to get a thumb between their bodies, stimulating her the way she'd always preferred and that set her off. At last. The ripples of her climax closed around him a moment before his answering climax exploded.

Sweet, blessed release. He shut his eyes and drove home one last time, drawing out the pleasure for them both. When he could feel his legs again, he swung her around and slid to the ground, still holding her in his lap. He tilted his head against hers, both of them breathless, chests heaving from exertion.

That had been…something else. Nothing like it had been before. It had been hot and erotic and the stuff of X-rated fantasies. She'd always been amazing but they'd never gotten so caught up that they couldn't make it to the bed. They were still in her foyer. He'd meant to be gentler, less frenzied. He'd envisioned a slow, sweet reintroduction to each other, but who could complain about a fast, unbelievably intense reintroduction?

Thankfully, they'd gotten that out of their systems.

"Maybe now we can concentrate," he muttered. But he didn't think so.

Cass ended up ordering pizza from the place around the corner. After the hallway gymnastics, her bones had melted away entirely and she couldn't stand long enough to cook. Gage had been amazing. Strong, tender, hot, sweet. Far more so than she'd expected or remembered.

True to his word, he got down to business and they read files while drinking a pitcher of the limey, sugary concoction he'd put together. It was delicious. But not as delicious as Gage. Or the conversation they fell into as they were reading. It was like old times—and her insides, which were not all that solid in the first place, mushed under the dual onslaught of sexy man and alcohol.

Names. She needed to focus on these names. She steeled her spine, hardened her heart and ignored all the sizzling sidelong glances he shot her way.

This was about sex and work. Only. After all, he'd practically dared her to prove she could separate business and pleasure. No emotions necessary for that.

She had Gage read the names out loud and as he did, she offered her impression of the person, their work ethic, any workplace drama she knew of. As she talked, she watched Gage carefully for any flicker of recognition. Nothing. Either he was very good at keeping his cards close to the vest or the leak's name wasn't on this list.

Of course, deep inside she recognized the possibility that he wasn't involved. The longer they spent in each other's company, the more she'd started to hope that he wasn't. Because if his interest in the formula was innocent, then it changed everything between them.

And she wanted that. Oh, how she wanted things to be different, with the possibility of throwing their agendas out the window and just connecting as man and woman.

It was madness. Gage could not be trusted under any circumstances and obviously sex had only confused things, not clarified them. She kicked him out before she started imagining things that were impossible, like asking him to stay and hold her all night.

He left without arguing, which dug under her skin and sat there irritating her for no apparent reason. Why? He'd done what she asked—what more could she want? Gage did not belong in her bed. That was reserved for men who wanted to stick around and he wasn't the type. A few days and then *gone*.

She knew that. But that didn't stop all the needy dreams during the long night where he curled around her in bed and stroked her hair and told her everything was going to be okay, that he was here for her and she didn't have to be strong with him. That he understood her and cared about her.

Clearly a dream—Gage Branson wasn't marriage material and she didn't need a man who whispered pretty lies in her ear about the state of things. There was no guarantee even one blessed thing in her life would turn out okay. The investigative work she'd done on her own time hadn't amounted to much and Gage hadn't given up any information either, which meant she was still at square one.

Around 5:00 a.m. she crawled from the big, lonely bed and tried to rinse Gage off her body and soul with a hot shower. It was Friday. Reckoning day. Trinity had scheduled a meeting with the four executives to hear Cass's progress report on the leak. It was shaping up to be a short meeting because she had nothing to report.

It took twice as long as normal to do her makeup, partly due to her shaking hands and partly due to the necessity of taking extra care to present her best "I've got this" face to the world. Then, she dressed carefully in a black suit with a knee-length skirt and red silk shell. The look radiated power and control and she needed both today.

By nine, the other ladies filed in to take their customary seats around the conference table. Cass had been in her chair for fifteen minutes, going over nonexistent notes, and calming her nerves. It should have been the other way around. Lots of progress, cool as a cucumber.

There was a distinct possibility she might throw up.

New fine lines around Harper's eyes spoke to the heightened level of stress on Fyra's chief science officer. She'd been clocking long hours in anticipation of presenting Formula-47 for FDA approval, perhaps in vain if Cass didn't get with the program. Trinity tapped one foot, impatient and ready to draw blood the moment someone presented their jugular. *Someone* was about to be Cass, she had a feeling. Eyes on her legal pad, Alex wore a slight frown, as if this boardroom was the last place she wanted to be and Cass had interrupted the CFO's more important agenda items for the day.

"Thanks for taking time from your busy Friday to hear my progress report," Cass began smoothly and squared her tablet, trying to get her emotions under control. She'd failed to do her job and her partners needed to know it, no matter how hard it was to admit she didn't have it all together.

If only she'd gotten some sleep last night, her emotions wouldn't be riding so close to the surface. If only she'd checked her mushy heart at the door when Gage came over, she could have gone all night with him and maybe extracted something useful. Instead, she'd kicked him out because she couldn't control anything, let alone herself.

"I'll cut to the chase," Cass said and met the gaze of each of her partners in turn. "I haven't found anything yet."

The three women's expressions ranged from disbelief to anger.

Alex spoke first. "What do you mean, you haven't found anything yet? You've had all week." She sank down in her chair an inch, as if Cass's news had physically added weight to her shoulders, which increased the general despair in the room. "This is awful. We should have involved the authorities from the beginning."

"We couldn't have," Cass reminded her. She cleared the catch from her throat. They'd had this discussion on Monday when the trade magazine had hit the industry and again on Tuesday in their board meeting. "Mike said the article was too vague, remember? We don't have any recourse but to investigate ourselves."

"Which has failed miserably." Alex crossed her arms and stared at Cass. "We trusted you with this. We could have all been working on it but you said you'd handle it. What, exactly, did you do all week?"

Cass took the harsh question without flinching. "I have a list of suspects. Everyone who's had their hands on Formula-47 over the past two years and could reasonably understand how it works."

The betrayer's name was on that list—she knew it like she knew her own face. How else would Gage's additional information about Fyra's yet-to-be-released product offering be so accurate? It was the only explanation. Now she just had to find a way to prove it. And convince the others to give her more time.

Trinity's chair squeaked as she swiveled it toward Cass. "So the article is too vague to involve the authorities, but when your old boyfriend shows up with more detailed information, that's not enough to go to the cops?"

Heat flushed through Cass's cheeks. Blushing? Really? She never did that. Thankfully, Harper's color-correcting foundation should hide the worst of it. "I'm working that angle. In case he's involved."

"Oh." Light dawned in Trinity's expression. "I thought that whole consulting thing was weird. I was convinced Gage was hanging around in hopes of swooping in for another chance to break your heart. It never occurred to me that you were the one working him. Good for you."

Alex's brows snapped together. "What, like you're sleeping with him to find out if he coordinated the leak? That's horrible."

A squeak of denial almost escaped Cass's clamped lips.

But she couldn't deny it. That was exactly what she was doing, but hearing it from Alex did make it sound horrible. Something sad crawled through her chest and she couldn't breathe.

Why? They were just fooling around anyway. Nothing serious was going on, so it wasn't as if he was going to get *his* heart broken. She wasn't even sure he had one to break.

And *how* in God's name had her friends figured out so quickly that she and Gage weren't strictly business associates this time around? Somehow this whole conversation had become a cross-examination of Cass's sex life.

"It's brilliant," Trinity insisted. "Men do stuff like that all the time and no one thinks anything of it. About time we turn the tables. Screw him and then screw him over, Cass."

Finally Trinity was defending her, and if only she hadn't been so enthusiastic about Cass's new status as a ballbreaker, it might have made Alex's accusations more tolerable.

"It's true," Cass admitted. "I'm keeping my eye on him from close quarters just in case he lets something incriminating slip."

"Was that before or after he seduced away your good sense?" Alex asked derisively. "You'll forgive me if I find your investigative techniques suspect. No one can fully separate business from sex. It's impossible."

Not for me.

Cass started to say it out loud, to defend herself against Alex's blatant charge that she'd compromised Fyra due to her personal relationship with Gage, such as it was. She should tell them unequivocally that she wouldn't allow a naked man to distract her from what she knew she needed to do.

But she couldn't say it. What if Gage *was* involved in the leak and she missed it because she was too busy daydreaming about him magically transforming into someone she could count on? That very possibility was exactly the reason the board meeting had descended into girl talk about the man Cass was boinking—because everyone thought she might be compromised.

Ridiculous. She was compartmentalizing just fine. The person responsible for the leak was keeping a low profile, that was all. If Gage knew anything about it, he'd trip up before long.

"Give me a few more days," she pleaded. "I know what I'm doing."

Throwing her pen down on her pad with considerable force, Alex shook her head. "No. We don't have a few more days."

Heart in her throat, Cass evaluated the other two girls,

who glanced at each other. Trinity shrugged. "I'm game for it. I kind of want to see what happens with lover boy."

Harper narrowed her gaze and flipped her ponytail over her shoulder. "Gage Branson treated you like dog food in college, Cass. While he's lighting your fire, don't fool yourself into thinking he's changed."

Red stained Harper's cheeks, likely as a result of holding back her legendary hot temper, which Cass appreciated. Alex's hostility was heartbreaking enough without adding another longtime friend to the other side of the fence.

"I've got that under control, too," Cass assured them, ignoring that sad ping inside that had only gotten worse the longer the conversation went on.

Of course Gage hadn't changed. Fortunately, Cass's eyes were wide open and soon she'd be watching him disappear down the highway. It was a fact, and wishing things could be different didn't mean she was fooling herself.

Alex's sigh was long-suffering. "This is a mistake. Have all of you forgotten that Gage runs a company that eats into our profits every stinking quarter? He's our competition, just as much as Lancôme and MAC."

And that was the bottom line in all of this. How fitting that Fyra's CFO would be the one to point that out. In marked contrast to the last time they'd been in this room, Alex's contrariness and lack of confidence had roots in reality, and that sobered Cass faster than anything else could have.

"No one's forgotten that, least of all me," Cass countered quietly. "Why do you think I'm cozying up to him? Give me a few more days."

"Fine," Alex conceded wearily. "I don't see how you're going to prove Gage is involved in the leak while he's got his tongue in your mouth, but whatever. We don't have a lot of choices."

As victories went, it felt hollow. With the leak still undetected, the company could come down like a house of cards. She got that. But it twisted her stomach to have her strategy so cold-bloodedly laid out for her. Yes, she'd planned to keep Gage close for exactly the reasons they'd discussed, but all at once, the idea didn't sit well. Gage had been…fun thus far. Almost like a friend. A confidante. Everything a lover should be. What if he *wasn't* involved?

She liked it better when her partners had been in the dark about her covert plans.

Abnormally quiet, they left the boardroom, and miraculously Cass made it all the way to her office before the shakes started. Nothing helped calm her nerves—coffee, water, a brisk walk at lunch. She had to get it together, had to find a way to produce results.

If Gage was involved in the leak, she had to figure out a way to prove it. To prove she could compartmentalize and that he wasn't affecting her ability to do her job, once and for all. She buckled down and pored over files and personnel records until she thought her eyes would bleed.

Around three o'clock, her phone vibrated and Gage's name flashed on the screen. She read the text message.

I'm in the parking lot. Ditch work and play hooky with me.

For God knew what reason, that put a smile on her face. That sounded like the perfect short-term solution to her problems.

Nine

The dark green Hummer sat in the same parking spot as it had the first time Gage had visited Fyra, under a large oak tree saved when the developers poured the concrete for Fyra's new building.

Shade nearly obscured the monstrosity of a vehicle, but Cass found it easily. With a heightened sense of anticipation, she dashed across the parking lot in hopes of hopping into the Hummer before anyone saw her.

After the unproductive day she'd had, the last thing she should be doing was leaving work at three o'clock. In her current mood, it was the only thing she could have done. Besides, this was exactly where she was supposed to be. She'd promised the others she'd make progress with Gage and the leak. No one had to know she was happy to see him.

Hooky. It used to be one of their favorite code words and it still had the same punch. Maybe more because she was skipping out on the enormous pressure inside the walls of her company instead of a boring lecture in a drafty hall. A little thrill shot through her as she clambered up into the passenger seat of Gage's car.

God, this sucked. She'd rather pretend they didn't have any more complications between them apart from where to go so they could spend an illicit couple of hours together. Strictly in the name of sex, of course. Instead, she'd spend their time together with both eyes wide open for any signs of his involvement in her company's troubles.

"Hey," Gage said, flashing her a mischievous smile. "I thought I was in for at least a couple of rounds of sexy text messages designed to get you out of your purple cave. Silly me. If I'd have known all it was going to take was one, I'd have been by at lunchtime."

"It's Friday." She waved it off as if she left early on Friday all the time, which was a flat-out lie. "I needed the break."

Especially if the break involved the man she should be sticking to like Velcro—and not because he was lickable. Which he was.

Concern filled his gaze as he pulled out of the Fyra lot. "Rough day?"

God, she was slipping. How had he realized that instantly? Gage shouldn't be the one person who saw through her, the only person who looked at her long enough to see her internal struggles.

She started to deny it but couldn't. What would be the point? "Yeah."

He drove in silence for a few minutes, but veered off the road after only a couple of miles. The Hummer rolled to a stop under the shade of a large oak tree near a deserted park.

"Come here," he commanded as he pulled her into his arms easily despite the gearshift and steering wheel.

She should have struggled more. Should have pushed him away. Sex only, nothing more. That's why she was here—for a much-needed release at the hands of a man very capable of delivering it.

But his soothing touch bled through her and nothing else could penetrate the little bubble surrounding her and Gage as he held her. *Nothing*, not the various parts of the car, not all the weight of Fyra's troubles, not the difficult past between them.

Everything faded under his tender strokes against her skin. She'd needed this, needed him. Needed someone to be there to catch her when she fell, to be on her side. His shirt was soft against her cheek and his woodsy scent filled her head, spreading the oddest sense of peace through her chest.

A tickle in her hair alerted her to the presence of his fingers a moment before both chopsticks slid free, releasing the tight chignon. Her scalp nearly cried in relief as her hair billowed down her back. He gathered the strands in his strong hands, winding them around his palms. Threading them through to his knuckles. Caressing her back.

It was relaxing and stimulating at the same time. How was that possible? But with the binding hairstyle gone, a weight lifted, almost as if he'd studied her and pinpointed precisely what she'd needed.

A groan rumbled in Gage's chest, vibrating her own, and in a snap, the atmosphere shifted. Awareness spread across her skin, sensitizing it. Switching cheeks, she rested her head in the hollow of his shoulder, but oh look, there was Gage's ear just a millimeter from her lips.

Grazing it lightly, she inhaled him, letting his powerful masculinity wash through her. The slow tide picked up speed, flowing like lava toward her toes, heating her in its wake.

Riding the flood, she arched her back, pushing her aching breasts against his chest, seeking more of his touch. She nipped at his throat, slowly working her way back to the tender lobe. When her teeth closed around it, he exhaled hard. It was ragged and thrilling, filling her with bold desire.

She licked him and oh, yes, he tasted amazing. *More.* And then his mouth was on hers and she drank from him, drawing out even more of that essence she craved. Hot and masterful, he kissed her back, meeting her tongue thrusts with his own, changing the angles to go deeper, and she moaned under the onslaught of sensation and Gage and everything she'd been missing for so long.

"Cass," he murmured against her mouth. "Let me take you to my hotel. It's five minutes away."

Five whole minutes? Too long. She didn't bother to respond and pulled him half into her seat as she went on a survey of that wicked, gorgeous body.

He sucked in a breath as she dipped into his pants and found the heated length of flesh she craved. So hard and thick and she wanted it. "Now, Gage. Don't make me wait."

With a curse, he pushed her hands off his body and moved from behind the steering wheel to slide into her seat, shoving her against the door. He promptly picked her up and resettled her on his lap, facing him, and watched her with a hooded, wicked glint to those hazel eyes as he pushed his palms against the hem of her skirt. The fabric gathered under his hands, riding up to her waist where he grabbed on and fitted their hips together, aligning his hard shaft against her center.

Perfect. Almost. Not enough. She rolled her hips, grinding against him and the answering shadow of lust shooting through his gaze heightened her own pleasure.

Without another word, he cupped her head with both hands and pulled her against his mouth, ravishing her with a long, wet kiss. Frantically, blindly, she worked at his pants until he sprang free into her eager hands. Her very own velvet-wrapped present. With her first stroke, his head fell back against the seat, flopping his too-long hair against his forehead and he groaned, eyes tightly shut.

That was…inspiring. She did it again, awed that she could command the body of such a powerful man.

"Back pocket," he rasped. "Hurry."

She wasted no time rolling on the condom. Pushing up on her thighs, she guided him to her entrance and plunged until they joined fully in one swift rush. They moaned in tandem as he flung his arms around her to hold her in place, rocking her so sensuously, so soul deep, she felt tears pricking at her eyelids. He filled her body, filled her head, filled every millimeter of *her*.

"So good." His breath fluttered in her ear as he read her mind. "Open for me."

To demonstrate, he widened her hips, nestling himself even closer to her.

Slowly, more slowly than she'd thought possible for a man on a mission, he drew her mouth to his and laid his lips against it. Savoring. He explored her as if they had all the time in the world, and as if she wasn't about to scream, and just as she thought she'd come out of her skin if he didn't move, he thrust his hips, driving deeper inside her.

She gasped and the rush overwhelmed her, pounding in her chest, at her center. Her vision darkened as he slid home again and again, and then his thumb found the true center of her pleasure, swirling against it with exactly the right pressure to set her off like a lit stick of dynamite.

The release rolled through her thickly, gathering power as she exploded over and over. She slumped against his chest as he cried out her name hoarsely, tensing through his own climax.

He held her gently, wrapped tight in his arms as if he never planned to let go. She sank down into the ocean of Gage. He surrounded her and she couldn't kick her way to the surface. Didn't want to. This was sheer bliss and it wasn't just due to the sex.

It was Gage. Only him.

"That was amazing," he murmured into her hair. "Now can we go to my hotel?"

"No." She snuggled deeper into his embrace, her nose against his neck where it smelled the most like well-loved man. "Take me home. And stay."

A mistake. He'd cracked open something inside her that should have been sealed shut.

Except she was so tired of pretending she didn't feel anything. So tired of bottling up her emotions and trying to prove she had it all together when in fact, she didn't.

Gage didn't care. He was leaving soon anyway, so why keep up pretenses? It was kind of freeing, knowing how it would end. She didn't have to worry about him breaking her heart because she wasn't going to give it to him. He didn't have to know she harbored all these feelings for him.

"That sounds like an idea I can get behind," he growled. "Or on top of, in front of, against the wall, in the shower. All of the above."

Too late to take it back now. And besides, she should have had the presence of mind to invite him deliberately. Because what better way to keep tabs on him than if they were together around the clock? That's where her mind *should* have been at.

"Stay the weekend. I know you have to go back to Austin Sunday night but until then? We'll order lots of takeout and never get dressed."

"That's a deal, Ms. Claremont."

His slow, sexy smile felt like a reward and she planned to grab her spoils with both hands. She'd spend the weekend enjoying herself and, as a bonus, she'd make solid progress on investigating Gage's involvement in the leak, just like she'd promised her partners. With the man in question in her bed, surely she could sneak a glance through his phone or keep an ear out in case he talked in his sleep. It was the best of both worlds and she didn't even have to feel guilty about it because she was looking out for Fyra first and foremost.

The other stuff—the emotional knot—wasn't a factor. She wouldn't let it be. She had to buckle on her armor a bit tighter while around Gage, that was all.

Gage untangled their clothes, hair and bodies, helping her resituate everything and then climbed back into the driver's seat. Fortunately, the park was still deserted or that would have been a helluva show.

She had one short weekend to get results on her quest for a name…before the other girls made a motion to relieve her of her position as head of the company she'd helped build from nothing.

Gage stopped by the hotel to pick up Arwen and his luggage, then checked out while Cass waited for him outside.

When he got back to the Hummer, he opened the back to stow his bags and waved for Arwen to hop in. That's when he realized this was not going to go well. She sat on her haunches and stared at the sky, the ground, a bug flying by. It was her way of saying she wasn't riding in the back like chattel.

"Don't be ridiculous," he growled. "There's a human in the front seat. You're a dog. Ride in the back. That's what they make this part of the vehicle for."

Nothing. He shook his head. They both knew she wasn't just a *dog* and this was one of the worst times in recent memory for her to remind him of it. He treated her like she was human, and she lapped it up as her due in true lady-of-the-manor style. Just because Gage had a real human to spend time with for a change didn't alter the fact that he'd spoiled her rotten due to his own lack of companionship over the years.

"What's going on?" Cass asked, her hair still loose and delicious around her shoulders.

The sight of her in that passenger seat, where she'd so sweetly offered him a fantasy weekend four seconds after giving him what he'd already thought was the ultimate encounter—amazing. He couldn't wait to dive in again.

"Arwen. In the car. Now," he muttered. "I've got a date with a shower and a wet woman and you are not going to mess it up." Louder, he called, "Just having a discussion about the proper place for a dog. One sec."

Extra motivation must have done the trick because he manhandled Arwen into the back on the first try and shut the hatch before she could leap out, which he wouldn't put past her. She gave a mournful cry that he heard even with all of the doors closed.

When he climbed into the driver's seat, Arwen had already weaseled in between the front seats, paws on the gearshift. She stuck her nose in Cass's face, clearly bent on discovering all the secrets of the woman who had usurped her spot.

Uh-oh. Arwen had never deigned to check out a woman

Gage had brought into her world. Usually she ignored them. Of course, Gage always introduced her to someone off Arwen's turf and it was rare that Arwen saw the same woman twice. Gage couldn't even remember the last time he'd had a woman in the Hummer, let alone at the same time as the vizsla.

"She's so sweet," Cass exclaimed as she rubbed Arwen's ginger head enthusiastically, earning a smile from the dog.

Gage eyed Arwen suspiciously and with no small amount of shock. She never approved of anyone female, let alone someone she'd already singled out as a rival. "Yeah, that's one word for her."

Arwen muscled her way into the front seat, right onto Cass's lap before Gage could grab her collar or even warn Cass that forty pounds of dog was coming her way.

Great. It wasn't as if Cass was wearing a fifteen-hundred-dollar suit or anything—not that he'd shown much more care when he'd crumpled it up around her waist. But still. There was a place for Arwen and it wasn't on top of Gage's...date. Former lover. Current lover. Partner in crime. Whatever.

"Sorry," he threw out. "Arwen, get in the back!"

"It's okay." Cass shot him a smile as she rearranged Arwen's paws off her bare legs. "I don't mind. It's not that far to my house and she's used to riding in the front, I would imagine."

"She is. Doesn't mean she should get her way." He started the car with one last warning glare at the dog who was predictably ignoring him. "I can drop her off at a pet hotel on the way."

Both woman and dog shook their heads.

"That's not necessary," Cass said, patting Arwen's back. "She's welcome in my backyard. I have some sad little hydrangeas that would probably benefit from being eaten."

"Really?" This time, he eyed Cass suspiciously. "She'll dig up your grass. I'm not kidding."

"So? She's been cooped up in a hotel all week, hasn't she? My yard overlooks the lake and there are always lots of birds. No reason why she can't have a nice weekend, too, is there?"

Arwen's ears perked up at the mention of birds and that seemed to decide it. Casually, as if it had been her idea all along, the dog picked her way to her own seat and lay down on it without bothering to glance at Gage.

A little dumbfounded, he drove toward Cass's house and wondered what had just happened. "Okay. Thanks. Apparently that plan got the thumbs-up from Her Royal Highness."

And from Gage. He snuck a sidelong peek at Cass. There'd always been something special about Cass but he hadn't realized her skills included dog whispering.

Warmth spread through his chest. Did Cass have any clue how much he appreciated her good humor over his bad-mannered dog? The invitation to let Arwen skip the dog hotel had earned *mucho* points with both man and beast. And neither of them gave points easily.

Arwen heartily approved of Cass's massive backyard. The moment Cass set down the bowl of water, Gage's diva of a dog gave Cass an extra nose to the hand, which was the equivalent of a rare thank-you. Would wonders never cease?

Gage followed Cass into the house, mystified why she'd be so welcoming of his dog. And why his dog was so welcoming of the woman.

Cass needs a big, fat thank-you. Immediately.

"Show me to your shower," he commanded, his body already hardening in anticipation of a hot and wet Cass.

She raised a brow. "That's the first thing you want to do? Take a shower?"

"You say that as though I'll be by myself."

"In that case…" She pivoted on one stiletto, then climbed the wide hardwood planked staircase at a brisk trot.

He raced after her, effortlessly taking the stairs two at a time, laughing as she ducked into a room and then popped back out as if to make sure he was following her. As if he'd be foolish enough to lose her.

"You're not getting away that easily," he promised as he entered what was clearly her bedroom. He made short work of whirling her into his arms so he could strip her slowly for a much-needed round two.

When her gaze met his, it was full of promise and his breath hitched in his chest as he drew off her suit one luscious piece at a time. Never one to hold back, she got him out of his clothes lickety-split and when they were both bared to each other, he picked her up and carried her into the en suite bathroom he'd spied earlier.

She flung her arms around his neck, her own breath coming faster as she nuzzled his ear. Heat swept across his skin. Would he ever get tired of her? Usually he was done by now. Once, maybe twice, was generally enough with one woman.

Not this one. She kept drawing him back and he kept not resisting.

Gently, he set down the armful of long-legged blonde on the black granite vanity so he could turn on the water in the shower. Six showerheads spurted to life and he let them run in the cavernous enclosure that had the perfect seat for what he had in mind.

Cass perched on the counter, blinking at him dreamily, and it was so sexy, he crossed back to her while the water heated. He wanted to touch her.

Stepping between her legs, he gathered her against him, flesh to flesh. She clung to him, wrapping her limbs around his waist. Her hair was still down, golden and curly against her back, tempting. So he indulged himself in what had become one of his favorite sights—her hair wound up in his fist.

A six-foot-long mirror spread out behind the vanity and Gage had a front row seat for viewing the gorgeous woman reflected there. Sensation engulfed him, sending a blast of blood to his groin so fast, it left him lightheaded. He groaned and his eyelids drifted shut. *No bueno.* There was no way in hell he was missing a minute of this.

Prying his eyes open, he gorged himself on the sight of the lovely naked woman in the mirror, and the man who was poised provocatively between her legs. And that's when he realized this was the first time he'd seen Cass fully unclothed. They'd made love in a couple of inventive spots that had been, oh, so very hot, but it hadn't given them the time to undress.

This was a first. And he planned to enjoy every second of it.

Reverently, he soaked her in. Then he was kissing her, delving into the moment with every fiber of his being. She made him ache, down deep inside where it couldn't be salved. Except by her.

They undulated together, physically and in their reflection. Steam from the shower gave the picture of the two of them a dreamlike quality, and it was the most erotic scene imaginable.

When they'd both shuddered to an intense, unbelievable release, he gathered her in his arms and took her to the shower, where he ministered to her like a slave doting on his mistress. It was as much an act of making love as what had happened on the vanity, though the thorough washing could never be remotely construed as sex. Didn't matter. Here in the shower as he rubbed soap over her skin and slicked shampoo through her hair, he wanted to make her feel as good as she made him feel, to connect on a higher level. Maybe somehow, he could open her up enough to know the ice was gone for good.

He couldn't stand it if things went back to being frozen between them.

Because he liked this Cass. More than he should. Far more than he had in college. This time was totally different, but he couldn't put his finger on what caused it to be that way. When he was inside her, his heart beat so fast, he thought it might burst from his chest, and when he wasn't with her, he thought about her. And not just about the physical stuff, though that was never far from his mind. No, he thought about how she'd come into her own as a woman. As a CEO. She'd grown far beyond his decade-old counsel.

The water grew cool and he shut it off, drying her tenderly. When he swiped the last of the water away, she grazed his cheek with her hand and lifted his lips to hers for the least suggestive kiss of his life. There was nothing sensual about it, just her laying her lips on his, and he couldn't have ended it to save his life.

Finally, she pulled back with a smile.

"Get dressed and let's eat something," he suggested, shocked at the roughness of his voice. He'd like to chalk it up to the explosive encounter on the vanity but that had happened thirty minutes ago. He suspected the source was Cass. Always Cass.

"Tired of me naked already?" she asked saucily.

"Never. I need nourishment if I want to have any hope of keeping up with you."

Dinner consisted of Chinese takeout eaten at the long island in Cass's kitchen. They sat on barstools, legs entwined and heads bent together as they laughed over failed attempts to use the included chopsticks.

Later that night, after a worthless attempt to watch a romantic comedy on Cass's wide-screen TV, he curled around her in her big fluffy bed, skin to skin. Moonlight poured in from the large triple bay window opposite the bed, where Cass had drawn the curtain to reveal the silvery lake. It was a million-dollar view but he only had eyes for the woman in his arms.

He stroked her hair, letting her essence wind through him and he had to know.

"Cass," he murmured. "Why did you agree to talk to the others about selling the formula?"

She stiffened and he regretted bringing it up. But weren't they at a place where they could be honest with each other? He hadn't sniffed out her agenda so far; the only thing he hadn't tried was flat-out asking.

"It doesn't matter. We haven't found the leak yet."

The bleakness in her voice reached out and smacked him. "We will. We'll spend all day tomorrow on it."

"Yes. We have to. Otherwise, I'll lose my job."

"What? They can't fire you. You own one-fourth of the company."

"Yeah," she allowed. "But if they say I'm out, I'm out. It's a vote of no confidence. I'd sell them my share and find something else to do with my life. That's the downside of being on a team."

He rolled her to face him in the dim moonlight. "You're not giving yourself enough credit. You've done amazing things with Fyra *because* you're a team."

He'd never been part of anything and he felt the lack all at once. Cass and her friends had been together for a long time. Longer than he'd known her. He'd never connected with anyone like that.

What would it be like if he did? If he hung on to someone longer than a couple of nights? Not as business partners, but as lovers. Would it always feel like this, like he felt with Cass? As though he could never get enough, never get tired of her, never run out of things to talk about?

It couldn't. Could it? Maybe for other guys who didn't have promises to their long-lost brothers to keep. Who would he be if he settled down?

She gave him a small smile. "Be that as it may, if I don't plug that hole, Fyra's profits could plunge. I have to answer to the whole company, as well as my executive team. Who are also my friends."

She was making herself accountable, like a great CEO should. It was inspirational and a little moving.

Her firm resolution spoke to something inside that he had no idea was there. Awed at the wash of emotion, he took in the serious expression on her beautiful face and everything shifted.

Cassandra Claremont wasn't just a fun distraction. He was starting to fall for her. How was that possible? He'd never let his emotions go like this. And what was he supposed to do with it—offer her his heart? Make her a bunch of promises?

Fall was definitely the right word. He'd fallen so far out of his depth, he'd need a thousand-foot ladder to climb his way out.

A bit panicked, he tried to get back on track. "So we'll find the leak. That's the only answer."

Get that squared away and then get the formula. That's what he was doing here. The crazy talk, that wasn't him.

He had nothing to offer Cass but a few laughs and a hundred million dollars. Then he'd go home and be done here. Like always. Like he was comfortable with.

She smiled. "Easier said than done, apparently."

"Double down, sweetheart." He kissed her temple. "I'm still a good bet. Get some sleep so we can spend all day tomorrow finding your name."

"I've heard that one before," she said wryly.

She'd meant it as a joke, but it sat heavy on his chest. He'd spent far more time focusing on pleasure than he had business with absolutely no thought to how their lack of progress might be affecting her. He could do better.

"Really. You can count on me. I promise we'll get there."

She didn't argue, though he understood why she might have a case for not believing in him.

As she drifted off to sleep, he gathered her in his arms and tried not to think about how natural it felt to be her go-to guy, how it made him want to stick to the problem until it was solved. How it made him want to stick to her.

Coupledom. Love. Living with someone under the same roof, sharing a bed, bank accounts—that was definitely an adventure Nicolas had never gotten to have. Gage had been avoiding anything that even remotely looked like that under the pretense of living life to the fullest on behalf of his brother. But in reality, the whole concept made him want to run screaming in the other direction.

Or at least it used to. He'd developed the strangest urge to stop running.

And he was truly daft if he thought for a moment that settling down was in the cards for someone like him.

Ten

A mournful howl woke Cass in the morning. She blinked. Sunlight streamed through the window and Gage's heavy arm pinned her to the bed.

Arwen apparently wanted them both to know she was awake and bored. But only one of them seemed to notice. Gage still slept like the dead, a fact she'd not forgotten. He'd never been the type to let the pressures of life keep him from something he enjoyed as much as sleep. He'd need a dictionary and autocorrect to spell *stress*.

One of the many reasons he fascinated her. It was a trick she'd like to learn. She openly evaluated his beautiful face, relaxed in sleep. How did he shut off everything inside so easily? Or was it more a matter of truly not caring and therefore, there was nothing to shut off?

The latter, definitely. She'd lost count of the number of times she'd labeled him heartless. It was starting to ring false. Any man who clearly loved his dog as much as Gage did couldn't be heartless. And he'd been so sweet in the Hummer yesterday before rocking her world, then again last night.

She shook her head. And therein lay his danger. Instead of uncovering his involvement in the leak, he'd uncovered *her*, in so many ways, reminding her why she'd fallen for him in the first place. He'd taken everything she'd dished out and come back for more.

He lulled her into believing he might be someone different this time around, someone who would be there tomorrow and the next day, growing closer as they grew older. Someone who could be trusted. She had no evidence of that.

Didn't stop her from yearning for it, though.

Gage stirred awake and smiled sleepily at her. "Morning, gorgeous. You better stop looking at me like that or we're going to get a very late start on our investigation. That's our top priority for today, no ifs, ands or buts."

"Oh, that's a shame. I do enjoy your butt." She snickered as he waggled his brows.

And somehow, she ended up under him and panting out his name before she'd scarcely registered him moving.

Finally, they rolled from bed at nine o'clock, the latest she'd gotten up since…college as a matter of fact. Gage was truly a terrible influence on her.

But then he took over her Keurig and brewed her a giant cup of coffee, exactly the way she liked it, which hadn't changed in a decade, but still. How had he remembered that? Trinity never remembered that Cass hated sugar in her coffee, and Trinity had watched Cass make it every weekday morning for years and years.

Gage elbowed her aside as she tried to put some breakfast together, insisting on scrambling eggs and frying bacon himself, despite never having set foot in her well-equipped kitchen before. Of course, she rarely set foot in it either. The pan he'd scrounged up from under the Viking range didn't even look familiar.

After Gage filled a plastic bowl with food for Arwen, they sat outside on the flagstone patio at the bistro set she'd purchased shortly after buying the house five years ago, and yet had never once used. It was a gorgeous morning full of fluffy clouds flung across a blue sky, but Cass was busy watching the man across from her as he tossed an old tennis ball he'd pulled from Arwen's bag. The dog raced after it time and time again. In between tosses, Gage shoveled eggs and bacon into his mouth in what was clearly a practiced routine.

It was all very domestic and twisted Cass's heart strangely.

She'd dated a guy… Tyler Matheson…a year or so ago and she'd have said it was bordering on serious, but she'd never once thought about inviting him to her house for the weekend. It had felt intrusive. As if men and her domain should be kept separate at all times. When they'd broken up, Tyler had accused her of being cold and detached, but she'd brushed it off as the ranting of a rejected man, just like she'd ignored the hurt over the unkind, unnecessary accusation during what should have been an amicable split.

Now she wasn't so sure he'd been wrong.

In contrast, Gage had flowed into her life effortlessly. As if he'd always been there and it was easy and right. As if they'd picked up where they'd left off. She'd been holding her breath for almost a decade, waiting for her heart to start beating again. And now it was.

She stared at him as if seeing him for the first time.

She'd never gotten over Gage Branson and chalked it up to having endured such a badly broken heart. But that wasn't it at all. She'd never gotten over him because she was still in love with him.

She shut her eyes for a beat. That was the opposite of a good thing. And this was a really bad time to discover it. He might be involved in the leak. Hell, he might have even orchestrated it and at this rate, she'd never find out. If he flat out denied involvement, she'd never believe him. He'd proven he couldn't be trusted personally, so what was to say he could be trusted professionally? She would not give him the opportunity to destroy her or her business all over again.

Even if he got down on one knee and proposed, which would happen when monkeys learned to pilot a stealth bomber, she'd say no. Her own self-preservation overrode everything.

"I did some more digging into our files. Ready to talk through them?" she asked after she cleared the emotion from her throat. Not only was it a horrible time to discover she still had very real, very raw feelings for him, it would be a disaster to tip him off. God knew what he'd do with it. Twist it around and say she owed him something.

He glanced at her, ball in hand, as Arwen barked to show her displeasure at the interruption. He threw it to the far end of Cass's property, a good hundred yards, and managed to make it look effortless. Like everything else he did.

"Sure. We've got all day and most of tomorrow. Let's make good use of it."

That was her deadline to somehow work through her emotional mess, too. A day and a half to get him out of her system for good and move on.

"I'm curious." She drank deeply from her coffee mug for fortification. "When I talked to you about planting false information, you seemed to know a lot about how digital forensics works. How did that come about?"

The best way to get him out of her system was to prove his involvement in the leak. Then she wouldn't have to remind herself he wasn't trustworthy. Because he'd be in jail. Her heart squeezed. Surely that wasn't going to be the result of all this.

But even if it wasn't, Gage's presence in her life was still because of the formula. He wasn't falling in love with her. He was only here to squash his competition.

Gage shrugged. "You learn stuff over the years. I read articles and such. But really, the reasons that wouldn't have worked are common sense."

Carefully, she raised her brows. "How so?"

"Because. Like I said, you don't have that kind of time. And you're assuming that the person responsible for the leak would actually be transferring files. What if they take handwritten notes? Memorize files? Take photographs? There are dozens of ways people can access information, especially if the person doing it is authorized in the first place."

All said very casually, while still throwing Arwen's ball. She'd watched him over her coffee cup, growing more frustrated by the minute at his clear hazel eyes and relaxed expression. He was supposed to be letting his guard down enough to say something he shouldn't.

Maybe he hadn't because she was being too subtle.

"Is that how you'd do it?" she asked, just as casually. Good thing she had a lot of practice at keeping her voice calm even when her insides were a mess. "Take photographs?"

"For what? To steal proprietary information?" He laughed and she'd swear it was genuine, not the kind designed to cover nervousness. "No reason for me to resort to underhanded tactics. If I want something, I buy it."

Yeah, as she well knew. Her coffee soured in her mouth. The problem with this line of questioning lay in the fact that she didn't have a clue if Gage was blowing smoke to distract her from his crimes or truly not involved in the leak.

How would she ever know for sure?

Maybe she was still being too subtle and the best way to resolve this was to flat out ask *Gage, are you involved?*

Surely she could read him well enough to recognize truth in his response. She opened her mouth to do it, once and for all, when his phone rang.

Frowning, he glanced at the screen. "Excuse me a sec. Someone from this number has called a couple of times but never leaves a message. Otherwise, I wouldn't take it."

Cass nodded as he stepped away from the table, her pulse pounding in her throat. So close. She'd almost blurted out the million-dollar question and she hated being forced to wait now that she'd made up her mind to go this route. But Gage ran a billion-dollar company. Of course people were vying for his attention.

She'd hoped to get her hands on his phone at some point this weekend, but snooping through his private life felt a little dirty, so she hadn't. So far. If he gave her any reason to, though...

Gage thunked back into his chair, his expression completely transformed from the relaxed, easygoing one he'd worn earlier. Thunderclouds had gathered in his eyes, turning his entire demeanor dark. "I have to leave. I'm sorry to cut our weekend short."

"What's wrong?" she asked before she thought better of it. They weren't a couple. They didn't share their problems. And no amount of yearning for that type of relationship would change things.

"Something's happened." Bleakly, he met her gaze, and suddenly it didn't matter if they weren't a couple. She reached out and captured his hand. In comfort, solidarity, she didn't even know. She just couldn't stop herself from touching him.

"What, Gage?" she asked softly, envisioning an accident involving his parents, a fire at his production facility. The pallor of his skin indicated it must be something bad.

"That was… I don't know for sure yet. I have to go home." He scrubbed his face with his free hand as he gripped Cass's with his other. "Someone I used to date died. Briana. That was her sister on the phone."

"Oh, I'm so sorry." Cass's heart twisted in sympathy. The woman must have been someone special for Gage to be so visibly upset. The thought of him caring about a woman so deeply set her back a moment. Was she missing something here? When had Gage become the committed sort?

"Thanks, I hadn't spoken to her in a long time. A year and a half."

Cass eyed him. "Then why would her sister have called you, if you don't mind me asking?"

Maybe *that* was the million-dollar question. Her curiosity burned. What if he truly had turned into someone who stuck around, growing close to this woman, and she'd been the one to dump him? Maybe *he* was nursing a broken heart.

After all, they'd never really talked about what the future between the two of them could look like. Maybe everything was within her reach if she just—

"She called because Briana had a son." Gage blinked. "My son. Or so she says."

* * *

Gage's two-story house overlooked Lake Travis just outside of Austin. It was one of the main reasons he'd bought the house several years ago and the water had always spoken to him. After driving straight home from Dallas in less than three hours—a record—he stood on the balcony, hands braced on the railing surrounding the enclosure and stared at the gray surface of the lake without really seeing it, wishing like hell the view didn't remind him of Cass.

But it did because her house was similarly situated near White Rock Lake in Dallas. He should be there with her right now, but wasn't because his world had shifted into something unrecognizable, where a paternity test was suddenly a part of his reality.

The woman who had called him was on her way over to discuss that very thing. It was bizarre. If what she'd said was true, he'd fathered a child with Briana.

Briana Miles. The name conjured up the image of a diminutive brown-haired waitress he'd met at a sports bar not far from his house. Beautiful girl. She'd come home to Austin after five years in LA and had started waiting tables so she could put herself through college, hoping to graduate without debt.

They'd struck up a conversation because Gage had expressed curiosity about how the University of Texas had changed in the almost ten years since he'd exited graduate school. That had led to a great couple of days that had ended amicably. He hadn't heard from her since.

The doorbell pealed through the house, and Gage opened the door to a short brown-haired woman with the swollen eyes and messy ponytail. Lauren Miles shared features with Briana and he could see their family resemblance even though he hadn't laid eyes on her sister in a year and a half.

"Come in," he said woodenly.

"The courier dropped off the results of the paternity test you took." She handed Gage the sealed envelope with her free hand. "I guess it's true that if you have enough money, you can get anything done quickly."

He ripped the envelope open and his vision went a little gray. No question. He was a father.

Lauren perched on his couch but he couldn't sit down, not until he got the most important question answered.

"Why?" he burst out as he absently paced the strip of hardwood between the couch and the fireplace. "Why didn't she tell me? I would have helped her with the medical bills. Paid for diapers and teddy bears. I would have—"

His throat seized.

Liked to be involved. But he couldn't finish the thought, not with the way his chest had gotten so tight that he couldn't breathe. All this time. Briana had been raising a baby without his help. Without even bothering to tell him he'd fathered a son. He'd have supported her if he'd known. She shouldn't have had to worry about anything.

And now it was too late.

Lauren bit her lip. "I argued with her about that. I really did. But she insisted you wouldn't want the baby and she was scared you'd make her have an abortion."

Gage's vision blacked out for a long minute. Rage tore through his chest and he thought he'd lose it if he couldn't punch something. *Make* her terminate her pregnancy?

Life was precious, so precious. That core belief was the one sole gift Nicolas's death had given him. The fact that Briana didn't know that about him infuriated him. Except how could he blame her? It spoke to the shallowness of their relationship that she'd assumed he wouldn't want his son.

Gradually, he uncurled his fists and breathed until he could speak.

"Fine, okay. I get that she didn't tell me because she—wrongly—assumed I wouldn't support her decision to raise her child. Nothing could be further from the truth. The baby is my responsibility and I appreciate the fact that you've come to me so I can do the right thing."

His vision went dim again as he processed what the *right thing* actually translated into. After years of cutting all ties with women as quickly as possible, one had managed to hook him with the ultimate string. For a guy who had no practice with commitment, he was about to get a crash course.

He was a father. A *single* father. His child's mother was dead and he had to step up. His carefree days of living life to the fullest had just come to a screeching halt with a set of brakes called parenthood.

And he'd never even held his son. What was he going to do?

All at once, he wished he'd asked Cass to be here with him. It made no sense. But he wanted to hold her hand.

"About that." Lauren scooted to the edge of the couch, brow furrowed as she leaned closer to Gage. "I'd like to formally adopt Robbie."

"Adopt him?" he parroted because his brain was having a hard time processing. Lauren wasn't here to pass off Briana's son to his father?

"That's actually why I contacted you, to discuss the paperwork that my lawyer is drawing up. You'll have to sign, of course, because you're the legal father on record. But it's just a formality," she said quickly. "I'm not asking for any child support or any split custody. He'd be all mine and you can go about your life. I'm sure you're totally unprepared to be a father."

It was as though she'd read his mind.

Something that felt an awful lot like relief washed through him. He'd give her money, of course. That was nonnegotiable. But Lauren could pick up where Briana left off and all of this would go away.

And the relief kicked off a pretty solid sense of shame. "So you want me to sign away all rights to my kid?"

"Well, yeah. Unless Briana was wrong and you are interested in being a father?" she asked tremulously, as if afraid of the answer, and tears welled up in her eyes. "You've never even met Robbie. I love him like my own son. He's a piece of Briana and I can't imagine giving him up. It would be best if he stayed with the family he's always known."

"I don't know if that is best," he admitted and his stomach rolled.

He should be agreeing with her. He should be asking her for papers to sign. Right now. What better circumstances could he have hoped for than to learn he had a son but someone else wanted him? It was practically a done deal.

But he couldn't. Somehow, he'd developed a fierce need to see this kid he'd fathered. He needed it to be real, and meeting his flesh and blood was the only way he could sign those papers in good conscience.

"I didn't know my son existed before today," he heard himself saying as if a remote third party had taken over his body and started spitting out words without his permission. "And you're coming in here like it's all already decided. How can I know what's best for him? I want to meet him first."

Gage had a significant number of zeroes padding his

bank account, which wouldn't be hard to figure out, even for a casual observer. This could still be an elaborate ploy for a seven- or eight-figure check. But he didn't think so.

She nodded once. "Can it be in the next couple of days? Briana didn't have much, but her estate needs to be settled. Robbie's future being the most critical part, of course."

Settled. Yeah, all of this needed to be settled, but unfortunately, this was the least settled he'd ever been. What an impossible situation. And he didn't have the luxury of shrugging it off like he normally did.

Grimly, Gage showed Lauren out and sat on the couch, head in his hands. And he didn't even think twice about his next move. He pulled out his phone and dialed Cass.

When he'd left her in Dallas, it was with a terse goodbye and a promise to call her, but he'd never imagined he actually would, at least not for personal reasons. It should have been a good place for them to break things off and only focus on the business of Fyra's formula. He'd planned for it to be the end, but nothing with Cass felt finished.

Besides, he needed someone with a level head who knew him personally to stand by his side as he met his son for the first time. Someone who wouldn't let emotions get the best of her. Someone he hoped cared enough about him to help him make the right decision. Someone like Cass.

Too late, he realized none of that actually mattered. He wanted Cass because *she* mattered. Yeah, it scared him, but he couldn't deny the truth. The formula had ceased to be the most important thing between him and Cass.

Cass answered on the first ring and he didn't even bother to try and interpret that. Too much had shifted since they'd last talked for petty mind games like guessing whether she'd missed him like he'd missed her. Or whether she'd realize the fact that he'd called her had earth-shattering significance. It did. She could do what she wanted with that.

"I need you," he said shortly. "It's important. Can you come to Austin?"

Eleven

Cass went to Austin.

There really wasn't a choice. Gage had said he needed her and that was enough. For now. Later, she'd examine the real reason she'd hopped in the car ten minutes after ending his call. Much later. Because there was so much wrapped up inside it, she could hardly make sense of it all.

When his name had come up on her caller ID, she'd answered out of sheer curiosity. You didn't drop something on a woman like a surprise baby and then jet off. Of course, she'd also been prepared for some elaborate plot designed to see her again so he could coerce her into either giving him the formula or getting naked, at least until he got tired of her again. She'd planned to say no and spend the weekend crossing the finish line on the leak's name.

She had to be close. The list of potentials wasn't *that* long.

But instead she'd found herself saying yes to the surprising request to accompany Gage as he met his son for the first time. He wanted *her* to be by his side as he navigated this unprecedented situation. The sheer emotion in his voice had decided it. What if Gage wasn't involved in the leak and she missed her chance to find out what might happen between them?

Cass held Gage's hand as they mounted Lauren Miles's front steps and wondered not for the first time if he'd literally come apart under her grip. The new, hard lines around his mouth scared her, but the fragility—that was ten times worse. As if the news he'd fathered a child had replaced his bones with dust. One wrong move and he'd blow away in a strong wind if she didn't hold on tight enough.

Just this morning, they'd been drinking coffee on her back porch and she'd been desperate to work him out of her system. So she could let him go and move on. Clearly that wasn't happening. But what was?

Less than four hours had passed since she received Gage's troubling and cryptic phone call and their arrival on this quiet suburban street. The slam of a car door down the way cracked the silence. It felt as if there should be something more momentous to mark the occasion of entering the next phase of your life. Because no matter what, Gage would never be the same. His rigid spine and disturbed aura announced that far better than any words ever could.

"I admire what you're doing," she told him quietly before he rang the doorbell. "This is a tough thing, meeting your son for the first time. I think you'd regret signing the papers if you didn't do this first."

The fact that he'd asked her to come with him still hadn't fully registered. Because she didn't know what it meant.

"Thanks." Gage's eyelids closed and he swallowed. "I

had to do it even though I feel like I'm standing on quick-sand. All the time. I needed something to hold on to."

He accompanied the frank admission by tightening his grip on her hand. He meant her. She was the one holding him up and it settled quietly in her soul. In his time of need, he'd reached out to her. She wished she could say why that meant so much to her. Or why the fact that he was meeting this challenge head-on had softened her in ways she hadn't anticipated. Ways that couldn't be good in the long run.

But what if there was the slightest possibility that they might both put down their agendas now that something so life altering had happened? That hadn't felt conceivable in Dallas, but here...well, she was keeping her eyes open.

He rang the doorbell and a frazzled woman answered the door with a baby on her hip.

"Right on time," the woman said inanely, and she cleared her throat.

Gage's gaze cut to the baby magnetically and his hazel eyes shone as he drank in the chubby little darling clad in one of those suits that seemed to be the universal baby uniform.

"I'm Lauren," she said to Cass. "We haven't met."

"Cassandra Claremont." Since she wasn't clear what her role here was, she left it at that. She and Lauren didn't shake hands as there wasn't any sort of protocol for this situation, and besides, they were both focused on Gage. Who was still focused on the baby.

"Is this him?" he whispered. "Robbie?"

"None other." Lauren stepped back to let Gage and Cass into the house, apologizing for the state of it as she led them to the living room.

A square playpen sat off to one side of the old couch surrounded by other baby paraphernalia that Cass couldn't have identified at gunpoint. All of it was tiny, pastel and utterly frightening.

That was when Cass realized she knew nothing about babies. She'd always known they existed and murmured appropriately over them when other women who had them entered Cass's orbit. But this was a baby's home, where the process of living and eating and growing up happened.

Gage had told her in the car on the way over that the baby's aunt was seeking to adopt Robbie. Really Cass was floored Gage hadn't signed the papers to give up his rights on the spot. Why hadn't he? The solution was tailor-made for a billionaire CEO who thought commitment was the name of a town in Massachusetts. Give up your kid and go on living life as though it was one big basket of fun with nothing to hold you back.

Sounded like Gage's idea of heaven to her.

The fact that he was here meeting his son instead… well, she wouldn't have missed it for anything in the world.

Crossing to the mat on the floor, Lauren set the baby upright in the center of one bright square and motioned Gage over. "Come sit with him. I can't honestly say he doesn't bite, but when he does, it doesn't really hurt." She laughed without much humor. "Sorry, that was a lame joke."

Then Gage knelt on the mat and held out a hand to his son. The baby glanced at the stranger quizzically but then reached out and grasped his father's finger with a small baby sound.

Cass forgot to breathe as a wave of tenderness and awe and a million other emotions she couldn't begin to name broke over Gage's expression, transforming it into something that tugged at her soul. She almost couldn't watch as the moment bled through her, blasting away the last of her barriers against a man whom she could never call heartless again. It would be a lie.

His heart was all over his face, in his touch as he ruffled his son's fuzzy head. In the telltale drop of moisture in the corner of his eye.

She couldn't watch and she couldn't look away as her own heart cried along with Gage. That's what love looked like on him and she wanted more of it.

Thirty minutes passed in a blur as Gage held his son in his strong arms and laughed as the baby pulled at his father's too-long hair. He pumped Lauren for information, demanding details like what Robbie ate, whether he'd taken his first step, what he did when he rolled over. Robbie's aunt answered the questions to the best of her ability but it soon became clear she hadn't spent every waking minute with the boy like his own mother had.

A somber cloud spread over the four of them with its dark reminder that this wasn't strictly a happy occasion of father meeting son. Gage had a decision to make and he needed to make it soon so Robbie could get settled in the home where he'd live for the next eighteen years with his permanent parent.

Lauren announced it was Robbie's nap time. She left the room, disappearing into the back of the house to perform the mysterious ritual of "putting him down" and returned after ten minutes, her eyes puffy and red, as if she'd been crying.

"He's so precious." She sniffed. "It's so unfair. I can't tell you how it breaks my heart that he's lost his mother."

"It's hard for me, too," Gage admitted quietly. "My son should have a mother. Yet if Briana hadn't died, I might never have known about Robbie."

It was the most brutal sort of turnabout and it was definitely not fair play. But Cass couldn't argue that fate had set that pendulum in motion. And the swings had widened to encompass her, as well.

Gage held out his hand to Lauren. "Thank you for opening your home to him."

"I wouldn't have done anything else." Lauren shook Gage's hand solemnly and didn't let go as she caught his gaze to speak directly to him. "I love him. He's my nephew, first and foremost, and we will always share that bond of blood. But you're his father. That's something I can't be to him and I'm prepared for whatever decision you make. Please, take twenty-four hours, though. Make a decision you can live with forever."

Nodding, Gage squeezed Lauren's hand and turned to go, ushering Cass out the door ahead of him. His touch on her back was firm and warm and it infused her with the essence of Gage that she'd be a fool to pretend she didn't crave.

The best part was she didn't have to pretend. Instead of spending the weekend working Gage out of her system, something else entirely was happening and she couldn't wait to find out what.

He drove back to his mansion on the lake and helped her out of the Hummer, leading her up the flagstone steps to the grand entryway flanked by soaring panes of glass… all without asking if she planned to stay.

No way in hell was she going anywhere.

Throwing a frozen pizza in the oven passed for dinner, and an open bottle of Jack Daniel's managed to intensify the somberness that had cloaked them since leaving Lauren's house. They pulled up bar stools at the long, luminous piece of quartz topping the island in Gage's kitchen and ate.

Or rather, she ate and Gage stared into his rapidly diminishing highball filled with whiskey.

"I'd ask if you were okay," Cass commented wryly, "but that would be ridiculous under the circumstances. So instead I'll ask if you want to talk about it."

"He looks like Nicolas." Gage tossed the last of his Jack down his throat and reached for the bottle. "Robbie. He's the spitting image of my brother at that age. My mom had a shrine to her firstborn lining the hallway. Literally dozens of pictures stared down at me for eighteen years as I went between my bedroom and the bathroom. Today was like seeing a ghost."

"Oh, Gage." *More alcohol needed, stat.* Her own Jack Daniel's disappeared as she sucked the bottom out of her glass through a straw. "That's…"

She didn't know what it was. Horrible? Morbid? Unfortunate? Gage had talked about Nicolas in college on occasion, so she knew the tragic story well. It had shaped a family into something different than might have been otherwise.

"It's a miracle." A small smile lit up Gage's features. "I never would have imagined… My son is a gift that I don't deserve. A piece of myself and my brother all wrapped up into one amazing little package."

The love and tenderness she'd seen at Lauren's house when he looked at his son appeared again in his expression, and it pierced her right through the heart. It was breathtaking on Gage, a man she'd longed to look at *her* that way, a man she'd been sure didn't care about anything. The fact that he'd shown a capacity for it was a game changer.

And she had a strong feeling she knew what that look signified. "You don't want to give up Robbie."

Gage shook his head. "I can't. It never sat quite right with me anyway, but once I saw him… I don't need twenty-four hours to decide. He needs me."

He wasn't going to walk away from his son. And she'd never been more proud of someone in her life.

That burst Gage's dam and he started talking about Robbie. How was it possible that a man becoming a father before her very eyes could be so affecting? But it was. Gage's decision opened up a part of her inside that flooded with something divine and beautiful.

They drifted to bed where they lay awake, facing each other in the dark, as she listened to Gage's plans for his impending fatherhood. There was no subject too inane, from the color of the walls in his son's new room to what kind of car Gage would buy him when he turned sixteen.

Cass smiled and bit back a suggestion that he let his son pick out his own car. Far be it from her to interrupt his flow. This was his way of working through it and her job was to be there for him. It was nice to be needed by the one man who had never needed her. Heady even.

"Thank you," he said abruptly. "For coming on short notice. For holding my hand. For not heaping condemnation and a sermon on top of me. I had to figure this out and I couldn't have without you."

What, like he was expecting her to shake her finger at him and give him a lecture about accepting responsibility? She shook her head. "You're giving me too much credit. I just responded to a phone call. You did the hard part."

"No. I don't do hard." His voice went scratchy but he blazed ahead. "I get out before anything difficult happens. Back at your house, that was supposed to be about burning off the tension so we could focus. It wasn't supposed to be the start of something. I don't do relationships. You know that, right?"

That was the first time she'd ever heard him admit he had a commitment problem. Admitting it was the first step toward curing it, right?

"Yeah. I knew it wasn't anything more than sex."

"What if I want it to be?" he asked, sincerity warming his voice and curling through her in the dark. It was as if he'd read the same question in her heart and voiced it out loud.

"What if you do?" she heard herself repeat when she should have been saying *so what?* Or *this is goodbye right now.* "Have things changed?"

Please, God. Let that be true and not a huge mistake.

His hand found hers, threading their fingers together, and the rightness of it drifted through her like a balm. She could listen to him talk all night long if this was the topic.

If she hadn't gotten in the car when he asked her to come to Austin, she'd never have gotten to watch this monumental shift in Gage.

"So many things," he repeated quietly. "I'm not even sure how yet. The formula… I wasn't going to give up. I wanted it and I was going after it. But somewhere along the way, I started to want more."

The earth shifted beneath the bed, sliding away faster and faster as her mind whirled, turning over his words, searching for the angle, the gotcha. "What are you saying, Gage? That you want to keep seeing each other?"

He spit out a nervous laugh. "Why not? I like spending time with you. I'm pretty sure the feeling is mutual or I'm much worse at this kind of thing than I think I am."

"You have a lot going on right now," she said cautiously. "Maybe this isn't the best time to be talking about this."

"I *am* worse at this than I thought if I'm not making myself clear. Let's see how it goes. I'll come up to Dallas. You drive to Austin. We talk on the phone during the week. Maybe a video chat late at night that involves some dirty talk. I don't know. I've never done this before."

She could envision it. Perfectly. Sexting during a conference call and naughty emails and rushing to throw her overnight bag into her Jaguar for a Friday night dash to the Hill Country in anticipation of a long weekend in Gage's bed.

But for how long? And what would happen when he ditched her again, as he surely would? "I don't know how to do that either."

His sigh vibrated through her rib cage. "Yeah. Robbie changes everything."

That was so not what she'd meant. "Why, because you think you being a father is a turn-off? Think again."

"It should be. My life will never be the same. It's ridiculous to even say something like 'let's see how things go.' I already know where I'm going. Play dates, preschool, the principal's office and Cub Scouts."

He was committing to his child. Didn't that give her some hope he might want to commit to her, too?

"Maybe it's not so ridiculous." Had that just come out of her mouth? It was madness. But honest.

"Stop humoring me," he said flatly. "I get it. Everything is up in the air, which is unfair to you. Besides, you might want to think about whether you'd like to be in the same boat as Briana. I don't know how she got pregnant. I used protection every single time."

Yeah, that had occurred to her. But he'd gotten it wrong. She was in a whole boatload of trouble regardless because she wasn't mother material. She ran a million-dollar company for crying out loud. Any conversation she and Gage had about seeing where things could go included a future with a baby no matter what. Now that she'd thought of it, she couldn't *stop* thinking about it.

But there was no point in heaping condemnation on him, especially not when it sounded as though he was doing a pretty good job of that on his own. "Of course you did, Gage. It was an accident. It happens all the time, even to smart, careful people."

Her heart twisted as they talked about subjects that shouldn't be a part of his reality. Gage embraced this challenge in a way she'd never have guessed—the king of disentangling himself from anything that smacked of the long-term had changed when she wasn't looking. Really and truly changed, which she'd just spent a considerable amount of effort denying over the past week.

What if she *could* trust him with her heart this time? A world of possibilities might be open to her. To both of them.

It gave her a lot to think about.

In the morning, she awoke before Gage. His sleeping form was close enough to touch but she didn't dare do it. He'd only slept for a couple of hours last night, which she knew because she'd been holding him when he'd finally drifted off.

Their conversation had meandered to every subject under the sun—how they'd gone without their first year in business, what kind of spices you could add to ramen noodles to make them taste like something other than cardboard, the first splurge purchase they'd made when their companies finally turned a profit.

It was like the old days, except Gage hadn't even tried to kiss her. Last night hadn't been about sex, a fact she appreciated. But at the same time, she couldn't help but try to categorize the night.

A turning point, perhaps. But one thing she did know for sure—she had to answer that million-dollar question about Gage's involvement in the leak. Soon.

Twelve

Cass entered this new phase of her relationship with Gage with equal parts caution and greed. She soaked up every second of laughing with him over Robbie's antics as Gage visited his son at Lauren's house, and she helped Gage shop for nursery items.

No task required to prepare Gage to take custody of his son was too small for her involvement, apparently. She didn't mind. Except for the part where they never picked up the conversation about where things were going. Whether there was a goodbye in their future or not. Was she simply a hand to hold until he found his footing?

Eventually, that question would have to be answered. But she was content, for now.

She shuttled between Austin and Dallas enough times over the next week that she could pick out roadside elements as mile markers. That weed formation meant it was an hour and thirty-six minutes until she'd be in Gage's arms again. The pile of rocks by the exit sign meant she'd see Gage's beautiful hazel eyes light up at the sight of her in seventeen minutes.

In between, she ran her company and hired a private detective to look into the leak. If she hadn't been so distracted, she would have done so earlier. The move was enough to satisfy her partners into giving her more time. And enough to satisfy herself that if Gage was involved, she'd find out before things went too far. She hoped.

On Friday, one week after she'd snuck out early to get busy with Gage in his Hummer—totally by accident, in her defense—she spent an hour at the end of the day frantically whittling down her email in anticipation of spending the weekend in Austin with Gage.

Her phone rang. Speak of the devil.

"Hey, sexy," she purred.

"It's done," he said. "The last of Briana's estate is settled and Robbie is officially mine."

She swallowed. Hard. "That's great news!"

Just in time for the weekend. They'd expected it to take a few more days, but Lauren had been instrumental in pushing things through once she saw how serious Gage was about being a father. She could have made Gage's life a living hell and he'd said he was grateful she'd chosen to take the high road for Robbie's sake.

Except now it was real. Gage was a single father.

Now that the estate was settled, Robbie would come to live with Gage permanently. Lauren would still be a huge part of her nephew's life, and she and Gage had already discussed potential arrangements for holidays. Gage's parents had put their house in Houston on the market and planned to move to Austin so they could spend their golden years with their new grandson.

The only person who didn't have her future mapped out was Cass.

"So I guess Lauren is bringing Robbie over tonight?" she asked. She'd planned to drive to Austin tonight to spend the weekend with Gage.

Things had just come to a head. What did Cass know about dating a single father? If things progressed, was she really ready to be a mother? The thought frightened her. She had a demanding job. She couldn't be calm and cool around a baby. The timing wasn't great for any of this.

One step at a time. What better way to figure out what came next than to spend time with the man and his child?

"No, she asked if she could keep Robbie until Monday so she could say goodbye, just the two of them. I couldn't say no."

"That was sweet of you."

Her heart opened a little more with each glimpse of the man Gage was becoming as he met this challenge. Each time, she had to reprogram a bit more of her thinking. She wasn't sure what to do with the result.

"So instead of you driving here, I'm coming to you. You've already put far too many miles on your car in the past week. Turnabout is fair play," he reminded her in case she'd forgotten about his strong sense of tit-for-tat. "I'll be there in three hours."

She ended the call with a smile and drove home instead of to Austin. The reprieve gave her time to review the email she'd received a few minutes ago from the background-check company. They'd finally completed new scans of all her employees.

Thirty minutes later, she kicked back on her sofa with her laptop, the report and a list of cross-referenced employees who worked in the lab. The scans she'd ordered included arrest records, of course, but that wasn't necessarily a good indicator of someone's propensity toward corporate espionage. A better one was financial records such as property owned and debt, which was the section of the report where she focused her attention.

Someone with a mountain of outstanding bills might be a prime candidate for thievery, particularly in light of what the formula was worth to someone like Gage. He'd never buy it from a shady Fyra employee, but the culprit might not realize that.

But Cass knew that about Gage. The thought settled into her mind as if it had always been there. Of course that was true. Why would he have bothered to come to Fyra's CEO with an offer to buy the formula if he planned to buy it on the black market?

Or was she missing the big picture?

Everything was mixed up in her head and the addition of his new status as a committed father wasn't helping. She just didn't know whether she trusted Gage or not.

Cass refocused and noted two lab employees with outstanding mortgages that seemed quite large for what Fyra paid them. Also not a blinking sign that pointed to criminal activity. But a curiosity all the same, considering neither of them were married according to the scan. Inheritance, maybe, but Cass couldn't be too careful.

Next, she moved on to her employees' former employers and known associates. GB Skin leaped off the page almost instantly. Cass's gaze slid to the employee's name. Rebecca Moon. She worked for Harper as a lab analyst. She'd worked for Gage before coming to Fyra. Also in his lab.

It wasn't uncommon. Many of Fyra's employees had previously worked for Mary Kay, too. That didn't make them criminals, just people with skill sets companies in the cosmetics industry sought.

But no one from a competitor had approached Cass about her formula, except one.

Cass sat up and started from the beginning of Rebecca's report. The picture was not pretty. She had a wide swath of credit card debt totaling well over a hundred grand and outstanding medical bills from—Cass tapped the line once she found it—her ex-husband's many elective procedures. So Rebecca had gotten divorced but was still saddled with an ex's debt.

Shaking her head over the things people did to each other, Cass eyed the woman's known associates and a sense of foreboding grew in her stomach. All of the people linked to Rebecca had addresses in Austin. Not a big deal. The woman had lived and worked in Austin when she was employed by GB Skin.

It just seemed odd that Rebecca Moon hadn't made any friends in Dallas in the…seven months she'd worked for Fyra. Not one person from her new neighborhood had asked her to lunch via text message or friended her on Facebook?

The background check hadn't extended to Rebecca's friends' information. So there was no way to know if the people she'd interacted with online and made phone calls to were employed by GB Skin—but logic would dictate that she'd made friends at Gage's company and kept them.

If Gage had found that out somehow, would it have been a temptation to lean on that connection? *No*, she couldn't assume that. Could she?

Her stomach rolled again as she recalled how convenient the timing had been when he'd first shown up at Fyra. Yes, she knew the drive between here and Austin was easy. Someone could conceivably hop in the car with little planning and be here before lunch. It didn't mean Gage had known about the formula *before* the information hit the trade magazine, or that he'd used the leak as some kind of leverage to get her to agree to sell.

But still. Gage had been convinced Cass owed him something. But then he'd stopped reminding her of it. The formula rarely came up these days. Why, because he knew Rebecca Moon was going to steal it for him?

That was a stretch. But Cass couldn't get it off her mind. A leak was one thing, but the threat of the culprit doing additional harm was very real. As was the possibility she'd been played by the master, just like she had been in college.

She would drive herself crazy with that line of thinking. She used her time to thoroughly peruse the rest of the report but Rebecca was the only lead she had.

Who better to contradict whether he'd discovered the perfect mole in Cass's company than Gage himself? There was absolutely no reason she couldn't bring this information to him and get his explanation. They could be straight with each other. He'd talk to her and tell her she was being silly and then maybe she'd tell him that she'd hired a private detective. With the detective on the job, she and Gage could focus on each other. See what their relationship might look like with all the agendas put away.

Because if she couldn't trust him with business, what could she trust him with?

Halfway through the last page of the report, a knock on the door startled her. *Gage.*

She let him into her house and drank in the man's beauty and masculinity as she stood frozen in the foyer where he'd made love to her for the first time in a decade. A million powerful emotions washed over her. She'd tried to keep her distance. Tried to keep her heart where it belonged—in her chest and shielded from Gage—but as she looked at him, images flew at her, of him as he held his son, as he laughed with her, as he made love to her.

The addition of his baby had shifted things. Far more so than she'd have anticipated, and not the way she'd have thought. Gage was a father now. Did that mean he'd changed his thinking about commitment? Was he ready to find a woman to settle down with?

But he still said things like *let's see how it goes. We're having fun. You owe me. Turnabout is fair play.* He'd distracted her from the leak again and again with his talk of pleasure before business. Had he been afraid she'd find something?

Ask him about Rebecca. Go on.

The wicked smile he treated her to fuzzled her mind and then he swept her into a very friendly embrace that promised to get a lot friendlier.

She pulled away and crossed her arms over the ache in her midsection that wouldn't ease. This was why she shouldn't let her heart take over. Emotions only led to problems.

"That was fast," she said brightly.

He raised one eyebrow quizzically. "Not fast enough, clearly. What's wrong?"

"I'm hungry," she lied. Of course he'd picked up on the swirl of uncertainty under her skin. "I waited for you to eat."

"I had Whataburger on the way. I'll hang out with you in the kitchen while you eat something, if you want."

"Sure." Then they could talk.

Except she couldn't seem to segue into *by the way, did you happen to set up a deal with one of my employees to steal my formula for you?*

Gage sat on a bar stool and chatted about Robbie, absently sipping a highball with a splash of Jack Daniel's in it. As she woodenly ate a very unappetizing sandwich that didn't sit well in her swirly stomach, she couldn't stand it any longer. The best approach was to ease into it, perhaps.

"When are we going to check in with each other?" she asked during a lull in Gage's conversation. Because of course their relationship, the leak and the formula were all tied together. Without one, the others didn't exist, and it was time to get all of it straight. "About how things are going."

"Now?" he suggested mildly. "Is that what's bugging you? You don't have to dance around it if that's on your mind. How are things going, Cass?"

Right, jump straight to her as if she could possibly articulate what was going on inside. She made it a habit of pretending she didn't have any emotions and she certainly didn't spend a lot of time cataloguing them for others when she didn't fully understand them herself.

Besides, this was about Gage. About whether he'd planted a mole in her company. Whether he'd invented a relationship with her to get his hands on her formula. Whether he'd become a man she could trust.

She scowled. "I wanted to know how it was going from your chair."

He took in her dark expression without comment. "It's working. But it's only been a week and Robbie will be a big part of my life come Monday. So I guess I'm still seeing how things go."

And somehow, his perfectly legitimate response plowed through her nerves like water torture. "What does that mean? Once you become a dad, you might decide two is enough?"

It would be exactly what she'd been expecting. *Sorry, this thing between us has run its course.* That's what she'd prepared for.

His brow furrowed and he abandoned his drink to focus on her. "No, it means it's a complexity in an already shaky situation."

"Shaky how?" she whispered. "Do you have something you need to tell me?"

Oh, God, what was she going to do if he came right out and confessed? He was bound to have some kind of rationale, like he'd only planned to use Rebecca to gather information for leverage or he'd say that technically, he hadn't done anything illegal.

"Cass, you're trembling."

Clearly concerned, he tried to grip her hand but she yanked it away, whacking her nearly empty wineglass and sending it clattering across the granite bar. Gage, bless his honed reflexes, caught the stemware before it shattered on the travertine tile below, but the trail of wine across her light brown counters would stain.

Good. Something to occupy her hands while she gained control again. *No emotions*, she scolded herself. *Brazen it out. Don't let him know what's going on inside.*

"You didn't answer my question," she said, pleased at how calmly she delivered the statement. And how coolly she wiped up the spilled wine with careful, even strokes. "If our situation is shaky, what's making it that way?"

"The formula, for one. I was expecting you to tell me to go to hell when I called about Robbie. But you didn't." He watched her closely but she refused to meet his all-knowing gaze.

She would never have told him that. He'd needed her. Maybe she should have told him to go to hell twenty times since then, but dang it, she'd wanted to believe in him. In them.

Yes, it meant something that she'd come when he called. She'd been hanging around, thinking she'd hold on to her heart and dip one toe in, but really, she was pathetically, predictably wishing for him to fall in love with her. Just like last time.

But he'd given her no reason to trust him, no reason to believe that could ever happen. Becoming a father didn't automatically make Gage Branson someone he wasn't and that's why he wasn't suddenly spouting promises and pretty words. *Let's see how things go* was code for *I've found my Ms. Right-Now.* Until he got tired of her. Until something better came along. It was all fun and games until someone's heart got broken.

Or worse, until she found out exactly how good he was at keeping business and pleasure separate. A little thing like corporate espionage wasn't supposed to get between them while they were burning up the sheets.

Before she could argue the point, he skewered her with those gorgeous hazel eyes and she felt it all the way through her soul. He'd burrowed under her barriers, winding his way through her heart despite all her vows to refuse him entrance. At the end of the day, she was the problem here. Because against all odds, she *had* started to trust him in spite of it all. And she shouldn't have.

"You came when I needed you." He held her gaze and wouldn't let go. "And we fell into something that I was hoping would continue. I meant it when I said I wasn't ready for it to end."

The rawness in his voice sliced through her. She wanted to believe him. Believe *in* him. The past week had been so amazing and surprising and deep, and sex had only been a small part of that.

When had she lost her "it's only sex" mantra? When had this become a relationship and not just sticking to a man to learn his secrets?

Unfortunately, she could pinpoint it exactly. It had happened the moment she'd answered Gage's call and he'd said, *I need you.*

He'd ruined her for other men—Gage Branson was it for her. She realized that now.

And she had to know once and for all if she could trust him.

"Rebecca Moon," she blurted out and his expression darkened so rapidly that the rag fell from her suddenly numb fingers.

"Yeah, what about her?"

"So you admit you know who she is?" Cass squawked.

"Of course I do. She used to work for me," he acknowledged without a scrap of shame. "My company isn't so big that I've lost the ability to keep track of my people. Especially those who worked in Research and Development."

"Used to work for you?" she prodded. "But not anymore?"

Gage stood, unfurling to his full height a good three inches above Cass. He crossed his arms, leaning a hip against the bar casually, but his frame vibrated with tension.

"Since I'm pretty sure we both know she works for Fyra now, it sounds like you're the one who has something you need to tell me."

This was her opening. The other Fyra executives were counting on her to solve the company's problems and the last thing she wanted was for her team to accuse her of letting her feelings for Gage get in the way of justice. Alex, in particular, was already poised to lambast Cass. She had to pull this thread.

"I'm sure there's a rational explanation." She resisted the urge to back away. "But Rebecca's in a lot of debt and maintains contact with people in your area. You can see how someone might think that's a suspicious combination. It just looks bad, Gage."

"Bad how?" he asked softly. Lethally. "What exactly are you trying to say?"

The pressure of his accusatory expression pushed on her chest, stealing her ability to draw in air. He was going to make her spell this out. She swore. "Come on. You agreed to help me identify a probable suspect for the leak but have spent almost every second distracting me from that goal. Almost as if you wanted to steer me away from any evidence pointing to a name."

Of course she was the dummy who'd fallen for it. Half of the fault lay with her.

"You seem to forget that I had an interest in finding the leak, as well. The formula is worthless otherwise."

She waved it off. "Only if you don't have another way to get your hands on it."

"Cass." He huffed out a sigh of frustration. "We agreed you'd talk to the others about selling when we found the leak. We haven't yet. What other possible way would I get my hands on it?"

Did he think she was born yesterday? "Turnabout is fair play, right? That's what you said when you demanded I sell you the formula less than twenty-four hours after its existence was leaked to the industry. Tell me the timing is a coincidence."

"It's a coincidence." His knuckles went white as he contemplated her with clenched fists. "But you don't really think so, do you? You suspect that Rebecca's the leak and I'm pulling her strings like some kind of corporate raider puppet master. You think I've paid her to steal the formula."

"Well…in a nutshell, yeah." It didn't sound so concrete

coming from Gage's mouth and she wavered. He didn't look guilty. He looked furious. "Are you denying it?"

"Hell, yes." A muttered expletive accompanied the declaration. "Though why I have to is the real question here."

Instantly, her hackles rose. Was he that out of touch? "Really? It's confusing to you why I might have a problem trusting you?"

Obviously, he didn't see anything wrong with being there for her and giving her a place to get away from all the pressures of life, being understanding and strong and wonderful…and then taking it away at a moment's notice. Like he had the first time. "You dumped me in college like yesterday's trash with *no explanation*. I can't—"

She shouldn't have brought that up. Not now.

"No explanation?" He stared at her, his expression darkening. "Our relationship is one of my fondest memories, or I wouldn't have rekindled it. But it ended at the right time, once it had run its course. We talked about it. That's what I said."

"Oh, you said that all right. But you might as well have said, 'It's not you, it's me.' Either way, it's a lame line designed to brush off the person you're tired of." All of this had been bottled up for far too long. It came rushing out—the formula and the baby and *let's see how it goes* all muddled together into a big emotional mess she couldn't control. "Surely you didn't think it was an actual reason."

He'd broken her and she wasn't letting him do it again. Not personally. Not professionally.

"Wait just a minute." He threw up a hand as if to ward off the barrage of words. "We had a lot of fun in college. But that's all it was—fun. Are you saying you expected an opportunity to talk me out of it when I said it was time to move on?"

"No," she countered. "I expected that you'd figure out

you loved me as much I loved you and ask me to marry you."

She'd thrown up wall after wall to prevent a repeat of those feelings. Unsuccessfully. Because at the end of the day, that was still what she wanted.

And she knew now it was an impossible dream.

"Marriage?" The pattern of Cass's granite countertops blurred as Gage processed that bombshell on top of the Rebecca Moon accusation. "You wanted to get married? To *me*?"

Of all the things he'd thought about their time together, her in a white dress and diamond rings and…other together-forever stuff that he couldn't even fathom right now—none of that had ever crossed his mind. None of that had ever crossed his mind with *anyone*, let alone back in college when he'd just begun to spread his wings.

He'd vowed to himself, and to Nicolas, to have the quintessential college experience—drink a lot of beer, sleep with a lot of women, have a lot of esoteric conversations at coffee houses with foreign exchange students. No one got *married* in college.

He and Cass had totally different viewpoints on their history. How was he only discovering this now? *And* in the midst of a conversation where apparently, he was being accused of planting an employee at Cass's company. His temper simmered again, which was not a good sign. He never got angry. Mostly because he never had much of an emotional investment.

Looked as if he was going to experience yet another first with Cass.

"I guess this is news to you," she said and her voice broke.

There were no tears, no hard lines around her mouth,

but he could tell she was upset about their relationship ending. *Still* upset. The bitterness radiated from her and he caught it in the gut.

"Completely. Jeez, Cass. We were kids with our whole lives—our whole careers—ahead of us."

But that wasn't true now. If that was what she'd wanted then, what had she wanted this time around? The same? While he was trying to reconcile and explore these new, unprecedented feelings she'd evoked, had she been waiting for a proposal? The thought put his chest into a deep freeze and none of the beating and breathing that should have been going on inside was working.

She crossed her arms over her abdomen as if to protect herself. From him. "So what's different this time that makes you say things like *let's see how it goes*? Am I suddenly more palatable now that I have power and money? Or is my allure strictly related to your bottom line?"

His anger mounted. How dare she accuse him of not only consorting with a former employee to steal from Fyra but then playing other angles, too. As though he'd faked his attraction and feelings for Cass strictly because of her formula?

"My offer to buy your formula is legitimate and legal. And I didn't bring up extending our affair because of it," he told her truthfully.

Maybe the affair had started as a way to make sure the odds fell in his favor. But that had changed a long time ago. She had their relationship all wrong—the first one and the second one—and somehow he was the bad guy in all of this. As though she'd had expectations of him that he'd stomped all over and God forbid he be given a second chance.

"Then why?" she pushed, her expression darkening

more with each passing second. "Why keep seeing each other? Why not end it like you always do?"

Because…he had all these feelings he didn't know what to do with. Because he liked being around her. Because he couldn't imagine saying goodbye.

But all at once, he couldn't spit that out. Heaviness weighed down his chest. If they didn't say goodbye, what then? He wasn't marriage material.

"Yeah, that's what I thought," she said derisively when he didn't answer her. "You haven't changed. You're another broken heart waiting to happen."

Another broken heart? Something snapped inside.

All this time… Cass had been in love with him. And he'd broken her heart because he'd ended their relationship, despite never making any promises. No wonder she'd been so frosty and uptight at first. Obviously, their past had colored her agenda and explained why he could never put his finger on what she was up to. Why he could never find his balance with her.

"Are you still in love with me?" he demanded.

She laughed but it sounded forced and hollow. "Boy, someone sure packed their industrial-sized ego for this trip down memory lane. What do you think?"

That cool exterior was a front, one she did better than he'd credited, but he knew the Cass underneath it. Very well.

Sarcasm meant he'd hit a nerve.

"I think you didn't deny it." Eyes narrowed, he evaluated her.

Of course, that question would remain unanswered because, at the end of the day, she didn't trust him. And he was still angry about it. The unfounded accusations about Rebecca Moon still stuck in his craw and he was having a hard time getting them loose. "I guess I should have ended things. Especially if you're convinced I'm out to steal from you."

"It doesn't matter," she cut in swiftly. "We both know your interest in me starts and ends with my formula. So I'll make it easy for you. This...whatever it is...is over."

So that was it? Because of how things had ended between them the first time, she chose to believe that he was involved in the leak and didn't have any intention of listening to him. She was operating under a decade-old hurt and refused to give him an opportunity to explore what he wanted this time. That was crap and he was calling her on it.

"What if I asked you to extend our relationship because I want to see what happens when we don't end things right away? It's totally unfair of you to say *adios* when I'm genuinely trying to figure this out. Almost as unfair as accusing me of being involved in the leak with literally no proof."

She stared at him, her eyes huge and troubled. "Yeah, well turnabout is fair play, Gage. Spend the next decade thinking about *that*."

Thirteen

Gage drove back to Austin, his mind a furious blur. Cass had found the ultimate way to get him back for breaking her heart—by accusing him of betraying her.

Turnabout is fair play.

If it had happened to anyone else, he'd have appreciated the irony.

As it was, his chest ached with unprocessed emotions. If it wasn't for the layer of mad, he might understand what had just happened. But he couldn't get the heaviness in his chest to ease or the anger to abate. She hadn't believed him when he said he wasn't involved. Because she didn't trust him.

In Cass's mind, he was guilty simply because he hadn't fallen to one knee and declared undying love. Stealing a competitor's secrets was apparently as much a crime to her as not proposing. It was ridiculous. He cared about Cass. Of course he did. Who suggested they keep seeing each other? *Gage*. Who had called Cass when he'd been at his absolute lowest? Still him. Didn't she get that he'd been falling for her all along and had kind of freaked out about it?

Obviously not.

He'd given as best as he knew how. And his best wasn't good enough.

Fine. That was the way it should be, anyway. Clearly this relationship business wasn't for him. But what if that meant he couldn't be a father either? What if he was completely flawed in some way?

Gage spent the remainder of the drive home nursing his wounds and then drowned them in a quarter of a bottle of Jack Daniel's. He tried to go to bed, where it smelled like Cass and everything good and hopeful in his life, and that was the breaking point.

He vaulted out of bed, scaring the bejesus out of Arwen, who was enjoying the rare treat of sleeping at Gage's feet. Head cocked at a curious angle, she watched him throw on jeans but elected to stay put when Gage stormed from the room.

Twisting open the whiskey again, he got started on what was probably a vain attempt to drink enough to forget the stricken look on Cass's face when she'd said *this is over*.

He'd hurt her. He got that. But it had happened a long time ago. This was all on her and her inability to forgive and forget. There was no reason for Gage to reevaluate anything, yet here he was, doing it anyway.

He groaned and let his head fall into his hands. Who was he kidding? He'd screwed up, too.

Whether it was fair, whether he'd made mistakes with Cass due to his unquenchable desire to best his competition, whether Robbie made his life unduly complicated—

none of that mattered. He'd lost something precious and he missed her. Cass should be in his arms at this moment and she wasn't and it sucked.

Before he dissolved into an unmanly puddle of regret, he palmed his phone and flicked through pictures of Robbie. The boy's face was so reminiscent of Gage's brother, it was almost eerie. Genetics. That's all it was, not a message from beyond the grave.

He's going to be a handful.

Gage smiled. Yeah, his son was pretty great. What did Nicolas know about kids, anyway? It was a sobering thought. His brother had guided him for so long. Who would be the voice of his conscience now that Gage was moving toward something new and different?

You'll figure it out. After all, you already know what not to do.

He definitely knew that. Gage would raise Robbie with no boundaries. Carpe diem and full speed ahead, unlike how his own parents had raised him. If Robbie wanted to run with scissors, Gage would put plastic tips on the sharp ends and lead the way. If Robbie wanted to climb trees—or mountains—Gage would be behind him every step, ready to catch him when he fell.

He'd say yes to every "Hey, Dad, can I...?"

Mom and Dad didn't put restrictions on you to keep you from having fun.

Yeah, he knew that. They loved Gage, fiercely, even to this day, despite their disappointment that none of Gage's childhood limitations had resulted in a son who played it safe. He lived his life unapologetically, reveling in all the experiences Nicolas couldn't.

Like falling in love?

Gage drained the highball and flipped it over instead of

refilling it like he wanted to. When his conscience came up with gems like that, it was time to lay off the sauce.

Except the thought wouldn't go away.

For his entire adult life, he'd avoided anything that smacked of permanence. Even with Cass, who made him feel alive and amazing and as though he wanted to be around her all the time. He couldn't just come out and commit. Why?

Because he feared losing someone who mattered—like his parents had. God, why hadn't he ever realized that? With Robbie, it had been easy. There hadn't even been a choice in his mind. But he had control over whether he committed to Cass and he'd exercised it by walking out the door instead of fighting for what he wanted.

You live life to the extreme but it costs you. You have no personal relationships. No one to lean on. What are you going to do when parenting gets hard?

Gage frowned. His parents were moving here. His mom would give him advice.

The same woman you just vowed not to emulate when raising your son? Good thinking. Besides, don't you want someone to be there for you who gets you? Who's your equal? Someone you can count on and vice versa?

"Shut up, already. I get it," he muttered. "I messed up with Cass and instead of figuring out how to fix it, I'm sitting here arguing with a ghost."

But was it even possible to fix it? Cass's frozen routine was a safeguard against *him*, after all. He'd started their relationship solely with the intent of leveraging their attraction to get his hands on her formula, and she was forcing him to reap what he'd sown. Which was no less than he deserved. The rift between them was as much his fault as hers.

He'd wanted something more and had been too chicken

to lay it all on the line, disguising his thirst for Cass as a drive to beat the competition.

And by the way...if you've never done permanent, never been in love, never figured out how to sacrifice and be selfless, you know being a father will be that much harder.

His chest squeezed again. Nicolas was right. Gage's closest companions were Arwen and his conscience disguised as his long-gone brother. He had no idea how to do relationships. And he needed to. Gage couldn't be a good father if he flitted between commitment and freedom. He'd already realized that but now he knew how to fix it.

He had to learn how to stick. He *wanted* to. Cass and Robbie were both worth it.

Somehow, he had to prove to Cass that she could trust him this time. That he wasn't responsible for the leak.

He wanted Cassandra Claremont in his life, living it alongside him, giving him the ultimate experience he'd yet to have.

But as difficult as it was to admit, Gage had no basis for figuring out what it took to be a good partner or a good father. He'd never had a relationship before—with *anyone*, his family, a lover...what was different this time? What could he offer Cass to convince her to give him one last chance?

After a long night of tossing and turning, Gage sat up in bed as the perfect answer came to him.

Phillip Edgewood.

Cass frowned as she listened to the detective spout more rhetoric about how the investigation was ongoing, nothing concrete to report, blah, blah. She switched her phone to the other ear but the news didn't get any better.

At the end of the day, Rebecca Moon either wasn't the culprit or she had been very, very savvy about her movements over the past few weeks. Nothing pointed to the woman as the source of the leak, nothing pointed to a link between her and Gage, and Cass was tired of beating her head against this wall.

She was even more tired of missing Gage and wondering why she was beating her head against that wall, too. The man wasn't interested in a relationship—which she'd known from day one. She'd done everything in her power to keep her emotions out of it, trying to convince herself she was sticking to him like glue so she could keep tabs on him.

It hadn't worked. She'd fallen in love with him all over again thanks to those quiet moments when he was the man she longed for, who believed in her but didn't care if she wasn't strong and capable 24/7, who'd demonstrated his ability to commit to his son.

None of that mattered. She couldn't trust him and that meant they were through. Forever.

That hole in her heart? It was there for good.

It almost would have been better to find evidence that Gage had been the one whispering in Rebecca's ear. At least then Cass could hate him for being a sleaze. Instead, she'd had to cut ties because, after it was all said and done, he only cared about the formula. When she'd told Gage it was over, he hadn't argued. Because he knew he'd end things eventually, so why not now?

A knock on her open door dragged her attention away from the detective's disappointing phone call and the regret burning in her chest. Alex stood in the doorway. Cass waved in the CFO and held up one finger in the universal "give me a minute" gesture as she told the detective to keep digging.

Alex sauntered into her office, but Cass could tell this wasn't a friendly visit.

"We need to talk," Alex said before Cass had even set the phone on her desk. "The prelim quarterly numbers are not looking good."

Cass bit back the groan. When it rained, it poured. "And now you're going to tell me they're down due to the leak, right?"

The hard line of Alex's mouth didn't bode well. "I don't think we can directly pin it on that. But it's clear we've got a problem, and not having that breach buttoned up isn't helping."

The accusation of fault hadn't been verbalized but it came through loud and clear. This was all on Cass and Alex wasn't pulling any punches. As the CEO, the buck stopped at Cass's chair and she should have found the leak's name long ago.

Helplessness welled up and nearly overflowed into her expression.

Push it back. Her throat was already so raw from watching Gage walk out of her life that she hadn't thought it could get much worse. Turned out she was wrong.

"I'm working on it," she said smoothly. Or what she thought would pass for smooth, but Alex scowled instead of lightening up.

"You've been saying that for weeks. I'm starting to wonder whether you've got a secret agenda you've failed to share with me."

Oh, God. She'd landed in turnabout hell. This was shaping up to be a redo of the conversation she'd had with Gage last week, except she was the one in the hot seat.

Being accused by *Alex*, who had been Cass's friend for years and years. They'd suffered through exams together in college, through Alex's man troubles, and of course, Cass's singular experience with Gage. Later, she and Alex had worked around the clock together, poring over financial statements for places to cut and bonding through the difficulties of starting a brand-new company.

Except Alex was in Cass's office in her capacity as one-quarter owner of that company. It was her right to call Cass onto the carpet. But she did not have the right to make this about something other than Cass's inability to do her job.

"I don't have a secret agenda. Don't be ridiculous."

"Why are you always so dismissive of me?" Alex's un-manicured fingernails drummed against her leg in a rest-less pattern as she stared at Cass with a small frown. "I run this company alongside you, not beneath you."

Confused, Cass shook her head slightly.

There was more here than a reproach about Cass's per-formance on the job. This was personal. She did not get the lack of trust and animosity wafting in her direction. It wasn't as though she'd done something horrible to her friend that would make all of this justified. Not like what Gage had done to Cass, for example.

"What are you talking about?" Cass asked. "I'm not dismissing you. I—"

A brisk knock at the door cut off the rest and Cass glanced up sharply to see Melinda, Fyra's receptionist, hovering in the hall outside her office, practically wring-ing her hands.

"Sorry to interrupt." Melinda's eyes were so wide, it was a wonder they didn't fall out of her head. "But not really. You've got a visitor and, well, he's not the kind of person you make wait around. Besides, I'm afraid he's disrupted the entire office and I thought—"

"Who's the visitor?" Cass asked as patiently as possible.

The timing was the worst and whoever it was could wait. She wanted to get to the bottom of what was going on with Alex, once and for all.

"Phillip Edgewood," Melinda blurted out. There might have even been swooning. "*The* Phillip Edgewood. The *senator*," she stage-whispered in case Alex and Cass lived under a rock and might not know the popular United States senator. "He's even dreamier in person than he is on TV. Oh, and Mr. Branson is with him."

Cass stood so fast, her chair shot across the low-pile carpet and crashed into the wall. "You could have told me that first. Send him back right away."

A compact. There was a compact around here somewhere. Pulse thundering, Cass fished blindly through her desk drawer, fingers closing around three lipstick tubes, a bottle of Fyrago perfume and then a foundation brush before she finally located the powder case. She flicked it open and used the mirror to slick on a fresh layer of lipstick, which predictably went on crooked because of how badly her hand was shaking.

Gage was here. In this building. He'd come to apologize, to throw himself at her feet. To declare his undying love…

Now *she* was the one being ridiculous. Her heart deflated. Gage wouldn't have shown up after a week of radio silence with a US Senator in tow if he was here to step back into her life. He was here about the formula.

Business. Of course. The man separated business and pleasure like a pro.

"Hot date?" Alex asked wryly and Cass peeked over the compact.

God, she'd forgotten all about Alex and, lucky girl, she was about to witness Cass's complete breakdown.

"Actually, Gage and I aren't seeing each other anymore. We—"

He swept into the room and she forgot to breathe. The sharp, dark navy suit he wore would make an Italian tailor weep. His too-long hair was somewhat tamed and smoothed back, leaving his gorgeous face the focal point it should be.

She scarcely noticed the handsome dark-haired man at his elbow. Because next to Gage, Phillip Edgewood might as well have been invisible.

"Ms. Meer." Gage nodded to Alex as she rose. "This is my cousin, Phillip Edgewood. Phillip, Alexandra Meer, Fyra's chief financial officer."

The CFO and the senator shook hands politely, exchanging pleasantries while Cass shot Gage a look and hissed under her breath, "Senator Edgewood is your *cousin*? Since when?"

"Since I was born?" he suggested mildly. "His mother and my mother have been sisters for almost sixty years."

"You never mentioned that."

He shrugged, messing up the lines of his gorgeous suit, which was a shame. "I never mentioned a lot of things. Which, not so coincidentally, is why I'm here."

With that cryptic comment hanging in the middle of everything, Gage repeated the introductions between Cass and Phillip and swung his attention back to Cass. "Phillip has graciously agreed to help Fyra navigate the FDA process required to get your formula to market. I came by with him today so you could meet him personally and get the ball rolling. Oh, and he'll also help you grease the wheels at the patent office. The sooner you get going, the sooner the leak will become a nonissue."

Cass's mouth fell open. "We're not—I mean…what?"

"That's amazing, Gage," Alex said, with a withering glance at Cass. To the senator, she said simply, "Thank you. We're honored to have such expert assistance."

"Yes, of course." Cass nodded woodenly, her faculties still scattered. "Thank you. We appreciate the assistance."

And now she sounded like a parrot instead of a savvy executive. Gage *still* fuzzled her mind.

The senator smiled at Alex, and it took over his entire body, as if he was lit from within. Charisma radiated from him like the corona around the sun. Cass started to get an inkling of what the fuss over him was all about.

"It's no problem," Phillip said, but he was looking at Alex as if Cass didn't exist. "Is there somewhere we can go to talk? And of course, we should include your chief science officer."

"Dr. Harper Livingston," Alex interjected, and the two of them were off, their conversation deep in the details.

Looked as if Alex was more than willing to stay in the senator's orbit, though he was hardly her type. They were a study in contrasts with Alex's face bare of cosmetics and clad in a gray shirt and jeans. Senator Edgewood wore Armani and power, and not necessarily in that order.

They excused themselves to Alex's office, leaving Gage and Cass staring at each other.

"What was that all about?" Cass demanded. "Waltzing in here with a US senator and throwing him at Fyra like some kind of peace offering."

"You say that like it's a bad thing." Gage shoved his hands in his pockets. "Does that mean it didn't work?"

"That's what it was?" A little stunned, Cass sank into her chair. She'd been about to grill him on his angle. Without reason apparently. "A peace offering?"

"Yeah. I needed an 'in,' in case you wouldn't see me otherwise. Phillip was my trump card." He grinned and she fought to keep from smiling back. Too many unanswered questions for that.

"But why did you ask him to work with us on the FDA process? If we file for approval, that's a pretty clear indication we're not going to sell it. To you or anyone."

"That's why I did it. I don't want your formula any-more, but this seemed like the only way you'd believe me. Now it's not a factor between us." He took her hand and held it without making any other move, but that alone connected them. "I owe you, and turnabout is fair play."

"You owe *me*?" She shook her head, still dazed. "You've got that backward. You've been quite clear that it's the other way around."

"That was before I fell in love with you."

Her breath caught and she drank in the emotion spill-ing from his gaze. Love. Tenderness. All of the things she'd witnessed in his expression when he looked at his son. The same emotion she'd dreamed of seeing directed at her. And now it was.

Shell-shocked, she stared at him. "I...what?"

"Oh, am I stuttering again? Let me start over."

He swept her into his arms and laid his lips on hers, infusing his warmth into her dark and frozen soul. Ev-erything thawed instantly, blooming under his talented mouth as he kissed her senseless. All of her feelings for this man surged to the surface, spilling out of her heart in an endless flow. He was in love with her, and all of the sharp, painful places inside smoothed out as she united with him, body and soul.

No. No, no, no. She wiggled away, breathless and still fuzzled because, *oh my God*, she wanted to dive back in and forget the past miserable week had happened. But it *had* happened.

"When did you decide this?" she demanded, but he just grinned and yanked her back into his embrace.

"For such a smart lady, you're being very slow to catch on," he murmured into her ear. "I'm not letting you go again. So you might as well forget about throwing up your walls. I'll keep knocking them down until you admit you're in love with me, too."

"Why would I do that?" She scowled but he just kissed the line between her brows.

"Because I'm sticking around this time. Forever," he promised and crossed his heart, catching her gaze. The depths of sincerity in his expression put a slow tingle in her midsection. "And I'd like to know up front where we stand. No seeing how it goes. No agendas. Just two people in it for the long haul."

"That's not what you want." Eyeing him suspiciously, she tried to cross her arms, but he wouldn't loosen his grip on her waist enough to give her room. "You want the formula, not me. So what exactly is all this Gage-speak supposed to mean?"

He pursed his lips and contemplated her. "Here's the thing. I haven't given you any reason to trust me. So I've spent the past week convincing Phillip to clear his schedule, and then I cleared mine. Because I want you to go to market with your formula so we can compete head-to-head. May the best CEO win."

That sounded more like Gage. There was a gotcha in there somewhere. A yet-to-be-named angle she couldn't see. "Now you're just talking crazy."

"No, I'm finally sane, thanks to you." Tenderly, he tucked a chunk of hair behind her ear. "You *have* moved past my mentorship. Far past. And turnabout is fair play. Show me what you've learned since then. I fully expect you to win."

It was as if he'd opened her heart and read the words she'd longed for him to say like a script. Where was this stuff coming from? Because if he kept going, she was going to completely lose all her safeguards against a bad decision.

But it was far, far too late for that. She'd been sliding toward Gage since the moment she'd recognized him in the parking lot of her building.

"Oh, I see." She didn't. But she had to keep fishing. His real agenda was buried in these well-delivered lines somewhere. "You've given up your bid for the formula and forgiven the debt you've claimed I owe you. Out of the goodness of your heart."

"That debt never existed." His small smile wiped the one from her face. "In fact, I owe you. Because I didn't know I had such a bad habit of turning a blind eye to what was happening around me. Briana had a baby without me cluing in. You were in love with me and I didn't know. You didn't tell me because I was too busy pushing you away. And then when you did tell me, I handled everything wrong. I should have admitted I was falling for you then. But instead, I clung to my freedom, not realizing it was meaningless. I'm a serial idiot."

This couldn't be real. All her dreams of being with Gage forever were not on the brink of coming true. Her life was not a fairy tale and he was not the guy he was claiming to be.

"So you've climbed aboard the commitment train?" She shook her head. "I'm sorry, Gage, but I can't buy that."

"Then you're going to feel very silly once I do this."

He pulled a small box from his jacket pocket and flipped the hinged lid to reveal something that might look like a diamond ring to someone whose vision wasn't instantly blurry with tears.

His arm dropped from her waist and he pulled the band from its velvet nest to slide it on her finger. "That's the sound of the conductor yelling 'All aboard.' I love you and I want to marry you."

She went a little lightheaded. "You know that if the

senator is helping us get the formula to market, marrying me won't get you access to it, right?"

Gage just smiled. "No agendas here. Mine *or* yours. You know if you marry me, you have to trust me. No more dates where you pump me for information, or sleepover games designed to figure out my angle. When you have questions, we have to talk about things like rational adults. And when we spend time together, it'll be because we can't be apart."

Guilt crushed through her chest. "Did you know the whole time?"

"No. I figured out later that all the strange questions were because you suspected I was involved in the leak from the very beginning. It's okay. I realized why you thought that was necessary. I hadn't given you any reason to trust me, which I hope I'm fixing right now."

Finally, it started to sink in. He'd taken soul-searching to a whole other plane. And somehow figured out how to claim her heart in the process with a simple thing like forgiveness. She'd held him at arm's length, convinced he would break her heart, when instead he'd offered his up with no strings attached.

She shoved back the flood of emotion for a second time. Or was it a third? She'd lost count because he'd done exactly what he'd predicted he would—knocked down her barriers against him.

"No agenda," she repeated dumbly. "Then why *marriage*? You could hardly say the word the last time this came up."

He took that with surprising grace and nodded. "I've spent years running from anything that smacked of commitment under the guise of living life to the fullest and experiencing new heights. I've done it all, except one thing. You're my ultimate experience, Cass. Just you. Everything feels better when I'm with you. Why would I keep running from that?"

"Because you're a serial idiot?" she choked out, and he laughed, pulling one from her, as well.

That was the benefit of falling in love with a man like Gage. She was botching up his marriage proposal and he still managed to pull it off.

"I am a serial idiot. I hope that means we're a perfect match," he said, his voice clogged with emotion she'd never heard before. "Because it would be dumb of you to take a chance on me. I'm going to immediately drop a baby in your lap. That's a lot to ask. I get that. But if you hand me that ring back, I'm only going to keep coming around until you say yes."

It was real. The man she loved had just asked her to marry him. She curled her hand around the ring, holding it tight against her palm. "The best thing about us is that we're equals. Guess that means I'm a serial idiot, too, because I never fell out of love with you."

Yes, clearly she'd gone mad because she never would have imagined admitting that in a million years. Never imagined being a mother. Never imagined she'd be this happy.

Strangely, Gage becoming a father had been the tipping point. She could trust that he'd stick around this time because she'd seen what he was capable of with Robbie. What it looked like when he loved someone. She knew it was possible and could finally believe it was happening to her.

A smile split his face and when he kissed her, he nearly split her heart, as well. Good thing. All the emotion inside was too big to be contained in that little bitty organ. Looked like she was getting her happily-ever-after.

Epilogue

Phillip Edgewood threw a hell of party. His status as one of the nation's most eligible bachelors coupled with his deep Texas roots afforded him a wide circle of acquaintances. Gage had never socialized with his cousin. Shame it had taken him so long to reach out to a man he'd known since childhood. They'd had lunch a couple of times since that day Gage had shown up out of the blue to ask for help, and they might even be on the way to becoming friends.

But tonight, Gage only had eyes for his date. Cassandra Claremont put the Hollywood celebs, Texas oil royalty and glittery society wives in attendance at Phillip's fundraiser to shame.

And Gage had been apart from his fiancée for five long minutes. He crossed the crowded ballroom to the bar, where Cass laughed over something Alex had said. That was a welcome sight. Cass had mentioned she and Alex were at odds over Fyra's strategy and that Alex had been the main one speaking out against Cass's leadership.

Whatever had happened to cause the rift appeared to be repaired, which Gage knew was a load off Cass's mind.

"Ladies," he murmured as he came up behind the most gorgeous woman in the room, wrapping his arm around her.

He couldn't touch her enough. Sometimes he did it just to assure himself he hadn't invented this fantasy out of thin air. But every time he reached out, she reached back. Commitment had its perks. Lots of them.

"Alex, you look fantastic," he commented truthfully as Cass's arm circled his waist in kind. "Did you do something different?"

Cass smacked him playfully. "Spoken like a true man. Of course she did. It's a formal party and we spent two days getting ready for it."

The two women exchanged smiles and piqued Gage's interest. "Sounds like there's a story there."

He'd been privy to nothing as Cass had told him to butt out. Repeatedly.

"A boring one," Alex assured him with a careful nod, likely in deference to the gravity-defying swept-up hairdo that drew attention to her lovely face. "Cass volunteered to give me a makeover, that's all."

"That's all?" Cass squealed incredulously. To Gage, she said, "The woman works for a cosmetics company and never wears the stuff. So I taught her a few tricks and voilà."

Alex blushed becomingly. "It's not that I didn't want to wear makeup. But every time I did, I felt like I was trying too hard."

Phillip appeared at Alex's side, which was the most likely cause of her blush. They made a cute couple and Phillip deserved some happiness after the untimely death of his wife several years before. Of course, the senator and the CFO both brushed off their association as "working together" to secure Fyra's FDA approval. They weren't fooling anyone.

As their host whisked Alex off to the dance floor, Gage nestled his fiancée closer.

"So things are good between you now?" he asked.

Cass nodded. "Yeah. We had a heart-to-heart and she admitted she was feeling left out. I have a tendency to deal with issues on my own, and apparently that comes across as…cold."

Gage stuck his tongue in his cheek. "You don't say."

"No, really," she insisted, oblivious to Gage's sarcasm. "I was acting like the title of CEO meant I had to do it all with no help and as if letting anyone see that I was uncertain was like some big crime. I ended up confessing that to all the girls when I told them I hadn't found the leak and you weren't involved. It was a real turning point and now we're 100 percent united. I have you to thank for helping me learn that."

"Me?" That was a genuine surprise. "You're the one who's been mentoring me in how to do this long-term thing. What did I teach you?"

"That it's okay to use your head and your heart." She smiled. "In all things. I couldn't have fathomed becoming a mother otherwise."

Robbie had warmed to Cass instantly, so much so that his son cried inconsolably when Cass had to go back to Dallas on Sunday nights. It was only temporary until they could figure out the logistics of moving an entire company's headquarters. And until they finished arguing about whose company was doing the moving.

"I told you we're a perfect match," Gage insisted. "I don't know what took you so long to get wise to how good we are together."

Guess it turns out you can live life to the fullest with one woman, after all.

Gage smiled. Nicolas was right once again. Cass was the ultimate experience and he couldn't wait to get started on forever.

* * * * *